Combat Frame XSeed

Principal Characters

TESLA BROWNING: Self-taught engineer credited with inventing the combat frame. Licensed his work to Seed Corporation, where he now serves as head CF engineer. Left his native L3 to build combat frames on Earth for the Coalition.

ALAN COLLINS: EGE Major. Originally hails from Britain. Lives by the book and expects the same of everyone else. Attack helicopter pilot and executive officer to Colonel Larson.

ZANE DELLISTER: Enigmatic Coalition Security Corps pilot stationed in the occupied city of Chicago. Arrested after an extended period spent AWOL and remanded to a mental institution. The advanced combat frame found with him was sent to the nearby Seed Corp factory for study.

MAXIMUS DARVING: Seed Corp software engineer who defected to the EGE. His background and his advanced fighter jet prototype earned him the rank of captain. Divides his affections between his EGE Naval Intelligence handler Li Wen and his custom-made A.I. Marilyn.

JEAN-CLAUDE DU LIONE: Last heir to the throne of Nouvelle France. Came of age in the free city of New Orleans after his parents were killed during the Coalition invasion of his homeland. Awaits the day when he will return to lead his people. Pilots the custom dueling CF Veillantif.

SIEG FRIEDLANDER: Son of L3 Prime Minister Josef Friedlander. Graduated from L3's service academy but resigned his commission when his mother and sister were kidnapped by Sanzen Kaimora.

Impatient with the politicians' endless prattling, he has vowed to rescue his loved ones himself.

SANZEN KAIMORA: Exo-archaeologist and military history buff chosen as the first Coalition Security Corps director. Convinced that only victory over the earth can secure peace, Sanzen often butts heads with Secretary-General Mitsu Kasei, who favors a diplomatic solution.

GRIFF LARSON: EGE Colonel formerly of the Federated Mid-American States Militia. Accomplished combat frame pilot who serves as strategic advisor and confidante to General Edward McCaskey. Is said to use a knife for a pillow.

SEKAINO MEGAMI: CSC Director Sanzen's young protégé. Though publicly his assistant, Sanzen has given her responsibility for many of his office's daily operations. Most of Megami's personal data remains inaccessible even to Secretary-General Mitsu.

PREM NARYAL: Newly installed governor of the Coalition's Mideastern Administrative Region. Her sterling track record within the Coalition Commerce Ministry recommended her for the office. An accountant by trade, she maintains an avid interest in combat frame piloting.

TOD RITTER: Teenage freedom fighter who seeks to liberate Neue Deutschland from SOC rule and avenge his family. Grenzmark aficionado. Currently serving with a German expatriate force in Africa.

Glossary

Combat Frame: A bipedal armored weapons platform derived from construction equipment used to build the space colonies. The Coalition's deployment of combat frames on Earth drastically shifted the balance of power and sparked a new arms race.

The Earth Governments in Exile: A council of earth leaders deposed by the SOC. They maintain a modest military based from a small fleet in the Atlantic.

The Earth Sphere Colonization Commission: An economic trust set up by the first space colonists to oversee the colonies' development.

The Federated Mid-American States: FMAS for short. One of three major political bodies created from the breakup of the old American Empire. Located in the Midwestern and Western states and Canadian provinces. The FMAS Militia is known to conduct guerilla warfare against Coalition forces in North America.

Grounder: A derogatory term for a native of Earth.

The L3 Colonies: A federation of space colonies founded by settlers of Western European extraction. L3 is the only colony government not to sign the SOC Charter.

Seed Corporation: Originally a farming equipment manufacturer founded in the colonies. A combat frame contract with the SOC turned them into the Earth Sphere's leading arms developer.

Soc: A derogatory term for citizens of the Systems Overterrestrial Coalition sometimes broadly applied to all space colonists. Pronounced like "sock".

The Systems Overterrestrial Coalition: An association of colonies in L1, L2, L4, and L5 obligated by treaty to improve life on Earth. The SOC's governing authority is divided between the Coalition Council and the Coalition Secretariat, which is further divided into the Ministries of Commerce, Engineering, Agriculture, Education, Reclamation, Transportation, Terran Affairs, and General Affairs. The Secretary-General wields chief executive power.

The United States of North America: A remnant of the old American Empire consisting of the former East Coast states and Eastern Canada. Protectorate of the Atlasid Caliphate. Allied with the Coalition.

Zeklov Corporation: A Russian arms company that primarily serves the remnants of Earth's ruling class. Second only to Seed Corp.

Zone Demilitarisée Coloniale: ZoDiaC for short. A secret alliance of colonies, nearly all of which are located in L3, opposed to the Coalition's military actions on Earth.

1

The giant's approach shook the pines atop the low ridge where Sieg lay hidden. A flock of starlings took flight from the trembling boughs but found no sky. They rose over the treetops, through a patchy layer of cloud, and toward the sunlight reflected through the thirty kilometer window arcing overhead.

Sieg didn't linger on the flock spiraling into a pointillist corkscrew in the twisted gravity of the colony's axis. He trained his field glasses on the stocky, olive drab combat frame tromping through the woods below. Boughs halfway up the trees' thirty-five meter tall trunks scraped its domed head. The CF held its oversized machine gun at the ready.

ZoDiaC's intel didn't mention Soc patrols this far from the compound. But the demilitarized colonies' report had already proved less trustworthy than Sieg's own eyes. The giant approaching his team's position was a Grenzmark C, a last-generation Systems Overterrestrial Coalition combat frame rushed into production as a stopgap measure. Its presence meant the Socs had tightened security on short notice.

It's almost on us. Sieg slid back downslope across the fragrant needles blanketing the ridge. When the rocky crest stood between him and the Grenzmark's sensors, he sprang to his feet and ran downhill. His life—and the lives of his mother, his sister, and his friends—depended on him taking down the giant before it reached

1

Elliot and Werner. He leapt the last four meters to the ground and landed in a crouch at his work frame's feet.

"How bad are we screwed?" Elliot hissed from the cab of his work frame, which stood to the right of Sieg's.

"Grenzmark C inbound," Sig told him and Werner, who manned the third work frame at Elliot's right. Werner's dark eyes and pale face brooded in contrast to Elliot's ruddy-cheeked anxiety.

"The three of us can take a Grenzie," said Werner, "but not the reinforcements who'll answer the pilot's distress call."

Sieg climbed into his work frame's cab. The construction equipment, plus forged work orders, had gotten him and his friends inside Byzantium colony. But the compact, utilitarian machines were no match for their larger, better armed combat frame descendants. *Not in a straight fight.*

The work frame's window reflected Sieg's sky blue eyes glinting in his determined face under a crown of neatly trimmed blond hair. He started the machine and strode toward the cleft in the ridge.

"Where are you going?" Elliott asked over the comm. Sieg answered by extending his work frame's three-fingered hand toward his friends. He knew they'd take the hint and stay back.

Suck ups and hangers-on had flocked to Sieg since his father's election as L3's prime minister. But Elliot, Werner, and Chase—the pilot who'd stayed with their shuttle to ensure a fast exit—comprised the small circle of academy friends he'd known since childhood. No one else could be trusted with such a vital mission.

The Grenzie's approaching footfalls rattled Sieg's cab. *The Soc's coming right through the gap.* It stood to reason. The artificial hills ran to the massive windows that flanked Sanzen's personal land strip. Water covered the thick panes, forming artificial lakes. Neither the Grenzmark nor the work frames were rated for aquatic use, so the cleft was the only way through the ridge for over a kilometer in each direction.

Sieg fought the urge to rush his target and stayed behind the cover of an outcrop to the Grenzie's left. The secondhand work frame had no active sensors, which was a blessing in disguise since using radar would have triggered the combat frame's sensitive instruments.

Three more steps. Sieg drew a carbyne-reinforced utility knife from his work frame's hip-mounted toolbox.

Two.

One.

Sieg's work frame pivoted into the cleft. The Grenzie's head swiveled to glare at its smaller foe. The squat metal dome covered a circular array of high intensity LED panels interspersed with mini cameras. Three columns of five horizontal slits made the CF's face resemble a gladiator's visor.

Sieg jammed the control stick forward. His work frame charged the Grenzie with two jarring bounds. The CF swung its 110mm machine gun forward but failed to adjust for its unusually short opponent before Sieg plunged his utility knife through the cockpit hatch in the Grenzmark's chest.

The suddenly unmanned combat frame started to list, and Sieg propped it up against a tree. He relieved the Grenzie of its machine gun. The weapon—essentially a handheld automatic tank gun— proved awkward but useable in the work frame's three-clawed hands. He grabbed an extra magazine from the CF's skirt armor and rejoined his friends.

"I knew you'd pull it off," Werner said.

"Is the Coalition pilot...dead?" asked Elliot.

The weight of what Sieg had done pressed down on his chest. *Mom, Liz, forgive me. I had to.*

Werner knew how to interpret his friend's silence. "Let's move out," he said. "It won't be long until more Socs come looking."

By silent accord, the three childhood friends turned comrades-in-arms filed past the motionless Grenzmark. Their work frames navigated the woods more stealthily than the combat frame had managed, and they soon reached the forest's edge. A verdant field stretched from the tree line to a stark concrete wall that, according to Sieg's informant, encompassed Sanzen's house of horrors.

"A hundred meters of open ground looks a lot bigger in real life than on paper," Elliot said. "How do we cross it unnoticed?"

Sieg's hand sought his red and black flight suit's left breast pocket. His thumb and forefinger closed around a smooth strip of fabric, which he gently drew out. He stared at the pink silk ribbon—

one of two his young sister was fond of wearing in her long blond hair.

Which Sanzen sent my father as a warning.

"I passed the point of no return when I killed that Soc," Sieg told his friends with cold subdued wrath. "You two have done more than I had any right to ask. Withdraw to the maintenance hatch, call Chase, and wait for me. I'll go after Mother and Elizabeth."

Elliot's work frame stepped forward to stand beside Sieg's. "I promised to help rescue your family from Sanzen," said Elliot. "No use trying to change the terms now."

Werner lined up next to Elliot. Sieg didn't have to hear his explanation. His quiet friend's crush on the lively and beautiful Elizabeth Friedlander was an open secret.

"There are no combat frames visible on the ground," said Sieg. "We rush the wall at full speed, go over the top, and head straight for the research wing. If we meet any resistance..." Sieg brandished the oversized machine gun in his work frame's hands. "Keep going and leave them to me."

The only reply was a whispered, "For Elizabeth," on Werner's channel. It spurred the three friends like a starter pistol, and together their work frames charged from the safety of the trees toward the imposing wall.

Screaming fire rained down. Werner's cry cut off as his work frame vanished in a burning cloud. Sieg reflexively jerked his control stick hard to the left. The missile that had been meant for him detonated in the trees. Splinters drummed against his work frame's back like flaming hail.

The smoke cleared. A debris-lined crater yawned at Werner's last known position. Elliot's work frame lay slumped against a blackened tree, its right arm and leg blown away.

Sieg fixed his camera on the colossal window above. Applying a dazzle filter showed him the stocky outlines of six combat frames silhouetted against the sun's reflection in the colony's angled mirror.

Grenzmark IIs. The current-model combat frames had been waiting in the air over the compound, hidden in the sun. *They knew we were coming.*

Sieg's cold anger burst into white-hot rage. He punched his work frame's jump jet switch and fired a series of controlled bursts from his machine gun as he rocketed toward the enemy squad. Three of the six CFs went down trailing smoke from their ruptured cockpits.

The remaining Grentos opened up with their own automatic rifles. Huge bullets flew past the small, fast-moving target until one volley shredded the work frame's legs. Missing its thrusters, the critically damaged machine crashed to the ground. Emergency airbags deployed, sparing Sieg the full force of the impact that knocked the air from his lungs.

Sieg mashed the door release and tumbled from the work frame's cab. He landed on soft mowed grass, lurched to his feet, and bolted for the trees. The whine of the Grentos' thrusters harried him like onrushing thunder.

Elliot sat beside his ruined work frame, his left leg bent at an unnatural angle. The color had drained from his normally flushed face. "I'm done," he panted as Sieg ran to him. "Werner's gone. He was right next to me…"

"Don't talk," said Sieg. He bent down and slung his arm around his friend's back. With Sieg's help, Elliot rose to stand on one shaking foot. Together they hobbled into the forest.

"I'm sorry," Elliot said as they limped through the woods. Three searchlight beams swept the shadows of the canopy close behind them. "I tried my best. Just wasn't enough."

"It's not your fault. Someone set us up."

"We're trapped," said Elliot. "I don't know what to do."

Sieg knew exactly what to do. From the moment he and Elliot entered the woods, he'd been heading back toward the cleft in the ridge. They might have a chance if they could reach it before the Socs caught up—which would happen any second with Elliot slowing Sieg down. He gathered his injured friend in his arms and made a run for the ridge.

Time seemed to dilate as Sieg ran. But the trees parted, and his heart leapt when he saw the small pass between the hills. Summoning a final burst of speed, he sprinted through the cleft and set Elliot down at the Grenzmark C's foot.

Sieg's lungs and limbs burned, but the low roar of thrusters just behind the ridge drove him up the steel rungs set into the combat frame's armor. He reached the cloven cockpit door, pried it open, and fought his gag reflex as he dumped most of the dead pilot to the ground below. Elliot's cry sent panic stabbing up Sieg's spine until he saw that his friend was only reacting to the bloody mess that had landed a few meters to his right. They hadn't been discovered yet.

Good thing my suit's mostly red. Sieg took a deep breath and hoisted himself into the Grenzmark's cockpit. His knife thrust had destroyed the main monitor and split the pilot seat's back, but the controls mounted on the armrests remained functional. He lowered the combat frame into a crouch and set its left hand on the ground. When Elliot crawled into the giant metal palm, Sieg raised the CF to its full height and set off with the punctured door open.

"Chase," he called on the shuttle's frequency. "This is Sieg. Do you read me?"

After an agonizing moment, the line crackled. "Chase here," the shuttle pilot said. "Reading you five, Sieg. Didn't expect you so soon."

"I need an evac, stat."

"For five, I hope."

"Negative. It's just me and Elliot."

Chase's voice fell. "And Werner?"

"He didn't make it. I'm in a stolen Grenzie with at least three flight-capable Grentos in pursuit. What's your ETA to the maintenance hatch?"

"Give me ten minutes," said Chase. "And Sieg? Stay alive, or I'll fly this bird to hell and beat your dead ass. Over and out."

Sieg set the Grenzie's feet toward the access hatch partway up the curve of the colony's end cap. Negotiating the colossal bowl was like climbing the inside of a hollow mountain. The climb proved more difficult than the initial descent from the same hatch what seemed like a lifetime ago, especially with Elliot cradled in one of the CF's hands.

Equally relieved and wary that the Grentos hadn't spotted him yet, Sieg tuned in the Coalition Security Corps' dedicated frequency. From the three surviving CSC pilots' chatter, he soon learned that his combat frame theft had gone unnoticed. The Grentos were still searching the forest near Sanzen's compound for intruders fleeing on foot.

Sieg piloted the Grenzmark into the warren of enormous passages between the colony's inner and outer hull. Navigating by memory, he reached the CF-sized airlock that led to outer space and freedom.

"Seal your suit," he called down to Elliot, who pulled his helmet over his head. Sieg did likewise. His helmet magnified his heavy breaths of metallic-tasting air.

"Come in, Chase. This is Sieg. Elliot and I are in position. Do you copy?"

"Copy, Sieg," said Chase. "I'm parked just out of sight. It's a straight shot from the hatch to the shuttle. Come on out, and I'll have us home for supper, over."

Sieg's anger blazed like red coals in the pit of his stomach as he opened the airlock. "I'll come back for you," he promised his mother, his sister, and the unavenged ghost of his friend. He fired the Grenzie's jump thrusters and launched into the black.

What looked like a white dot soon resolved into the blunted bullet shape of the shuttle's hull, which grew to dominate Sieg's vision. Within moments, he and Elliot would be safely aboard and bound for L3, where the wayward son would face his father's displeasure. *I'd rather fight the Socs again.*

Sieg had come alongside the shuttle and was reaching the Grenzie's free hand toward the bay door when a nasal male voice came over the CSC channel. "Gamma One to Control: Unauthorized shuttle confirmed twenty klicks to spinward off the end cap. Transmitting live feed from my Grento's optical array."

"Acknowledged, Gamma One," a brusque voice replied. "Target lock acquired."

"Chase," Shouted Sieg. "They spotted you. Get out of here!"

A point of light streaked from the colony and connected with the shuttle amidships. The resulting blast reduced the spacecraft to a hot vapor. Sieg barely managed to turn his Grenzie aside before the shockwave hammered the combat frame, sending it hurtling away from the colony at an acute angle.

Sieg feared the damaged chair to which he was strapped would break loose and eject him into space. It held, but he almost wished it hadn't when the tremors rocking his CF threatened to batter him into paste. The shaking subsided, leaving him bruised and in shock with cockpit alarms blaring.

A frantic thought shattered Sieg's respite. *Elliot!*

Sieg's throbbing hand gripped the control stick and commanded the Grenzmark to raise its left arm. Nothing happened. He repeated the process twice before a dread realization penetrated his numbed mind. Against his muscles' protests, he released his harness, leaned forward, and craned his neck outside the cockpit.

All of the Grenzmark's limbs had been blown off.

Despair drove Sieg back into his seat. He sat motionless for what could have been seconds or hours, until a familiar voice intruded on his daze.

"Gamma One to Control: Detonation confirmed. Target vaporized. Request authorization to search for CF spotted before impact, over."

"Negative," said an icy female voice Sieg couldn't quite place in his near-delirium. "Break off pursuit and return to base. This mission was a total success."

Mother, thought Sieg as he tumbled through space. *Liz. I failed you.*

2

"The institute is entrusted with caring for the most extreme cases—those who exhibit disorders not seen in the colonies since before the Collapse."

The doctor's pedantic droning filtered into Zane's cell and roused him from his brooding. He eased himself off his bed's foam mattress, crept across the spongy floor, and crouched beside the narrow slit in the padded steel door.

"I see." The stern male voice kindled dim recollections in Zane's mind. "Tell me, Doctor. How do you deal with these prisoners?"

The voices were getting closer, along with the click of footsteps on the hallway tile. *There's three of them. Two are about the same weight, wearing men's dress shoes. One's a lot lighter, in boots with raised heels.*

"We refer to them as *patients*," Zane's doctor said. "Sadly, the cases in this ward pose a danger to themselves and others. The best we can do is keep them confined to their rooms."

"You mean *incarcerated in their cells*," said a girl whose soft voice took a harsh tone. The sound flowed like ice water down Zane's back.

"I was speaking to your father, young lady," the doctor said. "I'll thank you not to interrupt."

"My responsibilities to the Coalition afford me no time for children, Doctor," said the second man, annoyance creeping into his stony voice.

"I apologize, Director Sanzen. I'd assumed this young woman was your daughter."

Sanzen Kaimora? The head of the Coalition Security Corps? Zane wondered if he really was psychotic and the conversation in the hall was just a hallucination. He risked a peek through the slot in his door.

Zane already knew the graying, lab coated figure of Cody, the facility's head of psychiatry. Facing the doctor in the middle of the hall stood a tall lean man who, unlike most in the Coalition, looked used to manual labor. The only hair on his head was a severe black goatee. The lapel of his charcoal gray suit bore a gold O'Neill cylinder pin—the emblem of the SOC. *Definitely Sanzen. But who's that with him?*

A petite young woman stood behind Sanzen in a matching skirted suit. Black hair with a deep blue sheen fell past her shoulders to the small of her back. Dark eyes set in a pale narrow face scanned her surroundings with the calculation of an artic she-wolf. Her gaze met Zane's, and he recoiled from the door.

"This is my assistant Sekaino Megami," said Sanzen. "She is here to advise me on my decision."

"Yes, of course," the doctor stammered. "As per your request, I've assembled a list of all patients who were originally part of Block 101. The first is right down this hall. His name is Zane Dellister. He's been with us for several months.

"The name sounds familiar," said Sanzen. "What's wrong with him?"

"Zane developed a strange form of obsessive-compulsive disorder," Cody said. "Oddly, symptoms manifested after he arrived here in Chicago but before his unit saw combat. He was arrested in an abandoned warehouse following a rash of thefts from Seed Corporation. Evidently he'd built his own combat frame out of parts stolen from Seed's factory, the CSC's own inventory, and even destroyed enemy units."

"I remember now," said Sanzen. "He refused to cooperate with Browning's analysis. Why wasn't he confined to the stockade?"

"Zane harbors an unhealthy attachment to this black combat frame. He put three security personnel in the infirmary during his removal from the warehouse. Since then, he's displayed behavior verging on dissociative identity disorder."

"Fascinating," Sanzen said dryly. "Put him down as a candidate for transfer to Metis, and let's move on."

"Who's next on the list?" asked Megami.

The doctor's stylus tapped on his tablet's screen. "That would be Eiyu Masz, our most violent case. I advise proceeding with caution."

The Doctor's words faded as he led his guests down the hall. "Did you hear that, Dead Drop?" Zane asked his absent combat frame. "They're transferring me and Masz to that asteroid base in L5." Zane didn't get along with people—Masz least of all. He always seemed to be breathing down Zane's neck despite being locked in another cell. "They're not sticking me with Masz," he told Dead Drop. "And they're not sending me back into space without you!"

A high time preference was among the personality traits that Cody said aggravated Zane's dysfunction. That didn't mean Zane was incapable of long-term planning. He could be patient when necessary. He just didn't like it.

Zane waited almost a whole hour after Cody, Sanzen, and Megami passed back down the hallway and out of the ward before he enacted the escape he'd been planning for months. He stood before the mirror embedded in the wall behind a thick polymer sheet and pulled his light blue pajama shirt up over his head of buzzed, platinum blond hair. Then he stuffed the shirt down the drain of the small sink built into a wall recess and opened the taps.

His slippers came off next. These he wrapped in plastic hoarded from weeks' worth of prepackaged meals and jammed down the tankless ceramic toilet. The water flow valve was hidden in the white padded wall, so Zane kept flushing as cold water sloshed onto the floor. He knew security was watching him over the pinhole cameras installed in his room, and he knew they'd send orderlies to deal with his misbehavior. In fact, he was counting on it.

It didn't take long for the overflowing fixtures to flood the small room five centimeters deep. Zane lay face down in the rising water and held his breath. He was floating, and his lungs starting to burn, before the heavy door hissed open.

"He'd been like that for five minutes when the second shift guy came on and saw the monitor," said a male orderly who burst into the room, fighting the outflow of water.

"Get him up," said another man behind him. "If he drowns, it's our asses on the line!"

Zane pushed up from the flooded floor and drove both feet into the first orderly's stomach. The air escaped the man's lungs in a pained gasp, and the torrent swirling around his shins assisted in knocking him backwards into his coworker.

Drawing a deep sweet breath, Zane sprang to his feet and rounded on the orderlies who lay in a sodden tangled heap outside. The man on top struggled to rise, but Zane leapt from the doorway and stomped on his chest, driving both orderlies back down. He knelt, bounced both men's heads off the tile floor, and ripped the security badge from the top man's white scrubs.

The exit from the ward lay down the hall to Zane's left and around the corner to the right. But the keycard alone wouldn't get him out. The exit used an airlock system with two doors and a small booth in-between. Only one door could be opened at a time, and the whole booth could be remotely locked down to hold an escapee till security showed up.

Which Zane was also counting on. He hauled the first orderly—a pudgy man with short brown hair—off his unconscious counterpart, bound his hands with his shirt, and stood him up. Zane positioned himself behind the semiconscious orderly and encircled the man's neck with the chain from his extendable badge clip. He held the makeshift garrote closed with one hand while pushing him forward with the other. The fat man sputtered as they slogged down the hall.

When they reached the heavy airlock door, Zane opened it with the orderly's keycard. A beige steel box waited beyond with an identical door on the far side—a door that couldn't open until Zane shut the one behind him.

12

Security was certainly watching Zane's every move. They knew he was in the airlock and that he had a hostage. The smart move would be to lock down the room when he closed the door and wait him out, regardless of the risk to the hostage. But Zane's time on Earth had acquainted him with a fundamental difference between himself and other colonists. Socs couldn't stomach making hard decisions. Instead, they jumped straight to excessive force.

Zane shut the door behind him. He tightened his feebly struggling hostage's chain and waited. Sure enough, the facing door slid open to reveal four guards in dark blue CSC uniforms. They all carried carbon polymer batons, but they hadn't taken the time to don riot gear.

Big mistake.

"Release the hostage and get on the floor with your hands behind your head, now!" said a security officer with tan skin and a short crewcut.

"I'm crazy-ass spaceman," cried Zane. "I'll do what I want!" He released the chain and kicked the orderly through the door. The security officers jumped aside, and Zane charged right between them into the outer hallway, stepping on his former hostage.

The two rearmost guards lunged at him. Zane grabbed the guard to his right by the wrist, kicked his leg out, and levered him toward his oncoming friend while prying the baton from his hand. As the second guard struggled to prop up the first's dead weight, Zane spun to intercept the two guards who'd stood near the door but were now charging him. He ducked under a vicious swing from the guard on his right and drove the butt of his own baton into the man's stomach.

With the man on his right down on all fours struggling to breathe, Zane launched himself at the guard on his left. His new opponent's brown eyes widened, and he froze as Zane's baton crashed into his temple. He folded to the ground.

The first two guards regained their feet. The one who still had a baton brought it down in a whirring arc at Zane's head. Zane angled his body to one side, let the stick blur past, and punched his attacker in the throat. That made three guards writhing on the floor.

Zane let the last guard run down the hallway yelling for help while he took a detour to the right. A short sprint brought him to the commissary for low-security patients. He rushed through the pajama-clad dinner crowd, past a wall cluttered with disturbing finger paintings, and into the steamy, savory-smelling kitchen. The mostly female staff shrieked, and trays crashed to the floor as Zane bolted for the back of the room and plunged down the trash chute.

The dumpster where Zane landed smelled decidedly worse than the kitchen above, but this air was free. *Almost. I just need to cross the yard and get through the fence. Then I'm out, and no one will keep us apart, Dead Drop!*

Zane didn't bother rummaging through squishy trash bags and soggy cardboard boxes for the baton he'd dropped upon landing. He vaulted out of the reeking metal bin and took off running across the cracked asphalt of a loading dock. Broken glass stabbed his feet, but he ignored the sting and fixated on reuniting with this combat frame.

A wide green lawn sloped down from the low gray building that housed the institute. The cool grass soothed Zane's tortured feet as he ran for the razor wire fence encircling the campus. A pair of wheeled gates flanked an enclosed guard box thirty meters away. Zane sped up, dashed across the road leading to the gate, and dove at the box.

The panicked guard inside shot at the window, sending the reinforced glass sliding away in a spiderwebbed sheet. Red hot pain engulfed Zane's mind as a bullet slammed into his right leg. His momentum carried him through the broken window and into the screaming guard, whose head collided with the opposite window before he got a second shot off. He slumped back into his chair.

Breathing like a furnace, Zane hammered the gate button. More gunshots cracked behind him, and bullets ricocheted off the guard box and the fence. He ducked out of the box and rushed through the gate. But his wounded leg betrayed him. Zane stumbled and went rolling the rest of the way downhill. He splashed down in a drainage ditch at the base of the slope. A concrete pipe yawned to his left. Without thinking, Zane scrambled into the filthy darkness.

3

"Ritter!" Schwarze barked from the dirt path at the combat frame's feet. "Quit tinkering and prep that Grenzie for action. We're moving out."

Tod Ritter, soldier of the Black Reichswehr, closed the access panel in his prized Grenzmark C's cockpit and poked his head out into the sultry African morning. Exotic birds and insects filled the air with song. He took in the lush green carpet of jungle rolling away from the hill where the German expats' CFs were parked before lowering his eyes to Schwarze's scrawny figure.

"Already?" asked Ritter. "Is General Kopp sending us into a real battle this time?"

A scowl pinched Schwarze's gaunt face. "Are you questioning the General's command decisions?"

Ritter hopped down from the cockpit, using the Grenzie's olive drab knee and foot as stepping stones to reach the muddy ground. He fixed his brown eyes on Schwarze's beady, slate gray irises and said, "I'm questioning how raiding African settlements and caravans is supposed to help us restore Neue Deutschland!"

"Have some patience for once," said Schwarze. "It took a hundred and fifty years to drive the Caliphate from our lands. The Socs and their lickspittles overthrew Kaiser Maximilian just three years ago. Marshaling a proper resistance takes time."

"What's the target, then?"

"There's a small village nearby. The General believes they have a cache of parts, fuel, grain, and ammunition."

Fury welled in Ritter's chest. "I joined up to liberate my homeland from the Socs, not to terrorize innocent villagers!"

The way Schwarze's travel-stained fatigues hung from his lank frame led many to misjudge him as weak. Ritter got a reminder that Kopp's toady was made of lean muscle when Schwarze grabbed him by his frayed green collar.

"You should know," Schwarze spat in Ritter's face, "that the caravan leader you urged us to spare sold out this village. The battlefield is no place for sentiment, boy! It will get you killed. I'm inclined to do the job myself before you take someone else down with you."

Ritter grunted as Schwarze's tightening grip constricted his throat. He cocked back his arm to strike his superior, but his punch smacked into a firm gloved hand.

"Stand down," said a breathy male voice. The new recruit, known only as Blondie for his wild golden hair, stood to the right gripping Ritter's balled fist.

Schwarze inclined his head to the newcomer. "Here to help me enforce military discipline, Private?"

"I was talking to both of you," Blondie said as he released Ritter's hand.

Schwarze's brow furrowed. He shoved Ritter down and rounded on Blondie. "I don't care if you supplied your own combat frame," said Schwarze. "That's a contribution we're all obliged to make for the Fatherland. It doesn't earn you extra privileges, and it sure as hell doesn't justify insubordination."

Ritter sprang to his feet and jabbed a finger at Schwarze. "It's two against one. That's all the justification we need."

"Schwarze is right," said Blondie.

Ritter's jaw dropped. "But you're the one who convinced them not to slaughter the caravan. Now they want to massacre a whole village!"

Blondie removed his aviator sunglasses and fixed his gaze on the younger soldier. On closer inspection, he was only a year or so older than Ritter. But his sky blue eyes held even more loss and sorrow. *Did the Socs murder his family, too?*

"Everyone in an outfit like this has two choices," Blondie said, "fight or run. What's yours?"

Ritter clenched his teeth to contain the cry of frustration that threatened to burst from his mouth. His white-knuckled fists fell to his sides.

"I'll take silence for assent," said Schwarze, mussing Ritter's shaggy dark hair. "Be ready to roll out in ten minutes." He turned and strolled down the dirt path. After ten paces he looked back over his shoulder. "I was talking to both of you."

"I can't believe you just folded like that," Ritter shouted at Blondie when Schwarze had disappeared around the curve of the hill. The older Private had become Ritter's mentor, even helping him with the new Grenzmark design he hoped to build one day. Ritter had thought the two of them saw eye to eye. Now he realized he didn't understand Blondie at all. "Are you bloodthirsty or just a coward?"

Blondie weathered the verbal assault. "There's a difference between surrender and picking your battles. Like I said, we all have a choice. Choose well." He replaced his shades, stuffed his hands in the pockets of his red and black jacket, and strode down the path toward his Grenzie.

"The only battle I want to fight is for my homeland," Ritter said to himself.

"This village is under the protection of the Black Reichswehr," General Kopp announced over his Grenzmark II's PA. "You have no need of weapons. Surrender your arms, along with your food, fuel, and equipment stores." The mostly Chinese villagers ignored his gruff German words and continued their shrieking flight through the muddy roads between hovels.

Schwarze's Grenzmark I, with its bullet-shaped head and earth tone desert paint scheme, pulled up alongside Kopp. "We're wasting time," Schwarze broadcast on the Reichswehr's channel. His CF raised its machine gun. "Let's clear this place out."

Ritter urged his Grenzie forward from the tree line to confront his superiors at the settlement's edge. "They don't understand us. Gunning them down would be murder!"

The grill covering Schwarze's sensor array swiveled toward Ritter's CF. "Do you speak Mandarin?"

Frustration burned Ritter's blood. "No. But if we just kill these people and take their property, we'll be just like the Socs."

"The Coalition took Deutschland," said Kopp. His Grento's domed head with its backswept command antenna never turned from the village. "We have the same objective. Why shouldn't we emulate their methods?"

"Well said, Sir." Schwarze's Grenzmark I took an earthshaking step into the village and angled its gun barrel toward the street. Like a school of fish, the panicked mob retreated as one from the steel giant.

"That's a language they understand," said Blondie, who advanced his olive drab Grenzmark C from the jungle to join his squadmates. His Grenzie's metal hand pointed to each side of the roughly square settlement. "If we position a CF at each side of the perimeter and have them all move in toward the center, we can herd the villagers into that building there."

Ritter studied the long, warehouse style structure Blondie indicated. Made of whitewashed steel walls running east to west under a peaked wooden roof, the building dominated the prefabricated huts and plywood shacks surrounding it. Colorfully painted panes filled the small windows. Two simple beams intersecting at right angles hung over the double door. *It's a church.*

Kopp took only a moment to decide. "Schwarze, keep driving them from the south." His Grento's left arm swept in a westerly arc, taking in the Reichswehr's other Grenzmark I. "Heinz, move in from the left. Blondie, the right. Ritter, circle around and herd our sheep from the north. I'll deal with any stragglers."

Ritter breathed a sigh of relief. As the Black Reichswehr members broke off to fulfill their assigned roles, Ritter's Grenzie snapped a salute at Blondie's, which crisply returned the gesture.

Intimidating the frightened villagers into taking refuge in their church pricked Ritter's conscience, but it beat the alternative. He flinched whenever Kopp's 115mm machine gun thundered from the surrounding woods.

"That's most of them," Schwarze reported when the Black Reichswehr reconvened in the small unpaved square in front of the packed church. "Or at least enough to let us search this shithole at our leisure."

"Start searching, then," said Kopp. "Blondie, Ritter: You stand guard here. If any of these church mice so much as set foot outside, don't hesitate to make an example."

Kopp, Schwarze, and Heinz set to their task with gusto, tearing down rickety dwellings and sifting through the wreckage.

Ritter opened his cockpit to the humid, reeking air and turned his CF to face Blondie, who did the same. "Thanks," Ritter said over the racket of his squadmates ransacking the village.

Blondie nodded, his face unreadable behind his mirrored glasses.

"You're a hard guy to figure out," said Ritter. "Why are you with this third-rate outfit, anyway?"

"Have you ever failed in your responsibilities, Ritter?" Blondie's stony expression never changed as he looked to the cloudless sky. "Did you ever let someone important to you down?"

Shame warmed Ritter's face. "I was sixteen when the Socs overran my town. More than old enough to fight back. My father said it was best to do nothing; that if we kept our heads down, it would all sort itself out in the morning. I listened to him. Now I'm the only member of my family left alive."

Blondie's deep but airy voice softened. "I bet you'd do anything to make up for that mistake."

"Nothing!" Schwarze's Grenzmark I came stomping toward the church. "We leveled this flyspeck to the ground, and we've nothing to show for it."

"Serves us right for terrorizing innocent people," Ritter said.

"You're so naïve it's a wonder you're still breathing," said Schwarze. "If these people are innocent, I'm Tesla Browning. They're holding out on us, and by process of elimination, there's only one place they can be hiding their stash."

Ritter sealed his cockpit and imposed his Grenzie between Schwarze and the church. "These people have suffered enough. This church is all they have left. I won't let you destroy it!"

"Does anyone else hear that?" asked Blondie. "It sounds like a jet, but I'm not getting anything on radar."

The Grenzmark I lunged. Its armored shoulder slammed into the Grenzie's chest and sent it reeling backwards. A jolt stabbed up Ritter's spine as his CF landed in a sitting position against the church doors.

Schwarze drew the curved axe from his Grenzmark I's hip. The air around its blade wavered with steel-melting heat. "Looks like I'll have to cut through you to crush that church and everyone inside. The smell of your charred corpse will add savor to the work."

Rhythmic tremors coursed through the ground as Heinz's Grenzmark I and Kopp's Grento tromped into the square. "We've coddled these peasants enough," said Kopp. "Heinz, Blondie: Take down that church."

Not good, thought Ritter. His Grenzie's early warning system chirped an instant before he heard the roar of jet engines approaching from the west.

"This is Captain Maximus Darving of the Earth Governments in Exile," a mellow tenor with a flippant edge radioed in American English. "Move away from the building, exit your combat frames, and surrender."

Ritter rotated his CF's head to scan the sky behind him. A white, hard-edged plane with blue markings on its forward-swept wings screamed toward the village. He couldn't visually identify the aircraft, and he found no match in the Grenzie's admittedly outdated CSC database.

Kopp pointed his oversized machine gun at the sky. "Shoot down that plane!"

Heinz obliged. His gun joined Kopp's in splitting the air with bullets as big as milk cans. The jet rolled between both streams of fire and answered in kind with the twin Vulcans mounted in its nose. Kopp's Grento danced aside from the double row of divots spraying out of the ground, but the rotary cannons' fire chewed up Heinz's slower CF like aluminum foil. The perforated Grenzmark I crashed backwards into the ruined village and lay smoldering.

Kopp's Grento steadied itself, took aim, and fired a controlled burst as the jet flew overhead. Smoke trailed from the aircraft's port wing.

Ritter used the distraction to haul his Grenzie to its feet. He drew his own heat axe and swung at the head of Schwarze's Grenzmark I. His target's grill swiveled toward the incoming axe, and Schwarze's superheated blade intercepted Ritter's with a ringing clash. Ritter's axe went flipping from its hand to disappear in the wreckage.

"Still too weak, boy!" gloated Schwarze as he raised his CF's heat axe for a blow to Ritter's cockpit. A staccato burst of thunder punctuated his last word as a volley of 110mm slugs reduced the Grenzmark I to jagged scrap.

Ritter swept his main camera to the left. Blondie's Grenzie stood, gun smoking, over the burning remains of Schwarze's CF. "Thanks, Blondie," Ritter said between heaving breaths.

From the corner of his eye, Ritter caught a blur of motion as Kopp's Grento spun at the waist and leveled its gun at Blondie's CF. Ritter fired his Grenzie's rifle from the hip. The jungle ate most of the volley, but one round grazed the Grento's arm. Kopp's barrage flew wide of its target.

Blondie pivoted toward Kopp. He couched his gun's stock against his Grenzie's pauldron, aligned the sights with his CF's sensor grill, and squeezed the trigger. Six rounds punched through the Grento's chest in a pattern confined to the general's cockpit door. The idle Grento remained standing with a ragged hole drilled straight through its torso.

"I didn't expect to pay you back so soon," said Ritter.

"We're not even yet," Blondie reminded him. "You still owe me one."

Ritter's proximity alarm pinged again. This time a beat passed before what sounded like a giant weed trimmer echoed over the western horizon.

Blondie moved his Grenzie to the church's front wall and propped his gun up on the long roof, aiming at the sky. He motioned for Ritter to join him.

"Inbound helo," Blondie told Ritter when both men had positioned their CFs facing the church's east wall with their cockpits open. "She's coming in hot and heavy. Gunship, probably."

"No problem," said Ritter. "Kopp sent that jet packing. We can take a chopper down, easy."

"That *helicopter* is more maneuverable at low altitude, is probably carrying an arsenal of anti-armor ordnance, and has a team of gunners that can scatter us across the surface of a smoldering crater faster than we can react. Stay alert and don't do or say anything till I give the word."

The gunship hovered over the jungle canopy like an overfed green and brown hornet. A pair of tiered transparent blisters swelled from its nose. Ritter counted three Vulcans and a 70mm cannon mounted on turrets at the front of the fuselage. A pair of missile pods dangled from its stubby wings.

Ritter shut his cockpit against the lashing wind and piercing whine of the rotors. A higher register male voice with a Received English accent spoke over the radio. "This is Major Alan Collins of the EGE. Exit your combat frames and surrender."

"That's what the guy in the jet said," Ritter replied. "Didn't go too well for him."

Blondie groaned.

"The guy in the jet is still combat-capable," said the more laid-back, American English speaker whom Ritter recalled as Captain Darving. "And trust me; you want to do what the Major says. He's way less gentle than me."

"I repeat," said Major Collins. "Exit the combat frames. I won't warn you again."

Blondie kept his Grenzie's rifle trained on the chopper. "Negative. Your weapons are still locked on to us. Tell your gunners to stand down, and we'll accept your terms."

"I'm not blind," said Collins. "Or daft. My gunners won't stand down while you're pointing a 110mm automatic rifle at my aircraft. And it's no good using that warehouse as cover. I will shoot your cockpit right through it unless you stand down."

"This is a church," said Ritter. "It's full of people!"

"I know," the Major said flatly.

"Collins!" said Darving. "Have you gone apeshit? You're not firing on a church."

"I will use any means necessary to protect the men and equipment in my command, Captain," said Collins. "Contradict me again, and I'll have you in the brig for insubordination. Is that clear?"

The gunship was close enough for Ritter's main camera to get a good shot of Collins' face. The Major looked to be in his mid-twenties with short brown hair and green eyes with a scar bisecting his left eyebrow. He wore a bulky headset and a khaki uniform with a flag on the sleeve consisting of a red cross on a white field. Nothing in his demeanor hinted that he was bluffing.

"Listen," said Blondie. "I can respect your devotion to your crew, but I'm on an important errand that can't wait. My friend and I didn't destroy this village. We helped take down the cretins who did. Why don't we end this standoff and go our separate ways?"

"I don't give a toss about your itinerary," Collins snapped. "Whether or not you took part in the carnage here is for a military tribunal to decide. Now put down your guns and exit your bloody CFs!"

Ritter's screen flashed red and an alarm trilled, indicating a missile lock on his Grenzie. *He's serious!*

"My name is Sieg Friedlander," Blondie said through gritted teeth. "Former L3 Prime Minister Josef Friedlander was my father."

Ritter felt as if he were in freefall. *He's who!?*

"I know who Josef Friedlander was," Collins said, irritation edging his voice. "It's only been a few months since the accident. My condolences if you really are his son, which I doubt."

"Not an accident," said Sieg. "An *assassination*. It's part of the reason I'm here on Earth." His Grenzmark rifle thudded to the ground beside the church. "I've already compromised a highly sensitive mission by telling you this much. Now tell your men to stand down, and let me get on with trying to save you idiotic grounders from yourselves."

Ritter's monitor shifted back to green, and he released a breath he didn't remember holding. The helicopter descended into the square.

Sieg leapt down from his kneeling Grenzie's cockpit and gestured for Ritter to do likewise. The landing gunship pelted the pair of them with dust and debris as Ritter joined the man he'd called Blondie on the church steps.

"Is it true?" Ritter asked. "Are you really Josef Friedlander's son?"

"Yes," said Sieg. "Now be quiet."

Collins approached from the makeshift landing pad accompanied by a thin man with a light brown mop of hair and a stockier soldier with a similarly colored crewcut; both carrying assault rifles. According to their uniforms, the first man was named Zimmer and the second Edmonds. All three wore khaki uniforms with stylized globe patches on their upper right sleeves.

"Up against the wall," Collins said.

Sieg complied, and Ritter grudgingly followed suit. Collins' men handcuffed the two Black Reichswehr survivors, subjected them to rough, thorough searches, and relieved them of anything that could be remotely considered a weapon. The soldiers spun their prisoners around, and Ritter grunted as the cold steel bracelets bit into his wrists.

Collins stood at parade rest facing Sieg and Ritter. "You gentlemen have earned a free cruise aboard the ES *Yamamoto*," the Major said, "with complimentary shuttle service. The duration of your voyage will depend on the outcome of your trial."

"You don't have jurisdiction," Ritter objected. "I'm a German citizen."

"A shame Germany no longer exists," said Collins.

Ritter struggled fruitlessly against his bonds. "We didn't do anything wrong!"

Collins nodded to his men, who marched the prisoners to the helicopter. The Major strode behind them.

4

"Esteemed delegates of the Commission," Sanzen's harsh voice filled the gray oval of the Coalition Secretariat Chamber in L1's Byzantium colony. "Honorable secretaries; especially Secretary-General Mitsu. I am humbled to address such a distinguished body."

Adopting a diplomatically neutral expression came easily to Mitsu Kasei as a skill honed by long practice. But sitting quietly amid her colleagues on the raised Secretaries' Platform while the barbaric Security Director spread his dangerous rhetoric taxed her patience.

Sanzen's rough hands gripped the podium centered on the red semicircle of carpet directly below Mitsu. He looked half-presentable, but a mercenary in an expensive navy blue suit was still a mercenary.

"I speak for of those who labor to secure the great strides we have made," Sanzen said. "They toil thanklessly below to realize the Colonization Commission's dream of a united and prosperous mankind. Many of these dedicated public servants will not live to see that dream fulfilled."

Uneasy murmurs and the crisp shuffling of papers arose from the tables that radiated from the podium to the gallery's edge in concentric rings.

"Your protectors in the Coalition Security Corps have persevered despite this council's neglect," Sanzen accused. "They ask for little and receive even less because more prestigious ministries are given higher priority. This inequitable resource allocation has exacted a toll in our citizens' blood. One hundred and twelve casualties have resulted from combat frame armor reductions required by budget cuts."

The subdued grumbling escalated to shouted denials and fists pounding on tables. "Order," Mitsu called over the din. "Director Sanzen, please correct whoever furnished you with those figures. The CSC's budget has increased year-over-year since its inception, if less drastically than your lavish proposals call for."

Sanzen kept his eyes locked on the gallery. "Will you say the same to Terrestrial Affairs Secretary Gohaku? What about Commerce Secretary Satsu? Is there any other department in the SOC whose wanton spending is not rubber stamped by the Secretariat?"

Seated on either side of Mitsu, portly graying Gohaku and rail-thin Satsu cast identical looks of displeasure at their chief executive. *How did I miss that obvious trap?* she rebuked herself.

"We colonists endured a brutal trial after the Collapse," Sanzen continued. "Perhaps we sacrificed our humanity to survive, as the grounders claim. I contend that our ordeal forced us to advance beyond every prior human society. Yet, while the Secretariat basks in luxury, the unsung heroes of the Security Corps fight and die on Earth."

The chamber fell quiet. A knot tightened in Mitsu's stomach. *They're hanging on his every word.* Even, she noted with distaste, the offensive slur for Earth natives.

"Let us not become desensitized to the suffering of our own people," said Sanzen, "our guardians and defenders! I implore you on behalf of the countless voices which cannot be heard across the gulf of space: Lend us your full strength that we may defeat the insurgents who endanger our lives...and our dream!"

The gallery erupted in applause while Sanzen's last syllable hung in the sterile air. Mitsu saw her goal of Earth's bloodless pacification recede further out of reach.

Sanzen forged ahead. "It is not only the halfhearted support of an indecisive administration that has condemned our brothers below to suffer. It is the SOC's foolish entanglements with the so-called governments of Earth. We have always sought to carry out our mission with their cooperation. But how often has our generosity met with deceit and betrayal? How many of earth's self-styled leaders have revealed themselves as greedy shiftless criminals?"

Discontented muttering emanated from the gallery. But this time Mitsu sensed that the discontent was directed at the Secretaries' Platform and her in particular. *Sanzen is a glorified thug,* she reminded herself. *But he's playing the chamber like a veteran political hand. Someone's been coaching him.*

"My solution to this twofold problem is simple," the Director said. "The Coalition Secretariat must show it is willing to lend full support to the Security Corps while extracting itself from all ruinous agreements with illegitimate governments.

"To that end, I submit to you Operation Oversight. Prepared by myself and my finest security advisors, this initiative will unleash the Coalition's full might against the criminal syndicates masquerading as Earth's governments!"

Applause still thundered from the chamber as Mitsu retreated down the curving, blue-carpeted hallway to her private office. It wasn't just the sting of defeat that hastened her steps, but humiliation at an outsider's hands.

Originally from L2 beyond the moon's orbit, exo-archaeologist Sanzen Kaimora had spent most of his working life on Mars. The infamous paper presenting his findings had been suppressed by L1's government before the SOC's founding, but its contents had won Sanzen a chief researcher position on the Colonization Commission's shadowy Project S. Five commissioners had nominated him for CSC director, forcing Mitsu to approve his appointment.

Mitsu would have given anything for such powerful benefactors. She'd have given more for an uncensored copy of Sanzen's paper and access to records from his tenure as a Project S lead. As chief executive of the Systems Overterrestrial Coalition, Mitsu Kasei of L1 wielded more authority than any president, prime minister, or queen in Earth's history. Yet all the powers of her office couldn't unlock her opponent's secrets.

Someday I'll find the key, she thought. Like everyone else, Sanzen's past contained the seeds of his undoing.

Mitsu stepped into her secluded office and stifled a gasp. A slight young woman in a black sweater, a blue plaid skirt, and dark green leggings stood before the glass bookshelf set against the opposite wall. The girl giggled as she thumbed through an antique volume.

"Excuse me," the Secretary-General said. "You're not—Oh!"

The girl's waist-length black hair whipped as she turned, and Mitsu found herself meeting a familiar dark-eyed gaze.

"Megami." Mitsu sighed with relief. "To what do I owe this unexpected pleasure?"

Sanzen's aide snapped shut Mitsu's first edition printing of *Alraune.* "I thought you could use some company after today's session."

Mitsu collapsed onto her cream-colored satin sofa and let the smooth cushions conform to her. "I suppose you're right. Sanzen completely blindsided me. Do you know who writes his speeches?"

Megami crossed the small room and pressed a dainty index finger to the security panel. The door slid shut with a soft hiss. "Probably an intern. But the sentiments were definitely his. Do you find them disturbing?"

"I just don't understand why he always pushes for the military solution."

"Humans don't have to check their natural aggression to survive in space anymore," said Megami. She seated herself in a matching chair across from Mitsu, crossing her legs in ladylike fashion. "The SOC's prosperity has given them time for previously wasteful pursuits, including Sanzen's penchant for military history."

Mitsu sniffed. "A strange hobby."

"That hobby got him nominated to head the CSC," Megami said. "No one expected Sanzen to become like the grounders he studied— least of all you—but he's internalized their violence."

It makes sense, thought Mitsu. She'd always harbored fears that the earth's backward ways might somehow infect the colonists. But one doubt lingered. "You're the Director's aide. Why are you sharing his confidential information with me?"

The girl's sharp face fell. "I never asked to be Sanzen's pet. He thinks the earth can only be pacified through victory over it. He's blind to the worldwide bloodbath his conquest would entail. You want the Coalition to take custody of Earth's people through peaceful negotiation."

Mitsu's heart leapt. *Finally! Someone understands.* But her elation soon passed. "Operation Oversight has me in a bind. If I deny Sanzen outright, I validate his claim that I'm neglecting the Security Corps. But authorizing the operation is tantamount to declaring war on Earth."

Megami stood and smoothed her skirt. "If you're given two choices, make a third."

"How?" asked Mitsu.

"Why use force when projecting the threat of force can achieve the same goal?"

Mitsu couldn't see what the girl was implying, but she admitted herself intrigued. "Go on."

"Send envoys from the Terrestrial Affairs Ministry with a message for the leaders on Sanzen's blacklist," Megami said, running her hand over dusty books by Sun Tzu, Musashi, and Clausewitz. "Tell them the Coalition refuses to do business with warlords. Threaten to cut off aid unless their governments meet your demands. That way, you can support the CSC without giving Sanzen his war."

"What if the warlords refuse to negotiate?"

"I'll make sure Sanzen's plan for Operation Oversight is leaked through the right channels," said Megami. "If Earth's leaders think he's about to crush them, they'll beg to negotiate with you."

The plan seemed too good to be true, and a moment's thought showed Mitsu why. "By leaking Sanzen's plans, don't we run the risk of the warlords attacking first?"

"If that happens, the Security Corps will be hardest hit. Sanzen will overreact and make a mistake—one you can exploit."

Megami's words eased the agitation that had plagued Mitsu since Sanzen's address. She couldn't find fault with the girl's reasoning, but a pang of uncertainty remained in the back of her mind. *I'm being indecisive, just like Sanzen said.*

Mitsu rose and stepped around her lavender-colored desk to her secure terminal. "I'll make the arrangements with Secretary Gohaku," she said in defiance of her misgivings.

"I knew I could trust you," Megami said. "You've saved untold lives today."

The Secretary-General barely heard her door hiss open and shut as she rang the Secretary of Terrestrial Affairs' encrypted line.

Megami showed herself out of Mitsu's office and strolled down the empty hallway to a gray carbon polymer door like all the others. It opened onto a narrow corridor bearing the musty smell of disuse. The forgotten service passage led under the Secretariat Complex and into the substructure of the colony itself. Power had long since been routed to more vital areas, leaving the tunnel cloaked in the artificial dusk of emergency lights.

An imposing figure emerged from the gloom. The sort of familiarity that so easily bred contempt granted Megami instant recognition of Sanzen Kaimora. He sported the same dark suit he'd worn for that morning's address. His razor-straight goatee framed a tight line of a mouth.

"Mitsu didn't have you followed?" His question ended with a curt laugh.

"She's too innocent," said Megami.

"The seeds have been planted?"

A wry grin tugged at the corner of Megami's lip. "Mitsu will give us everything we want."

5

Sieg took the measure of his captors as he sat handcuffed in the cramped, noisy cabin of Major Collins' gunship. He looked past Ritter, whose tanned hands cradled his face, and through the left window. His and Ritter's Grenzies and Kopp's damaged Grento dangled like ripe fruit from the three transport helos flying beside them.

The Earth Governments in Exile claim to be legitimate, but they're just scavengers, too. I hope they'll listen to reason. Sieg brushed his jacket's breast pocket with his thumb and felt the silk ribbon tucked inside.

Edmonds sat on a canvas bench facing Sieg and Ritter. The EGE soldier's fleshy face betrayed no emotion as he kept watch on his prisoners. Behind Edmonds, Collins and Zimmer piloted the gunship from its double-decker cockpit. Through the forward bubble canopy Sieg glimpsed a massive ship with a flat, angular deck gliding on the azure sea below.

That carrier is older than some of the space colonies, thought Sieg. Sixteen Shenlong V/STOL attack aircraft—and Darving's oddball fighter—occupied the ship's bustling flight deck. It clearly wasn't a pre-Collapse American supercarrier. The ship had probably been a fleet defense carrier from a nation that had sat out the war between the Atlasid Caliphate and the seventh Holy League.

Collins brought the gunship in near the carrier's island, a forty-five meter tower sprouting a forest of antennas. The three transport helos hovered over a port-side elevator, where a deck crew helped unload the combat frames.

The gunship came to rest tilting slightly to the left. Edmonds, along with two men seated behind Sieg whose names he hadn't caught, escorted the prisoners onto the ship. The scents of saltwater and jet fuel assaulted Sieg's nose as he stood in the whipping breeze amid the controlled chaos of the flight deck.

Collins and Zimmer emerged from the cockpit and stood facing the island. An older man in a khaki uniform bearing an FMAS flag strode purposefully toward the gunship. His wavy hair and neatly trimmed beard matched the white clouds overhead. His light blue eyes took in the surrounding activity at a glance and settled on Collins.

"Who's the geezer?" asked Ritter.

"That's Griff Larson," Zimmer whispered behind his hand, "hero of the Mid-American Campaigns. They say he uses a knife for a pillow."

"Colonel Larson," Collins said with a crisp salute, "I trust you received my message, sir."

Larson eyed the prisoners while returning Collins' salute. "I didn't come above for a stroll, Major," he said in a gravelly voice. "Now, how about telling me why some damned squid spooks interrupted my meeting with General McCaskey?"

"Sir," said Collins, "I came into possession of sensitive information that OPSEC procedure dictates be screened through Naval Intelligence. I—"

"Get to the point, Colons, or start swimming back to Pansy Island."

"It's *Collins*, sir. And I wish you wouldn't refer to England that way."

"I wish I knew why the hell I'm standing out here holding my dick. Get on with it, Major."

"While en route back to the *Yamamoto*," said Collins, "I responded to Captain Darving's report of smoke rising from a small village. My crew and I found that a paramilitary group had razed the settlement using stolen Soc combat frames. Between Darving and my crew, we killed all of the hostiles except these two." He nodded to Sieg and Ritter.

One corner of Larson's mouth turned downward. "Colons, you don't need my permission to throw bandits in the brig. Hell, in the militia we'd have stood them in front of a trench they'd dug, shot them, and used the CFs to push the dirt back in. I'm not hearing why I got a visit from Omaka's snitches."

"Sir, I strongly advise having that prisoner, who identified himself as Tod Ritter, incarcerated before we discuss potentially global scale—"

"Major, I strongly advise spilling your guts before I reassign your bird as the maintenance division's hangar queen. The General's been riding me to solve our parts shortage."

Collins winced. He gestured to Sieg. "Sir, this man claims that his father was the late L3 Prime Minister Josef Friedlander."

Larson cocked a snowy eyebrow at Collins' copilot. "Throw the kid in the brig, Mike."

"Wait," Ritter shouted as Zimmer led him away. "Don't I get a trial?"

"We'll get around to it," said Larson. "Collins, you're with me. Bring towhead along."

Larson turned and marched toward the island. Collins stepped behind Sieg and nudged him forward. The three of them entered the ship's dim, crowded command center and descended a nearly vertical staircase to a narrow corridor with white and gray steel walls. They brushed past a steady flow of crewmen whose echoing footsteps filled the hallway. The Colonel stopped at the fourth door on the right and knocked.

"Come in," said a calm resonant voice only partly muffled by the door. Larson turned the knob and entered. Collins marched Sieg in after the Colonel.

Sieg found himself in an austere office painted off-white and furnished with a simple oak desk fronted by two steel chairs. Behind the desk sat a leather office chair occupied by a man slightly older than Larson. He had iron gray hair and a lined face with a strong chin. His tan uniform also had an FMAS patch with twenty-five stars and two vertical blue stripes flanking a larger red stripe. The black glass nameplate before him read *GEN Edward McCaskey*.

Larson planted himself two steps from the desk and saluted. McCaskey returned Larson's salute. His dark eyes focused on Collins. "Go ahead and uncuff him."

Collins complied. Sieg fought the urge to rub his sore wrists. Instead he kept his hands still and his eyes open.

"Thank you, Major," McCaskey said. "Dismissed."

Collins gave a textbook salute and left, closing the door behind him with a metallic thud.

"Are you sure we can trust this guy?" Larson asked McCaskey.

"Admiral Omaka cleared him." The General waved both men toward the chairs in front of his desk. "Take a seat, gentlemen. We have a lot to discuss."

Sieg took the chair on the right. Its firm support came as a relief after riding in a helo jumpseat. Larson shot a skeptical glance at Sieg before sitting down next to him.

"Be advised, Colonel, that this entire conversation is classified," McCaskey warned. "Do not share anything you hear in this room with your men—especially not Collins. But *especially* not Darving."

Larson folded his arms across his sinewy chest. "I got it. Darving's girlfriend works for Omaka, and he's two-timing her with his jet. Icebergs are less likely to cause leaks."

"If the preamble's over," said Sieg, "I'm sure the Admiral told you my mission is vital to the earth's independence."

"What's left of it," Larson scoffed. "Except for us and a few warlords, the planet's run from space by a nanny state on steroids."

Sieg locked eyes with the Colonel. "Exactly. The Coalition already controls most of North America and all of Europe. They just established a beachhead in the Middle East and are planning to expand from there. The EGE has been forced to abandon all its land bases. You still operate from your Atlantic fleet, but the Socs can come for you whenever they want."

"The FMAS Militia's kept a big swath of Middle America Soc-free," Larson said. "There'll still be at least one independent people on Earth as long as my boys keep up the fight back home."

"Wishful thinking," said Sieg. "The SOC hasn't gotten serious yet. Secretary-General Mitsu is still keeping Director Sanzen reined in, but his influence is growing. If he gains the upper hand, the Socs will roll over you in a week."

"That's truer than you know," said McCaskey. He leaned forward, planted his elbows on his desk, and laced his fingers. "Sanzen just gave a speech to the Coalition Secretariat. He outlined an aggressive foreign policy that would cut off the exiled royal families that are our main source of funding. And that's just for starters. There are rumors that Mitsu plans to endorse key parts of his plan."

"Alright, Golden Boy," Larson said, "where do you fit into this FUBAR picture?"

"I'm an operative with ZoDiaC," said Sieg.

Larson tilted his head to one side. "I take it you're not an astrologer."

"He's with the Zone Demilitarisée Coloniale," McCaskey explained. "They're a secret alliance of space colonies opposed to the Coalition's military intervention on Earth."

"I doubt ZoDiaC's working against the Socs out of neighborly concern for Earth," said Larson. "What's their angle?"

"Enlightened self-interest," said Sieg. "ZoDiaC's member colonies—particularly those in L3—know the Coalition will come for them when they're done with you."

"I think I see where this is going," Larson said. "The space frogs don't want to provoke the Socs, so we get to be their proxies."

"The EGE General Staff already signed the deal," said McCaskey. "In return for defending the sovereignty of Earth's nations, which we're doing anyway, ZoDiaC is supplying us with aid and weapons to resist the Coalition; including combat frames."

Larson perked up. "We get our own CFs?"

McCaskey nodded. "The delivery date hasn't been set, but they've sent some cash as a good faith offering. It's not enough to compensate us if Sanzen freezes our funds. That's where Mr. Friedlander comes in."

"The Coalition has installed a new Mideast Region governor sponsored by Commerce Secretary Satsu," said Sieg. "Her name is

Prem Naryal. She's got a reputation as a ruthless bean counter. Our sources say Mitsu's putting Naryal in charge of bringing the Mideastern and African 'warlords' to heel. I've been assigned to gather intel on her organization."

"Why were you prancing around the Congo with a troupe of German bandits?" asked Larson.

"ZoDiaC smuggled me planetside through the Coalition's Kisangani Spaceport," said Sieg. "I joined up with the Black Reichswehr for cover. I'd planned to travel with them to Sudan, where my handlers left an equipment stash. Collins threw a wrench in my plan."

"That limey rotorhead can be a real pain in the ass," Larson said, "but if his mother cut him a check, he'd ask for ID. You and your teen sidekick must've been pretty naughty to get on Major Anal-retentive's shit list."

"We did what we had to," said Sieg.

"With the crisis we're facing," McCaskey said, "I'm prepared to sweep that incident under the rug. In the meantime Friedlander, I'm granting you the EGE Army rank of staff sergeant and assigning you to Admiral Omaka's flagship. A helicopter will fly you to the *Lloyd George* at 0800 tomorrow. Naval Intelligence will instruct you from there. Any questions?"

"Just one, Sir," said Sieg. "What do you plan to do with Tod Ritter?"

McCaskey's chair creaked as he leaned back. "I honestly hadn't given him much thought." He looked to Larson and Sieg. "Suggestions?"

"Right now, he's just ballast that eats," said Larson. "Let's dump him on an island with a full canteen, a week's worth of rations, and a knife."

"I won't rule it out," said McCaskey. "Sergeant?"

"Ritter's competent with a CF," said Sieg. "He has the makings of a real pilot, but he lacks discipline."

McCaskey's lip twisted in a half-smile. "Lucky for him, we just acquired three combat frames. The *Yamamoto* will need its own CF teams when ZoDiaC comes through. We may as well organize one now to shake the bugs out."

"Please don't say what I think you're about to say," sighed Larson.

"Sorry, Griff," McCaskey said. "You've got more combat frame experience than anyone aboard. I'm assigning the captured CFs, and Private Ritter, to your command."

"I'll need some time to get my people organized," said Larson. "What if the kid doesn't want to enlist?"

"Then we find him an island," said the General. "If there's nothing else, you men are dismissed."

Sieg and Griff rose and saluted the General, who stood and returned the gesture.

"For what it's worth, Sergeant," McCaskey said, "I was sorry to hear about your father. He was an honorable man."

Sieg strained to keep the emotions warring in his heart from showing on his face. "Thank you, Sir."

"One more thing, Ed," said Larson. "If this caper ends in tears, don't forget I warned you."

McCaskey resumed his seat. "I'll take it under advisement."

Larson stepped to the door and opened it. The cacophony of the hallway flooded in. The Colonel exited. Sieg followed and closed the door behind him.

I've thrown in with another quixotic company, thought Sieg. His hand delved into his breast pocket, and he ran the silken ribbon between his fingers. *Hopefully the EGE fares better than the others.*

6

Zane felt his way along the grimy wall of a narrow alley in near-total darkness. Thick clouds blanketed the strip of sky between the five story buildings on both sides. The only real light shone from the street ten meters ahead, where harsh LED lamps hung over an empty intersection. The lack of traffic meant the city was probably under curfew.

"Won't be long now, Dead Drop," Zane promised. He'd have recovered his stolen combat frame already if the guard at the institute hadn't shot him in the leg. He'd tied off the burning wound with a rag, but warm sticky blood still seeped through his light blue pants. Both his legs felt cold, and the once-throbbing soles of his bare feet had gone numb.

Two meters from the alley's exit, Zane pressed his back against the right wall and sidled to the corner. He peered around the bend and saw a Grenzmark II standing in the middle of the next intersection to the right, its domed rotating head sweeping a blinding beam across the neighborhood like a bipedal lighthouse.

That makes eight, thought Zane, mentally counting the Coalition CFs stationed in a five-block radius of his position. *They're fencing me in. I need to get past their cordon.*

Tires sped over damp pavement to Zane's left. He turned his head to see a pair of headlights approaching the intersection. The streetlights revealed the vehicle as a white van with a Seed

Corporation logo on the side. Wet brakes squealed as the lights turned red and the van came to a stop in front of the alley's opening.

As soon as the Grento's face grill turned in the opposite direction, Zane picked up a loose brick, hobbled to the van as quickly as his wounded leg allowed, and smashed in the front passenger window.

A feminine yelp sounded from the driver's seat, and the van lurched forward. But Zane crawled through the shattered window and threw himself down on the glass-strewn passenger seat. "Stop," he ordered.

The van screeched to a halt less than a meter from the red light. The driver, a young woman with shoulder-length almond hair and brown eyes wide with fear, looked over Zane's bloody pants and filthy undershirt. "You're the escaped mental patient," she said in a trembling voice.

Zane twisted around and scanned the back of the van. Step ladders and bales of electrical cord lined the walls. The dingy confines smelled of stale machine oil. A blue jacket and a matching cap, both bearing Seed Corp patches, hung on a hook behind Zane's seat. He snatched them up, put them on, and laid a tool belt over his bloody pant leg.

Green light spilled in through the windshield. "Drive," said Zane.

"Where to?" the woman asked.

"You were headed to the factory, right?"

"I work third shift in the infirmary." The woman's eyes darted to a plastic card that hung on a lanyard from the rearview mirror. The card bore a snake-entwined winged staff and her picture above the name Dorothy Wheeler, RN.

Essential Seed personnel must be exempt from the curfew, thought Zane. It explained why a nurse was driving a maintenance van. They'd lent her a company vehicle to get past the cordon, which meant *he* could get through the same way. "You'd better drive to work, then."

Dorothy eased off the brakes and rolled slowly through the intersection, but her brow furrowed. "The Coalition's looking for you. Shouldn't you leave the city?"

"I go where I want," said Zane.

"But what do you want at Seed Corp?"

"The Coalition stole my combat frame. I'm taking it back."

"Oh." Dorothy's voice fell. "I understand. The Socs that run Seed Corp denied me bereavement leave when my dad died in a factory accident. They take from everybody."

The van pulled alongside the Grento's stubby green foot. Its 115mm rifle barrel yawned just above the motor vehicle's roof. Blinding light slanted down from the middle row of five slits in the CF's hemispherical head. Zane's muscles tensed, but the Grento made no move to stop the van as Dorothy continued through the intersection. In the rearview mirror, the CF's searchlight roamed over the silent block.

Made it, thought Zane. *I'm coming, Dead Drop.*

"That wound looks pretty bad," said Dorothy. "How'd you get it?"

"A guard shot me."

"Do you want me to take a look at it?"

"I want to find Dead Drop."

Dorothy fell quiet and fixed her eyes on the darkened road ahead. A towering fog bank rolled off the lake, engulfing whole buildings and dividing the city's heart with a wall of cloud. A sense of peace enfolded Zane like a blanket, and though his legs were almost numb with cold, he leaned back in his seat to relax for the first time in days.

White light filled Zane's vision. *It's a Grenzmark,* he thought with a start. But he felt himself lying on a padded table. *I'm back at the institute. They recaptured me!*

Zane sat bolt upright on what proved to be an exam table under an operating light in a small, astringent-smelling room. Charts and safety posters plastered the white tile walls.

"Easy." Dorothy rushed to Zane's side from the room's back left corner and laid her soft hands on his arm. "I can't believe the sedative wore off that soon!"

Zane glared at the nurse, who now wore a set of gray scrubs. "Where am I?"

"You told me to go to work, so I did. This is an emergency treatment room in Seed Corp's infirmary."

"Seed Corp?" Zane swung his legs over the side of the table and slid off. The pain that stabbed up his right leg when his feet hit the tile floor forced a grunt from his chest.

Dorothy's arms encircled his shoulders. "Careful! I removed the bullet, treated the infection, and stitched you up, but you lost a lot of blood. You should stay off your feet for a while."

Zane freed himself with a firm push. "I'm going to look for Dead Drop."

"Dressed like that?"

Only when Dorothy pointed at him with a bemused smile did Zane realize he was only wearing a hospital gown. "Get me some clothes," he grumbled.

"Already did." Dorothy grabbed a blue bundle from the stainless steel table behind her and dumped it in Zane's lap. The wrinkled ball of fabric turned out to be a Seed Corporation jumpsuit. "If you insist on ignoring my advice, throw that on and we'll head down to the factory."

"We?" Zane asked as he donned the sturdy garment.

"Yeah," said Dorothy. "*We*. I won't let a recovering patient wander around a factory alone. Besides, I know the plant's layout."

Zane slipped his smarting feet into a pair of brown work boots on the floor next to the table. "Fine. Show me where Dead Drop is."

"The plant's on a skeleton crew right now," Dorothy said as she moved to the door, "but we still need to be careful. There's a terminal in Product Testing where we can do an inventory search. Come on."

Zane followed Dorothy from the empty infirmary. Their footsteps echoed as they traversed a series of concrete hallways with bare gray floors and color-coded walls under ceilings overgrown with pipes and cables. A short ride in a lift with brushed steel walls brought them to an open warehouse style room rife with plastic-wrapped machinery stacked on wooden pallets. The warm air smelled of metal and hard rubber.

Dorothy stepped up to a mobile terminal perched atop a rolling black steel cabinet. A half-wall of plastic drums and a couple of parked forklifts gave her reasonable concealment. Zane joined her as she hunted and pecked on the plastic-covered keyboard.

"Where is it?" he asked over her shoulder. Her hair smelled like a purple flower he'd seen while fleeing through the forest preserve near the institute, but he didn't know its name.

"Hang on a second," Dorothy said in a harsh whisper. "I'm not finding—darn! My session expired, and I don't have a password to log back in."

Zane turned on his heel. "I'll have to do a visual search. Where do they store the combat frames?"

"Wait!" Dorothy urged him. "That area's off limits. If we're caught, we'll get in serious trouble."

"I'm already in serious trouble."

Dorothy sighed. "Don't say I didn't warn you."

Five more minutes of navigating Seed Corp's maze of corridors and two more elevator rides later, Zane stood on a narrow steel catwalk suspended over a warehouse floor spanning three city blocks. Though the combat frames arranged in ordered columns below stood over seventeen meters tall, the catwalk passed half again as high over their heads.

Dorothy leaned over the railing beside him. "Do you see it anywhere?"

A company's worth of Grenzies and twice as many Grentos stretched from wall to wall below him, but no black, square-shouldered CF stood out from their ranks. "Dead Drop's not here," he grumbled.

Slow footsteps clattered behind them and sent slight tremors through the catwalk. Dorothy gasped. Zane rounded on the approaching figure, revealed in the glow of an overhead light as a lab coated man in his early thirties with dull brown hair.

"Dead Drop," the stuffy-looking man said in a calm, oddly boyish voice. He adjusted his wire frame glasses. "Seed Corp designation XCF-08D-1."

Dorothy stepped forward. "Dr. Browning! We were just—"

Browning interrupted her with a raised hand. "The inventory management system alerted me to your search for Mr. Dellister's combat frame. You are Zane Dellister, correct?"

Zane pushed past Dorothy. "That's right. And you're Dr. Tesla Browning, the guy who invented combat frames."

"I'm not really a doctor. Tesla Browning is my nom de guerre, or it would be if I'd ever used a weapon. Instead I attached one to a work frame and licensed the design to Seed Corp."

"Where's Dead Drop?" asked Zane.

"On a cargo plane to Kisangani, Africa. I should congratulate you on creating a one-of-a-kind prototype."

"Africa?" repeated Zane. "What's Dead Drop doing there?"

"The advances in energy weapon technology Dead Drop incorporates helped us break through the dead end in CF evolution," said Browning. "The next generation of CSC combat frames will be based on your prototype. As such, it's being shipped to the space colonies for further study."

Zane pounded the railing. The vast space swallowed the loud clang. "You won't keep Dead Drop from me. If it's in Africa, then I'm going to Africa!"

Browning stood aside. "Far be it from me to stop you. In fact, I'll arrange transport for you on a Seed Corp barge."

"A barge?" repeated Zane. "Why not a cargo plane?"

"Because the security is far laxer," said Browning.

"Why are you helping Zane?" Dorothy asked.

"The new combat frames inspired by Zane's design will make the Coalition's victory inevitable," Browning said. "I don't see how they can begrudge him his freedom. I've also taken the liberty of purging Nurse Wheeler's security breaches—and her relation to an anti-SOC militia leader—from the record."

Dorothy's mouth worked soundlessly for a moment before she could form words. "You know about my uncle?"

"No need for alarm," said Browning. "I'm from L3. My working relationship with the Coalition is simply a marriage of convenience. Your family's politics are none of my concern."

"Thank you," Dorothy stammered.

"Don't thank him yet," said Zane. "A river barge won't get us to Africa."

"Not all the way, no," said Browning. "Norma, the barge's pilot, will take you to the free city of New Orleans. Seek out a man named Jean-Claude du Lione. He'll be easy to find. Tell him what I told you, and I'm certain he'll give you passage to Africa."

43

"When does the barge leave?" asked Zane.

"Under the current circumstances," said Browning, "it's best if you leave right away. The barge is parked in the canal that runs past this complex."

Zane bolted for the exit. He hardly felt the dull ache in his leg. Pursuing footsteps shook the catwalk. "Wait," cried Dorothy. "You're still my patient! I'm not letting you out of my sight."

"Whatever," said Zane. "Just try to keep up."

7

Upon his release from the brig, Ritter made a beeline for the *Yamamoto's* cavernous hangar. Walking across the matte black deck that spanned two-thirds of the ship's length, he felt like a solitary ant deep within a bustling colony. Members of the ship's company navigated artificial canyons between mountains of metal crates while steering clear of the forklifts that rumbled back and forth bearing supplies.

The buzz and whine of power tools led Ritter to an open area where several Shenlong jets sat parked. The machine shop smell made him feel at home. One plane stood out: a white and blue collection of acute angles and sharp edges.

A smooth male voice emanated from below the open canopy. "Increase fuel flow to the starboard engine by ten percent." Ritter had heard the same voice over his Grenzie's radio.

"Okay, Max," a tinny-sounding woman replied. "Projections show that the increased thrust should compensate for the damaged stabilizer."

"That's my girl!"

Is someone in there with him? Ritter wondered, craning his neck to examine the cockpit.

"Max," the woman said, "Someone is eavesdropping."

A handsome man with brown hair spilling almost to his shoulders popped up from the jet's front seat. He wore a brown flight jacket with an old American flag patch on the sleeve. His hazel eyes zeroed in on Ritter. "Hey, kid." his soft voice took a mischievous tone. "You lose your tour group?"

Ritter snapped to attention and saluted. "Sir, Private Tod Ritter reporting!"

"Captain Maximus Darving." Max casually saluted with a screwdriver, which he pointed at Ritter. "Judging by your grungy fatigues, you must be one of the irregulars Collins brought in. Shouldn't you be in the brig? For that matter, why are you reporting to me?"

"I was released and assigned to Major Collins' unit under your direct command," said Ritter.

Darving rolled his eyes, but his irises veered up and to the right as his face brightened. "You know how to sling a spanner?"

Ritter couldn't suppress a grin. "I was a CF mechanic in the Black Reichswehr, and I've been tinkering with anything that has a motor since I was twelve."

"Perfect," said Darving. "Six months' experience is plenty to be my assistant."

"I'm nineteen."

"Just joking. You ever overhaul a jet engine?"

Ritter approached one of the two oblong nacelles below the jet's wings. "Not like this one."

"That's not an engine."

"Is it a weapon pod?"

Darving bit his lip. "Something like that. Let's just say it's for emergencies."

A long octagonal tube mounted under the plane's nose caught Ritter's eye. "What's that—some kind of spy camera?"

"That's the Thor Prototype's electrolaser."

Ritter gaped. "Electrolaser!?"

Darving puffed out his chest. "It ionizes the air with a laser to project an artificial lightning bolt. It'll annihilate anything that's a better conductor than the ground. I call it Mjolnir."

"Max," the tinny female voice called from the cockpit, "I'd appreciate you not sharing classified design details with strangers."

"Private Ritter's not a stranger, honey. You heard him. He's with the EGE now."

"I don't see anyone in the aft seat," said Ritter. "Who else is in there?"

"That's Marilyn, the Thor Prototype's integrated A.I. She handles navigation, diagnostics, and even flight and fire control. I coded her myself."

"You're a fighter pilot *and* a programmer?"

Darving set down the screwdriver and wiped his oily hands with a rag. "I was the youngest engineering team lead in Seed Corp's history. Wrote their flagship transport app. But the Socs and I developed irreconcilable differences, so I defected to the EGE and brought Marilyn along. Or more accurately, she brought me."

"I brought a combat frame," said Ritter. "I'm even designing my own CF, but they didn't make me a captain."

"Do you have advanced degrees in aeronautical and software engineering?"

Ritter shook his head.

"That's why they made you a grunt," said Darving. "But don't sweat it. Command is a headache. I only took the job for the perks— like fielding my own custom equipment. Speaking of which, Marilyn took a hit from your Reichswehr friends. The damage they caused will be a bitch to fix. How about lending me a hand?"

"I'd love to," said Ritter, "but I came down here to work on my Grenzie. Can you tell me where they stowed it?"

Darving bent down to fiddle with his jet's control panel. "Sorry, kid. Collins ordered your CF scrapped to fix that Grento for Colonel Larson."

"He can't chop my Grenzie like a stolen Mercedes! It's my property."

"I bloody well can." Ritter felt Collins' hot breath on his neck. "And by international law, that Grenzie belongs to the EGE."

Darving climbed down to face Collins. "Give the kid a break, Major. You know how a pilot can bond with his machine."

"Not as well as you do, Captain. As for Private Ritter, the sooner he learns his place, the less likely he'll be to get someone killed."

"Relax," said Darving. "It's not like we're in combat."

47

"We may be tomorrow. General McCaskey has formed a new unit consisting of a combat frame team and air support. Colonel Larson and Private Ritter are the former. You and I are the latter. We're scheduled to go wheels up at 0900 tomorrow."

"What's the mission?"

"It's to do with the Socs' Operation Oversight. Governor Troy, the Coalition's man in Western Europe, is flexing his muscles against a Sardinian gangster called Carlos the Scorpion. Carlos plans on moving his not inconsiderable arms smuggling operation to Algiers."

"How is that our problem?" asked Darving.

"The Scorpion couldn't be arsed to ask Algeria's warlord Kazid Zarai for permission."

"They say it's easier asking forgiveness," said Darving. "Let me guess. Our intel guys expect this neighborly spat to turn hot."

"The Scorpion has asked the EGE to ensure it doesn't," Collins said. "He and Zarai will be having a sit-down tomorrow in Algiers. McCaskey's agreed to send a delegation to act as third party observers. That's us."

Darving winced. "Great. What kind of firepower can we expect if the talks go south?"

"Zarai has five hundred militiamen armed with Kalashnikovs and RPGs. Plus he's got around fifty technicals."

"Battlewagons," Darving said with a grimace. "I hate those bargain bin tanks!"

"Then you'll be glad to learn that The Scorpion has a used Zeklov tank, along with two dozen technicals of his own and two hundred men equipped with stolen CSC rifles."

"And McCaskey thinks our unit can handle that cluster if the shit hits the fan?"

"The *Yamamoto* will of course be offshore on full alert," said Collins. "But our objective is to prevent violence breaking out."

"Why even bring our hardware?" asked Darving.

"These warlords respect strength," said Collins. "We're only to make a show of force."

Ritter wheeled on Collins, who stood with his arms crossed over his ribbon-bedecked khaki shirt. "How can I make a show of force if my Grenzie's scrap?"

"To be frank, Private," Collins said, "Colonel Larson objected to your assignment with this unit, and I agree with him. He's placed you under my supervision for the entirety of the mission."

"You mean I'm supposed to sit there in your chopper and keep quiet like a civilian?"

Collins' face became a rigid mask. "I pilot a helicopter. It is not a toy for giving tourists joyrides. It is a sophisticated death machine that's worth a hundred useless gits like you. Now drop and give me thirty. And the next time you call a helicopter a chopper, you'll give me sixty."

Ritter barely contained the obscenities that strove to burst from his mouth as he fell prone and repeatedly pushed himself up from the deck with angry pumping motions.

"See that he finishes," Collins told Darving as he turned to leave. "And I'll see you on the flight deck at 0900."

"He's gone," Darving said a moment later. "You can get up."

Ritter stood and shook his sore arms. "Collins needs to lighten up."

"Yeah, so you'd better be a model passenger tomorrow."

"I've got a better idea," said Ritter. "If I fix the Grento, I can pilot my Grenzie tomorrow."

"There's a couple problems with that," said Darving. "First of all, the EGE's always short on parts. Unlike your former associates, we don't steal from civilians."

"No, you steal from me."

Darving sucked air through his teeth. "Fair enough, but even if your Grenzie's operational tomorrow, unlike the Grento it's not capable of sustained flight. Besides, Larson will never let you pilot it solo."

"What if I repair his Grento's cockpit on my own?"

"You might get on Griff's less prickly side," said Darving, "but that brings us right back to the problem of where to get the parts."

"He can strip the cockpit from my Grenzie," said Sieg.

Ritter and Darving turned to the right, where Sieg stood beside a stack of cardboard drums in his red and black jacket.

"Geez, man," said Darving. "My girlfriend's a Navy spook, and even she doesn't sneak up on me like that."

"Is anybody else spying on us?" asked Ritter.

"Sorry," said Sieg. He removed his sunglasses and ran a hand through his blond hair. "I was looking for Collins, and I overheard your problem. I might be able to help."

"Fantastic," said Darving. "Who are you?"

"If your girlfriend works for Admiral Omaka, there's no point keeping my real name secret. I'm Sieg Friedlander."

Darving's eyes widened. "The son of L3's prime minister? I heard you and Collins' radio banter, but I didn't believe a VIP like you would be slumming with us."

"Is it less likely than a Seed Corp team lead defecting to the EGE?"

"Touché," said Darving.

"Thanks for the offer," Ritter told Sieg, "but what will you pilot?"

"I've been reassigned," Sieg said. "I won't need my Grenzie where I'm going."

Ritter approached Sieg. By an unspoken understanding, both men extended their hands and shared a firm handshake. "It's been an honor fighting beside you," said Ritter.

A smile cracked Sieg's stony face. "Likewise. This era's drawing to a close, but I have a feeling we'll fight together again before the end." He replaced his mirrored shades. "I look forward to seeing how much your skills improve."

Ritter watched Sieg cross the busy deck to the lift. The steel doors slid closed, and he was gone.

"He's a cool customer for someone who's had it so rough," Darving said.

"I heard his dad was assassinated," said Ritter.

"That's just the last bite of the shit sandwich. Before that, his mom and little sister were kidnapped. Sanzen held them hostage to silence L3's opposition to the Socs. Folks who're paid to know this stuff say they were killed when rescue plans went south."

"Sieg asked if I'd ever failed someone important to me," Ritter thought aloud. "Losing his family must've been the mistake he meant. He'll stop at nothing to correct it."

Darving threw his arm around Ritter's shoulders, interrupting the Private's train of thought. "We've both got our work cut out for us," said Max. "So tell you what: If you help me fix Marilyn, I'll help you switch out the Grento's cockpit for Sieg's."

"Deal!" Ritter said.

8

Ritter squinted as the main port side elevator carried him from the *Yamamoto's* hangar to the sun-drenched flight deck. The good ache of a night spent at honest labor suffused his body, but the warm sea breeze got his blood pumping. Darving stood with him. Thanks to Max's help, Larson's Grento and the Thor Prototype both sat fully repaired behind them.

Larson strode toward the elevator from Collins' gunship. A gray flight suit covered his muscular frame, and his silver hair poked out from under his helmet's raised visor. His voice carried over the whine of the helo's rotors. "I was about to send the MPs after you."

"Sorry we're late, sir" said Max. "Your Grento needed more work than we thought, but Ritter and I got it running."

Larson gave Max a slight nod and climbed up to the CF's cockpit. "Darving, you and your waifu take point. Collins will follow. I'll bring up the rear."

"What about me?" asked Ritter.

The Colonel lowered his visor and frowned at Max. "Captain, did your helper monkey just talk to me?"

"Hear him out, sir," said Max. "Your CF wouldn't be combat-ready without him."

Larson sighed. "Permission granted to speak freely, Private. So spill it, and make it good."

"As a trained pilot, I should be manning a combat frame, sir!"

"I don't repeat myself," said Larson, "so shut up and listen hard. I decide where you should be, when you eat, sleep, and shit, and what you think. If I decide you'd be more useful nailed to the bow, you'd better grab a hammer. Understood?"

"Yes, sir," said Ritter, "but—"

Larson pinched the bridge of his nose. "Apparently not. I'll spell it out for you, with big block letters in crayon. For the duration of this mission, you will be warming a seat on Collins' helo. You are not a pilot. You do not get your own command. You are one step above a bush bandit, and if it were up to me, there'd be a tiny rock out there with a population of crabs, bird shit, and you, in descending order of social status."

"Sir," said Max, "I advise you to reconsider. The MOA is highly unstable, and a second combat frame would be a significant force multiplier."

"Darving, how'd you get to be a whiz kid programmer when you can't even count? There's only one CF on deck. What's Ritter supposed to do, sit on my lap?"

"Not to contradict you, sir, but we have two operational CFs." Max pointed aft to the secondary elevator, which had just arrived on deck with Ritter's Grenzie. Its freshly polished olive drab armor glinted in the sun.

Larson looked from Darving to Ritter. "If it will shut you two up, fine. Report to your Grenzie, Private. And you'd better haul ass. I'd like to start this op before Christmas."

Ritter couldn't keep from smiling as he saluted. "Yes, sir! Thank you, sir."

"Belay the ass-kissing," said Larson. "You're basically acting as a decoy. Now get ready for takeoff, or get left behind."

"Private Ritter's Grenzie is not flight capable, sir," said Max.

"I'm aware of that, Captain." Larson spoke into his helmet mic. "Collins, attach a tow cable to that Grenzmark C on the elevator. Ritter's riding bitch."

The deck crew coordinated with Collins and Ritter to tether his Grenzie to the helo. Within minutes, Darving's jet blasted off from the carrier, followed by Collins' gunship. A thrill surged up Ritter's spine as his monitor showed the *Yamamoto* shrinking below his CF's stumpy feet. True to his word, Larson took the rearguard position in his Grento.

Ritter kept his 110mm machine gun at the ready and constantly scanned his surroundings. He wanted to earn his keep. And besides, if the gunship went down over deep water, he'd be buried at sea in a Grenzie-shaped coffin.

A sheer, sunbaked coastline rose from the clear blue waters up ahead. Collins followed the shore. Ruined hotels watched over the golden beaches to Ritter's right. The mostly overgrown buildings blurred into a green and silver wall as the helo sped past. Larson's Grento seemed to hover like a parade balloon behind them. Max's far faster jet had long since flown out of sight.

"We're two hundred klicks from Algiers," Collins told Ritter over the radio. "Should be smooth flying, but keep your head."

"This is Darving," Max cut in. "Marilyn says someone's transmitting a radar signal from the coast."

"Is it the control tower at Algiers Airport?" asked Collins.

"Negative," said Max. "The source is about a hundred klicks too close. It's a good bet whoever's running that transmitter saw me."

"Looks like someone's rolled up the welcome mat," said Larson, "Everybody stay sharp."

Ritter strained to see over the horizon. Darving hadn't reported any hostile contact, but enemies lying in ambush often let the point man through and surrounded the next in line—which in this case was Collins' gunship and him.

"I'm picking up a transmission on multiple channels," said Zimmer. "There's a lot of power behind the signal."

"Put it through," said Larson.

"...unauthorized aircraft: This is the Coalition Ministry of Terrestrial Affairs. North Africa has been declared an SOC protectorate. You are to leave our airspace immediately. Repeat: You are violating Coalition airspace. Withdraw to at least one hundred kilometers offshore immediately, or you will be designated enemy combatants."

"Bloody Socs," muttered Collins.

"Your comm's better than mine, Major," said Larson. "Patch me through to General McCaskey on a secure channel."

"Aye, sir," said Collins. "We're connecting you now."

A heavy silence fell. Ritter's grip tightened on his control sticks.

"The EGE brass can't reach the Ministry of Terrestrial Affairs office in Rome," the Colonel said after a few minutes that had felt like hours. "They conferred with Zarai and the Scorpion. Both deny cutting deals with the Socs. We're to stay on course. The *Yamamoto* is prepping a Shen squad to back us up just in case, but watch the skies."

Ritter swiveled his Grenzie's head for a 360 degree view of his surroundings. Puffy clouds scudded across the blue sky, but he saw no signs of incoming aircraft or missiles. His radar screen was clear. But trouble could break out before even Shenlong fighters could reach them.

"Could Zarai or the Scorpion have issued the warning as a ruse?" asked Collins.

"It's possible," said Larson. "Maybe one warlord figures he's got the upper hand in a turf war. Better to duke it out and take it all than make concessions for a peace deal."

"If someone's dealing in bad faith," said Collins, "these negotiations will likely be short."

Three blue-white streaks zipped across Ritter's screen. Fire blossomed beneath the gunship's wings, and Ritter's stomach leap into his throat as his Grenzie entered freefall. The severed tow cable whipped past the combat frame's face as the heavy machine plummeted toward the ocean. Ritter's brain went numb. He worked the control stick to no effect as alarms trilled.

"I'm hit," Collins reported.

"The shots came from seven o'clock below us," said Zimmer.

"Damage to both wings," said Collins, "but I'm not losing lift. The cable must've snapped."

Ritter's bones rattled as his Grenzie hit the water. An infinite blue vista filled his main screen. His chest heaved as if the water was pressing down on him. Sweat loosened his hold on the controls. "I'm sinking fast," he shouted over the comm.

"Ritter, heads up!" Zimmer said. "I've got three CFs converging on you from behind."

Ritter took a deep breath to focus his thoughts and turned the grilled opening in the Grenzie's sensor dome to face behind him. Three bulky humanoid shapes that blended in almost perfectly with the water were shooting toward him. Aside from their blue paint scheme and the strategic application of fins and hydrojets, they resembled his own CF.

"I see them," he reported. "They look like Grenzmarks."

"They're Grentos modified for marine use," Max chimed in. "Seed Corp calls them Mablungs. They're probably packing heat swords and handheld railguns."

"Collins, pull out," Larson ordered. "Darving, get your ass back here and help me sink these bastards."

A burst of 115mm shells cut spiral trails through the water as Larson opened fire on the Mablung approaching to Ritter's right. Three rounds punched gaping holes in the marine CF's torso, and it exploded in a flashing cluster of bubbles. The center Mablung raised its railgun's rectangular barrel and returned fire. The machine gun volley ceased.

"Colonel!" Ritter called over the comm. "Are you hit?"

Ritter's own problems interrupted before he got an answer. The third Mablung kept charging him, firing as it advanced. Turning his CF underwater was like dancing while drunk. Two railgun darts hammered into the Grenzie, shredding its right shoulder pauldron and left skirt armor, before Ritter faced his opponent.

The Mablung had already entered close combat range. It drew a spade-shaped short sword, and bubbles streamed from the superheated blade. Ritter leveled his machine gun, but only water spurted from the barrel before the Mablung's blade sliced the gun in half. In desperation, Ritter dropped his useless weapon and grabbed his opponent's descending arm, stopping the fizzing blade less than a meter from his Grenzie's head.

Red lights strobed in Ritter's cockpit. Text flashing on his screen warned him that ambient pressure levels were exceeding the Grenzie's design tolerances. Unless he ascended soon, his CF would be crushed like a soda can.

The Mablung's pilot clearly didn't have the same problem. He holstered his railgun on his CF's back, gripped his sword in both hands, and doubled his effort to split the Grenzie's head. With his right shoulder servos damaged, the reduced strength of both his CF's hands couldn't keep the superheated blade from descending closer.

Chatter from Ritter's teammates flooded the comm, shouting that they were taking fire from the first Mablung and urging him to disengage so they'd have a clear shot at the second. They didn't see that clinging to his enemy was all that spared Ritter from a crushing death in the black ocean depths.

Which gave him an idea.

Ritter pulled the Mablung in closer, letting the sword bite into his CF's already damaged shoulder and locking the aquatic CF in a bear hug. He flipped open the clear plastic cover of the jump jet ignition switch on top of his control stick and whispered a prayer. "Please let this work!"

Had the Grenzie's jump boosters been airbreathing jets, Ritter would have been screwed. Luckily, they were in fact chemical rockets. He set the thrusters to full burn and pressed the ignition. Much like his machine gun, the rocket nozzles discharged pressurized jets of water. The Grenzie rose slightly. A massive blast followed that propelled Ritter's CF upward like a bullet, taking the Mablung along for the ride.

The grappled combat frames broke the surface in a fifty meter geyser of seawater. Ritter kept the throttle mashed down, sending them rocketing into the sky.

"What the hell is that?" Max called over the comm.

"That would be Ritter," said Larson. "He did something incredibly stupid, and you're just in time to watch it kill him."

Ritter's secondary cameras showed Collins' retreating helo trailing black smoke. Larson's Grento bobbed and weaved, staying one step ahead of the railgun darts lancing upward from the sea while he returned fire. "It's too deep for standard rounds," grumbled Larson.

A point of light gleamed on the horizon and soon resolved into the sharp, angular fuselage of the Thor Prototype. "Ritter might be reckless," said Max, "but he gave me a clear shot at that Mab. Marilyn, charge up Mjolnir and give me a firing solution."

The jet's chin-mounted, lens-like barrel angled toward the sea. A blinding column of light stabbed into the water, flash-boiling millions of liters into a billowing white cloud. A second explosion far below sent another plume of water and steam fountaining to the surface.

"Target is tango uniform," Max declared. "Nice work, honey."

"You can sweet talk your calculator when *all* hostiles are tits up," said Larson. "Right now, the last one's tangling with Ritter at two thousand feet."

Larson's words barely registered with Ritter, whose attention was focused on his losing battle with the heat sword-wielding Mab. The Grenzie's waterlogged arm servos squealed as its left hand, which gripped the Mab's right wrist, was forced down by both of the marine CF's arms. An actuator in the Grenzie's elbow blew with a puff of black smoke, and the shimmering blade collided with Ritter's sensor dome. His main screen went black.

While he was pulling up feeds from secondary cameras installed throughout the Grenzmark's body, the jump jets stalled. The sickening sensation of weightlessness intruded once again on Ritter's panic.

Plaintive alarms warned of the Grenzie's imminent impact with the water's surface. This time, there would be no escape from the smothering depths.

Ritter unstrapped himself, drew his sidearm, and opened his cockpit. Howling, salt-scented winds strove to tear him from his seat. The Mab's cerulean blue chest blocked his view of the ocean rising rapidly to meet them. *Max said that Mabs are modified Grentos. Hope they didn't change the emergency release!*

Ritter reached across the screaming gulf between the entangled CFs. Fighting the wind resistance was like forcing his hand through a block of gelatin. With a final push, he grabbed the central bar traversing the circular access handle on the Mab's cockpit. His aching fingers twisted the slick handle twice to the right and once to the left.

The hatch retracted, revealing a wetsuited pilot whose eyes widened behind his diving helmet's goggles. The whipping wind threw off Ritter's aim, and he shot the Soc in the hip instead of the chest. But Ritter got the opening he needed to release the pilot's harness and yank him out of the cockpit. Furious air currents blew the Soc away from the grappled CFs and into the open sky.

Dragging himself from his crippled Grenzie and into the Mab's cockpit took most of Ritter's strength and all his luck. He threw himself into the pilot's seat and sealed the hatch. The Mab hit the water before he could strap himself in.

9

Max banked north around the rising vapor cloud he'd made of the Mablung and the surrounding water. He lost sight of Ritter's Grenzie and the Mab it was grappling in the rising cloud but kept tabs on the battle via his comm. *That kid's a wild man,* he thought. He hoped Griff was wrong about Ritter getting himself killed.

The howl of the wind, followed by a gunshot, came over the comm. A moment later, the Grenzie's channel went dead.

"Ritter," Max belted into his headset. "Do you copy? What is your status? Over."

No reply came.

"You're wasting your breath, Captain," Larson said. "The Mab decapitated Ritter's Grenzie, and they both hit the water."

"We have to pull him out of there!" said Max. "If the Mab doesn't get him, the pressure will."

"Negative," said Griff, his voice heavy with resignation. "I've got just enough fuel to coast home on fumes. Collins already turned back. I'm scrubbing the mission. Return to base."

"Look," said Max, "I'm looping back around, anyway. Let me make one more pass over the splashdown zone."

"You are to proceed back to the *Yamamoto* ASAP," Griff insisted. "Do you read me?"

"I helped get the kid into this," said Max. "Let me make one more pass. I owe him that much."

"One more pass," said Griff. "Then you get your ass back to base, no matter what. If you find Ritter, radio ahead, and we'll dispatch a rescue team. No lone wolf stuff. Are we clear?"

"We're clear, sir." Max ended his transmission and toggled Marilyn's verbal interface back on.

"Hello, Max," the A.I.'s dulcet but somewhat tinny voice greeted him. "Current air temperature is twenty-seven degrees centigrade. Humidity sixty percent. Wind speed is eight knots from the southwest. Visibility is forty kilometers. All in all, excellent flying weather."

"That's great, honey. We're gonna be doing a flyby ocean scan. I need you to calibrate all sensors for maximum depth. Can you do that for me?"

"Of course," Marilyn said through his headphones, though it sounded as if she were sitting right next to him. "Sensors calibrated."

"That's my girl. Now keep an eye out for a sunken Grenzmark C. We've only got one shot at this."

Light g-forces pushed Max back in his seat as he completed the turn and leveled out his jet's flight path. His eyes searched the sparkling blue water through the wedge-shaped canopy. The vapor cloud had dissipated, leaving the ocean's surface calm and glassy.

"Metallic object located at a depth of four hundred meters," Marilyn said. "Its configuration matches that of a standard CF-05 Grenzmark C."

"What's the Grenzie's status?"

Marilyn paused. "Inoperative," she said at last.

Max slammed his gloved fist down on his armrest. "Damn it! I should have listened to Griff. This is my fault."

"Combat frame detected five kilometers to the southwest traveling away from our position at forty knots. Model confirmed as CFM-07 Mablung."

"It's the bastard that deep-sixed Ritter. Plot an intercept course, sweetheart. We're going dynamite fishing."

The Mab appeared as a moving red dot on Max's HUD. He pointed the Thor Prototype's nose downward and opened the throttle. The jet's afterburners roared, and sheer-sided islands rushed past the canopy. The long gray hull of the *Yamamoto* rose into view from beyond the ocean horizon, with smaller vessels in-between. The dot was a klick away and headed straight for the carrier.

Max eased back on the throttle. "Attention, Coalition combat frame," he barked into his headset. "You are trespassing in EGE waters. Reverse course now, or you will be fired upon."

The Mab only accelerated.

"Marilyn, call the *Yamamoto* and tell them they've got incoming. I'll try to catch this Soc before he gets in firing range of the ship."

The water column between the Mab and the Thor Prototype interfered with the jet's fire control, and Max strained to keep his targeting reticle centered on the red dot. Firing Mjolnir was too risky with the *Yamamoto* as a backstop, so he pressed the release for his Vulcan cannons and covered the trigger.

"The *Yamamoto* acknowledges the warning, Max" said Marilyn. "One of her escorts has a bead on the Mablung and is prepared to blow it out of the water."

Max smiled behind his mask. "It's my job to make sure they don't have to." He squeezed the trigger. A double row of small geysers erupted across the ocean's surface toward the submerged CF.

"No damage," Marilyn said. "Standard ammunition is ineffective at that depth."

The negative number representing the Mab's depth rapidly dwindled. "Looks like the Soc pilot's solving that problem for us," said Max. "Is he an idiot?"

"Target within effective weapon range," said Marilyn.

Max covered the trigger but held his fire. "He could've tagged us anytime with that railgun. Something doesn't add up."

"One of the *Yamamoto's* escort cruisers is preparing to launch an anti-submarine missile," Marilyn warned. "They advise us to clear the area."

The Mab surfaced. It bobbed in the water like a blue giant. The cockpit opened, and a tiny figure emerged, waving his arms.

"Marilyn, zoom in on the Soc pilot," said Max. The magnified screen showed a clear close-up of Ritter's dark hair and eyes.

A ball of light shot up from the distant cruiser's armored superstructure, trailing a column of smoke. "Missile inbound," Marilyn said. "It has a lock on the Mablung."

"Shit!" said Max. He centered his reticle on the rising fireball and opened fire. The missile's countermeasures kept him from locking on, and the Vulcans sprayed bullets into the missile's exhaust trail. Max struggled to reacquire his target as the missile reached the top of its arc and plummeted toward the sea. If its homing torpedo payload hit the water, there'd be nothing to do but watch Ritter die.

Lightning flashed from beneath the jet's nose, and the missile detonated less than fifty meters above the waterline. The blast kicked up concentric rings of waves that nearly sent Ritter tumbling out of the Mab's cockpit and buffeted the Thor Prototype as it passed overhead.

Shock and relief warred for supremacy in Max's brain. "Marilyn, did you fire Mjolnir without my authorization?"

"Yes," the A.I. said. "Voice stress analysis clearly showed that you prioritized Private Ritter's life over all other concerns. The missile was 1.2 seconds from impact, but it would have taken at least 2.6 seconds for me to request and receive firing clearance."

Max blew out a deep breath. "We'll have a talk about that later. For now, tell the carrier to hold their fire and inform them that Private Ritter is in command of the enemy CF."

"Yes, Max."

"And honey? Nice shooting."

10

"What is a Soc's favorite drink?" the barge pilot asked in her precise, tinny voice.

Zane's head tilted back against the wheelhouse's steel wall with a soft thud. "I don't know."

"A Dirty Russian on the rocks."

"I don't get it," said Zane.

"The joke refers to the five hundred cubic meter ice block dropped on Siberia from the SOC's lunar mass driver in 2228."

"Oh." Zane squeezed his eyes shut and sighed. Most of the pilot's jokes went over his head, and after a week spent drifting downriver with no other entertainment options, he was getting tired of humoring her.

"I'm detecting exasperation in your voice. Would you prefer a trivia challenge or a riddle contest?"

Zane stood, crossed to the swivel-mounted touchscreen in two strides, and set the A.I. pilot's audio to "do not disturb" mode. *This wasn't what I expected when Browning called our pilot* Norma.

The Noetic Operations Route Management Application had steered them safely down the Mississippi all the way from Chicago, but her grating personality left much to be desired. Zane decided to complain to NORMA's programmer if they ever met.

Screw that. When I get Dead Drop back, I can flatten Seed Corp.

"Come look at *this*!" Dorothy called from outside. Zane opened the creaking watertight hatch. Stepping from the cramped wheelhouse to the barge's deck was like escaping from an old rusty vault and walking face-first into a hot damp towel. The heavy air smelled of brackish water, and shrill bird calls filled the sky.

Dorothy stood at the bow in the tan, short-sleeved blouse and denim shorts she'd grabbed from her work locker before they'd left Chicago. She clutched a box of energy bars from the boat's cargo—Seed Corp still had their fingers in the food industry—and stared into the distance.

Zane approached to stand behind her. A wide stretch of muddy water spanned from the barge's bow to the horizon. On the right, a bracket-shaped gray and silver flood wall carved out a dismal tract of marshland from the river. To the left, the crumbling walls of city blocks long since reclaimed by the river sprawled as far as Zane could see.

This grim view earned short shrift from Zane, who chalked it up to Earth's lack of weather control. The dun-colored towers looming around the river's next bend captured his attention. Unlike the drowned remnants of a once-great empire that surrounded him, the distant city still breathed.

"You ever been here before?" asked Zane.

"The Socs treat their grounder populations like indentured servants," said Dorothy. "You need a transit pass to leave your district, and they almost never approve travel to the free cities."

Zane clenched his teeth. "How are we gonna find this Jean-Claude guy?"

Dorothy clasped his arm. "Browning said he'd be easy to find. Have a little faith."

"I don't have much choice," said Zane.

Dorothy's faith was rewarded when NORMA docked the barge at a pier of new, white concrete, and a bald stout man exited a black luxury sedan parked beside the levee above. He wore a seersucker suit the color of sugary milk over a black shirt. The left lens of his round glasses was blacked out. "M. Dellister," he called down to the barge in a robust baritone, "Mlle Wheeler, welcome to New Orleans!"

Zane marched up the steel steps built into the levee and stood beside the car. Dorothy followed.

"Who are you?" Zane asked the one-eyed man. "How do you know our names?"

The stranger's mouth curled into a smile under his brown mustache. "I am Fr. Edward Cleon, confessor to His Royal Highness Jean-Claude du Lione. Dr. Browning informed us of your imminent arrival through our back channel contacts."

"Jean-Claude is *royalty*?" interjected Dorothy.

"His Highness is the last heir to the throne of Nouvelle-France," said Fr. Cleon. He opened the car's back door and motioned the new arrivals inside. "The Dauphin waits to receive you."

Zane reluctantly got in the car. Dorothy eagerly joined him. The leather-trimmed interior felt refreshingly cool compared to the muggy air outside. A hulking man with mocha skin dressed in a black business suit sat behind the wheel. Fr. Cleon took the seat beside the driver, who pulled away from the dock as soon as the priest's door closed.

The car sped down a straight road bounded by a high wall on the right and rows of rundown warehouses on the left. After a few blocks, the driver turned left onto a narrow street lined with small boxlike houses.

"What's a French prince doing in America?" Dorothy asked at length. "And what's his connection to Dr. Browning?"

The burly driver answered in a rumbling Midwestern accent. "The Dauphin's family has owned property in New Orleans for years. He fled here when the Socs' Caliphate thugs overran his kingdom and murdered his parents. Don't bring it up again."

"Benny is highly protective of our young master," said Fr. Cleon. "Nevertheless, he is correct that the pain of His Highness' loss is still quire fresh. The Dauphin has joined other deposed leaders in supporting the Earth Governments in Exile. You must keep this information in strictest confidence, but Dr. Browning maintains a number of contacts within the EGE."

"So Seed Corp is playing both sides," scoffed Zane.

"Let us say rather that their chief designer prefers to remain flexible," said the priest.

The car slowed as it approached a square, three-story mansion. Balconies supported by wrought iron pillars clung to its white walls, and an elaborate fence of the same black metal enclosed its small green lawn. Benny turned right into a gated driveway between a high hedge and a brick wall. Two men in black suits armed with shotguns opened the iron gate, and the car rolled into a small courtyard paved with red brick.

Benny parked the car facing a rectangular swimming pool. Fr. Cleon exited the vehicle and helped Dorothy out of the car. Zane let himself out. A honey-like floral scent hung in the air. A stone fountain babbled nearby.

Two men stood facing each other beside the pool. One towered over the other. They both wore mesh masks and padded white vests. Each man held a spindly sword in his right hand. Zane watched as the swordsmen engaged in a formalized sparring session. Their blades blurred and clashed with rhythmic precision. The match ended with the shorter man's sword bowed against his larger opponent's chest.

The shorter man removed his mask, revealing a head of long brown hair tied back with a black ribbon. His tan complexion set off his deep blue eyes. "*Merci,* Lucien," he said. His opponent bowed his shaved, dark-skinned head and withdrew to the house as the victor turned to acknowledge his guests.

"M. Dellister," Fr. Cleon said, "Mlle Wheeler, it is my honor to present Jean-Claude du Lione, Dauphin of Nouvelle-France."

"I can't believe I'm meeting actual royalty," Dorothy said breathlessly.

Zane studied the slender, fine-featured prince. *This guy doesn't look that important.*

Jean-Claude met Zane's eye without wavering. "Welcome to my court in exile, such as it is. I apologize for receiving you in such a disheveled state. If you would like, we can adjourn to freshen up. Changes of clothes will, of course, be provided for both of you."

"Thanks," said Zane, "but I'd rather get down to business."

Benny had filled a glass of water from a poolside kitchenette. Jean-Claude accepted the offered drink, took a sip, and handed the glass back with a nod. "If you wish," said the Prince. "You have made a long journey to see me. Though not my subjects, both of you are fugitives from the Coalition, my sworn enemy. As a Christian nobleman, I am obliged to entertain your petitions. State your grievances."

"The Socs stole my combat frame," said Zane. "I built it myself. It's mine. They shipped it to Africa, and I want it back."

Benny approached the Dauphin's guests with two fresh glasses of water. Zane declined. Dorothy accepted with a skittish bow.

Jean-Claude cupped his chin. "I sympathize with your plight. The SOC has despoiled my family and threatened my person. However, I must consider my people's welfare. Were I to confront the Coalition head-on, my subjects scattered around and above the world might face reprisals. I am prepared to offer compensation for your loss and asylum at my court for you and the mademoiselle."

"I don't want compensation," growled Zane. "I want Dead Drop. If you won't help me get back what's mine, I'll take it back on my own."

Dorothy clutched his arm. "Zane…"

"You're quite determined," Jean-Claude said. "Take care that determination does not become rashness. The Coalition cuts down the stalk that stands up."

Grim amusement twisted Zane's lip. "You think you can just lay low and ride this out? The Socs will cut you all down with the new CFs they based on Dead Drop."

Jean-Claude's eyes narrowed. "The Coalition is preparing to field a new generation of combat frames? Browning's agent said nothing of this."

"Must've slipped his mind," said Zane. "If the Socs have put Dead Drop's energy weapons tech into mass production, the EGE's as good as dead."

"Benny," Jean-Claude said, "contact the harbor and have my ship's crew make ready to depart." He spoke again to Zane. "In the meantime, all of us shall repair to the house. My staff shall tend to you and Mlle Wheeler. We shall reconvene in the dining room at nine. Dress for dinner. Tomorrow, we sail for Africa."

11

"There must be a bug we missed," Max shouted as he bent over the diagnostic readout in the *Yamamoto's* noisy hangar. A bundle of cables ran from the terminal on its wheeled cart, up the side of the Thor Prototype's fuselage, and into the open cockpit. "Recheck lines 819 through 5347."

"Check complete," Marilyn said through the diagnostic terminal's speakers. "No coding errors found."

Max unconsciously stuck his pen in his mouth. The soft plastic was already pocked with his tooth marks. "We'd better find some kind of glitch. Otherwise I'll have to tell Collins and Larson you were in your right mind when you fired Mjolnir across our escort cruiser's bow."

"Incorrect. I fired at, and hit, a missile three meters above and 2.4 kilometers to starboard of the cruiser."

"I dare you to see how far that excuse flies with Griff," said Max. "Forget handling fire control for the Thor. You'll be lucky if he lets you run a fryer in the galley. I only avoided a court-martial because we kept Ritter alive to bring in the Mab."

Darving glanced at the cargo truck parked against the wall to his left. The powerful marine combat frame's blue bulk lay supine on the flatbed since the hangar's ceiling was too low for a CF to stand upright. *Nice catch, kid.*

A mechanical whine echoed from Max's right. One of the massive elevators was descending from the flight deck bearing a transport helicopter whose tail markings identified its home base as the EGE carrier *Lloyd George*. A deep metallic boom rang out as the elevator arrived on the hangar deck. A petite woman showing toned calves below the hem of her skirted service blues stepped from the helo and strode toward Max carrying a black briefcase.

"Wen," Max said as he stepped forward to meet her. "This is a surprise." He smoothed his stained jumpsuit. "You should've told me you were coming."

"As it happens, Captain Darving," the Naval Intelligence officer said as she straightened his collar, "I sent you four messages this week. Let me guess. You were too busy working on that jet to check them."

Max returned the favor by adjusting the skewed Roman Orthodox cross pin on her lapel. "Right again, *Lieutenant Li*. Marilyn's been taking liberties with the Thor Prototype's weapon systems. I'm still trying to figure out why."

Li Wen shook her head. "You've always been more interested in things than people."

"Marilyn's kind of a person."

"Then perhaps you should keep her company while I deliver my findings to Larson and McCaskey."

Max stuffed his pen in his pocket. "I needed a change of scenery after staring at this screen all week. Glad you're here to pretty up the place."

Wen failed to suppress a laugh. "It's good to see you too, Max. Now if you don't mind, I've got official business." She resumed her walk across the hangar. "Are you coming?"

"The Mab's transmitter is still broken," said Max. "Almost got Ritter killed. Did Omaka send you to pull the data off its systems?"

"You really have been out of it. Collins sent every bit of data in that CF days ago. I just finished analyzing it, and the Admiral sent me to brief McCaskey."

Wen proceeded to the galley deck lifts, and Max squeezed into a cramped metal car with her. She smelled of jasmine, which reminded Max of coming to in the *Yamamoto's* infirmary feeling like he'd been run through a rock crusher. But beholding Wen's celestial beauty upon waking had been worth the pain.

"Sorry I missed your messages," said Max, "but I remembered that today's our anniversary."

Wen tucked a stray, raven-black hair behind her ear. "We've only known each other for six months."

"*Exactly* six months," said Max.

"Are you counting my time as your handler while you were still at Seed Corp?" The elevator door opened, and Wen merged with the foot traffic filling the narrow hall.

Max followed her, twisting and weaving between crewmen hustling in both directions. "No, counting from the end of my coma after crash-landing on the flight deck. You were there when I woke up."

"Of course. I had to debrief you."

"And it led to something beautiful," said Max. "Now you're here in an official capacity again. Who knows where it'll lead this time?"

Wen arrived at McCaskey's door and knocked.

"Come," the General's muffled voice called from the other side.

Max followed Wen into the General's spartan office but hung back as she officially greeted McCaskey. Larson and Collins stood to one side conversing with a sharp-looking private first class in a service uniform with a German flag on the sleeve. Max didn't recognize the enlisted man until he turned to face the newcomers. "Ritter?"

The PFC faced Max and saluted. "Captain. Glad you're here. I wanted to say thanks for saving my skin."

"Don't mention it," said Max, returning the gesture. "You clean up nice. I hardly recognized you."

Ritter pointed to his still relatively long but much neater brown hair. "It's probably the haircut. Plus, I finally got my clothing bag. The Major said this meeting's important, so I thought I'd dress for the occasion."

"Mission accomplished," said Max. "You make me look like a bum."

"That's a pretty low bar," said Larson. "You just get off shift moonlighting as a janitor, Darving?"

Wen defused the tension by exchanging greetings with Ritter. "You must be the pilot who captured the Coalition CF. I'm Lieutenant Li Wen, EGE Naval Intelligence. Outstanding work, Private."

"Thank you, ma'am," said Ritter. "Honestly, I was just trying to survive."

"Let's not overlook the fact that he lost a Grenzmark C in the process," Collins said.

Ritter grimaced. "Don't remind me. I feel like somebody shot my dog."

"A fair price to pay for a superior combat frame and wealth of intel," said McCaskey, "which the Lieutenant is here to brief us on."

"Shouldn't Private Ritter be dismissed first, Sir?" asked Collins.

"Admiral Omaka gave him a security clearance," McCaskey said.

Wen laid her briefcase on the side of the desk, unlocked it, and produced a matte gray tablet emblazoned with a winged Eye of Providence superimposed over an anchor: the EGE Naval Intelligence logo. "Ritter was the first to discover that the Mab was carrying encrypted files. Besides, the information they contained has direct ramifications for the EGE's first CF team, which includes all of you."

"'Direct ramifications' sounds bad," said Larson. "I'm even more convinced that forming this team was a mistake."

"Believe me, Colonel," Wen said, "if my analysis pans out, the whole earth is headed for a historic crisis. Your team will simply bear the brunt of it."

Max exchanged uneasy looks with Ritter, Collins, and Larson. "The brunt of what?" asked Darving.

Wen read from her handheld screen. "Comm and sensor log analysis confirmed the captured Mablung as part of a Coalition CF team stationed at Tenes. All three Mabs were in communication with an SOC listening post near Tipasa 130 klicks to the east. They were deployed to shadow you when Tipasa's radar picked you up. When you ignored their warning to withdraw, the SOC commander at Tenes ordered you shot down."

"What were the Socs doing in Algeria to begin with?" asked Collins.

"Based on transmissions recovered from Ritter's Mablung," Wen said slowly, "there's a high likelihood the Coalition Security Corps is establishing advance bases for an invasion of North Africa."

The ensuing silence was broken by the creaking of the General's chair as he leaned forward and rested his elbows on the desk. "The Coalition's Ministry of Terrestrial Affairs just sent diplomatic missions to every warlord along the southern Mediterranean coast. Why would Secretary-General Mitsu give the local leaders a chance to go straight if the CSC's just going to invade anyway?"

Wen bit her lip, which Max recognized as a sign she was deep in thought. "If I were planning to occupy the region," she said at last, "I'd send envoys to the local leaders with a list of onerous demands made under threat of invasion. Their real objectives would be to put the warlords off balance and gather intel on potential targets."

"You're talking psych warfare and espionage," said Max. He caught himself chewing on his pen and jammed it back in his breast pocket. "Since when have the Socs used anything but linear command and control tactics to beat grounders into submission?"

"Director Sanzen is a military history buff," McCaskey said. "He may have gained the upper hand on Mitsu."

"If Sanzen's calling the shots," said Griff, "you can bet he'll invade. The question is, do we warn the locals?"

"Of course we do," said Max. "What other option is there?"

Wen's face fell. "There's a high probability of a warlord striking the SOC first if we share this intelligence."

"Warning the Socs' targets means starting a war," said Collins.

"But on the locals' terms," added Larson, "not the Socs'."

"I concur with Colonel Larson and Captain Darving," McCaskey said. "The local leaders deserve to know they've got targets on their backs."

"But Sir," argued Wen, "The EGE's mission is to ensure world peace; not to start wars!"

"Your objection is noted, Lieutenant," said McCaskey, "but the General Staff has already discussed this scenario. The Socs intend to make war regardless of our actions. We currently lack the strength to confront them directly, so it's best to leak the intel with plausible deniability. That way we can maintain our objectivity and adopt a supervisory role."

"We're gonna let the locals take a swing at the Socs so we can referee the fight," Max thought aloud. "When do we break news of the invasion to Zarai and the Scorpion?"

McCaskey folded his hands as if in prayer but glanced at Wen. "Knowing Admiral Omaka, we already have."

As the Coalition's Mideast Region governor, Prem Naryal could have let her sizable staff prepare her administration's financial reports. But the penchant for ruthless diligence she'd learned under Commerce Secretary Satsu compelled her to sift the raw data personally.

Naryal sat at a terminal in the cool darkness of her Jeddah mansion's server room, reviewing her administration's books line by line. No sound intruded on her meditation except the humming of fans and the clacking of keys.

The numbers add up, she thought—and not without frustration, because a small voice in the back of her mind told her they shouldn't. With a sigh, she expanded the first of 365 spreadsheets and started again from line one. She was contemplating an audit of all the transactions between Jeddah, other SOC protectorates on Earth, and Coalition facilities in the colonies, when someone knocked on the mahogany door.

Naryal ignored the knocking, but it came again, and more urgently. "What do you want?" she called out.

The electronic lock clicked open, and a blue-uniformed Coalition Security Corpsman threw open the door. "Governor Naryal," the young man said breathlessly. "You should see this, ma'am."

Being interrupted galled her, but Naryal's security detail had learned better than to bother her with trivialities. She logged off, swept her long black hair back over her shoulders, and stood to face the guard. "*What* do I need to see?"

"It's Kazid Zarai, ma'am. He's delivering an address on live global television."

Naryal rushed past the guard and down the blue-carpeted hallway, her yellow silk gown swishing with each rapid step. She burst through a set of double oak doors and into her spacious office. Floor-to-ceiling windows curved along the left wall, giving the Governor a commanding view of the inlet whose blue waters lapped against the palace's foundation below.

A line of monitors hung above the windows. Each screen showed a man standing at a podium in a wood paneled room in front of a green, white, and red flag. The weathered face below his bald pate was engraved with a sneer. He wore a dark green jacket adorned with military ribbons. His nameplate read, "COL Kazid Zarai" in Arabic script. The unsteady camerawork betrayed a hasty, amateur production, and the picture looked pixelated and grainy.

Zarai's people must have hacked into one of the old satellite nets.

"Greetings to all the people of the world," Zarai said in a bastardized mixture of Arabic and French. "For those who do not know me, I am the legitimate president of Algeria. It has come to my attention that the Systems Overterrestrial Coalition is scheming to usurp my people's sovereignty."

The floor under Naryal's feet seemed to become shifting sand. *What has Sanzen done?*

"On behalf of the people of Algeria," Zarai continued, "I declare war on the Coalition. Let them—"

The transmission cut out. A clap of thunder in the clear desert sky rattled Naryal's windows.

"Look!" The Security Corpsman stood in the doorway, pointing across the harbor to a black pillar of smoke rising into the sky. "That blast came from the desalination plant."

We're under attack! Naryal considered ordering her personal combat frame prepped for battle, but she thought better of it. "Get me Security Chief Davis."

Megami knew when an emergency broadcast interrupted Zarai's pirate feed that the Jeddah operation was a total success. She curled up on the white plush sofa in her private quarters within Byzantium colony and savored breaking reports of the carnage.

Commander Davis will inform Governor Naryal that the blast originated from a van loaded with crude explosives, she thought. *An Algerian suicide bomber will be implicated. Sanzen will launch a counteroffensive in North Africa, and the last dominoes will start to fall.*

Masz entered from the bathroom, trailing humid, musk-scented air. He had one white towel wrapped around his chiseled waist and was drying his black curtained hair with another. "You look happy."

"Happiness is fiction," said Megami, "but I am pleased with the chaos the EGE caused by sharing the intel I leaked."

"Chaos," Masz said with a wolfish grin. "I should be down on Earth causing it."

"Be patient. Let our enemies kill each other a while longer. When the time is right, I'll send you to do my work on Earth."

Masz approached the sofa and knelt before her feet. "I'll make you proud."

Megami reached down and tousled his damp hair. "I know you will. I know you better than anyone."

12

Sieg knew he was nearing the combat zone's edge when a pair of Grentos flew over him, stirring up hot dust from the road beneath his aching feet. He raised his hand to the crown of his stolen helmet, shading his eyes from the desert sun, and watched both Soc combat frames descend toward a group of small buildings half a klick up the road. He spotted a couple of fuel pumps and a service kiosk with a plywood shack behind them.

CFs ran on cold fusion, not petrol, so the shack was probably a bar. The Algerians Omaka had acquired to drive Sieg to Jeddah were recalled when Kazid Zarai declared war on the Socs and Sanzen had answered in kind. Rather than turning back, Sieg had spent the past two days trudging through the Sahara.

I'm sure one of the Socs patronizing that establishment will give me a ride.

The shack wasn't much cooler than the desert. It was dark though, which along with Sieg's CSC combat uniform would help hide his identity. He entered, shut the flimsy creaking door behind him, and crossed the dirt floor to the rough planks on sawhorses that served as a bar.

Besides the two men whose blue flight suits identified them as the Grentos' pilots, the bar's only other occupant was an aged local man who must've owned the place. His back bowed under his dusty white thawb, and his face looked like a creased paper bag. He stood wiping the bar with a dirty cloth that only moved the dust around.

"Another round of whatever they're having," ordered Sieg. "And keep the drinks coming—on me."

The already bent barkeep dipped his hoary head even lower and hobbled into a small storeroom behind the bar to find another bottle. Both Socs turned to greet Sieg.

"Thanks," said the pilot on the left: a pale, dark-haired young man barely out of his teens who probably hailed from L2. His name patch read "Cowan". "Kindness is hard to come by down here."

"Seconded," said his sandy-haired teammate Voss, who was probably a year older. "What's your name and unit, friend?"

"Yonin," said Sieg, who'd long since removed the uniform jacket bearing its original owner's name. "I was with the Third CF Team out of Tenes. A technical packing an AA gun shot me down north of Chott Melrhir."

Sieg didn't mention that he'd actually been manning the gun, and the Soc pilot hadn't survived the crash.

The bartender returned with an unlabeled bottle filled with caramel-colored liquid that smelled like industrial degreaser when poured.

Sieg flipped a gold coin onto the bar. "Pour one for yourself, landlord," he told the old man.

Cowan and Voss raised their glasses to Sieg. "Here's to the colonies," said Cowan.

"And Director Sanzen," added Voss. "With him in charge, we'll stomp the grounders and be off their backward planet within a week."

Sieg drained his glass—the last full serving of the astringent liquor he would drink—and wiped his mouth on his undershirt's grimy sleeve. "Perhaps sooner."

The sun was nearing the horizon when Sieg left the humble watering hole beside the dirt road in the middle of nowhere. Both Soc pilots and the old bartender lay passed out inside.

Though Sieg felt a bit lightheaded, he'd regulated his drinking— continually asking for refills when his glass was mostly full and always requesting ice which, surprisingly, the shabby establishment had. He climbed up to the nearest Grento's cockpit, hoisted himself inside, and closed the hatch. Secured within the CF, he activated the sensors and rotated the domed head for a full sweep of the area.

The screen was clear. Besides the other Grento and the filling station, no other vehicles or structures turned up within sensor range.

Sieg pressed the Grento's ignition and gradually opened the throttle. The stout CF rose smoothly into the air. At 100 meters up, he trained its 115mm machine gun on the filling station and opened fire. The buried petrol tanks exploded, engulfing the other CF, the roadside bar, and its three slumbering occupants in a towering firestorm.

Turning the Grenzmark east-southeast toward Jeddah, Sieg accelerated to top speed. Shadows lengthened in the desert below as oily flames leapt skyward behind him.

Max circled the belt of farmland at the foot of the coastal mountains directly east of Algiers. If not for Marilyn's night vision scope, he wouldn't have seen the empty suburbs sprawling across the darkened plain below.

Cars crawled along the highway leading through the mountains to the port like a string of sequentially blinking Christmas lights. The CSC already held all the coastland to the west and were pushing toward the capital. Residents of outlying areas fled the Socs' advance in the hope of finding safe haven in the city, or with the lucky few granted refuge aboard an EGE ship.

Max could see the six carriers and their support ships—the entire EGE fleet—anchored offshore to the east. Helicopters were flying around the clock to evacuate asylum-seekers.

It won't be enough, Max brooded. Every other approach to Algiers was just as packed with refugees. Even if all six carriers' crews abandoned ship, they couldn't accommodate all the people displaced by the war.

"Damned Socs. Wish I could head west and call down the wrath of God."

"I could chart a course for the nearest Coalition advance base," Marilyn replied to Max's spoken thought.

"Thanks honey, but you can't go weapons hot till we find that glitch in your algorithm—Major Collins' orders. Just keep scanning the evac zone for Socs, and leave a channel open to friendlies on the ground."

"Yes, Max."

Darving suppressed a pang of envy for the Algerian and EGE forces on the plain below. Marilyn would spot approaching enemies long before he did, so he put his time to good use by checking a few more lines of her code. Within a couple of minutes, he noticed something odd.

"Marilyn, what's with all the activity in your comm processor?"

"Running scans and maintaining radio contact with our allies doesn't require my full attention," Marilyn said. "I'm currently streaming data from the FAST radio telescope in Guizhou, China."

The A.I.'s words tripped an alarm in Max's mind. "What kind of data?"

"Radio signals from deep space. I'm assisting the Chinese Academy of Sciences in searching for intelligent transmissions."

"Everybody needs a hobby."

"Max! A group of technicals is approaching from the west. Three Coalition Grenzmark IIs are in pursuit."

"Show me," said Max. A translucent, green-tinted image appeared in his HUD. Four pickup trucks armed with tripod-mounted guns sped across the fields alongside the congested highway. Three Grentos ran close behind them, covering almost ten meters per stride. The spotlights shining from the CFs' grilled faces stayed fixed on the modified trucks.

"Marilyn, alert our guys on the ground," Max said before he opened a channel to the Grentos. "Attention, Coalition pilots. You are entering a restricted area. Turn back now, or you will be fired upon."

The Grentos kept advancing. A gunner fired an anti-tank rifle from the back of a technical. The high-caliber round exploded against the target's thigh in a burst of light but didn't even slow CF down. All three Grentos responded by sweeping 115mm fire across the plain, blowing away three technicals and two civilian cars on the nearby road.

"Civilian vehicles taking fire!" Max shouted into his headset mic. "Requesting medevac."

"Negative," replied the *Yamamoto's* Air Boss. "The LZ is too hot."

Max clenched his jaw. "Collins will bust my ass for this, but those battle wagons can't even scratch a Grento, and innocents are getting caught in the crossfire." He ran his thumb over his weapon release.

The lead Grento's foot overshadowed a beat up station wagon on the gridlocked road when its torso disintegrated. The combat frame following behind and to the left only had time to turn its grilled spotlight toward the distant hills before its upper body flew apart. The last battlewagon's gunner finally got an RPG loaded and sent a molten copper-filled rocket blasting straight into the last Grento's cockpit.

"Where did those shots come from?" asked Max. A view of the forested hills rising from the plain filled his HUD. Marilyn's IR filter showed a light gray Grento-shaped blur aiming a glowing white machine gun downrange.

A gravelly voice came over the radio. "This is Colonel Larson. The LZ is clear, *Yamamoto*. Have those medical corpsmen get their asses airborne, over."

Max visually measured the distance from Griff's sniper nest to the Grentos' smoking remains. *He nailed two CFs dead center from over four klicks away!* Nice shooting, sir," he told Larson. "I just wish we could take the fight to the Socs."

"You're preaching to the choir, Captain," the Colonel said. "Keep your panties on. We'll get our shot at the spacebugs."

13

Megami breezed into the Secretary-General's office to find Mitsu concluding a dialogue with her tablet. The tight set of Mitsu's jaw and the frazzled appearance of her brown hair suggested that the conversation had been heated.

"We'll continue this discussion later," Mitsu told her interlocutor—probably Terrestrial Affairs Secretary Gohaku. She tapped the screen to end the call, stood up from her desk, and addressed Megami. "I won't mince words. We have a real mess on our hands."

"Define *mess*."

Mitsu consulted her tablet. "In the three days since Algeria declared war on the Coalition, we've lost a dozen combat frames and almost two hundred personnel. Enemy casualties are approaching three thousand."

"Sounds like a good ratio," Megami said.

"There shouldn't *be* a ratio!" Mitsu punctuated the statement by tossing her tablet onto the desk with soft slap. "I implemented your plan to avoid a war. You said an implied military threat would prompt Earth's warlords to negotiate. Instead Kazid Zarai bombed Jeddah, Sanzen invaded North Africa, and now he's convinced Governor Troy to send the Roman garrison to Sardinia. Why didn't Zarai and the Scorpion negotiate?"

Megami seated herself on the office's comfy couch. "The attack on Jeddah proves the grounders can't be reasoned with. I acknowledged that possibility, remember? I also said that if the enemy was stupid enough to attack, Sanzen would overreach himself. He could have ordered limited reprisals. Instead he launched a full-scale invasion, and he's duped Troy into serving his ambitions."

Mitsu bit the tip of her thumb. "I'll grant you that Sanzen overstepped his authority, but his approval rating is over eighty percent. Even the Commission is praising his swift, decisive action. Publicly acting against him would be political suicide."

"You're thinking too linearly," said Megami. "Sanzen has given you the perfect opening to take advantage of the CSC's gains in Africa while undermining his credibility."

"How?"

"Have you ever heard of Block 101?"

Mitsu's brow furrowed. "No."

"It's a black site in L2 that the Commission gave Sanzen as his personal playground."

"That's not possible," the Secretary-General said. "They would have informed me."

Megami's face showed no hint of the cruel glee pulsing through her mind. "Check your tablet again."

Mitsu picked up the slim device. "There's a new anonymous message." Her expression shifted from confusion to outrage as she read. "It's a manifest for experimental research colony Block 101, updated this morning. Their inventory lists 200,000 general laborers!"

"I'll save you some time," said Megami. "You won't find any of Sanzen's workers registered with the Commerce Ministry's revenue service."

"Sanzen has the gall to criticize me for withholding resources while keeping his own secret labor force?" Mitsu furiously tapped her screen.

"What are you doing?" asked Megami.

"Requesting a Commerce Ministry investigation into Block 101."

"A reasonable response," Megami said, "but inefficient. An official investigation will give Sanzen time to cover his tracks. And even if you get him removed, he's staffed the Security Corps with fellow travelers. Sanzen's replacement would just continue his agenda."

Mitsu's hands slowly fell to her sides. "What can I do?"

Megami rolled onto her hands and knees. Clutching the couch's satin armrest, she leaned toward the Secretary. "Beat Sanzen at his own game. Declare victory in North Africa, and announce an aid mission to rebuild the area." Ricimer's memory of Basiliscus' doomed invasion of the region surfaced from the abyss of her mind, and Megami allowed a venomous grin to emerge. "I think 200,000 aid workers should suffice."

"I see…" Mitsu bit her thumb again. "Won't using Sanzen's illegal workforce make me complicit in his crimes?"

Megami stood and straightened her dark blue skirt. "Who would accuse you—Sanzen? He couldn't without implicating himself. If anyone asks questions, admit I told you about Sanzen's workers but not that he kept them illegally."

"Are you sure?" asked Mitsu. "You'd be placing yourself at grave risk."

"I know you're disappointed with Operation Oversight," Megami said. "Consider this my way of compensating you—and fully committing myself to your cause."

Mitsu sat down in her desk chair. "You're confident this plan will work?"

"I'll stake my future on it," said Megami.

"It's my future too," the Secretary-General said. "Don't forget."

Megami bowed her head. "Not in sixty million years."

With a final burst of effort, Sieg's sweat-slick hand gripped the top of the sheer concrete wall. His burning muscles strained as his other hand reached up to join the first on the hard ledge. Having found purchase, he put some of his weight on a block at his feet that jutted out slightly from the rest.

The night wind swirled around him, bearing the scent of the sea and the sweet fragrance of greenery—a rare luxury in that part of the world, which reminded him where he was and why. *I've crossed thousands of kilometers through jungle, air, sea, and desert. Now this retaining wall is the only obstacle between me and the Coalition governor's residence.*

And if ZoDiaC's intel was right, he'd find the full truth about his family's murder inside.

Against common climbing wisdom, Sieg looked down. He clung to a sheer rampart twenty meters above the restricted road that encircled the mansion. Wilting lawns blanketed the grounds from the road to an old sea wall at the compound's west edge. The lapping of water, the chirping of crickets, and the calls of night birds filled the air.

Jeddah had been on high alert since the bombing. Getting through the city had been as difficult as the entire journey from Kisangani to Algeria. The danger hadn't passed yet. A camera or patrolling guard could spot Sieg at any second.

Sieg hauled himself over the wall. He fell about three meters and landed in a crouch on patterned tiles. The scent of saltwater intensified.

The wall Sieg had scaled intersected with two others and the back of a white stone mansion to form a rectangular patio. Between Sieg and the house lay a two-lane lap pool. A woman stood beside the pool in a blue and yellow racing swimsuit. Water beaded on her cinnamon-colored skin, and her long black hair clung to her back.

She was staring right at him. Her eyebrows formed two angry arches. "Security!" she cried.

Sieg sprang across the four meter-wide pool. The second his feet hit the tiles next to the woman, he grabbed her slick wrist, spun her around, and trapped her arm behind her back. His free hand drew his sidearm and held the muzzle to her head as four guards in CSC uniforms burst through the French-style patio doors.

"Drop your weapons," Sieg ordered the fireteam who held their rifles at the ready without aiming at him or his hostage.

The Socs held on to their weapons. Time seemed to stretch out as the standoff continued. Sieg heard only his captive's breathing. Water from her swimsuit seeped into his dusty uniform shirt. *I have to get out,* he thought.

Sieg slid his foot backwards, felt his heel dangling over empty space, and remembered the pool directly behind him. The instant his balance wavered, his hostage rammed her elbow into his stomach. She struck repeatedly, eliciting spasms of pain he feared would disgorge the package he'd swallowed earlier. He took another reflexive backward step and teetered on the pool's edge.

The woman grabbed Sieg's gun hand, bent forward, and heaved. He flipped over her muscular shoulder to land hard on the pavement. The throw only dazed him for a moment, but it was long enough for the guards to surround him. This time they aimed their weapons at his chest.

Sieg tossed his pistol into the pool with a small splash. Two guards roughly turned him onto his sore stomach and cuffed his hands behind his back. A pair of bronzed bare feet stepped into his field of view. "Some might call you brave," she said in a precise L1 accent, "but you're foolish for invading my home and doubly so for assaulting my person."

The Socs' affinity for genetic modification was an open secret, and rumor had it that many within their military and elite classes were artificially enhanced. The woman's gloating confirmed Sieg's growing suspicions. *Governor Naryal.*

"Asking your identity and intentions now would only waste time," Naryal said as the guards hauled him to his feet. He met her calculating gaze. "We'll talk later under more favorable conditions." She nodded toward the house. The guards marched Sieg inside.

"Try the hydrojets again," Max said into his headset mic, "at full power this time."

The water twenty-five meters below churned white against the *Yamamoto's* hull. Max gripped one of the four wrist-thick chains that ran from a cargo crane to the Mablung beneath the surface. Vibrations surged through the warm metal.

"The reactor's still in the green at fifty knots," Ritter said excitedly. "We boosted engine output by twenty-five percent!"

I'm happier we fixed the Mab's radio, thought Max. "Don't be so modest. You did the heavy lifting. I just ran the numbers."

"Either way," said Ritter, "This Mab outclasses any Grenzmark." His voice fell. "Too bad I won't get to pilot her against the Socs."

Max looked out from the carrier's fantail to the port of Algiers. The setting sun painted the city orange and gold. A helicopter thundered overhead, ruffling Max's jumpsuit. The EGE had taken in six thousand Algerian refugees. With the Coalition's abrupt ceasefire, the fleet's helo pilots had been ordered to turn right around and transport all of them back. One reason Max had agreed to help Ritter was to avoid the understandably testy Major Collins.

"The SOC still claims the whole region and holds everything but the city." A sinking feeling pulled on Max. "This truce is temporary. You'll get your chance."

"Max," Marilyn's synthetic voice cut into his channel. "I've received a most surprising message."

"From deep space?" joked Max.

"No," said Marilyn.

Max stepped to the mobile terminal positioned against the rail. "Go ahead and patch it through."

"Considering the nature and origin of this message, transmitting its contents to a public terminal would violate OPSEC regs. Lieutenant Li Wen would not approve."

Max winced. *No she wouldn't.* "OK, honey. I'll be right down."

The hangar looked like a campground the day after a music festival. Max weaved through a maze of abandoned tents, overflowing trash bins, and the cloying stench of rotting food before he reached the port wall and his parked jet. *That's one reason to be glad the fighting's on hold.*

Max climbed into the cockpit, closed the canopy, and removed his headset. "We're all alone, darling," he said to Marilyn's built-in UI. "Now what's so important you had to drag me all the way down here to see it?"

Marilyn brought up her mail client, revealing a newly received message. The subject line was a string of seemingly random numbers, but Max's breath caught in his throat when he saw the point of origin.

That's an internal Seed Corp address! Not only that, the sender's profile indicated someone high up in the R&D division.

Max hadn't communicated with anyone at Seed Corp since he'd stolen their experimental jet and nearly got himself killed in the process. His hand shook as he tapped the screen to open the message.

"Yes?" General McCaskey's terse voice filtered through his office door.

Max rushed into the room and almost blurted out what he'd learned before he remembered to stop and salute.

"At ease," Captain," McCaskey said, returning the greeting. "The Lieutenant was just telling us that the Socs threw another curveball."

Max took his eyes off the General for the first time since coming in. Both chairs facing the desk were occupied. Colonel Larson sat on the left, and Wen sat on the right, directly under Max's nose.

"You might as well start over," Griff told her.

"Thirty minutes ago," said Wen, "Secretary-General Mitsu announced a relief mission to the war-torn regions of North Africa. Our sources say the Coalition plans to send 200,000 aid workers to Earth."

Dread tightened Max's chest. "It's a trick. The Socs are launching a wholesale invasion."

"I wouldn't put it past them," said McCaskey, "but can you tell us why we should treat this revelation as more than a hunch?"

"Tesla Browning just warned me that Seed Corp is rolling out a next-generation combat frame to replace the Grenzmark," Max said in one breath. "In five days the new CFs will be deployed from Kisangani as part of something called Operation N."

Wen lifted her dark, almond-shaped eyes to Max. "The SOC is calling the relief mission Operation Nightingale."

McCaskey and Larson exchanged a look. "How long have you been in contact with Browning?" asked Griff.

"Until today? Not for six months," said Max. "I was helping Ritter with the Mab out on the fantail when Marilyn told me I had a message. It could only have come from Browning. I read it and came straight here."

"Don't attempt to contact Dr. Browning," the General said. "I want you glued to your aircraft, and Lieutenant Li Wen glued to you, until further notice. The second you receive another message that you even suspect is related to Operation N, you are to inform me at once. Is that understood?"

"Yes, Sir," said Max.

"Is it really necessary for me to stay with Captain Darving's plane, Sir?" asked Wen.

McCaskey rested his folded hands on the desk. "So far, Browning has only made contact via the Thor Prototype. Since it was built at Seed Corp, it's possible he has some kind of back door access. He may have other communication channels, but we only know of one, and we can't risk missing vital intel. Do I make myself clear?"

Wen nodded. "Perfectly, Sir."

"Good," McCaskey said. "Report to the hangar. And send Private Ritter up here. I have a special assignment for him."

"Ritter didn't tag along for once," Larson said as Max started toward the door. "Where is he?"

Max froze. Cold sweat broke out on his brow. "He's—"

Larson rose and tugged on his khaki shirt. "Get back to your trigger happy digital assistant. I'll have someone pull the kid out of the water."

"Thank you, sir." Max swung the door open and hurried from the room.

14

Megami followed three steps behind Sanzen as they debarked from the shuttle to the colossal hangar carved into the cratered face of Metis. Other shuttles shaped like blunt white bullets were discharging orderly lines of men and women in dark gray uniforms.

The Kazoku, Megami thought with a flutter of affection. *Sanzen likes to think they're his private army. And he thinks he owns Metis.*

The Consortium had towed the two hundred kilometer-wide rock from the asteroid belt to L5 as raw material for the first colonies. Metis had later served as a manufacturing hub before the Colonization Commission let Sanzen use the mined-out asteroid as a secret CSC base.

As Megami and her self-styled mentor crossed the half-kilometer metal deck, she imagined the back of his bald head cracking open like a blood-filled egg. The noise of work frames unloading cargo and crews wielding power tools would drown out the sound if she did split his skull, but there were too many witnesses.

The CSC Director and his protégé entered a lift built into the far iron and silica wall. A blond Kazoku soldier pressed the button for the observation deck, and a muffled hum reverberated through the lift's brushed steel walls. The young man's appearance stirred up a strange longing in Megami, but the sentiment soon passed.

"Have all Block 101 personnel relocated to Metis?" asked Sanzen.

"All but the 200,000 you left behind," Megami said. "The Ministry of General Affairs took them into 'protective custody' on Secretary-General Mitsu's orders."

"Including two thousand Kazoku?"

Megami nodded. "I handpicked them myself."

The lift doors slid open to reveal a tall wide room. The opposite wall was a single long window that looked down on the vast hangar below.

Sanzen stepped from the lift, and Megami followed. The soles of her boots sank into the soft eggshell white carpet—newly installed, by the smell. A low table of polished black marble sat in the middle of the room. Sanzen sat down with his legs crossed on one of the square cushions surrounding the table. Megami sat across from him.

Before each of them lay a full place setting complete with fine china bearing the O'Neill cylinder and shield seal of the Coalition Security Corps. Megami unfolded a white linen napkin monogrammed in gold with the kanji for *three thousand* and placed it in the lap of her black skirt. A white-gloved Kazoku in dinner dress blues filled first Sanzen's; then Megami's champagne flutes with sparkling white wine.

Sanzen raised his glass. "To Mitsu, for taking our bait."

Megami joined in the toast but declined to drink the floral-scented wine.

"Still," Sanzen said after dabbing his goateed chin with his napkin, "it's annoying having to rely on the EGE. You're certain the necessary information will fall into their hands?"

"Browning is thorough," Megami said, "and our trial run proved the EGE can be reliably manipulated. They exploited the Operation O leak exactly as predicted."

"Not *exactly*," Sanzen reminded her. "You underestimated their restraint. How can we be sure they'll launch a preemptive strike on the shuttles?"

"The EGE fancy themselves the last legitimate government on Earth. Playing neutral observer to a limited retaliatory action doesn't threaten their group identity. An invading army equipped with next-generation combat frames will plunge them into existential crisis."

"Speaking of which," Sanzen said as the waiter served the soup course: a savory-smelling tomato bisque, "how is the Dolph rollout proceeding?"

"Mr. Huang contacted me from Kisangani during our flight," said Megami. "He assured me the first production run of Ein Dolphs will be ready ahead of schedule."

Sanzen held up his glass and peered through the tawny liquid at the busy hangar beyond the observation deck windows. "I have stood watch through the night. Now comes the hour before dawn. My Kazoku, armed with the deadliest weapons ever devised, will sweep away all opposition. I will at last bring order to the earth." He swirled his champagne thoughtfully. "This must be how Themistocles felt before Salamis."

Themistocles was vexed from arguing with his allies and lusting for his young male lover the night before Salamis, Megami recalled as if that warm September evening had been only yesterday. "It sounds glorious. I'd like to go down and witness your triumph firsthand."

"Don't be ridiculous," Sanzen chuckled. "I shall watch the Kazoku's victory from on high like Xerxes from the slopes of Mount Aigaleo. You, my dear, were made to stand at my side."

"Xerxes lost," Megami said.

"An imperfect analogy," said Sanzen. "My personal power so far outstrips the King of Kings' as to be incomparable."

The waiter returned, whispered in Sanzen's ear, and left. The Director laid his napkin on the table. "Excuse me, my child," Sanzen said as he stood. "Duty calls. Expect me back tomorrow. Until then, I wish you a pleasant meal and sweet dreams."

Megami watched Sanzen stride to the lift with cold hatred creeping through her veins. At last, the door slid closed. She broke her champagne flute against the black stone table, leapt to her feet, and threw the jagged stem after the Director. It shattered on the closed steel door. "Sweet dreams? Not since I met you!"

The carpet mostly muted the heavy footsteps approaching Megami from behind, but she knew they belonged to Masz. She turned and proved her intuition correct. "How long were you eavesdropping from the next room?" she asked.

"The whole time," said Masz. His midnight blue leather jacket and pants creaked as he approached. "Sanzen insulted you. Let me kill him."

Megami thought for a moment. "Okay. As soon as I pin Operation N's failure on Sanzen, he's all yours."

Masz's nostrils flared, but suddenly he frowned. "Do we really have to let two thousand of our brothers and sisters die?"

"Sanzen already set the plan in motion," Megami said with a pang of regret. "But their deaths won't be in vain. When the other Kazoku see how the EGE slaughters our brethren, they'll gladly cleanse the earth."

"As long as I get to kill Sanzen," said Masz.

Megami brushed her hand through his coarse dark hair. "You will."

"I'll ask again," said Naryal. She'd changed out of her swimsuit and into a green silk dress, but Sieg could still smell a trace of saltwater concentrated by the walk in closet-sized room. "Who sent you?"

Sieg shifted in the steel chair to which he was handcuffed. He glanced from the Governor, whose dark eyes gleamed with indignation, to the brooding silver-haired man on her right. His navy blue CSC uniform named him Commander Davis.

"And I'll tell you again," said Sieg. "I'm just a peeping Tom. If I'd known you were the governor, I'd have tried another house."

Naryal folded her arms. "Don't insult me. Of all the houses in Jeddah, you picked mine at random?"

"No," said Sieg. "Yours was just the easiest to find."

"With all due respect, Your Excellency," said Davis, "You weren't trained in interrogation. Let me call in some of my people to...*enhance* the process."

"No," said Naryal. "We're not savages like Kazid Zarai. Besides, it's obvious our little voyeur works for the EGE. His chief value is as a bargaining chip. I want him kept intact. Is that understood?"

"Yes, ma'am," said Davis.

Naryal turned to leave but paused. "Keep in mind," she said with her back to Sieg, "Your degree of cooperation determines the quality of your treatment. Sleep tight, Mr. Friedlander." She strode out of the small room. Davis followed. He glowered at Sieg as he shut and locked the hardwood door.

She knows who I am. Not surprising for someone of her stature. Sieg waited till the sound of retreating footsteps faded. "Don't sleep too soundly yourself, Governor," he whispered.

Calling on muscles he'd trained through long and unpleasant practice, Sieg regurgitated a small plastic pouch and spat it onto the tile floor to his right. He tipped the chair over. His induced nausea gave way to wrenching pain in his side and wrists when he struck the floor.

Halfway there. Sieg scooted across the tiles till his fingers touched the wet pouch. He eagerly tore it open and retrieved the lock pick he'd ingested in case of capture. *Good thing I didn't vomit it up by the pool when Naryal elbowed me in the gut.*

Within five minutes, Sieg had unlocked his handcuffs and his improvised cell. He opened the door a crack and glimpsed a long hallway carpeted in blue. No guard stood by the cell, which meant Davis had put more men on the mansion's perimeter while letting hidden cameras mind his prisoner.

That's fine, thought Sieg. The security and communications servers would be in the same place. Finding it would achieve both his goals.

Sieg scanned the walls, which were clad in waist-high oak paneling with green, ivy-patterned wallpaper above. His search continued upward to the plaster ceiling, where a bundle of cables ran along the left side.

The cables led Sieg up two flights of stairs and through two more locked doors. At last he stood on the mansion's third story in front of a hardwood door with an electronic keypad. *Picks won't work on that,* he thought.

Thankfully, Admiral Omaka had already provided Sieg with the key code. He entered the number, the lock clicked open, and he opened the door. The room beyond must have originally been a bedroom suite. Now it was filled with row upon row of blinking, humming server racks.

Sieg closed the door and moved to a compact desk against the wall to his right. Atop the desk sat a work station connected to the backbone of the SOC's diplomatic net. Omaka had also furnished him with an admin-level password.

I'll have to thank the mole in Naryal's administration. Sieg would know the mole's identity soon. The fact that Omaka was willing to burn a high-level asset tripped alarms in his head, but his aching need to know the truth drove him on.

The local drives were filled with dreary financial reports. Sieg widened his search to recently deleted items and found traces of a communication from the Ministry of General Affairs. The message itself was long gone, but its source gave Sieg a lead. A shock lanced up his spine when he laid eyes on a hidden folder stored on a server in the colonies labeled "Elizabeth" containing a single document.

These are orders commanding Security Chief Davis to stage a false flag bombing of the Jeddah waterworks!

The door lock clicked. Sieg leapt to his feet as Davis charged through the door with pistol drawn. Sieg dived between the server racks as a bullet blasted from Davis' gun and through the back of the empty desk chair.

Sieg wended through the forest of twinkling racks as Davis stalked into the room, leading with his pistol. The unarmed spy kept the servers between him and his pursuer, hoping the security chief shared the Soc tendency to value information over human life.

"Who discharged a firearm in my server room?" Naryal shouted from the doorway. Davis looked to her for a split second, but it was long enough for Sieg to lunge from the servers and grab the security chief's arm. He broke Davis' wrist, took the pistol from his limp hand, and repeated the maneuver he'd used to take Naryal hostage.

"Clear the doorway," Sieg ordered the governor while holding Davis' broken hand to the chief's back and the gun to his head.

"Do what he says!" Davis groaned.

Naryal's face was a mask of rage, but she complied. Sieg exited the room, goading Davis before him. Three other CSC guards stood in the hallway with pistols drawn.

"Let him go," Naryal told Sieg, "or you'll never leave this house alive."

Having surveyed the mansion before attempting his botched break-in, Sieg suspected she was right. *There might be one chance…*

Sieg spun to put Davis between him and the other four Socs. He backed down the hallway, pulling his hostage with him. After what seemed like forever, Sieg's back bumped into a smooth wooden door. He pivoted so Davis could reach the lock with his good left hand.

"Open it," Sieg said, keeping his eyes fixed on Naryal and the three guards, who were advancing down the hall.

The slow clacking of fingers fumbling with another keypad preceded a welcome click. Sieg backed through the double doors with Davis in tow and kicked them shut. He spared a look over his shoulder at the stylishly appointed room with its curved glass wall looking out on the harbor.

The doors flew open, revealing Naryal standing on the threshold with a predatory half-smile. "This is my office. The doors are biometrically keyed to open for me. You're either ignorant or desperate."

Sieg returned her grin. "And you're not as smart as you think." The crack of his pistol drowned out the shattering of glass as he shot out the window behind him. He put all his strength into a kick that sent Davis reeling toward Naryal. Her guards raised their weapons, but Sieg fell backward through the third-story window before they could fire.

15

The converted cargo ship that served as Jean-Claude's royal yacht pulled into the harbor at Pointe-Noire. The rusted port-side rail creaked in Zane's tightening grip as he stared across the African port's haphazard red tile roofs. He could feel Dead Drop waiting somewhere in the jungle beyond the sprawling city.

"Our voyage finds its end, M. Dellister," Jean-Claude said from behind Zane. "How did the man from space enjoy his first time at sea?"

The deposed prince sat on a wooden stool amid the white-painted deck with a welding torch in his hand. Before him stood a bronze lump that supposedly contained a sculpture. If Zane had learned nothing else from their time together, it was that his host had lots of weird hobbies. "I hate the sea," said Zane.

Jean-Claude rose and walked to the rail. He pulled the goggles down from his deep blue eyes and let their thick lenses dangle against the front of his sleeveless white shirt. The scent of a plasma fire followed him, heightening Zane's already overpowering urge to find Dead Drop.

"I suppose you wish to seek out your stolen combat frame," said the Prince. "Benny has been in contact with an EGE carrier on course for Moanda. She should be passing by within forty-eight hours. If you can wait, I will ask the commanding officer for assistance with your search."

A flatbed truck with Coalition markings pulled up to berth behind Jean-Claude's ship. An actual cargo vessel lay moored there, and a crane was unloading goods from its hold. The truck driver left his idling vehicle to engage in a lively discussion with a dock foreman.

"No more waiting," said Zane. He left the rail and hurried toward the gangplank.

"Zane!" He paused at the sound of his name. Dorothy stood at the top of the stairs leading belowdecks. She wore a white linen sundress, and her brown hair was tucked under a frayed baseball cap.

"What?" said Zane. "Don't tell me you want to come along."

Dorothy's eyes widened. "Oh, no. I'm staying here on His Highness' yacht. I just figured you'd be setting out again now that we're docked, and I wanted to say good luck."

"Most thoughtful of you, Mademoiselle," Jean-Claude said with a slight bow.

"Thanks," said Zane. "Good luck getting His Highness to make you his queen or whatever." He started down the ramp toward the pier.

"Hey," cried Dorothy. "I'm not some cynical gold digger!"

"If you say so," Zane replied.

"Farewell, my friend," Jean-Claude said. "Regardless of whether you succeed, I hope we meet again."

Zane dashed the rest of the way down the boarding ramp, sprinted to the Coalition truck, and jumped in the cab. He never knew if the driver saw him speed away from the dock and into Pointe-Noire's warren of congested streets. Having a large truck and no regard for traffic laws, Zane made good time through the city. Soon he merged onto the highway that would take him to Kisangani and, finally, Dead Drop.

Darving strode across the hectic flight deck toward the waiting Thor Prototype. The angular, white and blue jet was prepped to take off for Kisangani. General McCaskey had even authorized use of Marilyn's full capabilities—including fire control—out of necessity.

"Max!" Darving barely heard the cry over the cacophony of aircraft engines, crew vehicles, and the hot tropical wind. Delicate hands gripped the arm of his flight suit.

"Wen," Max shouted when he saw the slight young woman in her blue camo jumpsuit. For reasons his heart kept secret, her ethereal beauty struck him like a blow to the head. "Did Browning send ironclad proof of the Socs' dastardly plans while I was suiting up?"

"No." Wen's heart-shaped face turned to the forward port elevator, where the Mablung's blue-armored bulk was descending below the flight deck. "We're still counting on you and Ritter to get firsthand confirmation of the Coalition's new CFs. It'll be dangerous, but…"

Max cupped her chin in his hand and turned her face to meet his gaze. Her eyes glistened from more than gusting wind. "I understand," he said. "Operation N could be a mercy mission, or it could be the showdown the Socs have been spoiling for."

Wen closed her eyes. "I know the Coalition is ready for a fight. I'm just not sure we are."

"I'm ready to fight for the important people in my life," said Max. He gathered both of her hands in his. "You top the list."

A bittersweet smile half-lit Wen's face like the stray shafts of sunlight piercing the ragged clouds above. "Thank you, Max. I know what I mean to you. I've always known."

Max found himself overcome by a sudden wild impulse. "Marry me."

Wen's rosebud mouth fell open. "I need time to think," she said.

A piercing tone blared over the loudspeakers, warning Max that the mission was about to commence. Fighting to hide the pain her words had evoked, he winked. "Don't think too long. I'll be right back."

Wen removed the small gold cross from her lapel and pinned it to Max's flight suit. "Good luck!" she shouted. The wind swallowed her benediction.

Max climbed into the Thor Prototype's cockpit and strapped himself in. Marilyn's GUI already glowed with cool blues and greens. "Your heart rate and respiration are elevated," the A.I. said when Max had donned his helmet with its built-in comm.

"I'm just eager to crack some Soc skulls, honey," he lied. "What's the time to launch?"

"The operation will commence in two minutes," Marilyn answered in her sweet yet tinny voice.

Max keyed in Ritter's comm. "What's your status, kid?"

"Ready," said Ritter, "but I'd still rather fight the Socs head-on."

"Griff and Wen planned that water route to get you inside the spaceport unnoticed," said Max. "If you do get spotted, just holler. I'll strike down the Socs like fire from heaven."

"One minute to takeoff," said Marilyn.

"I've been thinking," Max said at length. "Our unit needs a nickname."

"Got something in mind?" Ritter asked.

"Considering the kinds of missions we get, I'm partial to 'The Suicide Kings'."

"I hate it," Ritter said.

"We are go for launch," said Marilyn.

Max eased the throttle open as he angled the Thor Prototype's vectored thrust nozzles and hinged afterburners toward the deck. The fluttering in his stomach as the aircraft ascended almost made him forget the aching in his heart.

Below, the Mab dove off the lowered elevator and into the deep green seas off the coast of Moanda, sending water spraying ten meters into the air. The aquatic CF's souped-up hydrojets sent it speeding toward the Congo River's broad mouth as it dived. Soon the Mab was lost to sight in the murky depths.

"The kid's going strong out of the gate," Max said to Marilyn. "The river will take him all the way to Kisangani. Plot me a course that brings us in under their radar within two minutes of the launch facility's airspace."

The route appeared on Max's HUD as a bright teal line stretching toward the forested horizon. "Good girl. Let's not keep the Socs waiting." He angled his thrusters full aft and shot out over the gulf.

Naryal centered Davis' convoy on her screen and eased her control stick forward. The sand-colored CSC vehicles fell behind as Jagannath, her personal combat frame, soared over the road to Jeddah's airport, stirring up a miniature sandstorm in its wake.

The four transports in the convoy sequentially skidded to a halt as Naryal brought the Jagannath down in front of the lead vehicle. Built unusually large to accommodate its high-output generator, the twenty-one meter tall combat frame's stance spanned three lanes.

Davis' deep voice boomed over Naryal's comm. "Sorry, Your Excellency. No time for combat exercises. I'm on urgent CSC business."

"This is no exercise." Four Grenzmark IIs landed behind Jagannath, flanking the road with their machine guns ready. Her wingmen's modified mass-production units, distinguished by their gold left pauldrons, had taken a moment to catch up with her custom CF. But Naryal appreciated their timing. "You're under arrest, Commander."

To his credit, Davis remained unfazed. "Under arrest?" he laughed. "On what charge?"

Naryal let a wolfish grin twist her lip. "All files accessed during a network breach are automatically forwarded to me. That should say it all. If you'd rather cling to formality, let's start with treason and espionage."

Jagannath's sensors screamed as a high voltage magnet aboard the rear transport powered up. Naryal barely raised the CF's reinforced shield in time to block the steel dart the truck-mounted coilgun fired at her cockpit. The hypersonic impact sent a shock up the giant CF's arm and left an ugly black splotch on its golden shield but inflicted no real damage. 115mm rounds thundered from the two forward Grenzmarks, reducing the armored truck to burning scrap.

The second vehicle in line made a break for the desert. Naryal almost missed it in the confusion, but she reached out at the last second and snatched up the fleeing car in Jagannath's gleaming gold hand.

"I know you're in there, Davis," Naryal radioed to the car in her CF's grip while the Grenzmarks secured the other two vehicles. "You taught me everything, remember?"

"Friedlander set me up," Davis growled.

"That's why you were fleeing me?"

"I was on my way to a meeting with Director Sanzen when you and your personal guard detained me—with combat frames, no less. Of course I tried to run. They fired on my men!"

"Only after yours fired on me!"

"I take full responsibility for their actions," Davis said. "I warned them to expect an ambush, and they jumped the gun."

"Interesting," said Naryal. "Why would they consider me a threat?"

"Because I suspected you'd buy Friedlander's false intel. That's why I was going to Sanzen—to straighten the whole mess out."

"And if I call the Director?"

"He'll only confirm our scheduled meeting," said Davis. "It's no mystery why I didn't tell him I've been framed for espionage on the diplomatic net."

Naryal gingerly set Davis' armored car back on the road.

"I'm glad you've seen reason," the Commander said.

Jagannath's foot pressed down on Davis' car, blowing out the bulletproof windows with a series of sharp pops. "This isn't reason," said Naryal. "It's anger. In fact, I'm getting angrier and less reasonable every second."

"I'm telling the truth," Davis cried.

Naryal drew an immense metal tube from the rack built into the Jagannath's skirt armor. The giant combat frame's right hand could barely encompass the cylinder. Thick braided cables connected the tube's pommel to the CF's oversized powerplant. "If a spy as clever as Sieg Friedlander wanted to implicate someone, he would have implicated me." She held the tube's open end to the trapped car's side. "Now tell me: Who executed the bombing?"

"Alright," barked Davis. "My men arranged for an Algerian national to drive a van filled with crude explosives to the desalination plant. They acted under my direction. Satisfied?"

"No," said Naryal. "Why did Sanzen put you up to it?"

Davis laughed like a man mounting the gallows with a secret he'd take to his grave. "It's not Sanzen you should be worried about."

Naryal sighed in frustration. "If you'd stoop to covering for a snake that bombed his own people, we should skip your trial and cut straight to your execution."

"Do it," Davis said. "I know you will. You've an accountant's brain and a killer's heart. But there's someone even smarter and more ruthless than you, Prem. Do me a favor and kill me now."

"You're bluffing," said Naryal. But a note of uncertainty tinged her voice.

"You know I'm not, and I know you're not. Act accordingly."

Naryal racked her weapon. Whoever was pulling Davis' strings scared him more than any physical threat she could make. Luckily, Naryal had a habit of acquiring leverage over potentially difficult people. "If this mastermind is as terrible as you say, I'll leave you to him. Now, would you rather your pension go to your partner in L1 or to your son in Riyadh?"

The pause that followed told Naryal she'd hit the mark.

"I don't have a son," Davis said, his voice trembling.

"You do," said Naryal, "with a grounder woman you met six years ago. She's ineligible to receive your CSC death benefits, but young Daisuke qualifies. Unless you didn't register him with the Commerce Ministry. But why would you make such an omission? It's almost as if you were trying to hide him."

"Please," Davis begged between rapid breaths. "You can't imagine what she'll do."

"*She*? Mitsu Kasei could never inspire such fear. Who ordered the bombing, Davis? Tell me, and I'll protect your son."

"No one's safe from her. There's nothing you can do to change that."

"Fine," said Naryal. "Give me your principal's name, or I'll leak your son's."

"You really are a vile bitch," spat Davis. "I hope I live to see Megami slap that smug look off your whorish face."

An exclamation halfway between a laugh and a gasp caught in Naryal's throat. "Megami?" she choked. "Sanzen's...what is she, exactly? His *intern*? I'll have to pull her tax returns. Whatever her title, I can't believe you're terrified of a little girl!"

"She's not a little girl," Davis warned. "She's a monster Sanzen made from the combined knowledge of humanity's most bloodthirsty conquerors."

Naryal finally did laugh. "That's quite a monumental achievement, even for such an avid scholar of military history as Sanzen." She removed Jagannath's foot from Davis' car. "Take the Commander and his men into custody," Naryal ordered her guards.

"We should execute the traitorous pigs right here," said Raskin, the head of Naryal's personal guard.

"Why do them the honor?" asked Naryal. "Secretary-General Mitsu will arrange fitting punishments for all who've betrayed us— including Sanzen Kaimora."

The disgraced Jeddah security chief crawled from his ruined vehicle at the point of a Grento machine gun, and Naryal took off into the dust-tinted sky. *Davis must be lying,* she thought. Interrogating him further would only waste time. Her efforts were better spent elsewhere. Friedlander's inside information had almost certainly come from Davis, but not directly. *Time to smoke out his source.*

16

Ritter followed the Congo River as it curved northeast from Africa's west coast, delved into ancient jungles, and cut through the heart of Kisangani. *Never thought I'd thank the Consortium,* he thought.

The old tech cartel had bribed the People's Republic of the Congo to make the equatorial city a spaceport. Chinese engineers and African workers had enlarged the riverbed to aid the transport of building materials to the site. Almost two hundred years later, those improvements let Ritter navigate the river at top speed.

With his Mablung's hydrojets running at peak efficiency, the trip lasted a little more than a day. Ritter took comfort knowing that Max and two of the EGE's Shenlong pilots were taking turns shadowing him between pit stops on the *Yamamoto.*

And a whole squad of them are coming after me to bomb the Soc base. Of course, bombing Kisangani wasn't the mission's main objective. The EGE lacked the hardware to take out the spaceport. Instead, the airstrike would serve as a smokescreen to cover Ritter's exit.

The river's murkiness forced Ritter to rely on sensors, especially thermal imaging and sonar. Using the Mab's spotlight would risk giving him away. Besides, the dense clouds of particulates in the water would just scatter the high-powered beam.

Ritter's GPS said he was coming up on the spaceport. He rotated the Mab's grilled face through 360 degrees, but his screen showed the same green-brown wall of water in all directions.

The Mab's sonar gave a plaintive ping. Proximity alarms wailed, and Ritter hastily reversed his hydrojets' flow. An imposing concrete wall loomed out of the turbid water, and Ritter extended the CF's left arm to keep from colliding with the barrier.

"Ritter to Max," the Mablung's pilot radioed to the jet soaring somewhere in the sky above. "I'm right outside the base, but there's some kind of dam in my way. Sonar shows it spans the whole river. Please advise, over."

"Stand by, kid," said Max. "This looks like a job for our resident strategists."

Silence filled the open channel. Every minute that passed heightened Ritter's unease. He was treading water ten meters from a key Soc installation in a stolen Mablung. His CSC combat frame might fool base security at first, but they'd inevitably ask questions he couldn't answer.

"Ritter," said a sweet, lightly accented voice, "This is Lieutenant Li. Colonel Larson, Major Collins, and I have confirmed the obstacle you mentioned."

"You couldn't take my word for it?"

"You're a newbie who just got the rocker on his mosquito wings," Larson cut in. "Be grateful we let you pilot a multimillion dollar war machine."

"That wall doesn't show up on current satellite images because they're redacted by the CSC," explained Li. "We had to dig up records from before the Collapse. According to environmental impact surveys made by the Chinese colonial government, that wall is part of a lock and dam system built to regulate water traffic. It also provided the spaceport with hydroelectric power until the Coalition installed a fusion reactor."

"Is there a way around it?" asked Ritter.

"The best way around is through," said Larson. "The Socs channel their reactor runoff through the old hydro plant pipes. Look around, and you'll find one of the outflow vents."

Ritter focused his Mab's sensors on the submerged wall and felt along the algae-coated concrete with the CF's left hand. Pressure sensors in the Mab's fingers alerted him to the presence of a metal grate. Thermals showed a plume of warm water pouring out.

"OK," Ritter said. "I found a vent, but it's only five meters wide. There's no way my Mab can fit through."

"The Mab doesn't have to," said Larson. "Just you."

"Hold on. You want me to swim up a drainpipe filled with nuclear waste?"

"It's a fusion reactor," Larson explained. "The only waste product is hot water. Now hop in there, get inside the base, and steal one of the Socs' new combat frames."

With a sigh, Ritter punched in the vent cover with the Mab's finger. "Looks like this is goodbye," he told the Mab. "It's a shame I never got to pilot you in combat." Ritter reached for the torpedo-shaped diver propulsion vehicle stowed behind his seat but decided against it. *Won't be much use in such close quarters.* He pulled up his wetsuit's hood, secured his rebreather in his mouth, and opened the cockpit door.

Sanzen stood at the Metis observation deck window, dividing his attention between the live video feeds of technicians readying the asteroid's immense engines and his personal view of its vast hangar. *The Operation N shuttles are en route to Earth with two thousand of my loyal Kazoku aboard,* the Director mused. His soldiers' presence had been leaked to the EGE. The fallout promised to be spectacular.

Metis would descend into the chaos following Mitsu's failure like the Second Coming from grounder mythology. The orbiting asteroid would be Sanzen's kingdom, the Kazoku his angelic host; the hangar below him the gate through which they would issue.

Sanzen glimpsed a point of light through the huge oblong aperture of the hangar doors. Dim and distant at first, the light intensified as it grew closer. "An approaching vessel?" Sanzen puzzled aloud. It couldn't be. The first shipment of Ein Dolphs wasn't due for three days, and no other arrivals were scheduled. "I want the approaching object identified," he barked into the comm.

"It's a shuttle from the Ministry of General Affairs," said a soft-spoken man standing behind the Director.

Sanzen wheeled on the speaker, who turned out to be a dark gray-uniformed Kazoku officer with short brown hair and an impassive face. "Mitsu's lackeys are on their way here?" marveled Sanzen. "Why wasn't I notified?"

"Because you're no longer in command," the officer said as if stating that grass was green. "The Secretary-General has stripped you of your post. She has also issued a warrant for your arrest on charges of gross negligence, espionage, and treason."

With a guttural growl, Sanzen turned back to the comm. "This is Director Sanzen. Shoot the shuttle down. That's a direct order!"

The only sound was the soft rush of air through the ceiling-mounted vents. Work continued on the asteroid's engines. The shuttle drew closer.

Sanzen slammed his fists on the control panel and bolted from the room, pushing the young officer aside. He raced down to the hangar as if he could smell the brimstone breath of pursuing hellhounds.

His panic only abated when he stood in front of his personal combat frame: a modified Grenzmark II painted navy blue and charcoal with a high gain antenna on its forehead. He rode the adjacent lift to the cockpit and climbed inside. "I'll destroy the shuttle myself. Then I'll restore discipline here and launch an invasion of L1." Sanzen grinned. "Mitsu thinks she can strip me of command? The CSC will show her otherwise."

Sanzen took off without asking for launch clearance or warning the soldiers at work on the floor. Several hit the deck as their commander's combat frame blasted across the hangar, out the door, and into space.

"There you are!" Sanzen gloated as his targeting reticle locked onto the inbound shuttle. He raised his Grento's machine gun and aimed at the center of the bullet-shaped vessel's blunt bow. At his command the CF's finger held down the trigger. 115mm shells raked the shuttle's nose. Sanzen reveled to see the cockpit windows blown out a second before the rest of the ship erupted in a ball of incandescent gas.

"So shall it be with all who betray me," Sanzen boasted. "Do you hear, Mitsu? You'll follow your bootlickers into oblivion!"

The Grento's comm crackled. Megami's airy yet grave voice spoke. "If you want revenge on everyone who betrayed you, I suggest you deal with me next."

Sanzen couldn't help laughing. "A poor jest, my dear. Then again, humor was never your strong suit."

"True," Megami said. "Elizabeth Friedlander, though—she had a delightful sense of humor."

Panic renewed its grip on Sanzen's heart. "You can't know that."

"You gave me new memories," said Megami, "but you looked in the wrong place when you tried to root out the old ones. I dream about the family you took from me. But that's okay. I have 300,000 new brothers and sisters, and all of them live to please me."

Impossible. That little bitch!

Sanzen's proximity alarm pulled him out of his dark reverie. Another combat frame was approaching fast from Metis. The angular pauldrons of its midnight blue armor flared up and outward like devils' horns. It carried a long staff in its right hand and a tapered shield in its left as it trailed bright fire across the black sky.

I wasn't aware of a customized Zwei Dolph aboard my station, Sanzen thought with growing dread. The Ein Dolphs hadn't officially rolled out yet, and their planned successor was still in the prototype stage. "Tell whoever is piloting that combat frame to break off and return to base," he ordered Megami.

"No," she said. "I promised Masz he'd get to kill you, and he's a pain in the neck when he's disappointed."

"Call off your attack dog and face me, coward!" Sanzen raged.

"You haven't earned death at my hands," said Megami. "The grounders are another story. A slight change to your plan should do for them. Not that you'll live to see it."

The Zwei Dolph entered weapons range. Sanzen spun his Grento and unleashed a hail of automatic fire with a visceral cry.

Sanzen put no stock in transcendence. He'd learned too much about man's true origins to believe in a benevolent creator. Yet he could only classify what he saw then as a miracle. Or perhaps it was black magic, because the Zwei Dolph's pilot flew like a demon. He danced between the shells Sanzen sprayed at him and halved the distance between the two CFs.

The last round in Sanzen's gun burst harmlessly against the Zwei Dolph's shield, the tip of which flicked upward to point at the Grento. Sanzen found himself staring down the black muzzles of the double-barreled plasma cannon mounted inside the shield.

"No," shouted Sanzen. "I was meant to conquer!" He spun the Grento about and punched the throttle. The blackness of space gave him no sense of forward motion, but the g-forces pushed him back in his seat. His aft-facing cameras caught two simultaneous flashes of blinding red light. Sanzen's combat frame and the air in his cockpit and lungs dissolved in white fire.

With a final heave, Ritter pushed the drain cover open and slid it aside. The heavy steel grate ground against the concrete floor. He climbed from the cramped dark tunnel, his wetsuit dripping with warm water and smelling of ozone.

I came to the right place.

Ritter stood in a colossal warehouse. A flat ceiling crisscrossed with white girders hung far overhead. Combat frames stood in recesses along the walls fronted by movable scaffolding. *Those aren't Grenzmarks!*

The unknown CFs exceeded nineteen meters in height. They were painted darker blue than a Mab, and unlike the Grenzmarks, squares and rhombuses dominated these machines' design. The stock of some new type of rifle jutted over each unit's right shoulder. Instead of grilled domes covering circular camera arrays, the new CFs had actual heads resembling blocky helmets with shoulder-length neck guards. Each unit's face featured a black, v-shaped visor.

These must be the Socs' new combat frames, thought Ritter. The sight filled him with awe, until he saw what waited at the hangar's far end.

The black combat frame superficially resembled its hangar mates, but its unique coloration and lack of Coalition markings suggested it was a custom job. A narrow purple visor covered its main camera array. The black CF carried no visible weapons but exuded menace like a coiled mamba.

Ritter knew enough about combat frame design to connect the dots. *That black one must be the prototype. It might still have design schematics and combat test data onboard. Larson will eat his words when I bring this beauty back!*

Making it to the black combat frame would mean crossing a hundred meters of open floor, almost certainly in full view of multiple security cameras. But taking any CF would blow Ritter's cover, so he figured he might as well go for the gold. He broke into a sprint across the hangar.

Ritter's pounding heart swelled with pride when he reached his target's glossy black foot. He hopped onto the steel mesh lift built into the adjacent scaffold, closed the chest-high gate, and slammed the "up" button. Hydraulics whirred, and the lift ascended.

The rising platform jerked to a stop at a catwalk that traversed the black CF's chest. Ritter dashed to the cockpit and reached for the lever. A bullet ricocheted off the railing to his right as a sharp crack echoed throughout the concrete and metal warehouse.

"Don't touch!" someone shouted from below.

The fevered command drew Ritter's eye to a white-haired man who otherwise looked only slightly older than him. Smoke curled from the pistol in his hand. He wore the dark green jacket and pants of a CSC Southern Africa Region uniform, but Ritter doubted anyone that intense could be a Soc.

The gunman took aim at Ritter. "Dead Drop is mine."

Ritter vaulted over the catwalk's railing and slid down a support beam. There was no point arguing, and if his intrusion hadn't alerted security, the manic stranger's gunshot certainly had.

Sure enough, alarms blared. CSC personnel stormed in through every entrance, including the far door that the black CF's owner had left open.

Ritter charged the oncoming guards, passing the white-haired gunman who dashed toward the lift. A volley of gunfire turned the hangar into an echo chamber, but Ritter kept running. A bullet grazed his shoulder, tearing his wetsuit and the skin beneath with a stab of hot pain. He slid the last couple of meters to the open drain and fell into the dark.

17

Zane basked in Dead Drop's embrace. The bank of monitors arranged to his personal specifications remained black, shrouding the cockpit in darkness. Radio chatter—mainly from base security ordering him out of the combat frame—faded to white noise.

I'm whole again. Zane could only compare his euphoria to having a severed limb reattached, even though Dead Drop hadn't always been with him. *But it always has been,* he realized. His labor had given the black combat frame physical form, but its design had existed long before he'd soldered the first two wires together.

A strange hollowness marred Zane's contentment. He'd fulfilled his quest to recover Dead Drop, but his peace was shaken by a hunger he couldn't name. He set the puzzling emotion aside for later consideration and reveled anew in his victory.

"I'll never let them take you again," he vowed.

The warm current almost pushed Ritter past his Mablung. He avoided being swept down the muddy river by latching onto a seam in the Mab's arm. He crawled along the outstretched limb to the combat frame's chest and fumbled for the hatch controls. At last his fingers closed around the door handle. He opened the cockpit and spilled in, along with a torrent of dirty water.

Ritter scrambled to orient himself. When he was secure in his seat, he closed the hatch and drained the cockpit. He spat his rebreather onto the main monitor, which bore a thin film of river slime, and savored a deep breath of coppery air.

Made it! He thought with a deep exhale. Only then did he notice the burning in his shoulder. *They'll patch me up on the* Yamamoto. *Too bad I'm coming back empty-handed.*

Ritter Powered up the Mab. His screens flashed to life, showing the broken grate in the submerged wall. His thumb was hovering over the hydrojet selector when a familiar voice came over the radio. "Come in, Ritter. This is Major Collins. Do you read me?"

"Loud and clear, Major. The mission hit a snag. I'm headed back to the ship."

"I'd hurry if I were you," said Collins. "Captain Darving's picked up six unknown combat frames heading overland in your direction."

Must be some of those new model CFs. Ritter's gut clenched—partly in fear, but also with eagerness. "Copy that. I'm pulling out now."

"Roger," said Collins. "A Shenlong squad is inbound, but you'll want to be far away when the bombs drop."

Ritter pushed his Mab away from the wall, spun it around, and engaged the hydrojets. An underwater blast slammed into the Mablung's back. Ritter lurched forward in his seat as alarms shrieked. *That can't have been a mine. Are they dropping depth charges from the wall?*

The proximity alarm trilled. Ritter jerked the control stick to the left just in time to avoid another blast on his right. The shock jarred his spine, but the Mab's armor stopped any real damage. One rapidly expanding pressure bubble after another filled the river basin. The shockwaves bounced off the channel walls, shaking the Mab like a can in a paint mixer.

Can't stay down here.

The Mab jetted upward at Ritter's command. Its domed head broke the river's frothing surface. As Collins had warned, six of the CSC's blocky new CFs stood along the concrete-clad shore in a widely spaced line. Each carried a large black rifle with a second barrel mounted under the square main muzzle. The six underslung barrels fired, and Ritter forced the Mab back as a line of explosions sent plumes of white water shooting from the river.

"Grenade launchers," Ritter cried. "I can't get closer or line up a shot!"

"Relax, kid," Max said over the comm. "The lifeguard's on duty."

Ritter's instruments chirped. A green dot appeared at the edge of his monitor and zipped across the screen toward the six red squares in front of him. "Light them up," Ritter cheered.

Max clicked his tongue. "Socs don't have the sense to steer clear of the water in a thunderstorm. Give 'em a spanking, honey."

The Mab's filters barely compensated for the bolt of light that slanted from the sky into the enemy CFs' line. One peal of thunder answered another as the Thor Prototype streaked over the heavy smoke cloud enveloping the shore. With the enemy's bombardment ended, the river resumed its dark smooth flow.

Ritter heaved a sigh of relief. "That's another one I owe you, Max. I take back wanting to fight those things."

"There's hope for you yet," said Max. "You survived the battle. That's a victory. Now get back to the ship, and let's celebrate with a six pack I picked up in Algiers."

A red beam lanced upward, given coherence by the smoke cloud. A white-orange light flared above the horizon to Ritter's left. "Max!" he shouted into the comm. "What's your status?"

"I'm hit," replied Darving, his voice strained. "Bastard blew off my starboard tail fin."

A giant stepped from the thinning smoke. Its paint had burned off, exposing bare gray metal. The cloud melted in a gust of wind to reveal the other five Soc CFs marching behind their leader; their blue armor darkened with soot.

"Shit," said Max. "Their armor's insulated."

All six enemy combat frames raised their rifles skyward.

"Max," cried Ritter, "They're aiming at you. Get out of here!"

"And leave you with these pricks? Not a chance." The white jet rolled right, just ahead of six read beams that pierced the hazy air. It pulled into a banking turn that brought the Thor Prototype about to face the Soc firing squad.

"We don't even know what kind of weapons they're using," Ritter warned. "Be careful!"

"Some kind of refined plasma projectors," said Max. "I thought Browning was years from that kind of tech. And yeah, I'll try."

The jet hurtled toward the enemy CFs, too fast for their pilots to keep the aircraft in their sights. Crimson rays passed over the Thor Prototype's fuselage, and it opened up with its twin Vulcan cannons. Ritter's heart sank as the 20mm rounds disintegrated against the CFs' armor without effect.

"Damn, they're tough!" Max cursed as he finished his second fruitless strafing run. The Soc CFs turned to track his flight, their rifles spitting steel-melting fire. They'd already connected once. It was only a matter of time before one of the Socs scored a devastating hit.

But they're distracted, thought Ritter. *Don't let Max's courage go to waste. Run while you can!* Ritter gripped the Mab's controls so hard his knuckles popped.

He didn't leave me.

Ritter drew the Mab's railgun from the charging rack on its back. He took a deep breath, centered his reticle on the gray lead CF, and pulled the trigger. His railgun's barrel pulsed with electric blue light. But he'd undercompensated for his aquatic firing position. Sparks flew from the leader's pauldron as the hypersonic dart grazed its shoulder.

The Soc leader and the two CFs beside him pivoted toward the river. Ritter jammed his stick forward and toggled the drive selector. His Mab hit the shore running. A cry burst from his chest as he fired again. The lead Soc's plasma rifle exploded, leaving its right arm warped and sparking.

Both CFs flanking their disarmed leader opened fire. Their wild shots blasted craters in the concrete to the Mablung's right and left. The Mab was aquatic, but it retained a Grento's mobility on land. Ritter drew his curved sword and closed with the leftmost Soc CF. He sidestepped to keep his target between him and the other hostiles as he slashed the superheated blade. A cloven plasma rifle barrel hit the ground.

"Not a bad idea," Max said over the comm.

The Thor Prototype descended in a smooth arc with a roar of vectored thrust. Its afterburners swung downward on hinged struts that reminded Ritter of chicken legs. His jaw dropped when the mystery nacelles under the jet's wings unfolded into a pair of combat frame arms. Each arm wielded a long, tapering heat sword.

Max had said the strange pods were for emergencies. *Right now definitely qualifies,* thought Ritter. He'd disarmed two hostiles, but they were still active, and their four friends had rifles that could burn holes through steel as if it were paper.

Max threaded the needle between the two rightmost enemies and struck with his heat swords as he zoomed past. Aided by his momentum, the superhot blades finally penetrated the enemies' armor. One dark blue CF clutched its gouged side while another lost its left arm at the elbow.

The hybrid CF-jet turned right and accelerated down the base's main thoroughfare, blasting cars with jet wash as it careened between buildings. Two armed CFs, including the one with the damaged side, lifted off on rocket thrusters and gave chase as screaming pedestrians hit the deck.

Ritter saw only a red flash as a plasma bolt slagged the left side of his skirt armor. One of the three Soc CFs with a working rifle had risked shooting past his teammate in a bid to take down Ritter. *I don't know if I should be terrified or flattered.*

Ritter's nearest opponent lunged, grabbed his sword arm with both hands, and pulled the Mab forward. The railgun's long barrel was pinned between the grappling CFs.

The last armed Soc CF on the ground moved in for a shot at the Mab's damaged left side. Ritter fired his trapped railgun and vaporized a parked car down the street. His encroaching foe stepped back. The two other hostiles circled around to his right.

"What do you think you'll accomplish?" a male voice mocked over the main CSC channel. Judging by the exertion in the Soc's voice, he was probably piloting the CF arm-wrestling with the Mab. "Your Mablung would be outclassed by a single Ein Dolph, and you're up against four."

"Only one that counts," Ritter said. "Your Dolph can take a beating, but it's got no offense without its sparkle gun."

The Dolph's hard-edged knee pistoned up into the Mab's torso. Ritter's cockpit hatch groaned as the impact threw him back in his chair. The Dolph pried the sword from his grip.

"Don't think our Dolphs can't brawl because they're the first energy weapon-optimized CFs," the Soc pilot said. "We're gonna tear your Mab apart. Then we'll pry you out and pull your limbs off like a bug."

"The first?" a voice quivering with rage repeated over the comm.

A purple flash blew away the front wall of the hangar across the street. All four Dolphs turned their helmeted heads toward the smoke-filled building.

"Dead Drop is the first." The voice on the comm rose from a growl to a bluster. "Your cheap knockoffs copied the tech I built with my own hands."

The black combat frame strode out of the flames engulfing the hangar. Its purple visor flashed as it raised its left arm. "No one steals from me."

"It's the prototype!" said the pilot of the Dolph to Ritter's left. The dark blue CF leveled its plasma rifle at Dead Drop.

A barrel popped up from Dead Drop's outstretched arm and emitted a violet flash. Gouts of fire and oily smoke belched from the Dolph's cockpit and back. The dark blue CF dropped its weapon and crashed to the ground.

"Retreat!" ordered the Soc CF team leader. All three surviving Dolphs, including the one grappling Ritter's Mab, disengaged and blasted into the air. Dead Drop followed. Ritter marveled at the black CF's blinding speed. A burst of white fire had turned it from a jet black colossus a hundred meters in front of him to a speck in the sapphire sky faster than his eye could follow.

"Negative," a Dolph pilot replied to his team lead. "We've got that hybrid aircraft on the run. Give us a minute to finish it off, and we'll regroup with you."

Ritter checked his screen. The Mab's radar was making intermittent contact with three high-speed craft flying through downtown, but the tall buildings kept getting in the way. His cameras caught sporadic red flashes and smoke rising from the glass towers.

He squelched the Socs' channel, which was mainly transmitting the Dead Drop pilot's wordless cries, and radioed the Thor Prototype.

"Max! This is Ritter. I'm still on the riverbank. Swing past me and see if you can make those Dolphs follow."

An uneasy silence fell. *Did they shoot him down?* Ritter pressed his transmit switch again, but the Thor Prototype—back in full jet mode and trailing smoke—came screaming out of the urban canyons to the Mab's left.

Ritter raised his railgun and held it steady on the jet's smoke trail. Two Dolphs soon emerged from the skyline, hot on Max's tail. At that distance, they resembled wargame miniatures held at arm's length. When the lead Dolph flew into Ritter's sights, he pressed the trigger on his control stick. A hypersonic steel dart blasted from the railgun's barrel.

An orange explosion against the Dolph's blue armor told Ritter he'd hit the mark. His rising spirits fell when the Soc CF merely slowed with a slight wobble but stayed airborne.

That armor is tough! Ritter's fear for Max became more immediate panic as the Dolph he'd hit rocketed straight toward him. Reflex overrode his shock, and the Mab leapt aside an instant before the bank where it had stood erupted in a red flash. Ritter returned fire, but his shot streaked over the onrushing Dolph's helmed head. The Dolph took aim for a point-blank shot.

A black blur swooped down and slammed into the Dolph, knocking it off course and into a squat concrete building across the river. Ritter lost sight of the dark blue CF under an avalanche of broken masonry and a roiling debris cloud.

Dead Drop landed next to the Mablung. Ritter swiveled the Mab's grilled face to the left.

"Hi," Ritter transmitted to the black CF.

"Hi." The reply came from Dead Drop's pilot, who sounded out of breath but still overflowing with rage.

"Thanks for the help. I'm Tod Ritter."

"Zane Dellister. I wasn't helping you. I was destroying *them*." The last word dripped with contempt.

"Oh," Ritter said. "I lost track. Was that the last one?"

With a whine of vectored thrust nozzles, the Thor Prototype descended and hovered by the Mab's right side in hybrid mode. "It was the last of the team the Socs launched against us," said Max. "Thanks for getting that Dolph off my six. The diversion let me shank his wingman."

"I didn't know your jet was part CF," said Ritter.

"Seed Corp is known for combat frames," said Max. "This wasn't just a jet prototype."

Dead Drop's visor fixed itself on the hybrid aircraft. "You work for Browning?" asked Zane.

"I defected to the EGE a while back," said Max. "We could use a pilot like you."

"The rubble pile across the river shifted. A dusty but intact Dolph rose from the wreckage and lifted its plasma rifle.

Ritter, Max, and Zane fired as one. The Dolph vanished in a rumbling fireball.

"See?" said Max. "We work great together."

"They're hardened against electrical attacks," said Zane, "and my shot breached the reactor before Ritter's kinetic round caught up."

"That's just bragging," said Max.

A red pulse from the heart of the spaceport sent Dead Drop reeling forward with smoke spouting from its back. Zane grunted over the comm.

The Thor Prototype jetted upward and hung in the sky facing the base. Max's words came over the line in a torrent. "Marilyn says the Socs just deployed five more Dolph teams."

"This is bad," said Ritter. He swung the Mab's railgun toward the base. Through the clustered outbuildings he saw a blue line marching toward him. Red bolts pulsed down abandoned streets wherever the Dolphs had an opening. Ritter's heart fell into his stomach as the back rank of Soc CFs took to the air while the frontline continued to advance.

Dead Drop spun to face the enemy. "I'll take them all!" yelled Zane as his CF's arm-mounted plasma cannon fired. His shot melted the third floor corner of a skyscraper.

"Those Soc pilots rely on their machines too much," said Max, "but thirty machines like those will roll over us like we're roadkill."

"You're underestimating Dead Drop," said Zane.

"Marilyn says you lost a maneuvering thruster. You're a sitting duck against those plasma rifles. We need to pull out!"

Crimson fire from above blew smoking craters along the riverbank. Dead Drop tried a rocket-assisted backward leap that failed to fully clear the blast zone. Smoke poured from its singed left forearm. Zane aimed his damaged cannon up at the offending Dolph. The violet flash from its muzzle burned away the armor on the blue CF's chest but failed to destroy it.

Ritter fired at another airborne foe. His kinetic darts were no match for the Dolphs' armor, but he hoped to buy time. For what, exactly, he didn't know.

The Thor Prototype's twin Vulcans laid down suppressive fire. The six Dolphs in the air descended. But their pilots soon learned their CFs were impervious to the 20mm rounds and resumed their advance.

This is a nightmare! Ritter knew running was the only hope. But the flight-capable Dolphs would catch him whether he fled by water or land. Zane seemed ready to fight to the death. Only one of them still stood a chance.

"You did all you could, Max," said Ritter. "Leave these guys to me and Zane."

"Bullshit!" said Max. "Get your Mab in the river and swim out of here as fast as you can. I'll cover you."

"Why don't both of you bug out, and *we'll* cover your escape?" said Zimmer. His transmission ended just as a flight of Shenlong fighters barreled across the battlefield, raining earthshaking fire. The bombs raised a flaming curtain between the Dolphs and their targets.

"It's the airstrike from the *Yamamoto*," Ritter cried.

"You heard Zimmer," said Max. "If you don't get your ass back to base, you deserve to get it shot off." The Thor Prototype rotated westward, reverted to jet mode, and took off like a bullet.

Ritter turned toward the river but paused. He swiveled the Mab's face to see Dead Drop firing into the wall of flame that bisected the base.

"Zane," Ritter said. "We're pulling out. Come with us!"

Dead Drop gave no sign its pilot had heard Ritter's plea. Its damaged cannon flashed violet again and again, striking at unseen foes. A red beam stabbed upward through the center of a Shenlong, which went corkscrewing toward the skyline.

"The *Yamamoto* is anchored off Moanda," Ritter told Zane. "I'll see you there."

Ritter charged into the river. The murky water closed over the Mab's head, and he engaged the hydrojets at full power as bombs thundered and crimson light filled the smoking skies of Kisangani.

18

After the Jeddah fiasco, Coalition Secretary-General Mitsu Kasei had anticipated fighting a pitched battle to save her career. Instead, her flagging political fortunes had completely reversed in a single week.

Each day had brought a new and unexpected victory, starting with the revelation of Security Director Sanzen's illegal workforce at Block 101. Governor Naryal's shocking report of Sanzen's role in staging the Jeddah bombing had soon followed, leading to the Director's utter disgrace and shameful death while fleeing arrest.

Today Mitsu sat with her fellow Secretaries, secure in her position as first among equals. She'd convened the Coalition Council for a most welcome task: to replace the late Sanzen Kaimora as CSC Director.

The gallery of concentric tables radiating from the central podium was packed with bureaucrats, rent-seekers, and even a person or two of importance. A low susurrus of whispered innuendos rose to the Secretaries' table on the top tier of the gray chamber.

"Good morning," Mitsu spoke into her microphone. She relished how the room fell silent at her word. "This Council session is called to order. Before we discuss the CSC directorship's vacancy, I'll open the floor to new business."

"Madame Secretary," plump aging Secretary Gohaku said, "we at the Terrestrial Affairs Ministry have overseen the Security Corps since its inception. In light of mounting threats to the safety of our citizens, including yesterday's attack on the Kisangani Spaceport, I feel it's time we restructured the CSC's relationship to the TAM."

Mitsu already knew the content of Gohaku's proposal. Still, she did as advised and played along. "What sort of restructuring do you suggest, Mr. Secretary?"

Gohaku laced fingers like pale mottled sausages and laid his hands on the table. "For all his faults, we believe Sanzen's estimate of the resources required to secure safe work and living spaces for SOC persons was correct. Earth's endemic violence now threatens to invade outer space."

A rumble of agreement arose from the gallery.

"It is our conclusion," Gohaku continued, "that the CSC's funding and organizational needs far exceed the legal limits of a Secretariat sub-department. I therefore move that the Coalition Security Corps be dissolved. I further move that its assets and personnel be transferred to a new Ministry of Defense."

Mitsu waited for the applause from the gallery to subside before she asked a question she already had the answer to. "Secretary Gohaku, has your Ministry prepared legislation to effect the CSC's dissolution and the establishment of a Coalition Defense Ministry?"

"My team drafted the resolution last week and forwarded copies to all Council members," Gohaku said. "All that's left is to bring the measure to a vote."

"Is one week sufficient time to consider such sweeping legislation?" Mitsu asked, taking care to inflect her words as a request for information instead of a rhetorical question.

"Emergencies call for swift decisive action." Gaunt, black-haired Commerce Secretary Satsu was Gohaku's physical opposite, but both men were equally opportunistic. "I second my honorable colleague's call for a vote."

"Very well," said Mitsu. "The Coalition Council will now vote on the Terrestrial Security Act sponsored by Secretary Gohaku."

Fear is a powerful stimulus, Mitsu recalled as the final tally came in. Just over two-thirds of the Council voted to enact Gohaku's law.

"The measure passes," Mitsu announced. "As per the terms of the act, the Terrestrial Affairs Secretary will oversee the transition with the Defense Secretary-elect. I move that we amend our original agenda and proceed directly to naming our first Secretary of Defense."

Gohaku and Satsu both seconded the motion.

"Precedent dictates that Secretary-level appointments be made by the Colonization Commission," objected Secretary Vier. The iron-haired Transportation Minister had smelled blood after Mitsu's failure with Operation Oversight, but his stubbornness kept him from recognizing her strengthened position.

"Standard procedure hardly applies in such extraordinary circumstances," said Mitsu. "Besides, the Commission is currently ill-disposed to assemble a list of candidates. Or perhaps you've been too preoccupied to follow current events."

Mitsu allowed herself a brief smile. The Transportation Ministry shared jurisdiction over Kisangani with the Ministry of Terrestrial Affairs. Mitsu's barb would sting all the deeper since opposing Gohaku's solution would be seen as crass brinkmanship on Vier's part.

But humbling her rival wasn't the only source of Mitsu's satisfaction. A series of scathing exposés had thrown the Commission into chaos. Five Commissioners—all Sanzen's benefactors—had been implicated in scandals dire enough to force their resignations. As chief executive of the Coalition, Mitsu now had free rein to appoint her own Defense Secretary.

"Filling a high office entrusted with our protection is not a choice to be made lightly," Mitsu said. "The only pool of qualified candidates is of course the CSC itself. Unfortunately, most of the Security Corps' senior personnel are tainted by their close association with Sanzen.

"There is only one candidate with intimate knowledge of high-level security practices and a history of selfless service to the Coalition. I nominate Miss Sekaino Megami."

The Council chamber fell quiet as the void. At length Secretary Vier broke the silence. "With all due respect Madame Secretary, isn't your candidate rather young to be trusted with our safety?"

"Secretary Mitsu herself was hardly a year older than Miss Megami when she accepted the burden of governance," Gohaku replied. "If you withdraw your discriminatory comments, I'm sure Her Excellency will overlook the insult."

Vier crossed his slender arms and sat back with an indignant grunt. "Objection withdrawn."

"Before we put the appointment to a vote," said Mitsu, "the nominee is invited to address the Council."

Gasps erupted at the back of the chamber as the smoked glass doors swung open to admit a slight young woman. In her midnight blue skirted suit, she looked like a schoolgirl who'd broken off from a field trip. Her black hair flowed behind her as she swept down the center aisle. A growing din of muttering voices followed in her wake.

Megami took the podium below the Secretaries' platform and spoke in an airy voice that nonetheless saturated the room like a thick mist.

"This isn't a victory speech," Megami said. "Look anywhere: North America, Africa, Arabia. You won't find victory."

A hush fell over the gallery. Even Mitsu found herself listening in puzzled fascination.

Megami pressed on. "Our coalition boasts a thousand space colonies with a combined population of a billion souls. We command the most advanced technology and the greatest wealth ever seen in human history. Every king, prime minister, and president who came before should envy our achievements. But they don't. Because we lack the most coveted product of any civilization: victory."

Mitsu began to wonder if she'd made a mistake. Megami sounded like Sanzen, but her words kindled a fire in Mitsu's heart like Sanzen's never had.

"Why have we suffered our people to be preyed upon, despoiled, and killed by those history left behind? We tell ourselves that answering force with force is stooping to their level. We say we're better than that. We are better—by any conceivable metric—and it's time we informed the earth of that fact."

Mitsu couldn't decide which surprised her more, the scattered mumbles of agreement from the gallery, or her own nodding along with Megami's speech.

"Our protectors have failed," Megami declared like a hanging judge. "They foolishly dealt with the earth as if its state of progress matched our own. Sanzen Kaimora at least spoke to Earth's people in terms they understand, but he succumbed to demons of his own making. I will confront those demons and bind them to the cause of universal peace. I will defeat the lawless regimes that butcher our people, and I will make our coalition victorious!"

Riotous applause resounded throughout the chamber as the Council members rose to their feet in the gallery. On the platform above, Mitsu joined her fellow secretaries in giving their newest colleague a standing ovation.

19

Naryal soared over the Sudanese desert. The blazing sun beating down on the parched dunes made her glad for her climate-controlled cockpit. The four modified Grentos flying on either side of Jagannath lacked that luxury, but none of their pilots complained.

Loyal subordinates are even rarer luxuries these days. Naryal thought of her former security chief Davis, found hanged in his cell that morning. *I should have passed his warning about Megami to Secretary-General Mitsu.*

Naryal knew her self-rebuke wasn't fair. She'd had no way to corroborate Davis' claims until Mitsu had appointed Sanzen's former aide Secretary of Defense. If she accused the new SecDef of planning the Jeddah bombing—and probably Sanzen's death—Naryal's warning would be dismissed as jealousy. She needed indisputable proof to challenge one of the most powerful people in the Coalition, and there was only one source left.

"Target acquired," Raskin radioed from the gold-shouldered Grenzmark at Naryal's right. The Grentos' sensors were slightly superior to Jagannath's, so it stood to reason one of them would spot her quarry first.

"Synch your targeting systems with mine," Naryal ordered. Raskin immediately complied. The data he sent showed a lone combat frame flying southwest 120 klicks ahead. Its transponder had been disabled, but its RFID smart paint identified the unit as a Grento stolen from the scene of a triple murder at an Algerian petrol station. "Intercept that CF and force it down. I want the pilot alive."

Naryal's personal guard opened the taps on their upgraded rocket thrusters and surged ahead. Jagannath could easily overtake them, but Naryal's encounter with Davis' coilgun had taught her restraint. *And Sieg Friedlander is far more dangerous than the late Commander.* She drew the prototype Dolph rifle from its rack inside her shield and let her guard pull ten klicks ahead before she matched their speed.

"The target is heading toward a small earthen structure on a dry lakebed," reported Arnov, Naryal's second most senior guard.

"Confirmed," said Raskin. "I'm picking up concrete and metal construction under that lakebed."

Naryal studied Raskin's cloned screen. Sensors couldn't identify what lay under the humble earthen hut, but she didn't want Sieg to reach it. "Shoot the target down," she said. "Aim for his thrusters."

Automatic fire from all four Grentos' machine guns converged on Sieg's fleeing CF. The stolen combat frame swung upside down and sailed backward with its domed head pointed at the ground. The storm of shells passed over its inverted feet. Sieg returned fire, raking two of his pursuers with 115mm bullets before righting his CF and falling backwards toward the dry lake.

"I'm hit," Raskin said with preternatural calm. "It's—" His combat frame vanished in a sooty orange fireball. The leftmost Grento entered freefall, smoke streaming from its punctured cockpit.

Naryal ground her teeth. *He shot down half of my men!*

"Captain!" Arnov cried. He and Rashid, his sole remaining teammate, dived after Sieg's Grento.

"You have no shame," Naryal spat over the main CSC channel, trusting that Sieg would hear. "I will teach you."

Naryal opened the throttle. Jagannath barreled past her wingmen with a clap of thunder. The golden CF touched down amid an artificial sandstorm as Sieg's Grento cushioned its landing with a last-second thruster burst. He fired a full-auto volley the second his CF hit the ground, but Naryal blocked the bullets with her shield and disintegrated the Grento's gun and right arm with one shot from her plasma rifle.

Sieg stood his ground. "Get off my back, Naryal!"

"I can't just let you roam free," she said. "You're quite a violent man."

"Your people fired on me first."

"Only to disable," said Naryal, "not to kill. I'd have shot your cockpit if I wanted you dead. Surrender, and we'll talk."

"I don't have time for you," said Sieg.

"If not me, what about Sekaino Megami? You've been on the run for a while, so you may have missed that she had Sanzen killed and assumed the post of Coalition Defense Secretary."

"She put that mad dog down before I did," said Sieg. "You trying to make me jealous?"

"Those files you accessed made for edifying reading," said Naryal. "I think you know who Megami really is. If you cooperate, I may be able to stop her."

Sieg drew his CF's heat axe. "To hell with you!"

Naryal sighed. "You need another lesson." She racked her rifle and drew the metal tube attached to her generator by a thick braid of cables. "Very well. I can't promise you'll survive."

Toggling a switch on her control stick sent current rushing to the metal cylinder. Emerald plasma flared from the hilt's tip, and powerful magnetic fields shaped the raw energy into a crackling blade nearly as long as the Grento was tall.

Naryal pounced. The one-armed Grento raised its axe to meet Jagannath's rocket-assisted charge. The gesture proved futile as Naryal brought her plasma sword down in a two-handed slash. Her green energy blade disintegrated the Grento's axe, arm, and torso with no more resistance than a steel rod stirring sand.

The Grento's charred wreckage crashed to the dusty ground. "A pity," Naryal thought aloud. "Finding another loose thread to pull will be difficult." She quenched her plasma sword, only to see a blond figure in a dirty CSC combat uniform flee into the earthen hut the Grento had hidden from sight.

Naryal checked her screen. Arnov and Rashid's Grentos were circling overhead. She had the hut's only door covered. Unless the subterranean structure was an underground railway, Sieg had no escape.

"Some people can't see reason," said Naryal. She switched her plasma sword for her rifle and aimed at the hut. The shabby structure exploded before she pressed the trigger, and the green bolt streaked through a cloud of shattered brick.

"Something blasted out of the ground," Arnov warned. A large object rocketed skyward in a plume of dust that dissipated to reveal gleaming silver beneath. "It's a combat frame!"

Naryal stared at her monitor, which showed a bulky machine facing down her wingmen a kilometer overhead. It resembled a Grenzmark, but heavier and with a squared, stubby head. Its shiny armor was unpainted, and two huge drum-shaped generators protruded from the backs of its blocky shoulders. "It's a prototype Grenzmark?" she chuckled.

"This is no Grenzmark," Sieg said over the comm. "The Type One is the testbed for all combat frames."

Naryal fought to stifle her laughter. "You're threatening me with a unit that predates internal fusion reactors? Falling from my window must have given you a concussion."

The Type One aimed a long-barreled gun attached to its right arm at Jagannath. The outdated weapon seemed to have the same bore as a Grenzmark machine gun but clearly wasn't designed for automatic fire. "This is your last warning," said Sieg. "Stand down, call off your men, and let me deal with Megami."

Sieg turned his antiquated CF's back on Naryal and her hovering guards. A long metal slab sharpened on one side clung to the Type One's back. The crude sword's hilt extended from the blade's base below the CF's shoulders to the top of its angular head. A double row of four thruster nozzles glowed blue-white under the reactor drums.

"Don't ignore me!" Naryal ignited Jagannath's rockets and hurtled toward the Type One. Sieg's antique wheeled about faster than she'd thought possible. Fire belched from a round aperture in the upper left corner of its chest, and Jagannath's cameras saw only blinding white light before Naryal's screens went black. *EMP grenade!*

Naryal's heart seemed to stop as she struggled to keep Jagannath's flight stable without instruments. At last her systems rebooted, and she heaved a sigh of relief. Cold sweat stung her eyes, but only clear skies stretched before her.

"Arnov," she spoke into her restored comm, "Rashid. What's your status?"

No answer came. The last static cleared from her rear view monitor, showing both Grentos lying in the sand: one with most of its torso blown away and the other seemingly torn in two at chest height.

Naryal turned Jagannath toward the Type One, which was speeding away to the southwest. Rage engulfed her brain in red mist, and she blasted off on an intercept course. Sieg's primitive combat frame rotated at the waist as Naryal fired. Her plasma bolt impacted the comically large sword in the Type One's hands, leaving a rainbow smudge on the silver blade.

It repelled a plasma bolt? What's that sword made of!?

Sieg charged, firing his arm-mounted cannon twice. Naryal pivoted Jagannath sideways and threaded the needle between both shells' paths. The maneuver brought her within range of the Type One's sword. She drew and ignited her plasma blade as Sieg swung. Reinforced alloy met coherent energy in a shower of green and orange sparks. The gold combat frame and its silver opponent hung high above the desert, their blades locked in ruthless struggle.

A deep red glow spread along the Type One's blade. Steam poured from rectangular openings along the weapon's spine. *Whatever his sword is made of,* exulted Naryal, *it won't stand up to mine much longer!*

"You shouldn't have missed," she gloated.

Sieg suddenly jetted backward. "I didn't."

Jagannath's proximity alarms warned Naryal too late. The same two rounds she'd dodged a moment before had somehow turned in mid-flight and homed in on their original target. Both shells exploded into her CF's back, hurling her forward in her seat. Emergency airbags kept her forehead from cracking her screen. The last sight she saw before Jagannath lost power for good was the Type One's back receding into the distance.

131

20

Ritter redlined the Mab's hydrojets in his frantic flight down the muddy river. He didn't know if Max, Zane, or Zimmer had survived the chaos in Kisangani, and he didn't dare send any comm transmissions to find out. He spent every moment clutching his control sticks like a climber clinging to a high ledge. He could feel the Socs' net tightening around him.

But the river stretched on, and so did the day. Night fell, and Ritter navigated the pitch black waters by sonar alone. The burning in his torn shoulder had worsened until the heat gave way to chills that racked his whole body and drenched the inside of his wetsuit with cold sweat.

I have to get to sea. Ritter repeated that mantra to focus his increasingly weary mind. When had he last slept? Not since sometime before his day-long trip up the Congo to the spaceport. Now he was retracing the same journey after fighting a grueling battle and taking an infected wound. If he wasn't careful, he'd run into a barge or another submerged dam. Then the Socs would find him.

I hope the other guys made it out, Ritter thought for the hundredth time as the night wore on. He didn't think he could live with himself if they'd died for his sake, especially since he'd failed to capture one of the new Coalition combat frames.

Those Dolphs are monsters. Ritter counted himself lucky he'd been facing security personnel with only basic CF training. In the hands of experienced pilots, a Dolph squad could probably engage an EGE carrier group and win. He hoped Li, Larson, and McCaskey had a plan to stop Operation N.

Ritter's head was swimming by the time sunrise melted the dark away. He fought to keep his eyes open as the silty water began to clear. Only his shivering kept him awake.

A wave of relief washed over Ritter when his sonar pings passed into the open sea. The Mab's sensors picked up two large vessels, and he risked surfacing for a better look. The *Yamamoto's* majestic gray profile against the blue horizon made his heart leap. A smaller ship lay anchored alongside the carrier, its white hull looking like a cross between a tanker and a yacht.

Not until he'd come within spitting distance of the *Yamamoto* did Ritter realize his Mab was still slicing through the waves at top speed. *Better slow down and radio the carrier,* he thought an instant before he blacked out.

Megami generally disliked dealing with engineers. Most of them regarded their specialized training as a license to opine on every subject from military science to ethics. They also tended to exhibit a strain of intellectual myopia that focused on particulars to the exclusion of the big picture. Though she often made good use of the latter trait, she tried to avoid involving herself personally.

Tesla Browning was a rare exception to the rule. Perhaps being self-taught or hailing from the less collectivist L3 colonies had spared him the vices of his craft. In any event, Doctor Tesla Browning—or should she say Mister Leo Brown—had earned inclusion in the small group chosen to execute the next phase of Project S.

The study in Sanzen's house at his L1 compound, which was now her house in her compound, still exuded the stuffy air of academia. Megami stood before a screen framed by overflowing bookshelves and placed a call to Browning's Chicago office. Seed Corporation's lead designer answered within three seconds.

"Madame Secretary," Browning greeted Megami. He looked like a young actor made up in a lab coat and glasses to parody the archetypal egghead scientist. Yellow sticky notes adorned the cluttered room behind him. "What problem can I solve for you today?"

"Doctor." Megami wouldn't begrudge him the courtesy. Browning genuinely relished exploring ideas to surmount new challenges, despite his somewhat limited talents. "Have you reviewed the specifications I sent?"

"Of course," Browning said after a pause due solely to the one-second delay between L1 and Earth. "But be advised, a combat frame built to these specs will be far too expensive for mass-production."

"That's fine. It's not a mass-production prototype."

"If you want a custom unit for personal use, I can modify another Zwei Dolph for you."

"Frontline combat isn't what I have in mind," said Megami. "That custom Zwei Dolph was good enough to deal with Sanzen, but let's face it; Masz could've done the job with a golf cart. I need a CF engineered for a specific mission role. Can you do the job?"

Browning adjusted his wire rim glasses. "To be honest, some of your requirements are a bit out of my league—especially the integrated A.I. Unassisted reentry capability is also a decade or two beyond current combat frame technology."

"I'll round up a team of specialists to handle the finer points," Megami said with a smile.

"That would certainly help," said Browning, "but can you recruit and vet the necessary talent within the target time frame?"

"My people have sent out feelers," Megami said.

"There are a few qualified candidates I keep in touch with," said Browning. "If you'd like, I can send you a list."

I bet it includes Max Darving, Megami mused. Did Browning know she'd falsified the Operation N data he'd shared with his wayward protégé? Her spine tingled at encountering a player whose intellect approached hers. The only other source of that rare joy was Irenae Zend, a girl of fine breeding and fascinating genetics.

"I'll handle staffing," Megami said. "In the meantime, get ready to relocate. I'll be in touch when it's time to move."

Browning raised an eyebrow. "You're canceling your contracts with Seed Corporation?"

"Those were CSC contracts. Since Coalition security is now in my purview, I'm making this an internal Defense Ministry project and moving operations to space. Any objections?"

"None," said Browning. "I'd planned on returning to space anyway."

"We'll roll out the red carpet," Megami said before ending the call. Again she amused herself by trying to puzzle out how much Browning knew. Not that it mattered. Two hundred shuttles carrying 200,000 relief workers, one percent of whom were her fanatically loyal Kazoku troops, would enter Earth's atmosphere in twenty-four hours. Admiral Omaka would ensure the EGE's military response and signal the beginning of the end for Earth.

Ritter felt as if he'd slept off a long bender. The sensation of floating gave way to awareness of lying in a hospital bed. His shoulder was sore but no longer burned. His sensitive eyes adjusted, and he recognized the white-walled room as part of the *Yamamoto's* infirmary.

A young woman with light brown hair falling to the shoulders of her lavender scrubs stood by a bank of monitors at Ritter's bedside. She glanced at him with a smile, tapped one of the screens, and said, "He's awake."

Ritter had spent every waking off-duty hour not devoted to servicing his CFs getting to know the ship's company. A brief stay in the infirmary after capturing the Mablung had acquainted him with most of the medical staff. Yet he didn't recognize the woman at his bedside. "Don't think I've seen you here before." His voice emerged from his dry throat as a raspy croak.

The woman handed him a plastic cup of water, which he drank greedily. The cool liquid soothed his parched insides.

"My name's Dorothy. I came over on Jean-Claude's ship and volunteered to help out here."

"That's kind of you," Ritter said less hoarsely. "Who's Jean-Claude?"

Dorothy pointed to the nightstand. "The man who gave you that."

Ritter turned his head and winced as dull pain radiated from his shoulder. Upon the particleboard tabletop sat a deep red velvet-lined case. Carefully positioned inside the case lay a medal shaped like a five-pointed star with silver rays over a green enamel wreath. A central bronze disc bore a stately woman's head in profile. Age had darkened bronze and silver alike. The whole was suspended from a red silk ribbon.

"What is it?" Ritter asked in wonderment.

"The Legion of Honor," said Max as he strode into the room in a gray flight suit. Li Wen followed in her Navy dress blues with her tablet tucked under one arm. The Captain and the Lieutenant both came to attention near the foot of Ritter's bed and saluted.

"Did I get promoted above you guys while I was out?" Ritter asked.

"In your dreams, Private," chuckled Max.

"You're a chevalier of the Legion of Honor," explained Li. "All uniformed service personnel under Nouvelle French law are required to salute Legionnaires regardless of rank."

"I thought we were the EGE," said Ritter, "not the French Army."

"It's complicated," said Li. "Jean-Claude du Lione is heir to the throne of Nouvelle-France. He's also a founding member of the EGE and one of our biggest financial backers. Since his ship joined the *Yamamoto's* group, we're sailing under his flag."

The faint memory of a white cargo freighter emerged from Ritter's mind. "I think I saw Jean-Claude's ship on my way in. Everything between then and now is a blank. I just know I failed to bring back a Dolph. And I probably rammed the ship, so I'm not sure how I earned a knighthood."

"Traditionally," said Max, "you get knighted for being famous and useless or stupid and lucky. I didn't think you'd take it literally when I named our team the Suicide Kings."

"Over my objections," said Ritter. "Now, are you gonna tell me or keep drawing out the suspense?"

Max and Li exchanged a look. "Show him," Darving said.

"Nurse…" Li said to Dorothy.

"You don't have to ask twice." Dorothy stepped briskly from the room. "It was nice meeting you, Ritter," she called back.

Li stepped over to Ritter's bedside and held her tablet's screen at his eye level. A tap of her slim finger started a video that had been shot from the *Yamamoto's* island. A large blue object tore through the water below trailing a white wake. Seconds before the speeding object hit the ship, a black combat frame swooped down and plucked what turned out to be Ritter's Mab from the sea.

"That's Dead Drop!" Ritter said. "Does that mean Zane is here?"

"Because you invited him," Max said wryly. "And let me tell you, he hasn't been the best company."

"He did agree to let us examine Dead Drop in return for the parts he needs to repair it," Li said as she returned to Max's side. "As the template for the Dolph series, it's an intelligence gold mine."

Ritter took the plush red case in his hands. "That's why Jean-Claude gave me a medal?"

"I may also have mentioned how you pulled my ass out of the fire back in Kisangani," said Max.

"Zimmer and the other guys in his flight bailed us both out," Ritter said. "Remind me to buy them a round next time we're in port."

Max stared at the deck and sighed. "They didn't make it."

A Shenlong trailing flame as it spun into the city came to Ritter's mind. The case fell from his grasp and landed on the bed with a soft clack. "What? You, me, and Zane were outnumbered two to one, and we got out."

"Barely," said Max. "The Shenlongs were outnumbered five to one. Some of them might've had a chance if the base's anti-aircraft guns hadn't come online. Now Kisangani's doubling their defenses for Operation N."

"I guess bombing the spaceport's out of the question," said Ritter.

Max scratched the back of his head. "Yeah…"

Ritter detected an unspoken "but" in Max's voice. "You two didn't come down here just to congratulate me."

"The data we pulled from Dead Drop confirmed our worst fears," said Li. "Two hundred shuttles are headed for Earth carrying a Soc invasion force. We don't have the strength to fight them after they land or to take out the spaceport. But the shuttles will be vulnerable once they enter the atmosphere. The whole EGE fleet has assembled off the West African coast. In one hour we launch all twenty fighter wings to shoot down the shuttles."

Cold dread seeped into Ritter's stomach. "This is it. We're going to war with the Coalition."

"It's gonna be an air battle," said Max, "so technically you won't be going to war with them unless I screw up. Collins wants you on standby, just in case."

"Taking on a whole army of Dolphs is a tall order, even for a knight," said Ritter.

"You won't be alone," said Max. "Zane's made it his life's work to wipe out the Dolphs and everyone who built them. Of course, we'll all have our hands full if even one shuttle gets through."

"Can 120 fighters shoot down two hundred shuttles?" asked Ritter.

"They may not have to," said Li. "During atmospheric entry the shuttle pilots switch from manual control to an auto-nav system. My team will attempt to hack the Coalition's data relay satellite net and throw the shuttles off course right before they hit the atmosphere. Best case scenario: They all burn up, and we don't have to fight."

"Hacking a Soc satellite net sounds tough," said Ritter. "Do you think you can pull it off?"

"The SOC networking protocols we gleaned from Dead Drop will give us a chance," Li said.

Only because I convinced Zane to join us, thought Ritter. *Can I live with 200,000 deaths on my conscience?*

"Don't worry," said Max. "If electronic warfare fails, my boys and I will do the job."

Li squeezed Max's arm.

"What if we contacted the Socs and told them we know about their plan?" Ritter asked. "They might call off the invasion if they think we'll shoot down their shuttles."

"Operation N has already passed the point of no return," said Li. "The closest place they could reroute the shuttles to is L1, and they've already burned too much fuel to get there. At this point, landing on Earth is their only option."

"Besides," said Max, "Admiral Omaka already accused the Socs of planning an invasion, and they denied it. They still swear up and down that Operation N is an aid mission. The Socs can't turn back, but if they follow through they might win."

Ritter stared at the silver and bronze medal lying beside him on the bed. "I guess you're right," he said. "But what happens if the Socs lose?"

21

Max strapped himself in to his pilot seat and flexed his gloved fingers to steady his hands. The Thor Prototype sat idling on the flight deck ahead of the *Yamamoto's* fourteen remaining Shenlongs. He'd be leading them in the EGE strike group's attack on the Soc invasion force—unless Wen's electronic warfare team took down all two hundred shuttles on reentry.

The sun had just risen over Africa behind the assembled fleet of six carriers with their retinue of support craft. The western horizon beyond Max's cockpit was colored pink-orange where the sky touched the glassy sea. A cluster of bright points shone far above like a new constellation. Max gripped his control stick and slowed his breathing to calm his racing heart. His mask magnified the sound. *Here they come.*

The Socs labeled Operation N a humanitarian mission to aid victims of the North African conflict. Naval intelligence had data that convinced them the aid mission was a front for a full-scale invasion. Max pushed his lingering doubts aside. The General Staff had decided those shuttles couldn't be allowed to land. He and the other EGE aviators would execute that decision. Thinking of anything else would just distract him.

"Coalition shuttles approaching atmospheric entry threshold," Marilyn told Max in her synthesized voice. "Five minutes to comm blackout."

140

Wen's pleasantly accented English followed the A.I. "My team is attempting to commandeer the enemy's data relay satellites."

"Roger," said Colonel Larson, who was serving as Air Group Commander. "If you can pluck those birds from the sky without us firing a shot, you'll never pay for a drink again."

The comm went silent. Max's guts twisted as the seconds ticked by.

"Two minutes to atmospheric entry threshold," said Marilyn.

"What's the word on those satellites, Lieutenant?" Larson asked.

"We've hit a complication, sir," said Wen. "The Coalition's TDRSS net is a few security updates ahead of Dead Drop. We need a little time to gain access."

"A little time is all we have," said Larson.

"One minute to atmospheric entry threshold." Marilyn's grim announcement drowned out the rush of blood in Max's ears.

"We're in!" Wen said. "Altering nav data now."

Max fixed his eyes on the distant points growing steadily brighter in the morning sky. "Atmospheric entry threshold crossed," Marilyn said as the artificial constellation flared to dazzling brilliance. "Estimated comm blackout duration: three minutes."

A cascade of blinding flashes burst across the sky like high altitude missile detonations. But Max knew there'd been no shots fired. The sobering realization of what those vivid flashes meant tempered his relief as cheers went up from the deck.

The brightest lights died, but a smaller constellation remained. *Is that burning debris,* wondered Max, *or…?*

"One hundred confirmed radar contacts," declared Major Collins, Larson's acting deputy. "They're still on course for Kisangani."

"Give me a sitrep, Lieutenant," Larson said.

"We confirm Collins' readings, sir," said Wen. "Half the shuttles received correct guidance data before we could crack the nav satellites. The other half burned up, but we've still got a hundred enemy craft inbound."

"There's no free lunch, Lieutenant," said Larson. "Collins, it's your show now."

Max took a deep breath of recycled air and awaited the inevitable order.

141

Collins' accented voice sent a jolt up Max's spine. "All fighters, engage and shoot down those shuttles!"

The Thor Prototype was first in line for takeoff. Max spared a quick glance to port, where Dead Drop's sleek black form stood next to Ritter's stout blue Mablung. *Both standing by in case I fail,* thought Max, *so I'd better succeed.* Both CFs had gone unrepaired so the techs could get every aircraft combat ready. The Mab raised its giant hand to its domed head in a serviceable salute.

"Factoring in the shuttles' speed and our time to intercept," Marilyn said, "we will have two minutes to shoot them down before they pass out of range."

"Then let's not keep them waiting, honey." Max aimed his thrusters at the deck and opened the throttle. The Thor Prototype leapt into the air. He smoothly angled the thrust nozzles to aft and pulled back on the stick, pushing himself into his chair as he accelerated into a steep climb.

Max's tension eased as the other members of his squadron called in. His rearview monitor showed the *Yamamoto's* fourteen Shenlongs climbing in formation behind him. Contrails rising from the fleet's five other carriers confirmed that the whole strike group was in the air and racing to engage the enemy. Thunder filled the clear sky as over a hundred fighters broke the sound barrier.

Collins had direct operational command, but as the leader of the foremost squadron, Max was effectively leading the strike group in the field. *Just pretend it's an airshow,* he told himself. The pretense rang hollow. In terms of relative mass and speed, Max may as well have been riding a motorcycle playing chicken with a bullet train white trying to derail it with a handgun.

"The lead shuttle is in effective weapons range," Marilyn said.

"Are you sure?" asked Max. The shuttle's bow looked like a glowing quarter-inch bolt head stuck to his canopy.

"You calibrated my sensors yourself," said Marilyn, "so I assume that question is rhetorical. We have ninety seconds to complete the mission as of the end of this sentence."

Max eased back on the throttle and brought Mjolnir online. Marilyn handled the targeting, and the reticle centered on the growing luminous hexagon turned red.

Grant me victory, Max prayed. *And grant me forgiveness.* He squeezed the trigger. Blue-white radiance flashed under his jet's nose. The enormous transport kept hurtling toward him.

"Target undamaged," Marilyn said. "The shuttle's shock layer bent the laser by 0.85 degrees. I'll compensate on the next shot."

"We might not get one!" Max agonized over whether to take another shot at his first target and narrow his already short window for engaging the others.

Violet light burned through the shuttle's cockpit. Its six-sided hull tumbled and exploded. Dead Drop pulled up on Max's right. A heat haze surrounded its arm-mounted plasma cannon.

A pebble fell from the millstone on Max's shoulders. "Who gave you launch clearance?" he teased Zane.

"I do what I want," Dellister said with deadpan gravity.

Trails of fire streaked past them on every side, driving the Shenlongs' missiles into the onrushing shuttles' cockpits.

Zane's agitated voice cut through the jubilant shouts filling the comm channel. "Something's not right."

"One minute warning," said Marilyn.

Missiles filled the sky like a swarm of monster hornets. Shuttles broke up and burned by the dozens.

"MTA shuttle forty-seven to EGE fighters!" a frantic male voice called over the comm. "We are on a humanitarian mission. Hold your fire!"

Panic seized Max's heart. He radioed Collins. "I'm feeling some bad juju, sir. What if the Soc's telling the truth?"

"He'd say the same if he were lying," said Collins. "Dellister, keep quiet or leave the battlefield. Lieutenant, jam the enemy's transmissions."

The Soc's pleading, which had continued throughout Max's call to the *Yamamoto,* abruptly ceased.

"Thirty seconds," said Marilyn.

The remaining shuttles' hexagonal bows had grown to the size of silver dollars. Max counted over fifty at a glance. *If even one gets through, we'll have a thousand pissed off Socs rolling up on us in Dolphs.* He targeted the nearest shuttle's cockpit and fired. The

143

electrolaser blew out the slim window strip, and the shuttle joined two dozen others in fiery oblivion.

Only twenty targets remained. *We're going to make it.* Max swallowed the lump in his throat, but Zane's wordless scream nearly made him choke. As the Shenlongs fired, a bright trail of rocket exhaust arced away from the Thor's starboard side and toward the coast.

"What the hell was that?" Larson demanded from his command station in the carrier's island.

"Dellister, sir," Max radioed back. "He got a wild hair up his ass and took off."

Alarms blared. "Impact imminent," Marilyn warned, her placid voice unchanged.

Max's attention snapped back to the sky in front of him. A shuttle's blunt, off-white nose filled the right side of his canopy. He rolled left, and the gigantic transport's hundred meter-long hull roared through the air beneath him close enough to touch. Which he did, deploying his right manipulator arm and letting his heat sword shred the shuttle's starboard rocket nozzle. A deafening blast shook Max's cockpit and sent his jet spinning sideways into the open sky.

"Right manipulator severed," said Marilyn. "Structural integrity at seventy percent."

"Darving, wake up!" Collins shouted over the comm. "The last shuttle is still on course. All the Shenlongs have overshot it. Only you can intercept in time."

Max fought through his vertigo and reached for the thrust vectoring controls. The Thor Prototype's hinged afterburners swung down and fired. He lunged forward as the jet shuddered to a halt. The shuttle was a bright dot over the African coast. Max shifted all thrusters to aft, aimed his nose at the receding target, and blasted off. The g's crashed into him like a wave as the sound barrier shattered.

"The shuttle's lead is widening," Marilyn said. Max flogged the engines till he hit Mach 2. He kept accelerating despite feeling like the air around him had turned to smothering mud. A black circle closed in on his field of vision.

Marilyn's voice was faint in Max's throbbing ears. "Structural integrity fifty percent. Number two engine failure imminent."

144

The speed indicator on Max's HUD was riding the edge of Mach 3 when the tiny glowing dot grew into a less tiny dot. His hand moved through air like drying cement to center Mjolnir's reticle on the still-distant shuttle.

"Unable to establish a target lock at this range," Marilyn warned from across a vast gulf. The green reticle jittered like a jumping bean in an earthquake.

Air's already ionized in the shuttle's wake. Should give me some wiggle room. Max's target hung at the end of a long dark tunnel. He pressed the trigger and saw the edge of Mjolnir's muzzle flash. There was no visible impact on the shuttle's blazing rockets.

Max's HUD flashed red. His foggy head whipped forward with a sudden drop in speed.

"Number two engine inoperative," Marilyn said with improved clarity as the transparent clay filling the cockpit turned back into air.

Max gulped down a deep breath that escaped as a cry of triumph when the glowing pinpoint on the horizon expanded into a fist-sized fireball.

"All targets destroyed," Wen announced, her voice exultant.

"Nice save, Captain," added Larson. "We finally gave the Socs a bloody nose."

Max slumped back in his chair and breathed. He stared out over the hazy green coastline below. *But we lost Zane—and a prototype combat frame full of military secrets.* Once word got out, the Socs and every tinhorn warlord on the continent would be looking for Dead Drop. *Unless we find it first, we're in for a shitload of trouble.*

"This can't be happening," Secretary-General Mitsu told herself as she stared down the polished ebony table where eight of the nine Coalition Secretaries sat in heated debate. Her eyes wandered to the lone vacant seat: the place normally reserved for the head of the SOC's newly created Defense Ministry.

Terrestrial Affairs Secretary Gohaku stood and slapped a sheaf of papers down on the table with a shake of his bald, jowly head. "There's no mistake. Contact with all Operation N shuttles was lost off the coast of Africa shortly after 7:00 a.m. local time. My people on the ground have confirmed the shuttles were shot down by EGE aircraft."

"Who in their right mind would attack a humanitarian mission?" Mitsu thought aloud. The question silenced her colleagues' muttering.

"I'm more interested in why there was no warning of the attack," said gray-haired Transportation Secretary Vier. "The EGE can't have decided to slaughter 200,000 Coalition civilians on a lark. Someone must have gathered advance intelligence." He cast an accusing glance at Mitsu. Why wasn't it shared?"

The heavy oak door slammed open against the gilded plaster wall. Megami stood in the doorway with a navy blue trench coat draped over her black, skirted suit. "I see you started without me. I'd apologize for coming late, but no one told me about this meeting."

Mitsu stood up and pointed at Megami. "The Defense Secretary bears responsibility for this disaster! Sending those aid workers to Earth was her idea."

Megami tossed her waist-length hair. "Using Sanzen's illegal workforce was yours. I just suggested a number."

A heavy silence fell. All eyes turned to Mitsu.

The Secretary-General spoke in a quivering voice. "You staked your future on Operation N."

Megami grinned like a devil from Dark Ages art. "So I did—on Operation N *failing*."

"That's absurd," said Vier. "You've practically admitted your guilt."

"Why not?" Megami laughed. "All of you are complicit.

"Complicit in what?" scoffed Vier.

"In the deaths of 198,000 civilians and two thousand Kazoku," Megami said.

"Kazoku?" repeated Mitsu. That single word was all she could say in her shock. A corner of her mind remembered that it meant *family*.

Megami stepped into the conference room. "Yes. My loyal brothers and sisters are understandably eager to meet you." She snapped her fingers. Two lines of men in dark gray uniforms rushed around Megami and into the room. They surrounded the table, pointing assault rifles at the visibly startled Secretaries.

"But I helped you!" Gohaku whined to Megami.

"We did everything you asked!" added gaunt Commerce Secretary Satsu.

Megami's hand waved in a gesture that took in the whole table. "Sunset them," she ordered the Kazoku.

Mitsu stood frozen as her colleagues were herded from the room at gunpoint. A rifle barrel jabbed her in the side, breaking her trance. "Who are you?" she asked weakly when the Kazoku marched her past Megami.

"I'm the Sentinel on the wall," the new Secretary-General said. "I stand guard against the stupidity and brutality of Earth. And thanks to you, my watch is almost over."

22

Ritter stood with Max beside the battered Thor Prototype on the *Yamamoto's* deck. A flight of helicopters thundered overhead toward the tropical coastline off the carrier's port side. Two turboprop recon planes followed. Their rotodomes looked to Ritter like flattened mushrooms growing atop the aircraft.

At length, Ritter spoke. "We should be out there looking for Zane."

"Why?" scoffed Max. "He had the right idea bailing on this dumpster fire."

"That's an odd way to describe a total victory," said Ritter.

"Megami used our turkey shoot to promote herself from SecDef to SecGen. The only victory was hers."

Ritter's spirits sank. "You think that Soc pilot was telling the truth? Was Operation N a mercy mission all along?"

"I'd rather not think about it," said Max. "But Zane tried to warn us before he bugged out. Somehow he knew the situation was fubar."

Major Collins approached and saluted Ritter. To judge by his helmet and tan jumpsuit, he wasn't out for a brisk constitutional. Ritter returned the Major's greeting.

"Joining the hunt for Zane, sir?" Max inferred. He still wore his flight suit but had stowed his helmet.

"Admiral Omaka wants all available aircraft sweeping the coast for Dead Drop," said Collins. "We can't let it fall into the wrong hands."

"Do you want our help?" asked Ritter.

Collins shook his head. "No. You men have done fine work lately, but the Thor Prototype is grounded pending repairs, and the Mab would just slow us down. I want you to get your air and watercraft combat ready ASAP. If we weren't on the Coalition's radar before, we definitely are now."

"Excuse me for being blunt," said Max, "but Zane could be in Ankara by now. Don't you think searching the coast is a wild goose chase?"

"Off the record, yes," Collins said. "The Admiral turned that black combat frame inside out looking for intel. I assume she has a lead on Dellister's whereabouts she hasn't seen fit to share with us. All I can do is my duty. I expect the pair of you to do yours."

"Sir?" Ritter called out as Collins turned to leave.

The Major paused and looked back over his shoulder. "I'm on a tight schedule, Private. Out with it."

"I'm sorry about Zimmer," said Ritter. "He died so I could make it home. I can't help thinking I could've done more."

"Have you figured what you'd do differently if you could relive that mission?" Collins asked.

The question caught Ritter off guard. "Not exactly."

"Then find the answer," said Collins. "And when your next chance comes, act on it." He strode toward his waiting helo.

Max ran his hand along the Thor Prototype's blackened right side. "Classic EGE strategy: We poke the Soc hive; then commit our forces to a snipe hunt. Come on, let's get back to work."

Ritter ambled to the forward port side elevator where his Mab still stood with a chunk blown out of its left skirt armor. Collins' admonition and Max's cynicism toward the EGE swirled in his mind. His troubled thoughts and the constant noise on deck kept him from noticing he'd picked up a tail until an accented male voice spoke directly behind him.

"Chevalier Tod Ritter?"

"Yeah. Who…?" Ritter turned to see a man—a term he applied loosely since the stranger looked even younger than him—with brown hair tied back in a long ponytail and deep blue eyes. He wore a blue jumpsuit with a sleeve patch showing two angels holding up a crowned blue shield on a field of white.

"I beg pardon if I startled you. My name is Jean-Claude du Lione."

"The crown prince of Nouvelle-France?" Ritter sketched a hasty bow.

Jean-Claude saluted. "And the grand master of your order."

"Oh. Right!" Ritter saluted back. "I'm a knight now."

"Doubly so, M. *Ritter*," Jean-Claude said with a wry grin. "I am pleased to make your acquaintance now that you are awake."

"Likewise," said Ritter. "Thanks for the medal."

"Thank *you* for your service to the EGE, and by extension, the nation of France."

Ritter shrugged. "I'm fighting to restore Neue Deutschland, but I don't mind helping the French along the way."

"Your flippancy does not conceal your ambition," Jean-Claude said. "As one who also seeks to liberate his homeland, I discerned a kindred spirit in Captain Darving's account of your deeds. Will you see your duty through to the end, no matter the cost?"

Ritter stood straight, squared his shoulders, and looked Jean-Claude in the eye. "Yes, I will."

"Such singular determination enabled the leaders of Mitrophan's Crusade to reconquer Europe," Jean-Claude said. "Those who distinguished themselves in battle and remembered the loyalty of their men were made kings—my forefathers included. The Supreme Patriarch called his sons to drive out the paynim. With God's help, you and I shall drive out the Socs."

"I like your optimism," said Ritter. "It'll be a while before I lead anybody, though."

Jean-Claude laid his hand on Ritter's shoulder. "A leader is one who serves from the front. Remember this, and all will be well for you."

"Got it," Ritter said. "That's the best pep talk anyone's ever given me. Is that why you came over here?"

"In part," said Jean-Claude. "I also came to arrange passage to Moanda, where I have hired a transport plane."

"What for?"

"Though I do not question Admiral Omaka's competence," Jean-Claude said, "I am doubtful that her search for Dead Drop will bear fruit. I have resolved to make my own search, taking a different approach based on my knowledge of M. Dellister."

Ritter scanned the bustling deck and pulled Jean-Claude behind the Mab's giant blue leg. "You know where Zane is?"

"Not for certain," Jean-Claude admitted. "But I kept company with M. Dellister long enough to know that he shares a strong bond with his combat frame—a sentiment with which I sympathize. I understand that Dead Drop was damaged in Kisangani. Zane will seek to make Dead Drop whole and so become whole himself."

"The Dolphs took out one of Dead Drop's maneuvering thrusters," recalled Ritter. "It won't be hard to replace. The damage to its plasma cannon is another story."

"Dead Drop's cannon is damaged? I had heard it shot down a shuttle."

"You should've seen what it could do before," Ritter said flatly.

"To my knowledge," Jean-Claude said, "there is only one arms trafficker on the continent who would deal in such advanced military hardware."

A name popped into Ritter's head along with some serious reservations. "Carlos the Scorpion."

Jean-Claude's tanned face brightened. "I was not misinformed when I heard you knew Africa better than anyone in the EGE. Will you accompany me to search for M. Dellister? I fear for his safety traveling the Dark Continent alone."

Ritter suppressed his misgivings for Zane's sake. "Sure, if you can get me out of my current assignment."

"General McCaskey has already granted my request for transportation and personnel," Jean-Claude said. "You are now assigned to my search team. Come, we depart at once!"

Sieg swooped down toward Kisangani. Anti-aircraft fire raked the clear blue sky, but the Type One weaved through the hail of shells in a fluid aerial dance to the music of booming guns.

The city was an inverted oasis of stark steel and concrete towers in a sea of green. Farther south in the city center, the spaceport straddled the muddy river. There Sieg would find transport back to space, where he would confront Sekaino Megami and perhaps earn a chance at redemption.

But first he'd have to avoid being blown to molten scrap by the five Dolphs the base had just launched. Five red lights flared in the sky a klick above the spaceport, missing Sieg and giving away the advanced combat frames' positions.

Sieg pressed the Type One's speed advantage, accelerating toward the concrete canyons below. Windows exploded in a shower of crystal as the prototype CF broke the sound barrier thirty meters above the gridlocked street. *Right turn. Veer left. Boost over that skywalk.* Sieg cheated fiery death only because the deceptively nimble CF translated his thoughts into action as fast as his hands could move.

Six blocks ahead, the skyline dwindled from looming towers to wide open flats. The Dolphs would be ready to ambush him as soon as he left the cover of the buildings. Sieg wouldn't have fired a plasma weapon into a crowded city, either. Luckily, his CF was packing a ramjet rifle loaded with smart rounds.

Sieg had a clear line of sight on a pair of blocky blue Dolphs hovering over the spaceport. The Type One's fire control system locked on, and he pressed the trigger twice. Two laser-guided shells streaked up between the surrounding buildings. A bright ball of fire erupted from each Dolph's chest, and both fell to Earth.

The Type One blasted out of the city center and across a kilometer-wide pavement ringed with gigantic scaffolds. All three remaining Dolphs hung clustered together to concentrate their fire. Sieg pulled up and pushed his CF's engines to full power, nearly doubling its already insane speed. Plasma bolts pockmarked the airfield below him with glass-lined craters. *At least the AA guns stopped firing.*

Sieg rocketed into the midst of the Dolphs' close formation. He drew his two-handed sword before the Soc pilots could back off. Sieg pressed and held a red rubber-coated button as he swept the stick 180 degrees. The recessed rocket nozzles in the blade's spine fired, adding brutal force to his already crushing swing. The carbyne edge bisected all three Dolphs like a chainsaw tearing through piñatas.

Now I need to steal a shuttle, thought Sieg. But a sudden realization forestalled his search. *The guns haven't started up again.*

Sieg reflexively raised his blade just in time to shield his cockpit from a plasma bolt that would have reduced him to shreds of charred meat. Instead, the impact set off his front airbag and rattled his spine. *Not a plasma bolt.* Two.

The smoke cleared, revealing the enemy CF hovering right in front of Sieg. It looked like a Dolph, but darker blue with flared pauldrons and a backswept crest above the black v of its sensor array. It gripped a metal staff in its right fist and bore a tapered shield on its left arm.

"Sieg Friedlander?" a fevered male voice cackled over the comm.

"Yeah. Who's asking?"

The custom Dolph's pilot laughed. "I serve Miss Megami. She asked me to confirm your identity before I duel you."

Sieg gritted his teeth. "So you're an assassin sent to remove a threat to the queen."

"You misunderstand." The custom Dolph held out its staff. "I'm to make sure you're worthy of her." The staff's tip ignited, forming a red plasma blade as big as the Dolph's arm. Megami's assassin flourished the incandescent spearhead in a mock salute.

Sieg swung the Type One's two-handed sword. The plasma emitter atop the Dolph's spear split in half, forming two parallel blades. With a smooth motion of its wrist, the blue CF caught Sieg's sword between the plasma fork's tines. Sparks flew as the carbyne-infused steel blade took on a deep red glow. Sieg ignited his sword's boosters. The rocket-driven blade forced the plasma fork aside.

The Dolph gripped the fork's shaft in both hands and pistoned it forward. The twin plasma blades slid down the Type One's sword and burned through the clenched fingers of its right hand. Sieg released the booster switch too late. His sword flew from the Type One's weakened grip, spun through the air, and crashed into a fueling depot at the spaceport's edge with an explosion that engulfed a city block.

Sieg fired his retrorockets and pressed his ramjet rifle's trigger twice. Both shots fragmented against the custom Dolph's shield, leaving dark smudges on the convex surface.

Megami's assassin leveled his shield, revealing a pair of plasma cannons mounted inside. Sieg dived a split second before two crimson muzzle flashes burst from the chisel tip.

I can't beat this guy head-on. Sieg Pulled out of the dive and circled the spaceport counterclockwise, flying sideways to keep the dark blue CF in sight. He sensed the pilot was about to fire again and opened the throttle. Twin red flashes blew off the top of a launch tower the Type One had been in front of an instant before.

Sieg charged his foe, who answered in kind. The Type One's sensors acquired a target lock, and Sieg fired twice more but aimed slightly over the custom Dolph's head. As expected, the blue CF dipped slightly instead of presenting its shield, from which it fired another double plasma burst. Sieg pressed onward but bent his CF's legs at the knees. The energy bolts melted the tips of the Type One's feet.

The two combat frames collided with a force that crashed Sieg's forehead into his screen. A lesser pair of impacts on his CF's sides told Sieg that the custom Dolph's stronger arms had grabbed the Type One.

Sieg smiled to himself despite the warm blood trickling down his face. *You Socs are all the same,* he thought as the cracked monitor showed his shells homing in on the Dolph's back.

The Dolph spun, switching places with the silver CF in its arms. Sieg's mind reeled as he fought with the controls to break free, but his own shells blasted into the Type One's back. Alarms blared as red text scrolled across Sieg's spider webbed screen warning him the main thrusters were gone.

"You lasted longer than I thought," Sieg's opponent crowed over the comm. "But the fun's over!"

The Dolph spread its arms wide. Sieg's stomach somersaulted as he entered freefall. *It can't end like this—not when I've come so far!*

The Type One hit the ground like a bomb, gouging a crater in the pavement. But the tough old combat frame held together. Sieg's side airbags saved him from all but a few bruises to his extremities, some hairline cracks in his ribs, and a deep wound to his pride.

Megami's assassin landed on the broken pavement. Sieg anticipated twin plasma blades piercing his cockpit. Instead the custom Dolph grabbed the Type One by its empty sword rack and dragged the wrecked CF to a shuttle on a nearby launch pad.

"Does this mean I'm worthy?" Sieg asked himself. With a sigh, he let his sore head fall back into his canvas headrest.

23

The mammoth transport plane Jean-Claude had hired sailed over the hills west of Algiers like a fat thundercloud. Ritter sat in the spartan cockpit behind the Prince, who manned the seat beside their pilot: a mocha-skinned mountain of a man named Benny.

Ritter watched the sprawling port city pass out of view below them. All three of the plane's occupants wore headset mics, but he still felt the need to shout over the thrum of the turboprops. "How come we're not turning toward the airport?"

Jean-Claude's ponytail whisked the back of his cracked leather chair as he turned his cheerful expression on Ritter. "Because we're not landing at the airport," said the Prince. He pointed out the right window. "We're landing *there.*"

Ritter craned his neck to follow Jean-Claude's gesture. The plane was descending east of the city proper toward a small horn of land jutting into sparkling blue waters. A cluster of red-roofed buildings surrounded by greenery stood at the compact peninsula's tip. A sand-colored line cut through the brown flats adjoining the compound.

"Carlos gave men and weapons to Kazid Zarai during the Soc incursion," Jean-Claude said, "so Zarai let him set up shop on the mainland. Naturally, his new estate has a private airstrip."

"Naturally," Ritter said more jovially than he felt. *Should I mention my history with Carlos?* In the end, the shame of making a humiliating and potentially unnecessary admission to the prince who'd knighted him sealed Ritter's lips.

Within minutes, the plane touched down on a dusty airstrip ending at a low but steep coastal cliff. The only buildings were a couple of prefab shacks. A small helicopter of the kind flown by traffic reporters sat parked to one side under a camo net propped up on wooden poles.

Jean-Claude manually entered a radio frequency. "I will contact our host."

Benny unstrapped himself and turned to Ritter. "Help me unload some stuff from the back," the man-mountain said in an accent that might have been American or Canadian. To Ritter, there was hardly a hair's breadth of difference between North American English accents.

Ritter followed as Benny squeezed through the cockpit door and descended a flight of metal stairs. Though the plane's cargo box stretched twenty meters long, their cargo nearly filled the whole space. Benny had to scoot sideways past the tarp-covered load. Ritter had just enough room to walk normally, but both men had to duck under the strange protrusions that stuck out in several places.

"This is a combat frame, right?" Ritter had avoided asking earlier to avoid embarrassment for not knowing what Jean-Claude and Benny clearly took to be obvious.

Benny surprised Ritter by asking, "Did you know the Dauphin is a sculptor?"

"No," said Ritter. "Is this a statue he made as a gift for Carlos?"

"You're a soldier," Benny said. "His Highness is an artist. He'd never give away his tools. Grab a box."

Benny stooped and lifted one of six steel crates stacked by the open loading ramp. The name "Zeklov" was stenciled on each crate in black Cyrillic script. Ritter could barely budge his and only managed to unload it with the aid of a dolly. Two more trips in and out of the hot Mediterranean morning saw the whole lot transferred to the sunbaked runway.

Ritter took a seat on one of the boxes to catch his breath and wipe the sweat from his face. "What's in these crates? It feels like canned food."

"Payment for the Scorpion." Jean Claude approached from beneath the plane's broad wing. "A professional deserves his wage. Carlos is an arms dealer, and today we deal with him for the most potent weapon of all."

"A nuke?" asked Ritter.

"Information," Jean-Claude corrected him. "Though rumor has it the Scorpion obtained a nuclear device from the FMAS Militia in exchange for combat frames."

Ritter swallowed to ease a sudden tightness in his throat. "Do you really think he knows where Zane is?"

Benny looked down the airstrip, shading his eyes with his meaty hand. Ritter did likewise. Glass and metal glinted amid a distant dust cloud that grew rapidly closer.

"Our host has sent a car," Jean-Claude said. "What a courteous fellow."

The gleaming object resolved into a ghost from before the Collapse, before the Caliphate devoured Europe; before the breakup of the American Empire. The white vehicle sported a tall silver grill fronting a long engine compartment flanked by fenders like rolling waves. The boxy cab reminded Ritter of even more ancient horse-driven carriages.

A rusting minivan emerged from the trailing dust cloud. Both vehicles pulled to a stop beside the plane. Two swarthy men in sleeveless shirts and worn jeans jumped out of the van and strode toward the stacked crates.

"Help these men load the merchandise," Jean-Claude told Benny. "Then wait with the plane. The Chevalier and I will deal with the Scorpion."

Ritter did his best to project an air of confidence as he followed Jean-Claude to the white car. The prince brushed his fingers across the hood ornament: a silver statuette of a woman leaning into the wind, her gown billowing like a pair of wings.

A fit young woman with caramel-colored skin dressed in a black peaked cap and matching suit sat behind the wheel. Jean-Claude spoke to her in French when he and Ritter had settled into the wood-accented back seat. She said nothing in reply but put the car in gear, made a U-turn, and whisked them back down the runway. Awash in the scents of lavender and shoe leather, Ritter looked back and saw the van bouncing down a westbound gravel access road.

The rest of the short trip passed in silence. Soon the car turned onto a private blacktop road that cut through suddenly green lawns. A brief stop at an electronically controlled wrought iron gate preceded the car's arrival at a one-story Spanish villa roofed with red tiles. The driver passed the circular driveway and took a narrow side route between the main house and a smaller brick outbuilding to park beside a broad concrete patio.

"Kazid Zarai sure puts his guests up in style," said Ritter, staring through the windshield at the breathtaking sea view.

"Their accommodations reflect their usefulness to the regime," Jean-Claude said. He stepped from the car as the driver opened his door. Ritter was also shown out. He did a double take when he saw one of the workmen from the airfield holding his door.

A circular table of white marble surrounded by three wooden chairs stood amid the patio. A lone man sat facing the cliff beyond the manicured yard with his back to the nearby house. His hair was a slick black cap combed back from his olive-skinned brow. His lean face had strong cheek bones and a pointed chin. He wore a khaki EGE Army jacket with long-sleeves despite the heat, though the top three buttons, and those of his shirt, were undone.

The man at table remained seated as Jean-Claude and Ritter approached. He offered no greeting but sipped red-brown liqueur from a cordial glass. Jean-Claude sat down and smoothed his green chambray shirt. "Carlos," he said.

"They say it is a faux pas for one woman to come dressed the same as another." Carlos extended the hand holding his cordial glass and wagged his index finger over Ritter's own uniform. "It is good we are not women." He partly covered his rakish grin with another swig.

Ritter found the Scorpion's accent even harder to place than Benny's. Some said Carlos hailed from the South of France. Others, Northern Italy. He was said to be Castilian, Syrian, or Persian depending on who told the tale. The only constant was his reputation for swift, brutal retribution against those who crossed him.

"Please," said Carlos, gesturing to the chair Ritter stood behind, "take a seat, and we will talk."

Ritter released his white-knuckle grip on the chair's backrest and sat down stiffly while Jean-Claude spoke. "We came to inquire about directed energy weapons."

The Scorpion remained still. Only his jacket stirred in the fresh sea breeze. "That means Coalition," he said at length. "I no longer handle their leavings."

"Of course," Jean-Claude said, "but if anyone does, you would know who."

Carlos set down his small glass and snapped his fingers at the man in jeans and sleeveless shirts who still stood by the car. "Let us see what you have brought for me, eh?"

The swarthy man loped from the car to the house and disappeared through the patio doors. He and his counterpart retuned a few moments later, lugging one of the steel crates between them.

Carlos drained his glass, motioned for his men to lay the crate on the table, and handed the small piece of stemware to the nearer of the two. He rubbed his lithe hands together and opened the lid. A grid of plastic inserts divided the crate's interior into several smaller niches. The contents were shaped like tin cans as Ritter had thought, but topped with pins and safety levers.

Carlos plucked one of the canister grenades from the box. "Ah, Zeklov. Much better than that Seed shit." He replaced the grenade and closed the lid. "Your gift is satisfactory."

"And the information we seek?" asked Jean-Claude.

"You have offered tribute," said Carlos. "In exchange for such knowledge, I will require payment."

"I may be royalty," Jean-Claude said, "but I am crownless and stripped of my lands. You would squeeze blood from a stone."

The Scorpion wagged his finger again. "Do not think me so venal. I do not wish monetary compensation."

"What, then?" Jean-Claude asked.

This time, Carlos did not hide his grin. "Grant me full membership in the EGE."

Jean-Claude laid his elbows on the table and folded his hands. "In light of your service against the Coalition, I have no objections. But the decision is not mine alone. I must consult with my fellow exiled sovereigns and the military General Staff."

"You bureaucrats and your formalities!" Carlos scoffed. "The EGE and SOC are not as different as they think. Give me your word that you will personally recommend me to your colleagues."

Jean-Claude nodded gravely. "You have my word."

The Scorpion held out his hand, into which his man placed a refilled cordial glass. "A Moroccan gang has forced out all the local players since the Soc offensive ended. Word is they are part of a secret supply line running advanced Coalition hardware to Kisangani."

"Thank you," Jean-Claude said. "Tracking them down should not be difficult."

"Your wayward friend had better hope not," said Carlos. "Someone with connections has placed a handsome price on his head."

He knows why we're really here, Ritter realized. *Jean-Claude was right to fear for Zane's safety.*

"Thank you for the warning," Jean-Claude said. He and Ritter rose to leave, but Carlos raised his free hand, palm outward.

"Wait," the Scorpion ordered, fixing his dark eyes on Ritter. "This delinquent does not leave until he pays what he owes."

Ritter's blood froze. He fumbled for a reply.

Jean-Claude's brow knotted. "You two have done business before?"

"This mendicant purchased a Grenzmark C from one of my sales agents in Kampala," said Carlos. "His term of credit expired last month. Either he pays me the final half of the agreed upon price, with interest, or tonight he sleeps in a hole in the desert."

Jean-Claude stepped in front of Ritter. "Private Ritter is a chevalier of my court who enjoys my protection."

Carlos' men stood on either side of their boss. Their hands moved toward their back pockets.

"Do not think to deter me from dealing with my debtors as I see fit," Carlos warned. "You would not be my first regicide."

"Understood," Jean-Claude said. "I will pay the debt."

"You don't have to—" Ritter began, but the Prince hushed him.

161

Carlos cut both of them off. "Is this chevalier a boy or a man? Let him settle his own debts."

"I'll pay you," said Ritter. "In fact, I was on my way to settle up, but the EGE put me under arrest."

"Many others in your position have made similar claims," Carlos said.

"If Jean-Claude isn't responsible for me," said Ritter, "don't hold me responsible for them. Give me one more day, and I'll pay you everything."

The Scorpion's eyes bored into Ritter's for several moments more. Carlos raised his finger. "One day," he said darkly. "Everything."

Ritter held the Scorpion's gaze until Carlos turned to the man on his right and spoke quickly in a language Ritter didn't recognize. The underling vanished into the house once more, only to return with an ancient automatic rifle.

"Algiers is a dangerous place," Carlos said. He tossed the weapon to Ritter, who caught it by the rough wooden stock. "Don't forget: You have till noon tomorrow. After that, no one—no prince or even the EGE army—can protect you from me."

Zane hurried down the dingy alley between ramshackle warehouses, ignoring the throbbing in his feet. He'd walked all the way from the outlying hills where he'd hidden Dead Drop, and according to the manifest stored in its systems, a secret Coalition supply chain ran through a warehouse on the next street. There he'd find the parts to make his damaged CF whole.

The alley funneled a hot wind from the nearby docks, concentrating the smells of saltwater, dead fish, and diesel exhaust. Rows of long steel buildings mottled with rust lined the empty streets. Zane crossed to a warehouse that looked identical to the others except for the number 436 painted above the front door in white. The aluminum shutter, large enough to drive a tractor-trailer through, wouldn't budge.

Zane proceeded around the side of the building to a normal-sized wooden door about five meters from the alley's opening. He tried the knob and found it unlocked. Corroded hinges creaked as he opened the door and barged inside.

The room beyond proved to be a small office furnished with dented red filing cabinets, a portable radio tuned to some kind of sports match, and a fake mahogany table that looked like it belonged in a bachelor's apartment. Four men with dark skin and shabby clothes lay slumped over it or splayed upon the floor. All clutched guns in their hands, and all lay in fresh pools of blood. The scent of cordite still lingered.

A gray and blue tote bag lay on its side amid the table with multicolored polymer slips spilling out. Zane picked up a crinkled note bearing the image of a baby-faced man with short wiry hair and a wide mouth. *Coalition Commerce Ministry bills.* Zane threw the money back on the table and approached a door on his left with a window covered by dusty plastic blinds. There was no lock, so he stepped right through.

Zane found himself inside a cavernous room under a peaked, ten meter-high ceiling. A yellow industrial work mount bolted to a diamond plate riser stood in the middle of the floor. Attached to the end of the articulated mount was a combat frame's arm. The CF arm resembled Dead Drop's, but painted white and blue. Its hand held a charcoal-colored gun the size of a tow truck.

It's a plasma rifle, Zane realized with growing excitement, *more advanced than a Dolph's.* His luck couldn't have been better. He'd go get Dead Drop, return for the rifle, and cannibalize it to repair his damaged plasma cannon.

Zane rushed back into the front office and came face-to-face with three scowling men standing just inside the door. One wore a yellow, red, and green jersey. Another sported a tan canvas jacket, and the third was clad in a red wool sweater. All three wore dust-stained jeans. The man in the jacket nodded to the radio on the shelf, and the man on his right switched it off.

The jacketed man spoke to Zane in a guttural language he didn't understand. His two cronies pulled handguns from their waistbands.

"Get out of my way," said Zane, "or get ready for trouble."

163

Zane heard a footstep behind him. He spun to see a tall man in a brown track suit jabbing the butt of a shotgun at his head. The room went black in a burst of pain.

24

Ritter dug into the hot sand. He took his time, turning each shovelful into a meditation that kept his mind off the scorching desert air and the burning in his muscles.

He still didn't regret his deal with the Scorpion. Since CSC forces under Governor Troy had seized Ritter's hometown three years before, he'd been seeking a way to take back what the Socs had stolen from him.

But they can't give back my family.

Ritter buried the thought under another spade full of sand dug from his growing roadside hole. He remembered his escape to Central Africa, where the Chinese colonies still hosted large Europeans populations whose ancestors had fled the Caliphate. His search for retribution had led him to Kopp, whose bold claims of liberating the Fatherland had mesmerized Ritter.

There'd been a final hurdle to overcome. Kopp had refused to enlist any man without his own combat frame. The self-styled general hadn't expected Ritter to spend the last of his family's reduced fortune as a down payment on a Grenzie. For his part, Ritter had been childishly naïve about the sort of men he'd been dealing with, Kopp and Carlos both.

Ritter paused to drink warm bitter water from his canteen. He lifted his legionnaire cap's neck cover and dabbed his sweat-soaked skin with a rag. *Good thing my old comrades couldn't keep a secret.*

165

The rest of the Black Reichswehr had thought Ritter a weak young fool and hadn't seen fit to guard their speech around him. He'd soon learned that Kopp and Schwarze had hidden stashes of fuel, ammo, cash, and other looted valuables all over the continent. Ritter had made a point of memorizing several sets of relevant GPS coordinates.

One of Kopp's caches lay buried beside a lonely desert road south of Algiers. Ritter had meant to raid the hoard and settle his debt after his last mission with the Reichswehr. He'd been delayed, but thankfully the Scorpion had allowed him a grace period.

Ritter clipped the canteen back on his belt, adjusted his assault rifle's shoulder strap, and resumed digging. Soon his excavation resembled a grave, and when he brought his shovel down again, its tip thudded into something solid.

His heart leapt. Ritter cast his shovel aside and crouched down to dig with his hands. Sweeping away a few more centimeters of sand revealed the black lid of a hard plastic case.

The whiny, syncopated strains of Moroccan dance music drifted on the hot wind, underscored by the rattling growl of a poorly maintained engine. Ritter threw the sand-colored tarp he'd brought over the hole. He gripped his rifle and crept toward the pit's edge as the source of the noise bore down on him.

The car skidded to a halt a stone's throw from Ritter's hole. The strident music ceased. Four doors opened and were quickly slammed shut. Four sets of feet hastened to the back of the car. The trunk popped open, unleashing muffled but familiar cries of rage.

Ritter popped up from hiding. Standing on the crate, his upper body just cleared the pit's rim. A sun-faded banana yellow taxi festooned with gaudy beads and garlands sat in the dirt road. Four umber-skinned men stood gathered around the open trunk, which held a bound and gagged Zane Dellister. His short white hair clung wetly to his scalp, and his gray eyes widened in surprise.

Zane's four captors stared dully at the young man in dusty fatigues who'd sprung up from the desert. All four held weapons ranging from machetes to shotguns. Ritter mowed them all down with a clattering spray of automatic fire before they could move.

One corpse slumped into the trunk. Zane cut his bonds on the machete still clutched in its hand. He leapt out, bolted to the driver's side door, and jumped behind the wheel.

Shock left Ritter acting on impulse. He sprang from the hole, which the tarp mostly covered behind him. He slid across the cab's searing hood and climbed into the front passenger seat. Zane hit the ignition, gunned the engine, and pulled a U-turn, kicking up a dusty rooster tail. The two of them tore down the road to the wailing thump of Moroccan club music.

Naryal descended the stairs from her private jet to the desolate airstrip. Leaving the air-conditioned cabin for the afternoon heat was like walking toward a firing afterburner. She adjusted the wide brim of her cream-colored hat to shade her eyes and studied the colossal cargo plane parked across the runway.

A burly man with light brown skin wearing a three-piece sharkskin suit stepped from the shadow of the cargo plane's wing. Naryal strode across the cracked pavement to meet him, holding down the skirt of her yellow dress in the salt-scented wind.

"What can I do you for?" he asked in a vulgar accent of the American upper Midwest.

He's the embodiment of the Coalition's meddling on Earth, Naryal mused. "I am Governor Prem Naryal. Tell His Highness the Dauphin I desire an audience."

The giant wiped his enormous hands on an oil-stained rag. "I know who you are. The Dauphin's occupied with important business. I can check his calendar if you'd like to make an appointment."

"It's alright, Benny," a youthful male voice spoke from the open hatch leading to the transport's cockpit. A young man in white pants and a matching cotton shirt with his brown hair tied at the nape of his neck emerged. He held her gaze with fathomless blue eyes. "Your Excellency. A pleasure to make your acquaintance."

"The pleasure is mutual," said Naryal. "I've been eager to meet you for some time. How fortunate that we're both in the market for Carlos' wares. I have no idea what's keeping him, but thankfully you're here to greet me."

Jean-Claude du Lione stepped down from his perch and crossed the blistering hot tarmac to stand before her. "To paraphrase my friend's question, how may I be of service?"

"It is I who would offer my services to you," said Naryal. "You are aware of Sekaino Megami's recent installation as Coalition Secretary-General?"

Jean-Claude's tanned face fell. "I am aware that she staged a coup d'état."

"Some in the SOC likewise view Megami's ascendancy as illegitimate," Naryal said. "Governor Troy has declared Western Europe an independent territory under his sovereign rule. Megami is mobilizing a second invasion force even larger than Operation N. Officially she intends to quash Troy's rebellion, but I believe her true motive is more sinister."

"How do you mean?" Jean-Claude asked.

"I have caught wind of certain high-level movements," said Naryal. "Rumors, mostly, but from sources I'm inclined to take seriously. There are whispers of secret arms projects—terror weapons capable of destroying whole colonies."

Jean-Claude raised an eyebrow. "Why would the Secretary-General of the Coalition want to destroy a space colony?"

"Not all space colonists support the Coalition," said Naryal. "And many in the SOC will oppose Megami's excesses. I fear she intends to hang a sword over our heads to keep the earth and the colonies in line."

"You have indeed rendered valuable service, Mademoiselle," Jean-Claude said. "When I have finished my errand in Algiers, I shall report the matter to the EGE General Staff."

Naryal took the Prince's unexpectedly coarse hand. "I propose something more," she said, "an alliance between my office and the EGE."

Jean-Claude gently clasped her hand in return. "Considering the urgency of the threat you've brought to my attention, I am willing to defer my current business for the sake of our alliance."

Naryal smiled. "I have an apartment in town. Perhaps you—"

A blue flash blazed through the warehouse district across the bay, accompanied by a thunderclap that silenced Naryal in mid-sentence.

Whole buildings went up in flames as the sapphire light cut a swath through the dockyards and continued out to sea, raising a trail of steam taller than the city's highest building.

Naryal gaped. "That blast came from a plasma cannon!"

Jean-Claude rounded on his hulking servant. "Benny, bring the Governor aboard and lower the cargo ramp while I prepare to sortie."

Benny moved behind Naryal. His bearlike hands encircled her shoulders. She stabbed her finger toward the west, where a wall of fire stretched to the sea. "You don't plan to fight whatever caused *that*!"

Jean-Claude strode toward the tail of the plane. "If my surmise is correct, I bear some responsibility for this disaster. It is my duty to intervene."

Naryal let Benny guide her toward the stairs leading up to the plane, but she couldn't tear her eyes from the Prince as he strode into mortal peril.

Ritter stood at the work mount's controls, keeping a lonely vigil over the destruction he'd unwittingly wreaked. He still stared at the flame-wreathed hole in the warehouse's north wall long after Zane had fled in his commandeered cab.

He's welcome to it, Ritter thought through the numbing fog that had settled over his mind. He doubted he'd ever wash the smells of spiced mutton and stale tobacco from his clothes. The reedy strains of foreign dance music drifted through his mental haze.

Ritter tried to pinpoint when matters had gotten out of hand. He and Jean-Claude had flown to Algiers for a meeting with Carlos the Scorpion in the hope of getting a lead on their AWOL comrade Zane. The Scorpion had issued an ultimatum, and Ritter had gone digging for an old Black Reichswehr stash to pay him off.

Zane's sudden arrival in the trunk of a Moroccan gang's cab had been a surprise. Ritter had gunned down the gangsters to save his friend's life, and Zane had sped them both back to the gangsters' warehouse. He'd planned to cannibalize the experimental plasma rifle to fix Dead Drop, but they'd decided to test the mysterious weapon before Zane retrieved his combat frame.

The cinder-colored gun had unnerved Ritter on sight. He and Zane had cobbled together a backstop from Dolph armor plates found in the same warehouse and hung it against the wall. Ritter had learned the reason for his fear when their test shot instantly vaporized the thick armor plates, the wall, and everything from the warehouse to the sea in a path of ruin that still held him enrapt.

I'd better run, he thought. Someone would arrive at ground zero soon—if not the local authorities; their criminal counterparts or someone worse. Yet his legs refused to move. He'd still been shaken from killing Zane's would-be killers when he'd fired the plasma rifle. Now thoughts of innocent people suddenly reduced to pink mist by sapphire light haunted him.

A loud whine overhead and a tremor running through the steel platform under his feet startled Ritter from his brooding. He fought to stifle a scream when a gothic monstrosity of bronze and burgundy crouched down beside the singed hole in the wall and leered at him with a giant, gargoyle-like head. His ears were still ringing from the blast, so he didn't know if he succeeded.

"Ritter!" Jean-Claude's amplified voice cut through Ritter's tinnitus. The monstrous combat frame gripped the hole's edge with a clawed hand. "What in heaven's name happened here?"

"I—" Ritter stammered. "We—Zane and I found this plasma rifle. He wanted it for Dead Drop, but we thought we'd better test it first."

"Such destructive power does not belong on Earth," Jean-Claude said. "I must confiscate this weapon for the EGE to study. Perhaps they can devise some defense against it."

The clawed metal hand reached into the warehouse to seize the rifle from the disembodied CF arm's grip. Another impact on the ground outside stopped Jean-Claude short.

"The EGE promised me the parts to fix Dead Drop," Zane's indignant voice echoed from a PA speaker. "You broke your word and murdered thousands of my brothers."

"Your brothers?" Ritter and Jean-Claude asked at the same time, though the gargoyle CF's speakers drowned Ritter out. His feet finally came unstuck from the floor, and he ran to the breached wall.

Dead Drop's sleek black form stood in the street facing Jean-Claude's winged CF.

"The colonies aren't like Earth," said Zane, "where everybody has a mother and a father. The Coalition makes batches of workers to order. I grew up in an industrial colony with the other mass-produced laborers in my block. We had more than a brotherly bond. I could feel them even when we were apart. I felt them die when we shot those shuttles down."

"It would appear Captain Darving was right," Jean-Claude said. "Secretary-General Megami has played us for fools."

"Yeah," said Zane. Dead Drop advanced a step and pointed a black finger as thick as Ritter's torso at the mounted rifle. "So tell me why I should let you get your hands on next-level weapons like that."

Jean-Claude's CF raised the delta-shaped shield on its left to its chest. "You have my condolences, M. Dellister, but I cannot surrender the weapon to you; especially not in your current agitated state."

"Duel you for it," said Zane.

Silence fell. Ritter held his breath.

"Your combat frame is still damaged," Jean-Claude said. "My Veillantif is in peak condition."

"Then you might have a chance." Dead Drop's left arm swept toward Veillantif with plasma cannon deployed. Jean-Claude's shield blurred in a rising arc that knocked the black CF's forearm up and to the right. The cannon's purple beam blazed skyward through the lingering smoke, barely missing its target's gargoyle-like head.

Veillantif spread wine-colored wings lined with barbed teeth and jetted backward beyond sight. Dead Drop followed in a burst of rocket exhaust that would've left Ritter's ears ringing if they weren't already.

"Men and their foolish honor," a lightly accented female voice said from behind Ritter's left shoulder.

"Only a certain kind of man," Carlos the Scorpion spoke from the corresponding position to Ritter's right. "Others know how to resolve disputes without violence."

Ritter turned. Carlos stood in his partially buttoned EGE uniform next to a cinnamon-skinned woman in a yellow sundress and a floppy hat. Both stared through the ruined wall. "How?" Ritter exclaimed. "When?"

"Carlos' helicopter," the woman said. "Shortly after Jean-Claude arrived."

"Where are my manners?" Carlos chided himself. He gestured deferentially to the woman beside him. "Private First Class Tod Ritter, allow me to introduce Coalition Mideast Region Governor Prem Naryal. Governor Naryal, Private Ritter."

Naryal smiled wolfishly. "A pleasure, Private. I've heard much about you."

"You're with the Coalition?" Ritter looked from Naryal to Carlos. "And you're in a warehouse owned by a rival gang. Shouldn't we get out of here before the police or more gangsters show up?"

Carlos gave a derisive snort. "The local gendarmes will do as they're paid. Zarai's police do not always stay bought, but they will since you have removed my only competition—which answers your other question, also."

Ritter's throat went dry. "You mean, those men in the desert..."

"Were the leaders of the Moroccan gang that had forced out the local operations,' Carlos said. "Along with some of the gentlemen in the other room who let their passions interfere with business."

The memory of why he'd been in the desert crashed down on Ritter like a cold wave. "I was going to pay you back! I just got sidetracked. Give me one more hour, and I'll bring you enough to settle my debt, plus interest."

Carlos raised his finger. "Such topics are not fit for mixed company. But you are young, so I am sure the lady will not take offense."

"I used to be a Commerce Ministry accountant," Naryal said from below the looming gun's barrel, which she was studying intently. "Trust me, I am incapable of being offended by discussions of debt."

Carlos clicked his tongue. "A most unladylike occupation. In any event, my men already found your roadside stash. Have no fear. They withdrew funds sufficient to cover what you owed; no more. They even filled in the hole and left an extra deposit of four Moroccans."

"Don't take this the wrong way," Ritter said, "but I can't believe a gangster would leave money on the table like that."

"Normally I would have robbed you blind, but I am thinking you are a useful associate to keep around." Carlos wrapped his arm around Ritter's shoulders. He smelled of hair gel and bitter wine. "Also, you and Dellister plucked a thorn from my side, and I too pay my debts."

"I never meant to rub out a gang of arms dealers," lamented Ritter. He feebly gestured toward the ticking hot hole in the wall. "Or to do that."

Carlos gave Ritter's shoulder a reassuring squeeze. "It is difficult to face one's youthful errors."

"What is that weapon, anyway?" Ritter asked.

"Trouble," said Naryal. She straightened her hat and returned to the platform. "It's derived from the Dolph series' plasma rifle but far more refined. A better question is, what's it doing here?"

"The Moroccans were funneling hardware to Kisangani," Carlos said. "And the Socs are scrambling to purge all traces of Operation N, which is why they ordered a hit on Dellister." He cast a sidelong glance at Naryal. "Don't pretend you did not know."

Naryal's brow knotted. "I didn't. If I'd wanted Dellister dead, he never would have made it to his combat frame. He honestly hadn't caught my notice, but in light of what he said to Jean-Claude, I'll have to keep my eye on him."

"Telling white lies is a woman's prerogative," said Carlos, "but I have my means as well. The price on Dellister's head was placed by your own Security Chief Davis."

"Commander Davis is dead." Naryal frowned pensively. "Megami had him killed before her installation as Secretary-General."

Carlos shrugged. "I have men who check the legitimacy of such transactions. Their lives depend upon their accuracy. These men assured me the order and associated account numbers resided within a secure folder on a General Affairs Ministry server labeled 'Elizabeth'. The data in question was uploaded using a command authorization code matching the birth date of Davis' bastard son."

"Friedlander accessed the same folder," Naryal thought aloud.

"You know Sieg?" marveled Ritter.

Naryal's expression darkened. "We've met." Her dark eyes fell on Ritter's EGE patch. She dashed across the warehouse floor to the front office. Ritter took off after her, and Carlos strolled along behind them. Naryal searched the grisly crime scene, producing a satellite phone from the cash-stuffed bag. She dialed a long string of numbers and pressed the speaker to her ear.

"What's she doing?" Ritter whispered to Carlos.

"I have no idea," the Scorpion said, "but I expect it will be good."

Naryal seemed to reach whoever she'd meant to call, and she spent several minutes conversing rapidly in an incomprehensible language. A long pause interrupted the discussion, which finally resumed only to reach a perfunctory end.

"Admiral Kei Omaka is Friedlander's EGE contact," the Governor said, her face beaming. "Multiple transmissions have been sent between the same office where the 'Elizabeth' folder is stored and Omaka's flagship the *Lloyd George*."

Ritter felt as if he'd stepped in quicksand. "How do you know?"

"Controlling practically all satellites in Earth orbit has its advantages," said Naryal. "I knew Davis was exchanging information with an unknown agent in the Secretary-General's office. I'd suspected that he leaked my security protocols to Sieg through a third party, but I didn't have proof. Now I know all three players in our little drama were in contact with Admiral Omaka."

"It makes sense," Ritter said. "She is our head of Naval Intelligence."

"More sense than you know," said Naryal. "All my efforts to unearth the identity of Davis' grounder paramour came to dead ends. I knew she had to be someone well-protected. The signs were right in front of me all along. Omaka is the mother of Davis' child!"

"That's why he conspired with her?" asked Ritter.

"That is why *she* betrayed *him*," Carlos corrected him.

Naryal nodded her approval. "Davis took her son. Megami found out and used the knowledge to turn Omaka. Now the Secretary-General is covering her tracks, and the Admiral has put a death mark on Zane."

Ritter broke the ensuing silence. "Can you call Colonel Larson on the *Yamamoto*?" he asked Naryal.

The Governor shook her head. "Reporting Omaka will do no good. Even if Larson believed you, we have no solid proof. I think Megami is about to make a move, and Omaka will likely be involved. Our best option is to catch her in the act."

Ritter made his decision and rushed through the side door past one of Carlos' men, who cried out in protest. A small, bubble-canopied helicopter stood in the middle of the street with the Scorpion's female driver at the controls.

"Where are you going?" Naryal called after him.

"To tell Jean-Claude and Zane," Ritter shouted without looking back. He hopped into the helo's cramped cabin and grabbed a headset. "Follow those combat frames!" he ordered the pilot.

25

Zane flew down the deserted street, chasing Jean-Claude's weird combat frame. To Zane's eye, his opponent's CF was a baffling collection of wasteful ornaments and inefficient stylistic touches. Its barbed wings, for instance, were too small to generate much lift and just seemed like dead weight.

"Let's clip those wings," Zane said to Dead Drop. The excitement of battle had tempered his rage at the slaughter of his brothers. Besides, Jean-Claude had helped him find Dead Drop, so Zane would try not to kill him. He aimed his arm-mounted cannon at the dark red wing behind Veillantif's left pauldron.

The bronze gargoyle ducked as Zane pressed the trigger. The plasma beam flew over its target and incinerated a soft drink billboard by the harbor. Jean-Claude's CF might've packed some extra weight, but it was agile.

And fast. Veillantif turned about, drew a thin two-edged sword, and rushed Dead Drop. Zane jerked his control stick to the right and felt a stab of panic at the unexpectedly sluggish response. Jean-Claude's thrust missed the Black CF's left side by a hair.

Gotta replace that maneuvering thruster! Zane rebuked himself.

Jean-Claude pressed the attack. He slashed his CF-scale rapier in a rising diagonal that barely missed the backward-jetting Dead Drop but sliced a corner off the steel warehouse to Zane's right. The cut's edges glowed red.

Zane stopped and righted Dead Drop with a burst from its main thrusters, cut the engine, and let the CF's feet slam down on the already cracked road. Standing on firm ground to steady his shot, he took aim at the onrushing Veillantif. Again Jean-Claude's monstrosity moved clear of the plasma cannon's barrel, swerving to the right just before Zane fired. The purple flash brought down an empty parking deck on the corner in a cloud of dust and smoke.

He knows not to be there when I fire, thought Zane. *Let's pin him down!*

Veillantif hurtled into striking distance. Zane anticipated the heat rapier's thrust and caught the gargoyle's sword arm in Dead Drop's right hand. Veillantif's arm jerked back, almost pulling Dead Drop off its feet.

That monster's as strong as it looks!

Zane pointed his cannon at the gargoyle's ugly head. Veillantif twisted its arm free and struck at Dead Drop's weapon. Zane angled his cannon upward at the last instant and blew off the rapier's superheated blade. Jean-Claude planted Veillantif's taloned foot against Zane's cockpit with a jarring thump, thrust out its leg, and sent Dead Drop reeling back.

Jean-Claude threw down his giant rapier's bladeless hilt and snapped his shield toward the ground. The sharp point detached, trailing a chain of back-barbed segments that coiled on the broken street. The asphalt bubbled and steamed in a hate haze. "This can end whenever you wish, my friend," the Prince radioed to Zane.

"You just figured out I've been toying with you?" Zane retorted. Not since his purge of the hateful Dolphs had he felt so alive. He catapulted Dead Drop off the ground with a short rocket burst and leveled his cannon at Veillantif's upper chest.

The barbed meal whip lashed out with a crack that shattered nearby windows. Superheated coils wrapped around Dead Drop's left arm above the cannon's barrel. Jean-Claude doubled Veillantif's grip on its shield and pulled. Dead Drop's feet crashed back to the ground.

A red chorus of alarms filled Zane's cockpit as the heat whip ate through his first layer of armor. With its left arm snared, Dead Drop's plasma cannon was next to useless. Zane pulled the barrel free with his CF's right hand. He flipped a switch that energized fingertip contacts fed by Dead Drop's powerplant, and a violet blade sprang from the black cylinder's mouth.

Veillantif released Dead Drop's arm and rocketed back from a vicious swing of Zane's plasma sword. A rush of adrenaline spurred Zane to ignite his thrusters and charge after the retreating machine. For all its agility, Veillantif couldn't compete with Dead Drop's raw speed. Dilapidated buildings blurred past on either side as Zane closed with his quarry.

The heat whip corkscrewed toward Dead Drop's right side. Zane parried and ran his incandescent purple blade down the metal coil's length as he surged forward, charring and fusing barbed segments. He gripped his sword in both hands, cocked the hilt back to his right shoulder, and aimed the coherent energy beam at the gargoyle's leering face.

Veillantif rotated at the waist. Curved spikes spun around its wings like the teeth of enormous chainsaws as its right pinion slammed into Dead Drop's left shoulder. The surprise blow knocked Zane off course and into a derelict storefront. He felt like a rag doll in a tumble dryer as Dead Drop rolled through the decrepit building. The dizzying ride ended when the whole structure collapsed on the black CF.

Zane hung in the red glow that bathed his cockpit and his mind. His chair's straps dug into his chest through his sweat-drenched shirt as gravity pulled him forward, which was now down. His burning lungs heaved.

"Do you yield, Monsieur?" Jean-Claude asked over the comm.

Zane fired Dead Drop's rockets and blasted blindly out of the rubble. Jean-Claude had clearly expected a different answer, because Veillantif was crouching to dig through the wreckage. The gargoyle brought up its shield, but Zane's plasma blade cleaved off the leading third of the rounded delta. Zane reversed Dead Drop's grip and stabbed at Veillantif's chest.

"You guys knock it off!" The boyish voice shouting from the comm wasn't Jean-Claude's.

Zane paused in mid-strike. "Ritter?"

Dead Drop's external mics picked up the whir of rotor blades. A small helicopter descended into view over Veillantif's left shoulder. Ritter and two brown-skinned women were crowded into the rotorcraft's cab.

"We need to talk," Ritter said.

Zane fixed his eyes back on Veillantif, which stood in a defensive stance behind its cloven shield. "I'm in the middle of something."

"Just listen," shouted Ritter. "Admiral Omaka is a Coalition spy. She's gonna help Megami attack the EGE. We need to get back to the fleet!"

"Serves 'em right," said Zane. "Now buzz off. I've got a duel to finish."

Veillantif's shield crashed to the debris-strewn ground. Its chainsaw wings stopped spinning, and the heat haze surrounding them faded. "I concede," Jean-Claude said.

"What?" Zane asked flatly.

"You have removed my primary weapons," said Jean-Claude, "and you know my technique. The odds of your next attack crippling or destroying my combat frame are overwhelming. I am beaten, M. Dellister. Congratulations on your victory."

"I've never won a fight where the other guy didn't end up unconscious or dead," Zane confessed. "How does this work?"

"The terms of your challenge specified that the victor takes the spoils—in this case, the experimental plasma rifle back at the Moroccans' warehouse."

"You're just letting me have it?" Zane asked.

"That would be a grave mistake," one of the women in the helicopter said with a faint Indian accent.

"I am a man of my word," Jean-Claude said. "I ask only that you return to the *Yamamoto* with Private Ritter and myself."

Zane turned off his sword and returned the hilt to its place as the plasma cannon's barrel. The whole weapon retracted into Dead Drop's scorched arm. "I'll think about it—after I fix Dead Drop."

"Wait—" Ritter said, but Zane fired his thrusters, shaking the dust from Dead Drop's armor as the black CF arced back toward the warehouse.

"Let us return to the airstrip, Chevalier," Jean-Claude radioed to Ritter. "We are needed back at the fleet."

"I'd like to join you as well," said Naryal. "The General Staff will want to hear of Megami's planned attack."

"You may accompany us as my honored guest," Jean-Claude said.

Ritter cut in. "If Megami is planning an attack, we could be heading into a battle. Should we see Carlos about patching up Veillantif?"

Jean-Claude chuckled. "The damage is mostly superficial. Besides, I have a spare heat rapier and shield aboard our transport plane. Come! Time grows short."

Max reached behind his pilot chair and stowed the duffel bag holding his few personal effects on the navigator's seat. The *Yamamoto's* flight deck was practically deserted with most of the air wing still out searching for Zane, so Max had no reservations about making his exit in broad daylight.

"Are we joining the search operation, Max?" Marilyn's synthetic voice filled the Thor Prototype's open cockpit. "I haven't received flight clearance. There may be some clerical oversight."

"No, darling." Max reached down and patted the plane's white, soot-streaked side. "This bird's too cooked for active duty, but she'll get us where we're going."

"Excellent," said Marilyn. "Where are we going?"

Darving's peripheral vision caught a flurry of motion below him and to his right. Wen advanced across the deck. The tropical wind whipped her blue jumpsuit and strove to undo the black bun atop her head. "Somewhere the Socs and the EGE can't find us," Max answered.

"Max," Wen cried when she entered shouting distance. "What do you think you're doing?"

"I'm showing myself out the same way I came in," Darving said. He calmly resumed securing his bag.

Wen reached the cockpit ladder and gripped the sides. "You're no quitter. This is a childish stunt meant to make me feel guilty."

"It's not a stunt," said Max. "You got something to feel guilty about?"

"I know the counteroffensive to Operation N shook your faith." "We did the best we could with the intel we had. It's not your fault."

Max bowed his head and sighed. "You know what? You're right. You spent months coming on to me—sorry, 'cultivating the asset'— when I was at Seed Corp. You convinced me to defect, and you talked me into committing war crimes. My faith's not shaken. My eyes are open."

Wen hesitated only a moment before climbing the ladder. She raided Max's bag for his spare helmet, threw the duffel over the side, and jumped into the navigator's seat. "Point taken. I've worked too hard on our relationship to let you dump me and fly away." She donned the oversized helmet. "I'm going with you."

"Emotional blackmail won't work," said Max. "I'm deserting. If you're on this plane when it takes off, you won't be able to come within sensor range of an EGE ship without Larson ordering you shot down."

"Seven airborne craft inbound," Marilyn interrupted. "The *Yamamoto's* radar has detected one cargo plane eight kilometers to the northeast approaching at five hundred kilometers per hour and six combat frames twenty kilometers to the east closing at twice that speed."

Max pulled up the main camera feed. Six dark shapes hung over the green eastern horizon. They soon grew from formless blobs to vaguely humanoid shapes. Max's stomach dropped through his chair. "Zoom in."

Marilyn trained her telescopic lens on the boxy dark blue combat frames. She had to steadily zoom out to keep the onrushing formation in the shot.

"Dolphs!" Max cursed.

"The Fifth Shenlong Squadron encountered an SOC combat frame team over the People's Republic of the Congo ten minutes ago," Wen said. From the sound of tapping keys behind him, Max deduced she'd pulled up the latest intel reports on the navigation panel. "The Socs shot down half the squadron while suffering zero casualties."

There goes my stealth exit, thought Max. He called the tower. "Darving to control. We've got six Coalition CFs coming in hot. Five are Ein Dolphs. The sixth has a command crest and custom armor."

"Roger, Captain," the Air Boss said. "You're cleared to sortie. I'll recall the wing."

"Time to go," Max told Wen as he brought the Thor Prototype's flight control systems online.

"I said I'm coming with you," insisted Wen, "and I meant it. Besides, you'll need live intel out there."

The Dolphs rushed closer. If Max didn't take off immediately, they'd be on top of him before he could launch. He closed the canopy and fired up the Thor Prototype's engines.

Fireballs blazed aboard the escort cruiser and two destroyers far off the carrier's port side. Missile contrails arced toward the inbound Socs: one for each Dolph. Six bright red flashes blew the missiles to burning fragments well before they reached their targets. The escort ships' Gatling turrets opened fire, but the Dolphs ignored the 20mm rounds and answered with a second plasma volley that engulfed all three ships' armored superstructures in flames.

"I've lost contact with the *Cole*, the *Hilarion*, and the *Naples*," Wen said.

"Max!" a familiar voice hailed over the radio. "This is Ritter. I'm here with reinforcements." A bulky cargo plane landed on the *Yamamoto's* deck. Max stared in admiration of the pilot's feat, which was like stopping a speeding semi at the dead center of a tennis court during an earthquake.

"You picked a hell of a time to show up, kid," said Max, "but I won't look a gift horse in the mouth. Where are those reinforcements?"

A nightmarish combat frame rose up from behind the cargo plane. The baroque monstrosity was mostly bronze with armor and two barbed wings the color of old blood. "Here, Captain," Jean-Claude radioed from the gargoyle-like CF. "We have grim news. Secretary-General Megami has ordered an attack on the fleet."

"I gathered that," Max shouted back as his fingers keyed in the Thor Prototype's launch sequence with the practiced speed of a concert pianist. "Winged Victory there better have a bite to match its bark, because those Socs ain't here for an art show."

"Veillantif boasts the finest Zeklov craftsmanship," Jean-Claude said.

"Zeklov?" Max replied.

"Yes," Jean-Claude said indignantly. "Armorers to kings."

"They're fine if you want ceremonial CFs for the Supreme Patriarch's Swiss Guard," said Max, "or an armored limo for a Chinese bureaucrat, but we're staring down the barrel of Seed Corp's top military hardware. I hope you're ready."

"I always stand ready to defend those in my charge," Jean-Claude declared. Veillantif struck its shield with a CF-sized rapier.

Most of the indicators on Max's HUD flashed green, though some glowed yellow. "Warning," said Marilyn, "right manipulator not detected. Overall structural integrity seventy-five percent."

"Good enough for bebop," said Max.

The engines hummed eagerly. "Thor Prototype ready for liftoff," said Marilyn.

"Too late!" said Wen as the six Dolphs rocketed into firing range of the *Yamamoto*. The five wingmen clutched their plasma rifles in both hands, while the leader carried a long metal pole and a shield like Jean-Claude's, only bigger and midnight blue instead of burgundy. 20mm Gatling fire bounced off the shield's convex surface. When the Dolphs returned fire, they'd scuttle the carrier for sure.

"Take cover," Max broadcast shipwide.

The Dolph team soared over the *Yamamoto* like a storm cloud. Their ear-splitting rocket exhaust buffeted the deck, but otherwise the EGE flagship weathered their passage unscathed.

"Somebody give me a sitrep," Colonel Larson ordered via radio.

"This is Governor Prem Naryal," a brusque female voice replied from the cargo plane. "Admiral Kei Omaka is a Coalition spy. That Dolph team is here to extract her."

"That's a hefty accusation, lady," said Griff. "I'll need more proof than the word of a Soc."

"Then simply wait," said Naryal. "You'll have your proof when the enemy absconds with their agent."

Max opened the throttle and pointed his jet's vectored thrust nozzles at the deck. "I'm not waiting." He matched altitude with the low-flying Dolphs—now distant blue specks—and cut in the afterburners, launching the Thor Prototype after the Soc CFs.

"The *Lloyd George* is ten klicks east of the *Yamamoto*," Wen said.

Max chuckled. "We can be there in ten seconds." But it was too late for the *Lloyd George's* escorts. Three enormous fireballs blossomed on the glassy horizon. *I'll pay them back for you,* Max promised the destroyers' murdered crewmen.

"CF approaching from five o'clock," said Wen.

Veillantif's stylized gargoyle head filled the right side of Max's canopy. "Looking to join the dance, Your Majesty?" Darving asked.

Jean-Claude laughed. "The correct style is 'Your Highness'. Let us say I am honor-bound to prove my mount's worth in battle."

"The more the merrier," said Max.

"Welcome to the team," Ritter said over the comm. "Does that make Jean-Claude a suicide prince?"

"Joining combat against a mortal foe is not suicide," Jean-Claude explained.

"Wait till you fight these Dolphs." Artificial thunder split the sky as Max accelerated to Mach 1. Surprisingly, Veillantif kept up. *Maybe Zeklov CFs aren't just status symbols for shallow bluebloods.*

The Soc CF team snapped into view one klick off the *Lloyd George's* port side. Max eased back the throttle and lined up Mjolnir's targeting reticle with the leftmost Ein Dolph. The energy weapon-optimized CFs' armor was insulated against Max's electrolaser, but he'd bet the family farm their exposed thruster nozzles weren't. A well-placed shot of weaponized lightning darkened the rockets on the Dolph's back.

The damaged combat frame fell behind its comrades and rapidly lost altitude. The other four wingmen came about with the single-minded precision of a school of spooked fish. "Take evasive action!" Max warned Jean-Claude.

Four plasma rifles flared red. Max was already bobbing and weaving to stay out of the line of fire. One red bolt buzzed the Thor

Prototype's left tail fin, searing the paint off and rattling the whole aircraft. Wen gave a startled squeal.

Max steadied the jet's flight and fired his Vulcans at the center-left Dolph's rifle. The weapon exploded, and Max screamed past the armless CF. The other three Ein Dolphs sped after him.

"You alright?" Max asked Wen.

"Just a bit shaken," she said breathlessly.

Veillantif resumed its position off Max's right wing. "Thank you for the warning," Jean-Claude said.

"Thank me later," said Max. "The leader used that diversion to reach the *Lloyd George*. Catching up won't be easy with his buddies on our tail."

"Then I shall employ a distraction of my own." Veillantif spread its barbed wings to decelerate and wheeled on the pursuing Socs.

Don't get yourself killed, you crazy frog bastard. Max spared a glance at his rearview monitor. Jean-Claude had used Veillantif's speed advantage to close with the three combat-worthy Ein Dolphs. He harassed them with his rapier, some type of whip, and his CF's chainsaw wings. The Socs couldn't get away, nor could they use their plasma rifles without risking friendly fire.

Just buy me enough time, Max silently urged his new teammate. The *Lloyd George's* stately, flat-topped hull grew to dominate his view. The lead Dolph with its flared pauldrons and backswept command crest orbited the supercarrier. A crewman could have thrown a wrench at it.

"What's he waiting for?" Max wondered aloud.

"A light transport helicopter just powered up on the *Lloyd George's* flight deck," said Wen. "Admiral Omaka is aboard."

"Show me," said Max. The image of a light gray helo, its rotors just starting to turn, filled his HUD. A middle-aged Asian woman in a Navy BDU sat at the controls. "How did she make it all the way from the bridge?" he pondered aloud. Gatling fire and missiles sprayed the sky in answer.

"The crew's too busy fighting for their lives to worry about the CO going AWOL," Wen spat.

Max's palms sweated as he narrowly slipped through the carrier's hail of defensive fire. The Soc leader deftly avoided the ship's guns while picking them off with his shield-mounted plasma cannons. He worked his way aft until his midnight blue CF hovered beside Omaka's helo.

"Naryal was right," said Max. "The Admiral's defecting, and this psycho's her escort." He flipped his weapon selector switch to ready Mjolnir and agonized over whether he should shoot his honest enemy or his traitorous former ally.

A blazing red blade sprang from the tip of the custom Dolph's staff and split in two. The Soc pilot swept his plasma fork across the deck and through the helo's cockpit, vaporizing the treasonous Admiral inside. A wall of flame erupted from the trench carved in the ship's hull.

"Fire on the gallery and hangar decks!" reported Li Wen. Her voice fell. "He hit the officers' quarters."

"The Soc leader fragged Omaka's helicopter," Max shouted over the comm. "This ain't an extraction. It's an execution!" He fired a wild shot. The custom Dolph's murderous pilot blocked the lightning with his shield and fired his twin plasma cannon with a flick of the same arm. The searing bolts hit the Thor Prototype like a train.

"Critical damage to drive systems," Marilyn warned over the shrill din of cockpit alarms. Max struggled with the controls as his plane spiraled toward the *Lloyd George's* burning flight deck. Wen screamed.

"You're wrong," an oily male voice giggled over the comm. "I'm here to extract *you*!" The custom Dolph's left hand reached for the falling jet. An instant before its metal fingers closed, the custom Dolph rocketed to the right.

A violet beam lanced through the curtain of smoke where the dark blue CF had hovered a moment before. Dead Drop burst through the inferno to hang in the hellish air, facing its bastard offspring.

"You," the lead Soc hissed.

Max's cockpit spun to face Jean-Claude's battle with the three Ein Dolphs. One of the Soc CFs pivoted behind Veillantif. "Jean-Claude!" Max cried helplessly.

A purple plasma bolt streaked over the water and blasted into the Ein Dolph before it could shoot Veillantif in the back. An orange fireball ripped the Soc CF into smoking chunks as the Thor Prototype whipped back toward the burning carrier.

"*Merci*, M. Dellister," Jean-Claude said.

"Hold on!" Max told Wen as he fought to land the damaged fighter. The world inverted, and the cockpit spiderwebbed against the *Lloyd George's* flight deck with a final shock that probably realigned Max's organs.

"You okay?" he croaked to Wen over the plaintive alarms. She didn't answer. He looked back and saw the fragile-looking woman hanging limply in her chair.

"This is Captain Maximus Darving," he shouted into the comm. "I'm in the jet that just crash-landed on the *Lloyd George*. Lieutenant Li Wen is with me. She needs a medic, ASAP!"

No reply came. "Communications systems offline," Marilyn said in a staticky staccato.

Max beat against the cracked canopy till blood soaked through his gloves, to no avail. The *Lloyd George* had taken severe damage. The custom Dolph and Dead Drop were about to cause even more. *I have to get us out,* he thought, barely stifling the onset of panic, *or we're as good as dead.*

26

The constant feeling, like someone breathing down his neck, had started when they'd locked Zane up at the institute. Now, in the smoke-filled sky above the *Lloyd George's* burning deck, what had been vague discomfort throbbed as if the Soc pilot were stabbing Zane's temples with icepicks.

"Masz," Zane snarled into Dead Drop's comm. "You helped Megami murder our brothers. Now you come here in that knockoff and insult me!"

Masz laughed. "I could never insult you worse than our sister. She chose me and left you to rot!"

Zane's twitching lip curled upward. "Megami did me a favor. If I'd been shipped off to space, I wouldn't have found Dead Drop."

"Your pathetic machine is nothing next to the Sentinel set over the earth!" Masz thrust his forked plasma blade skyward.

Zane detached the barrel of Dead Drop's cannon, ignited his plasma sword, and held the brilliant purple blade in a high ready position.

The custom Dolph extended its plasma fork horizontally as if to bar its opponent's way. A second red blade sprang from the other end and split in two. "It's not too late," said Masz. "Our sister will take you back. Rejoin our family and cleanse this infested world!"

"It was too late for you the second you stole what's mine." Zane charged, aiming his plasma sword's tip at Masz's cockpit. The custom Dolph darted right and swung its crimson fork as Dead Drop rocketed into the space it had occupied. Zane parried the blow with a twist of his CF's arm. Blood-colored sparks flashed from the locked energy blades.

Masz canted his fork's lower head upward. Zane fired reverse thrusters, saving Dead Drop's right arm from the burning red arc. He lunged for Masz's cockpit again. The custom Dolph levered its double fork in both hands and caught Dead Drop's blade.

Zane Jabbed his violet blade between the scarlet tines. Masz barely forced the rocket-assisted thrust aside. The custom Dolph's armored knee crashed into the black CF's side. The shock numbed Zane's hands, but he held tight to the controls.

A second kick, and a third, rattled Zane like the ball bearing in a can of spray paint. With a feral cry he opened the throttle. Dead Drop slammed against its opponent. The custom Dolph pushed back, but even its enhanced drives were no match for the black CF's thrusters. Both combat frames hurtled out to sea. Zane cut his main engine and fired reverse thrusters, bringing Dead Drop to a sudden stop. Masz's CF continued tumbling into the distance.

Zane wheeled around and flew back toward the burning carrier at full speed. His sensors picked up the Thor Prototype through the smoke. The crashed plane was lying upside down near the flaming rent in the deck. Zane landed, quenched his blade, and reached Dead Drop's hand down to right the wrecked jet.

Thunder rolled in the clear sky. A red streak that left a green afterimage in Zane's eyes slashed through the ship's mast, sending the antenna-studded tower plummeting. The severed structure hit the flight deck with a riot of metallic booms and squeals. Zane punched the ignition, but a ruby bolt exploded into Dead Drop's main thruster bank before it could take to the air. The black CF fell facedown onto the scarred deck.

"Get up!" Pleaded Zane. Dead Drop rose to its hands and knees as its pilot wrestled with the controls.

Masz's custom Dolph touched down beside the Thor Prototype and planted one midnight blue foot on Dead Drop's back, forcing it back down with bone-jarring force. Masz swept his plasma fork across the plane's inverted fuselage to shear off the cockpit and nose.

He racked his fork and reached down with his CF's right hand. His Dolph's giant fingers closed around the canopy over the navigator's seat.

"Let go, you Soc son of a bitch!" Max shouted.

Zane wrenched the control stick to no effect. He pounded his chair's padded armrests in frustration.

The custom Dolph pressed its shield-mounted twin plasma gun to Dead Drop's back. Zane felt the heavy thud directly behind him.

"Miss Megami doesn't tolerate defectives," Masz hissed. Capacitors hummed down two huge barrels.

The twin cannon and the surrounding shield blew apart in a blue-white flash. The blast threw Masz off balance, and Zane rolled Dead Drop out from under the custom Dolph's foot. Masz ignored him and fixed the black v of his main sensor array on a streamlined blue dot in the water off the port side.

"Ritter!" Zane radioed to the Mablung that had destroyed Masz's cannon. "What the hell are you doing?"

"What I should have done back in Kisangani," Ritter said. Dead Drop's main camera zoomed in, showing the Mablung aiming its railgun for another shot at Masz.

"Get out of there," yelled Zane. He pushed Dead Drop up and sprang, but the custom Dolph rocketed out of reach. Still holding the Thor Prototype's cockpit in its right hand, the midnight blue CF took its staff in its left and activated one set of forked plasma blades. Masz skimmed over the water, sending up a frothing rooster tail. He anticipated Ritter's shot and veered clear of the hypersonic dart.

The Mab didn't get off a third shot. Masz slashed his fork through its domed head and upper torso like a great red pendulum. Steam boiled from the sea, followed a moment later by an explosion that sent a geyser of white water and blue CF parts fountaining into the air.

Zane howled. He launched Dead Drop toward Masz on secondary thrusters. One of the two Dolphs still jousting with Jean-Claude broke off to intercept the black CF. Even with half its engines gone, Dead Drop closed before its imitator could fire. Zane ignited his plasma sword and jammed the immolating blade through the Soc wingman's cockpit. He maintained his course and speed as the unmanned Dolph splashed down. Masz receded over the waves.

It's no good. I can't catch him. Zane considered racking his blade and picking off Masz's thrusters with pinpoint plasma fire, but there was too much risk to Darving and Li.

Jean-Claude quit running interference. He danced clear of a shot from the last Ein Dolph and beheaded the Soc CF with his heat whip as he darted past it. Raking Veillantif's chainsaw wings across the headless Dolph's engines sent the disabled CF plunging out of the sky and beneath the waves.

The bronze gargoyle soared after Masz. Defensive fire from the *Yamamoto* slowed the custom Dolph enough for Veillantif to catch up. Jean-Claude switched back to delay tactics, avoiding the wicked plasma fork while keeping Masz boxed in with wavering hot rapier, whip, and wings.

Zane held his breath all the way from the *Lloyd George*. He only exhaled when he entered close combat range with Masz. Dead Drop's overtaxed thrusters shrieked, but Zane kept the throttle open as he readied his plasma sword and locked the custom Dolph's engines in his sights.

Veillantif charged the midnight blue CF head-on, drawing Masz's attention and creating the perfect opening for Zane. He thrust his plasma blade, but the custom Dolph suddenly dropped out of sight. Zane's heart missed a beat as Dead Drop and Veillantif sped toward a midair collision. Each pilot swerved to his respective left at the same instant. Veillantif's exhaust buffeted Dead Drop as they careened past each other.

Zane furiously searched his sensor screen for Masz. "Where is he?"

Jean-Claude's unintelligible curse gave Zane his answer. The custom Dolph appeared in his rear view monitor behind Veillantif. The gargoyle slashed its buzzing pinions. Each end of Masz's plasma fork blocked one wing.

The exchange bought Zane time to close with Masz again. He stabbed at the rocket nozzles on the Dolph's back. Masz slid left and pivoted to face his foes.

As if at a silent signal, Zane and Jean-Claude renewed their attack as one. Dead Drop's violet energy blade sought the custom Dolph's cockpit with a series of vicious thrusts while Veillantif's heat rapier probed the enemy's defenses for an opening. The spinning double fork denied them at every turn.

Smoke streamed between the fingers of the Dolph's raised right hand as the Thor Prototype's ejection system fired. Only the pilot's seat shot into the air above the blue CF's crested head. The navigator remained locked in the Dolph's iron grip.

Jean-Claude took a bold swipe at the hand holding the jet's cockpit. Masz darted left and swung his fork as Veillantif slashed thin air. Masz's precise backhand swing parted the overextended CF's gargoyle-like head from its winged body.

Zane saw his opening. He aligned the tip of Dead Drop's plasma blade with the hatch in the Dolph's unguarded chest and jammed his control stick forward.

He was a split second too late. The custom Dolph inverted its weapon hand and flexed its elbow, catching the purple energy sword in the tines of its fork. The three plasma blades spat sparks as Zane strove to pierce the cockpit that filled his screen.

Zane switched off his plasma sword. Suddenly lacking resistance, the red fork stabbed past the Dolph's right arm. He once again pressed the "fire" switch on his weapon control stick. Before the sword could reestablish a magnetic field, a backhand snap of Masz's fork cut into Dead Drop's left side. Another thruster bank died in a blast that hit Zane like a punch to the kidney.

Without enough thrust to stay aloft, the black combat frame fell from the sky. The sea swallowed Zane's curses.

27

Charcoal-uniformed Kazoku marched Sieg down a stygian tunnel that followed the curve of Metis' largest crater. Megami's shock troops kept their sidearms holstered yet prominently displayed—a silent statement Sieg heard loud and clear.

Masz had thrown him onto a shuttle after their duel at Kisangani. Sieg probably could have hijacked the flight and headed home to L3, but his burning curiosity about the Coalition's new SecGen had prevailed. Members of Megami's private army had met him upon landing. Now they escorted him to a long hoped-for reunion or his execution.

A meter-thick window of silicon alloyed with powdered graphite and aluminum replaced the wall to Sieg's left. The barren crater floor stretched ten kilometers from the curving glass to the far wall of striated blue-gray rock. A cluster of rocket nozzles the size of sport stadiums mushroomed from the crater's center. Work frames and spacesuited figures swarmed over the colossal engines like ants.

That's one cluster of the old fusion rockets they used to move Metis from the asteroid belt, thought Sieg. *Looks like Megami's making them operational again.*

The smooth stone tunnel opened into a wide gallery echoing with the distant snarl of industrial drills and the screeching of diamond-bladed saws. Fifty meters away, an improvised partition of I-beams painted with diagonal black and white stripes fenced off a jagged trench over which a drilling rig had been erected. Magmatic red light filtered up from below. The smell of burning stone completed Sieg's sense of having descended into hell.

"Sieg!" A lithe figure leapt down from a catwalk eight meters above. Her blue trench coat flared around her slim hips, and her long black hair fanned out as the low gravity brought her to a gentle landing before him. She regarded him with lupine eyes.

"Madam Secretary," Sieg said with a slight nod.

Megami probed Sieg's forehead with spidery fingers. Her touch stung as she traced the outline of his cut. "Masz showed atypical restraint," she said. "Or else your fight was closer than he let on. We'll get you something for the pain, plus a new uniform to replace those dusty old togs."

"Thanks for your concern," said Sieg, "but I expected you to grill me, not mother me."

Megami's hands fell to her sides. "I'm not our mother, Sieg. I'm your sister."

Hearing his hope confirmed evoked a reaction Sieg hadn't expected. He laughed. "You're lying. Sanzen Kaimora had my mother and my sister executed in response to my failed rescue attempt."

It was Megami's turn to give an unexpected reaction. Her wolfish expression softened, and what Sieg would have called pity in anyone else glimmered in her black eyes. "The guilt almost crushed you," she said. "It's still weighing you down."

A flash of anger burned away Sieg's mirth. "You have no idea how I feel!" he lied.

"What's in your pocket?" asked Megami.

The question caught Sieg off balance. "What? Is that some kind of sick joke?"

"I'm serious. You're my prisoner. Consider this a search. What's in your left breast pocket?"

Long habit overcame Sieg's trepidation. His fingers drew out the pink silk ribbon as if it were a venomous snake.

Megami produced an identical ribbon from inside her coat.

The strength drained from Sieg's hand. His silk strip fluttered to the rocky ground. Megami's joined it.

Sieg sought his last refuge in denial. "How did you get that?" he said, choking back tears. "It belonged to Liz. Did you tear it from her body after Sanzen's butchers did their work?"

"I am Liz, Sieg," Megami said, barely audible over the heavy machinery gnawing at the rock.

"Your hair," Sieg protested. "Your eyes."

"I won't deny there've been drastic changes since we saw each other last," Megami said, "but it's still me."

The enervating emotions that had weakened Sieg's hand coursed through his whole body. Tears long held back flowed forth. He swept his hand across the soldiers standing behind him. "This is none of their business. Get them out of here!"

"This is family business," Megami said, "and the Kazoku are family."

"What are you talking about?" Sieg snapped.

Megami opened her palm to reveal another object she'd pulled from her pocket: a compact syringe pen. The clear tube's contents glowed red as a live coal in the hellish light. "The answers to all your questions are here."

Sieg hesitated. *Another trap.* But he feared never knowing the truth more than death. He snatched the syringe from the SecGen's delicate hand and injected himself in the neck. The expected paralysis and blackout failed to manifest. One of the Kazoku took the needle from Sieg's hand.

Megami turned and strode toward a tunnel entrance in the far wall. "Come on. We'll get you freshened up. Then you can go see Browning in the lab."

Sieg and the Kazoku followed. *This army,* he thought. *Metis' engines. Megami claiming to be Liz. That needle. They're all related.* The realization, or perhaps the syringe's contents, chilled his blood. *What am I doing?*

"We're about to have the last word in human history," Megami said as if in answer to his troubled thoughts.

Max leaned over the railing up on vulture's row. Another returning Shenlong screeched to a landing, but he ignored the commotion on the *Yamamoto's* flight deck below and kept his eyes

195

fixed on Jean-Claude's yacht. A banana yellow crane fished the blue waters between the converted cargo ship and the carrier with steel cables as thick as Max's arm. A clear sky stretched forever above him.

I should be up there looking for her.

"You think he's still alive down there?"

Ritter's question roused Max from his brooding. He hadn't noticed the slim, dark-haired kid sidle up next to him. "The tower's in radio contact," said Darving. "It's only been a day. Zane's alright."

"Gotta hand it to him," said Ritter. "He built Dead Drop tough. Even my Mab would've imploded at those depths."

A bitter laugh escaped Max's chest. "He'd have been smarter to ditch his CF like you did."

"To be fair," said Ritter, "I wouldn't have cleared the blast zone if I hadn't stowed a DPV behind my seat after Kisangani."

"Proves my point," said Max. "You can be reckless, but you've still got a sense of self-preservation. Zane's perpetual hard on for his CF kept him from bailing out when he had the chance."

"You ejected," Ritter said.

"Not voluntarily," muttered Max. He wondered if Larson was right about a bug deep in Marilyn's code. He'd probably never find out since Marilyn had jettisoned him, leaving Wen and herself to be taken by Megami's bag man.

Orange lights strobed on the yacht's deck as the cargo crane reeled in its cables. Dead Drop's head and shoulders emerged from the sea. Its black armor glistened in the sun as the crane hauled it up to the yacht's deck.

"Darving!" Griff Larson's harsh voice rose above the scream of an inbound jet. "Figures you'd be up here eye-banging the aircraft."

Ritter snapped to attention and saluted. Max kept enjoying the view. "What do you want, Griff?" asked Darving.

"I want to hear from your own pouty lips that the rumors of you going AWOL are bullshit," said Larson. "Look at me when I'm talking to you."

Max turned. The Colonel's digital camo ACUs bore soot stains, his wavy white hair looked downright frazzled, and the bags under his eyes said he hadn't slept in at least twenty-four hours.

"I should probably go help out on the *Lloyd George*," Ritter said sheepishly. A black pillar of smoke still rose across the water off the *Yamamoto's* stern, where her sister ship sat adrift and burning.

"Good idea," Griff said with all the warmth of a November gale. Ritter hurried along the balcony toward the stairs.

"It is bullshit," said Max. "I'm not going AWOL."

"Good," said Griff. "We lost 237 men yesterday, along with two flights of Shenlongs, three destroyers, and a cruiser—probably that treacherous bitch Omaka's flagship too, before this shit show's over. We've still got fifty-six MIA. Report to Major Collins for search and rescue duty."

"You misunderstood me," Max said, trying to keep his voice level. "I'm not going AWOL, because I'm not coming back."

Griff's mouth compressed into a thin line framed by his silver beard. "I'm gonna say this once, so listen hard. Because you've served with honor, I'll overlook what a huge pain in the ass you are and give you a choice. Option one: You go back to your quarters, you hit the sack, and as of tomorrow this conversation never happened.

"Option two: You keep driving with your dick and go looking for your sweetheart. I don't know whether that means Li or your digital pillow princess, and I don't care. But get this through your egg-shaped skull. If you go, you stay gone. Because I shoot deserters on sight. Do you read me, Captain?"

"Five by five," said Max. "Now I've got a question for you. We got our asses beat like a second string JV squad. When does the EGE punch back?"

"When we're ready," said Griff.

"What are you waiting for?"

"For ZoDiaC to supply us with our own combat frames."

"That means *never*," Max scoffed. "I watched those bug men turn my hometown into a joyless gray hive. I knew they'd remake the planet as one big cube farm with a monogrammed concrete box for everyone. Wen gave me a glimmer of hope that someone could stop the Socs. But the EGE hasn't even slowed them down. Now I know the truth. You can't stop them, and you never could."

Griff's nostrils flared. "Think you can do better?"

"As a matter of fact, yes I do. That psycho in the Dolph didn't just come for Omaka. He came to extract *me*. Naryal says the Socs' new SecGen has greenlit all kinds of Bond villain weapons projects. She wants me for one of them. If I go along, I can find Wen and fuck up their plans from the inside."

"If the Socs want you building weapons for them," said Griff, "that's the best reason to keep your ass parked here."

Max brushed past his former superior. "That's why you always lose."

"Darving," Griff called after him. "She was just a spook working an asset. Or do you think she'd throw away her career to oversee your eternal blueballing?"

Max paused, forced down the torrent of invective he knew Griff wanted him to let fly, and stalked off down vulture's row.

28

"General," Naryal greeted McCaskey when he stepped into the spacious salon aboard Jean-Claude's yacht. "Good of you to join us."

McCaskey hung the peaked cap that matched his khaki uniform on a sandalwood rack near the door. "Governor," he replied before acknowledging Jean-Claude, who stood at Naryal's side. "Your Highness." The General paused when his gaze fell on the room's final occupant.

Carlos the Scorpion lounged on a white leather bench built into the curved wall to McCaskey's left. The arms dealer wore a uniform identical to the General's own, but with the top three buttons undone, exposing a toned chest similar in color to the bronze sculptures displayed throughout the room.

"The correct style is *General*," Carlos said with an unctuous grin.

McCaskey smoothed his iron gray hair with a sharp motion of his hand. "I'll address you by that rank because you've joined your private army to the EGE, not because you earned that uniform."

Carlos cocked an eyebrow. "You're welcome."

"Please, my friends," Jean-Claude said. "The enemy has sown enough division without our help."

"You're right," said McCaskey. "Indulging petty rivalries won't help morale."

Carlos waved his hand. "I take no offense, and I meant none."

"Good," said Naryal. She led McCaskey to a set of white easy chairs near the center of the room. He and Jean-Claude took seats while Naryal remained standing. "Because the situation is deteriorating as we speak."

"That's an understatement," McCaskey said. "We've taken heavy losses, including a General Staff member who turned out to be a spy. She left us with a carrier that's salvageable but might not make it to dry dock in Algiers."

"Governor Troy has retaken all the land Mitsu relinquished in North Africa," said Naryal. "The EGE has no safe port of call in the Mediterranean."

"It's those damned Dolphs," Carlos spat. "No one can compete with their plasma weapons."

"An arms race never stands still." Naryal gathered up her pale green dress, strode to the lavish bar, and poured herself a glass of Cognac. "Carlos' people smuggled that experimental plasma rifle out of Algiers before Troy's forces overran the city. My analysts determined it to be a full generation more advanced than the Ein Dolphs' standard weapon. It even outclasses the twin plasma cannon carried by the custom Zwei Dolph that decimated the fleet."

"I'd like to know what a prototype plasma weapon was doing in an Algerian warehouse," McCaskey said.

Naryal swallowed a smooth, vanilla and caramel-flavored sip of her drink and said, "Someone was using the mob to transport military hardware to Kisangani under the SOC governors' noses. I don't have solid proof, but the only Coalition official capable of setting up a secret supply chain to outer space is the Secretary-General herself."

"Is that why you've decided to help us?" McCaskey asked.

"I underestimated Megami once, General," said Naryal. "Her coup against the Secretariat dispelled my illusions. Now trustworthy sources report a massive military buildup in the colonies. I believe Megami plans to launch the invasion for which Operation N was just a feint. I do not believe she will discriminate between friend and foe."

"That could be a problem if she is building more weapons like the rifle Zane and Ritter found," said Jean-Claude.

"I have no doubt she's building far worse." Naryal drained her glass. The warming draft chased the chill from her blood.

"What can the EGE field to oppose such overwhelming force?" asked Carlos.

"Our fighters have proven ineffective against the Dolphs," McCaskey said. "Regardless, Captain Darving didn't improve matters by going AWOL with a Shenlong. Our attack helicopters might fare better."

"How many combat frames do you have in your inventory?" Carlos asked.

"Veillantif is severely damaged," Jean-Claude said. "Dead Drop even more so. The Mablung and the Thor Prototype have been destroyed. Colonel Larson's Grenzmark II is the only combat-capable CF remaining."

The Scorpion pursed his lips as if whistling. "You will need an equipment upgrade."

"ZoDiaC had agreed to buy us our own combat frames from Seed Corp," said McCaskey. "Omaka and Friedlander were our main links to the dissident colonists. Now she's dead and he's disappeared."

"Megami nationalized Seed Corp and moved all their assets to outer space," said Naryal. "Don't expect any help from them. As for Friedlander, he's reportedly turned traitor as well."

"Zeklov," Jean-Claude said.

"Yes," said Carlos with a twinkle in his eye.

McCaskey's brow furrowed. "The luxury weapons manufacturer?"

"They also produce combat frames." Jean-Claude rose, straightened his white blazer, and motioned to the winged form outside the window that towered over the deck like a headless colossus. "Including mine."

"Zeklov installed the armor on my combat frame's Seed Corporation chassis," said Naryal. "Jagannath is currently undergoing repairs at their Russian facility."

"If you're suggesting the EGE contract with Zeklov to supply us with combat frames, I'm afraid we're not budgeted for it."

"I cannot afford to outfit the entire EGE," Jean-Claude said, "but I am prepared to fund a dozen."

"That's generous of you," said McCaskey. "It's just not enough."

"I'll cover the rest," Naryal said.

McCaskey regarded her with narrowed eyes. "And in return?"

"Treat me as an equal partner in our alliance," said Naryal. "A bargain price, since I'm fronting an unequal share of the funds."

Carlos chuckled. "You are out of excuses, General."

McCaskey raised his hands. "This is one time I'm glad to lose."

"The Zeklovs are old family friends," Jean-Claude said. "I will accompany Her Excellency to conduct negotiations with their managing director."

"Your assistance is appreciated," said Naryal. "I'd like Ritter and Dellister to join us. They've both proven knowledgeable—and quite resourceful."

"I have no objections." McCaskey stood, walked to the door, and donned his hat. "Just make sure you bring my men CFs that can fight."

Somebody rained hell down on this place. From the air, Max surveyed the swaths of burned-out buildings and rubble-filled craters on Kisangani Spaceport's perimeter. "Maybe Zimmer and his boys left the Socs a parting gift," Max thought aloud. He paused out of habit to let Marilyn deliver her analysis and fell into brooding silence in her absence.

Shenlongs like the one Max was flying hadn't caused the devastation below. The pattern of destruction didn't match aerial bombardment, and he doubted a whole squadron of fighter-bombers could have wreaked so much havoc.

Good thing they're not firing triple-A guns or scrambling CFs. Max hadn't thought twice about invading Soc airspace in the Thor Prototype. Making a second incursion in a less powerful, mass-produced aircraft set his teeth on edge.

A crackle of static drew Max's attention to his radio. "EGE aircraft," a slightly distorted male voice hailed him, "you are cleared for landing on pad zero five nine, over."

What if it's a trick? Max pondered. The answer immediately presented itself. *Of course it's a trick. But the Socs are holding all the cards. I'll have to play along if I want to save Wen.*

Max set the VTOL aircraft down on a hockey rink-sized concrete pad in front of an oblong gray hangar. The Shenlong's bubble canopy gave him a clear view of the wide circular spaceport with its skeletal launch towers. He expected a company's worth of light trucks and personnel transports to close in on him, but the port remained empty to every horizon.

A moment passed before Max felt secure enough to power down the Shenlong. With the engine's whine silenced, he could hear the wind tearing across the paved plain. He raised the canopy and climbed down to stand under the overcast sky.

Still, no hostiles appeared. Max removed his helmet, tucked the carbon fiber shell stenciled with the king of hearts in the crook of his flight suited arm, and strode toward the hangar's open rectangular door.

Max's eyes adjusted to the building's relative gloom. Not that there was much too see. The cavernous space's only furnishing was a wheeled cart of black metal that rose to chest height with a flat monitor perched on top.

A face appeared on the screen as Max approached. He recognized the narrow female visage framed by long blue-black hair with precisely trimmed bangs. The teenage girl's dark eyes studied him like an insect she'd stuck on a pin.

"Megami," Max cursed.

"Hi, Max," Megami's greeting boomed over the hangar's PA. "I hope you had a nice flight."

The Secretary-General's voice raised his hackles like a straight razor down the nape of his neck. Something in her tone uncorked the building frustration Max had kept bottled up. "Shove the pleasantries up your ass! You wanna talk? Try a phone call before sending your psycho lapdog on a murder spree."

Megami shrugged. "We're talking now, aren't we?"

"Keep acting smug. I'll get right back in my aircraft, and you can eat my jet wash."

"I doubt it," Megami said. "If you walk away now, you'll never know what happens to Li Wen, and I know you couldn't live with the uncertainty."

Max balled his fists so hard his nails bit into his gloved palms. When he'd calmed himself enough to speak, he asked, "Where is she?"

"Here on Metis. If you're ready to listen, I have a job for you."

A chuckle escaped Max's throat. "You don't know shit about me if you think I'd help a Soc hive-queen build a weapon to conquer the earth."

Megami adopted the expression of a teacher explaining a simple concept to a slow child. "You still think that little of me? I've killed more Socs than you, Max. In fact, I gave you an assist on most of your confirmed kills. I'm approaching you now because you're the only one who might hate Socs as much as me."

Max's swelling sense of indignation deflated. "I don't get it. Why go to the trouble of becoming the leader of a people you hate?"

"Governments have been the leading cause of death throughout history." Megami's eyes drifted down and to her left. "Except for viruses," she said, seemingly to herself.

"If I take this job," Max said cautiously, "I get to kill Socs, and you'll let me see Wen?"

"Someone else is looking forward to seeing you, too." Megami smiled like a normal girl.

Somehow that's even more disturbing.

"Hello, Max," a synthetic female voice said from offscreen.

Max forgot himself. "Marilyn! Honey, are you alright?"

"We salvaged your jet's OS," Megami said. "Coding like that more than qualifies you for my special project. Dr. Browning needs an expert programmer."

"Browning is working for you?"

"Sieg, too. We really want you on our team, Max. There's a shuttle fueled and waiting for you on pad eleven. See you soon!"

"Wait," said Max. "What if I—"

The screen went black, but the blue LED in front said it was still turned on. Max approached the black metal cart in search of the mic he'd used to speak with Megami on Metis.

In L5.

From Earth.

Max dashed to the cart and frantically searched every inch for a microphone. He found only a media drive the size of a black die with one slender cable connected to the monitor and another running from the audio out—probably ending at the hangar PA's input.

The helmet slipped from Max's arm, thudded to the concrete floor, and rolled. He realized what had bothered him about Megami's speech. It hadn't been her words or her tone. *There was no delay.*

Radio waves took about a second to travel between Earth and L5. Every time Max spoke, there should have been a two-second delay before he heard Megami's reply. He took the black media cube between his thumb and forefinger; gingerly, as if the small drive contained a deadly toxin. *Her side of the conversation was prerecorded.*

Max turned and trudged from the empty hangar. Megami had known exactly what he'd say, just as she knew he'd take the waiting shuttle to Metis.

29

The lead transport plane circled a dark spot at the center of a gray crater in the green and brown wilderness. Ritter peered through the right side window and saw intermittent lines of light twinkling on the kilometer-wide pit's sheer walls. "That's where the moon rock hit?" he called over the hum of the propellers to Jean-Claude, who sat across the cockpit behind Benny.

"It was an aircraft carrier-sized block of ice," the Prince corrected him. "The Coalition fired it from the moon's mass driver to deter Russia from opposing their conquest of Western Europe."

A knot formed in Ritter's stomach. "I remember that day. The northeastern sky turned black. My father always said the other Holy League nations would help us, but no one came."

Jean-Claude wore a sad smile. His deep blue eyes glinted. "Russia does not fight the Coalition directly, but she aids the nations of Christendom in other ways."

Ritter sank back in his seat and fell quiet until they landed at an airstrip cut from the outer crater's glass floor. Ritter, Jean-Claude, and Benny's plane carried the headless Veillantif. The second plane, which landed behind them, transported Naryal, Zane, and Dead Drop.

"Glad I wore my cold-weather uniform," Ritter said when the crews of both aircraft had gathered on the tarmac. The chill wind blowing across the desolate crater sought any opening in his camo pattern coat.

Zane stood unflinching in black pants a white short sleeved shirt. "You think this is cold? Try outer space."

Ritter, Zane, and Naryal followed Jean-Claude down a paved path with a narrow set of tracks embedded in the center. The walkway ended at a steel and concrete ledge fronted by waist-high railings with a panoramic view overlooking the pit. The abyss drew Ritter like a magnet pulling iron. *The lights glowing down there are windows,* he realized.

Jean-Claude pressed a button on a metal box attached to the railing. A gate rose up from a seam in the concrete behind the group, connecting with the railings to fully enclose them. Industrial motors hummed beneath the platform, which shuddered before starting a smooth descent into the pit.

"This whole platform is a lift," marveled Ritter. "And those big boxes sticking out of the pit's walls—they're like sideways buildings!"

Jean-Claude extended his white parka-clad arms, taking in the oblong, window-speckled structures covering the shaft's cylindrical wall. "Welcome to Steklov, the City of Glass. The Tsar ordered her built in defiance of the Coalition. Zeklov assisted with the construction and established their corporate headquarters beneath the crater floor."

The lift continued its steady downward journey. Ritter anxiously shifted his weight. *Zeklov has to approve our design. I'd hate to have wasted a trip all the way out here!*

Skyscrapers whose tops reached nowhere near the sky rose to surround the descending lift. Orange lights flashed along the railings as the moving platform delved below the buildings' foundations in the crater floor.

The lift emerged from the shaft and ensconced itself in a large square slot. An underground forest of steel beams stretched as far as Ritter could see. Rows of scaffolds towered between the uprights, casting off showers of sparks and a metallic symphony of industry.

A tall thin man stood three paces from the lift's leading edge, facing the new arrivals. He wore a gunmetal gray suit with tails, and a gold chain dangled from the pocket of his matching vest. A triangular patch of white beard and severely trimmed mustaches bracketed his mouth. Pince-nez glasses perched on his aquiline nose.

"Your Highness, Your Excellency." The tall man bowed to Jean-Claude and Naryal. The longer white hair atop his head bobbed in sharp contrast to the closely shorn sides. "Other esteemed guests. Welcome to our factory."

Naryal sashayed forward. The skirts of her blue coat nearly swept the floor. "Our pleasure, Director Zeklov. Thank you for receiving us on such short notice."

Zeklov placed the back of his hand under Naryal's right palm and gracefully raised his arm to kiss her hand. "You and the Dauphin are among my best customers," he said. "Besides, you deserve to be informed in person that repairs to Jagannath have been delayed due to supply shortages. You have my sincerest apologies."

The corner of Naryal's painted lips curved upward. "Perhaps you can make it up to me. My friends and I have brought you a new proposition."

"Let us discuss the details in my office," said Zeklov. He turned and marched across the smooth gray floor, which turned out to be the same glass that lined the crater above. Jean-Claude and Naryal followed behind the Director. Zane fell in beside Ritter.

The trek took the visitors past several of the giant scaffolds. Only two of them held combat frames; both in early skeletal states. *Looks like they could use our business,* Ritter thought hopefully.

The managing director's office occupied a spacious, mostly dim oval room floored with blue marble. A row of seats upholstered in red velvet followed the curve of the near wall, fronted by an obsidian coffee table. Five meters away, a large aluminum drafting table stood under a ceiling-mounted spotlight. The drawing board's surface glowed with LED and holographic displays.

Zeklov proceeded directly to his work table. "Again I must apologize for failing to render prompt service, Your Excellency. The Coalition's new Secretary-General has imposed a total trade embargo between the colonies and the earth. We are seeking alternative sources of certain rare metals."

"I'd thought Russia retained her deposits of rare earth metals when the Consortium plundered the rest of the world's reserves," Jean-Claude said.

"You thought correctly," Zeklov said. His lithe hands conjured inventory lists from the table. "But some materials required for combat frame production are less expensively obtained from asteroid mines. As it is, Her Excellency's CF will be ready in three days. My men are unloading Your Highness' Veillantif as we speak. Luckily we have a compatible head in stock which requires only cosmetic alterations. Work will be completed in the same time frame."

Naryal beamed. "You never disappoint, Zeklov. Let's move on to new business."

"And you are never one to mince words, Madame," said Zeklov. "I am at your disposal."

"The EGE is in need of combat frames to repel the Coalition threat," Jean-Claude said. "I am here to offer Zeklov Corporation the contract on their behalf."

Zeklov tapped the table's surface. Figures scrolled across a built-in transparent monitor. "The EGE is rather late. Could it be that you contracted with Seed Corp before approaching me?"

"We meant no disrespect," Jean-Claude said. "ZoDiaC made the original arrangements. That is an explanation, not an excuse."

Zeklov dismissed the apology with a wave of his hand. "My fondest wish is for my customers' needs to be satisfied. Who could have known that Seed Corp would be nationalized?"

"Thank you for understanding," Jean-Claude said.

"How many combat frames does the EGE need?" asked Zeklov.

"One hundred," said Naryal.

Zeklov raised one snowy eyebrow. "I regret to inform you that we do not have that much merchandise on hand—not of a kind that can match the Coalition's Ein Dolphs."

"We anticipated as much," said Naryal, "so we prepared our own design. Private Ritter, if you would be so kind..."

Ritter's pulse raced as the moment of truth arrived. He took a deep breath, strode up to Zeklov, and handed him the micro-drive he'd kept in his coat pocket. The Director scrutinized the thin plastic strip momentarily and plugged it into the table. Specifications appeared on both screens as a 3D wire-frame model of a sturdy CF with a domed head floated above the drawing board.

Zeklov pored over the specs, and Ritter's palms began to sweat. He stuck them in his pockets as the director spoke. "A formidable design. Unless I'm mistaken, these files contain a full set of plans for a close combat plasma weapon."

"In light of the Secretary-General's lawless actions," said Naryal, "I deemed it appropriate to share the Coalition's technology."

Zane grumbled from the shadows to Ritter's left.

"Can you mass-produce this design?" Jean-Claude asked.

"Technically, no," Zeklov said.

Ritter's heart sank. "Why not? I've been working on those plans for months! Sieg Friedlander, Max Darving, and these guys helped refine them. What's wrong?"

Zeklov removed his glasses and cleaned them with his red pocket handkerchief. "Do not misunderstand. The design is sound, and you rightly call it the Grenzmark III, but my company does not hold the manufacturing rights for combat frames in the Grenzmark line."

"Since Secretary-General Megami nationalized Seed Corp, the Grenzmark and all related patents belong to the SOC itself." Naryal chuckled. "As a duly appointed Coalition governor, I hereby grant you a license to mass-produce the Grenzmark III."

"Most magnanimous of you," Zeklov said. "How much is the licensing fee?"

"Give us a twenty percent discount on the wholesale price," said Naryal, "and we'll call it even."

"Agreed," said Zeklov.

"Not to rush you," Jean-Claude said, "but Megami could strike at any time. Will your materials shortage delay production?"

A sly smile twisted Zeklov's lip. "The EGE are not the only ones with Coalition connections. I married one of my daughters to Dyer Zend of the Transportation Ministry. Their daughter Irenae is a close friend of the Secretary-General. My supply chain problems have already been resolved."

"This is fantastic," gushed Ritter. "We're arming the EGE with CFs based on a Soc design, and one of Megami's friends is helping us build them!"

"The first run of Grenzmark IIIs will be completed in thirty days," Zeklov said. "As a reminder, the Dauphin's and the Governor's combat frames will be fully repaired in three. If there's no other business, I bid you all good day. Go with God's blessing."

"I have business." Zane strode toward the table. "Dead Drop was damaged in a fight with Megami's stooge Masz. I need it fixed and upgraded for a rematch."

Zeklov replaced his glasses at looked down his hawkish nose at Zane. "Masz pilots a Zwei Dolph—the Coalition's most advanced combat frame—customized by Tesla Browning himself. He is the CSC's leading ace. You could not afford the modifications necessary to make yourself his equal."

"I'll foot the bill," said Ritter. All eyes turned to him.

"How do you propose to pay on a Private's salary?" asked Zeklov.

"The Black Reichswehr didn't have just one cache," Ritter said. "Kopp had loot stashed all over Africa. I know where most of it is."

Naryal frowned.

"Are you certain you want this, Ritter?" Jean-Claude asked.

"Dead Drop is our most powerful weapon right now," said Ritter, "and it'll be fixed long before the Grenzmark IIIs roll out. Like you said, Megami could hit us any time."

Zeklov sighed. "Very well. I shall have Mr. Dellister's Dead Drop brought down to the factory. Private Ritter will receive an estimate as soon as my staff perform a full diagnostic."

Zane's expression remained flat, but his eyes wavered. "You hear that, Dead Drop? Next time we're taking Masz down!"

30

Sieg sat bolt upright in bed, panting and covered in cold sweat. Waking stole the memory of dreaming, but the dread that followed him from sleep made him grateful to forget. Strange voices whispered in the dark. They faded as Sieg came fully awake only to realize he had no idea where he was.

"What is this place?" Sieg's words rasped in his burning throat.

"You're on Metis. You're been asleep for over twenty-four hours."

That voice he did recognize. "Liz?"

Light footsteps fell on thin carpet, and clothing rustled as someone approached. "Yes. How do you feel?"

"Like Metis fell on me. What was in that shot?"

Megami sat down at the end of the bed. "I'm sorry about the side effects. The memories should come soon. You acknowledge I'm your sister?"

A bitter chuckle forced its way through Sieg's parched lips. "No sense denying it. I can feel you. Do you expect me to forgive all the blood you've shed?"

Megami sighed. "Even I can't believe what I've done sometimes."

"I've made my own mistakes," Sieg confessed. "I failed you."

"Yes," Megami said, "you did. Does that sound cruel? The concept has lost all meaning for me."

Sieg sought his sister's delicate hand in the darkness and clasped it in both of his. "Abandon the Coalition, Liz. On Earth I learned that anyone can walk away and start over. Let's leave them all—the Socs, the grounders—and build new lives together."

Megami gave her brother's hand a startlingly strong squeeze. "My future was decided when Sanzen put the monster in my blood. I was too weak to stop it, but you might be strong enough to stop me."

Sieg pulled back. "I crossed heaven and earth to save you. I won't kill you."

"You're making a mistake. I'm about to unleash horrors humanity's never seen."

"I stopped being afraid a long time ago," said Sieg. "And I never stopped loving you."

"That's two more mistakes." Megami said.

"What the hell are you building for her?" Max wondered aloud.

Perched above the Metis factory floor on a cherry picker, Tesla Browning turned from the giant metal skeleton propped against the wall and peered down at the new arrival. "*We* are building a combat frame that exceeds all current technological limitations."

Max had slept off his mental fatigue on the flight from Kisangani. Upon arrival a team of uniformed Socs had brought him to the secret factory in the heart of Metis. He had no idea how to get out, but standing in the shadow of Megami's death machine incited a desperate urge to try. Instead he buried his concerns in work. "Save the ad copy for next investors' meeting. Give me some numbers."

"We've developed new composite armor consisting of layered carbyne and lithium plastic sheets," Browning said. "Test samples withstood the equivalent impact of a locomotive pulling ten fully loaded box cars at 150 kilometers per hour."

"Putting a weapon like that in Megami's hands will leave the blood of millions on ours," said Max.

Browning's platform descended to the polymer-coated stone floor with a hydraulic whirr. He swung the orange steel gate open and approached Max. "You're right, of course," Browning said softly enough for the ambient machine noise to keep the toiling Seed Corp techs from eavesdropping. "Project S began with Sanzen. Even the XSeed is just an intermediate step."

"*XSeed*?" repeated Max.

Browning jabbed a thumb over his shoulder at the looming humanoid mass of struts, cables, and motors. "The XCD-001-1, to be precise. This combat frame will be the last *from Seed* Corporation, since production began before the Secretary-General nationalized the company."

"Sounds like something one of the old tech oligarchs would've come up with."

"Perhaps," said Browning, "but this unit's capabilities are truly revolutionary. The plasma rifle that cut a path of destruction through Algiers was a proof of concept mockup of the XSeed's main armament."

The rock under Max's feet seemed to become mud. "And Megami considers this monster an 'intermediate step'?"

"The project's next phase is a multi-stage orbital weapons system capable of global-scale destruction."

Max sucked in a lungful of metallic-tasting air and slowly let it out. "How close is the XSeed to completion?"

"The only remaining design hurdle is the XCD-001-1's core operating system," said Browning. "Megami specified an artificial intelligence capable of real-time learning to enable adaptation during combat. Therein lies your one chance to avert democide."

"It's not much of a chance," said Max. "Megami will have her people go over my code with a scanning electron microscope."

"Undoubtedly," said Browning. "Perhaps the best way to influence a learning machine is with the right teacher." He produced a dark blue handheld device from his lab coat's inside pocket and handed it to Max. A familiar GUI flashed to life on the rectangular screen.

"Hello, Max," Marilyn's voice greeted him. "I hope you can hear me over this device's crude speakers."

"I can hear you just fine, honey," said Max. "And it's music to my ears." Concern tempered his joy. "Marilyn wasn't Megami's only hostage," he told Browning. "Do you know where she's holding an EGE Navy Lieutenant named Li Wen?"

Browning straightened his glasses. "The intelligence officer who convinced you to defect? She's not here on Metis to my knowledge. The only ones who've been brought up from Earth recently are you and Sieg Friedlander."

"Sieg's here? What does Megami want with him?"

"She brought him to test the XSeed, but so far he's been indisposed due to illness."

Browning and Sieg are here with me helping Megami build a next-generation murder machine. She lied about Wen, but she let Browning transfer Marilyn from the Thor Prototype. Max tried to arrange the pieces, but no coherent picture emerged.

"Did something I said distress you?" asked Browning.

Everything, thought Max, *mostly because I'm not sure I can trust you.* He slid Marilyn's temporary housing into his flight suit's front pocket. "Let's get to work. The sooner we're done here, the better."

A glimpse of blue amid the muted earth tones of the Siberian woods alerted Ritter to the Ein Dolph's position. His Grenzmark III's state-of-the-art sensors locked onto the Soc CF from half a klick away. Ritter aimed his 115mm rifle and fired on full auto. Deafening staccato booms resounded through the trees, many of which exploded into splinters in the giant shells' path.

The dust and waste heat dissipated. Ritter got a clear view of the Dolph thanks to the felled trees. The boxy Soc CF's blue armor bore a coating of sawdust but not a single scratch.

The Dolph's black visor fixed itself on the Grenzmark III, but Ritter fired his new CF's rockets before the enemy could level his plasma rifle. The g's crushed Ritter into his chair. *This'll help break it in!*

Ritter's view of the woods blurred into a panorama of gray clouds. He brought the throttle down to hover above the forest canopy, through which a red flash blazed. A line of trees stretching from where he'd just stood to the horizon disintegrated in a cloud of flame.

Where is he? Ritter's sensors reacquired the Dolph in the woods below. An orange-white burst on his thermograph told him the Soc CF was firing its thrusters. The Dolph blasted up through the leafy canopy, its plasma rifle trained on Ritter's Grenzmark. Ritter launched a warhead from each of the missile pods attached to his CF's legs. The Dolph obliterated one missile in a crimson flash, and the other streaked past the target's left shoulder.

Ritter slid left on maneuvering thrusters ahead of the Dolph's next shot. His return machine gun fire didn't penetrate the Soc CF's armor, but it did distract the enemy from Ritter's second missile, which had curved around to home in on the Dolph's back. The impact took out half the blue CF's thrusters and blew it toward its opponent.

Racking his machine gun, Ritter drew his plasma lance. He ignited the double weapon and impaled the Soc's cockpit on the longer front blade. The Dolph fell smoking into the trees.

"The Grenzmark III is even better than I thought! If the production models perform this well, the Socs won't stand a chance."

"Not a bad cockpit shot." Zane's voice over the comm and the Grenzmark's chirping proximity alarm interrupted Ritter's celebration. A bright speck on the rearview monitor suddenly grew into Dead Drop's hard-edged black form. "Let me show you how it's done!"

Dead Drop screamed toward Ritter's back, leading with its violet plasma sword. Ritter spun in time to block with his plasma lance. Humming sparks flew where his green blade and Zane's purple blade clashed. Ritter levered his lance's rear blade up toward Dead Drop's right side, but Zane bisected the lance's two-gripped hilt with a diagonal slash and jabbed his sword's blazing plasma column into Ritter's cockpit.

Ritter groaned as the hatch in front of him hissed open. The warm dry air and industrial clamor of Zeklov's factory inundated him. The recently upgraded Dead Drop stood in its maintenance dock across the wide aisle from Ritter's unfinished Grenzmark III. "I know you're itching for a fight," he shouted to Zane, "but did you have to gatecrash my simulation?"

Dead Drop's cockpit opened. Zane poked his platinum blond head out. "Anything can happen on the battlefield. I just threw in a wild card. You should thank me."

"Hey, Zane," a familiar feminine voice called from the floor below. Dorothy ran around an approaching column of EGE soldiers to stand at Dead Drop's feet. She wore the same olive jumpsuit as the soldiers, and her light brown hair peaked out from under a matching field cap.

Zane's brow knotted. "What are you doing here?"

"She tagged along with me." Major Collins signaled the column to halt between Dead Drop and the Grenzmark. The scar traversing his dark left eyebrow was visible from ten meters up. "Colonel Larson has ordered our new CF teams to train on Zeklov's simulators. I'm to oversee their training and liaise with Zeklov on the Army's behalf."

Ritter hopped out of the cockpit and climbed down the scaffold surrounding the incomplete Grenzmark III—one of many arranged in rows across the expansive factory floor. Bare of the improved armor he'd co-designed, the new CF resembled a burly steel skeleton with carbon nanotube muscles and a thick black halo minus a head.

Collins saluted when Ritter reached the ground. "We haven't had a chance to talk since the Socs attacked the fleet," the Major said. "I saw Dellister's recording of your action against that Zwei Dolph. Damn fine work. Somewhere, Zimmer is smiling."

Zane landed hard between Dorothy and Collins, preempting Ritter's reply. "What about me?" asked Zane.

"I'd commend you if you weren't just out for yourself," Collins said.

Dorothy clutched Zane's arm. "He's not selfish, Major."

"Thanks," said Zane.

"He's crazy," she explained.

"I won't argue," said Collins. "Look here. Governor Troy has seized North Africa and could strike at any time. Our Shenlongs are no match for the enemy's combat frames. McCaskey wants both of you, du Lione, and Naryal to reinforce the EGE fleet off the African coast."

"Dead Drop's almost ready," said Zane, "but who cares about this Troy guy? I want a rematch with Masz."

"See what I mean?" Dorothy said.

217

"I won't have a combat frame until the Grenzmark IIIs roll out at the end of the month," said Ritter.

Collins set his jaw. "Let's hope the Socs do us the courtesy of waiting."

31

Is this what I fought for? Sieg pondered in his seat on the blue-curtained stage erected in Metis' cavernous hangar. *Elliot, Werner, Chase. Is this what you died for?*

The stage had been set up by a small detail of the 300,000 Kazoku who'd assembled to hear the Secretary-General's address. Megami stood front and center at the glass podium with her back to Sieg and the handful of other dignitaries on stage. Her full attention remained fixed on the sea of gray-uniformed soldiers arranged in ordered columns on the wide deck.

Though seated above the crowd, Sieg couldn't shake the feeling of being surrounded. Perhaps the silence fostered his unease. As the son of a prime minister, he'd been dragged to countless speeches, rallies, and assemblies. The white noise of a thousand conversations always preceded the main event—except this time. The Kazoku waited in silent obedience.

"The Coalition has failed." Megami's breathy voice swept through the enormous room like a chill breeze. "Guilt drove them back to the barbarous earth. Fear made them too risk-averse to combat barbarism."

His sister's words came to Sieg as an epiphany. Maintaining skepticism took an act of will.

"My predecessors spent their careers fumbling to contain Earth's corruption," Megami continued. "Mitsu sought political and economic quarantine. Sanzen lusted for conquest. What blind fools!"

Sieg knew without looking that Eiyu Masz lurked just behind the giant screen traversing the back of the stage. Officially Masz was running security—not that Liz could get much more secure in the midst of her own fanatical army. *And they don't get more fanatical than Masz.*

Megami's already cool voice turned frigid. "What did Mitsu and Sanzen achieve besides the deaths of our brethren?"

The first faint murmurs arose from the crowd. Sieg felt their mounting anger as if it were his own.

"Man crawled from the primordial muck only to bathe in blood," Megami said. "Stumbling toward the stars made him no more able to curb his murderous appetites. His disease threatens to contaminate the stars. A force beyond man is needed to end man's brutal reign. That force stands massed here, today."

A susurrus of assent passed through the Kazoku ranks.

The skirts of Megami's blue trench coat swirled as she pivoted toward the towering screen, which cut to a live view of the asteroid's cratered gray surface. The frame was centered on a titanic cluster of rocket nozzles jutting from the rocky ground. "This moment marks the start of our triumph and the beginning of history's end. There is no past, no future; only an eternal now. I hereby decree that all dates be reckoned from this current and final year!"

A whiteout mercifully dampened by image processing enveloped the screen. Sieg felt himself, and everything around him, nudged forward. The picture cleared to show the colossal engines spewing pillars of fire into the black sky.

"Our task is clear," Megami told her Kazoku. "We will purge the human infestation from the earth and cleanse the sky."

Rapturous cheers filled the hangar as Megami left the podium. She nodded to Sieg, who rose and followed her into the hallway behind the stage. Personnel of every class from officers to technical crew lined the narrow corridor. They paused and stared in awe as the girl who'd led the Coalition—who'd now decayed into something monstrous—passed them by.

Sieg waited till his sister entered a door giving on an empty hallway before grabbing her arm. "What the hell was that speech, Liz?"

Megami spun to face him. Her face betrayed mild amusement. "The beginning of the end."

"You've become everything Dad spent his life fighting. He's spinning in his grave right now!"

"He doesn't have a grave," Megami said. "I made sure there wasn't enough of him left."

The strength drained from Sieg's hand. Megami slid free of his grip just before wrenching pain shot up his other arm. Sieg doubled over in agony as hands like iron forced him into a joint lock.

"I'm sorry he touched you," Masz said from behind Sieg. "I tried to stay hidden."

Through the red fog of pain, Sieg realized he'd lost his constant sense of Masz's whereabouts. The unnerving sensation returned with interest.

"It's okay," said Megami, circling Sieg's bent, helpless form. "He can't hurt me. He never could."

Sieg tried to struggle against Masz's grip, but he may as well have been arm wrestling a Grenzie. He could only emit a pained gasp.

"Disappointing," Megami said. Her voice reinforced the sentiment. "He's nowhere near your level, let alone mine. Genetics really is a throw of the dice."

The pressure on Sieg's arm increased, bringing unimagined levels of pain. "Should I kill him?" asked Masz.

A moment passed. "Let him go," said Megami.

Masz inflicted one more jolt of maddening pain before releasing his hold. Sieg straightened, rubbing his tortured shoulder, and glared at his sister.

"I'm taking you off Project S," Megami said. "Masz is the XSeed's new test pilot." She nodded to her bootlicker. "I'm putting you in command of Metis and moving Irenae Zend to Astraea. Put my brother on a shuttle to Byzantium colony. He tried so hard to get into Sanzen's compound. Let him wait for me there."

Masz grabbed Sieg's upper arm, more gently this time, and forced him down the hall toward the hangar.

Sieg looked back at his sister. "I wish I'd never found out you're alive."

Max had begun work on the XSeed's operating system under duress, but he'd soon come to savor the challenge. Megami wanted a strong A.I. that could supplement a pilot's skills by learning to make its own combat decisions. She coveted the same capability the EGE feared.

She'd also stipulated that Prometheus—as Max had christened his experimental OS—have the ability to coordinate XSeed's targeting systems with a command vessel via free-space laser. Max was strictly forbidden from discussing that feature, even with other techs on the same top-secret project.

Thanks to the extravagant resources the Socs had provided, Max had surmounted the technical challenges set before him in rapid succession. While he felt a swell of pride at having brought Prometheus to near-completion in record time, knowing that a genocidal tyrant would reap the fruits of his labor tarnished his achievement.

That was why today, when Max expected to finish work on the XSeed's OS, he also planned to throw a wrench in Megami's schemes.

Figuring out how to screw her over presented another dilemma. Max's workstation had no external connectivity, just a keyboard and a mic for verbal commands. Soc software engineers checked every line of code prior to insertion in Prometheus' architecture. A single guarded door secured with biometric locks gave access to the palladium glass-enclosed lab.

It was Browning who'd pointed Max in the right direction. An emergency override or backdoor in Prometheus' code would have been spotted. Instead, Max would give Megami the learning A.I. she demanded and give Prometheus the best possible teacher.

Marilyn still resided on Max's handheld. Outside devices were banned from the lab, but today the inhumanly vigilant Kazoku guards were scheduled to attend some kind of rally in the main hangar. Max bet he could sneak Marilyn in under the temp guard's nose for a quick chat with Prometheus. A fraction of a second would be long enough for his first A.I. to impart her wisdom to her successor.

Once they made it inside, the operation would be out of Max's hands. He'd be counting on Marilyn to sway Prometheus. Plus he had no way of knowing what she could convince him of and no say in how she'd go about it. He couldn't discount the possibility that the more advanced A.I. might talk Marilyn into joining the Socs.

The risks were high, but so were the stakes, and Max had no other options. He strolled down the polished stone hallway toward the microalloy glass door with the handheld's hard rectangle tucked in his belt. Max breezed past the bored-looking Soc guard and submitted his thumbprint and retina scan. The door hissed open, letting the low hum of cooling fans emanate from within.

"Aren't you forgetting something?" a breathy feminine voice called from the hallway.

The hairs on Max's neck stood up. He turned.

Megami stood ten paces behind him dressed in a Kazoku uniform and a navy blue trench coat. Her two-bit thug Masz leered at Max from over her shoulder, but the SecGen had locked eyes with the guard.

The round-faced Soc on the door snapped out of his malaise and stood up from his desk. "Empty your pockets," he ordered Max.

"Weren't you giving a speech today?" Max said as his mind raced. He put on a cocky grin, hoping to buy more time.

"I already did," Megami said. "I hate long speeches. You heard the man."

Max turned out his pants, shirt, and lab coat pockets, producing only a couple of chewed plastic pens. He shrugged.

"Use the wand," Megami told the guard. The dumpy fellow ran a spatula-sized metal detector over Max's body. The device squawked when it passed over the small of his back.

Trying not to show his panic, Max reached back and pulled out the blue oblong handheld.

"You always keep that back there?" Megami asked.

"I must've forgot," said Max.

"Right." The SecGen pointed to the guard. "Hand it over."

Max slapped Marilyn's current vessel into the guard's chubby palm. The suddenly conscientious sentry switched off the device and locked it in a drawer of his metal desk.

"You can have it back when you're done," Megami said. "I expect nothing less than greatness." She turned on her heel to leave. Masz skulked after her.

Max's anger boiled over. "Where are you keeping Li Wen?" he shouted at her back.

"You'll see her after tomorrow's successful test flight," said Megami. "The XSeed's OS had better be finished by then. And Max? Cross me again, and I'll slit your throat."

32

Naryal sat back in Jagannath's pilot seat and panted for several moments after the simulation ended. She lowered her green jumpsuit's zipper to dangle between her breasts and took some relief in the coolness of evaporating perspiration.

"You fought well, my dear." The main monitor showed Jean-Claude poised halfway out of Veillantif's cockpit, striking a naturally dashing pose with one foot on the open hatch.

Naryal opened her fully repaired CF's cockpit to face her opponent across the subterranean factory floor. A mechanical chorus drifted from the distance, where Zeklov's men hurried to finish the Grenzmark IIIs. "Thank you," she said, her respiration still slightly elevated. "If I didn't know better, I'd say you let me win."

Jean-Claude's muscled arms, bare to the shoulders in his white cotton shirt, bore only a light glow of moisture in the harsh overhead lights. He laughed. "If you desired victory, what man could withhold it?"

"Point taken," Naryal said, unable to suppress a wry smile.

A chime from her control panel drew Naryal's attention to an unexpected message. During the Davis affair, she'd assigned a rudimentary A.I. to monitor her late security chief's communications. The digital watchdog was programmed to alert her if anyone accessed a tagged account. She scanned the alert and blinked. Davis was weeks in his grave, but someone had just logged in to the "Elizabeth" folder under his main alias.

"You seem distracted," Jean-Claude called from Veillantif's berth across the aisle. "Is everything alright?"

The Prince's words barely registered as Naryal absorbed the message that had been left for her to find. She read the short but earth-shattering missive once more like a lottery winner double-checking the numbers on a ticket.

"Find Zane and Ritter," she told Jean-Claude as she unbuckled her safety harness. "Bring them to Zeklov's office in ten minutes."

"I am sure M. Zeklov will lend you his office," Jean-Claude said, "but why not receive us in your suite?"

Naryal stepped onto the catwalk positioned in front of her cockpit's hatch. "Because we need the most secure room in the factory. Tell no one else. I'll meet the three of you there."

Jean-Claude and Zane were already sitting on the red velvet seats lining the front wall of Zeklov's office when Naryal entered. Ritter stood by the drafting table, toying with a holographic Grenzmark III. Dellister stared into the shadows of the ceiling as if captivated by something only he could see.

The Prince rose to kiss her hand. "We have done as you asked, Mademoiselle. Perhaps now you will share the reason for this clandestine meeting?"

Naryal visually searched the mostly darkened room. Zeklov certainly had active recording devices, but he didn't concern her. In all likelihood, the Russian industrialist's factory was more secure than her own home in Jeddah.

"Minutes ago I received a sensitive message from deep within Secretary-General Megami's inner circle," Naryal said. "I believe the source is Sieg Friedlander."

Ritter looked up from the table, his jaw slack. "Sieg is with Megami?"

"She's in L1," Zane said to the ceiling.

The sight of Dellister, clad in black as if in homage to the combat frame he shouldn't have been able to build, raised Naryal's hackles.

She almost asked Zane how he knew, but her better judgment prevailed.

"It seems that Sieg and Megami had a falling out," said Naryal. "He's been confined to Sanzen's old residence in Byzantium colony. Lieutenant Li is being held in the same location."

"Does Max know?" asked Ritter.

"Captain Darving has been coerced into an advanced weapons development project at the Kazoku asteroid base Metis," said Naryal. "He is collaborating with Tesla Browning on a combat frame to make all others obsolete."

"It must be related to the plasma rifle Zane and I found," Ritter said. "Megami can't get her hands on that kind of power! By the way, what's a Kazoku?"

Naryal faced Zane and folded her arms. "Perhaps you should ask Mr. Dellister."

Zane kept his eyes on the ceiling and his mouth shut.

"The Kazoku are a private army engineered by Sanzen for fanatical loyalty," Jean-Claude said. "Now they serve Megami."

"That's even worse," groaned Ritter.

"I agree," Naryal said, "especially since Metis is headed for Earth."

Jean-Claude rose to his feet again. "That absolute maniac! What does she intend?"

"The extermination of human life on Earth," said Naryal. "An army of Kazoku equipped with Dolphs supported by this new CF called XSeed would go a long way toward achieving that goal. Sieg also suspects Megami intends to drop Metis on us from orbit."

"I know Megami's a bloodthirsty tyrant," Ritter said, "but why would she want to wipe out Earth's population?"

"Fear," said Zane.

Ritter's brow knotted. "Megami's afraid of us?"

Zane shook his head. "Not her."

"Who, then?" Jean-Claude asked slowly.

Dellister's heavy-lidded eyes snapped open. He sat up. "What?"

"We're wasting time," said Naryal. "Metis will arrive in Earth orbit in four days. Megami is currently in L1 negotiating a treaty with representatives from L3. Prime Minister Venn is expected to sign. If so, ZoDiaC's involvement in this conflict will come to an end. The EGE will be on its own."

Ritter broke the ensuing silence. "We need to hit Metis now—rescue Max and destroy this XSeed."

"I concur," Jean-Claude said. "It will be too late once Metis arrives and we are on the defensive. Who commands the asteroid in Megami's stead?"

"The same Kazoku pilot who executed Omaka, abducted Li Wen, and decimated the fleet," Naryal said. "Eiyu Masz."

Zane leapt to his feet and stormed out the door. "Stop him," Naryal shouted as she chased the mad pilot. Jean-Claude and Ritter followed her into the hallway.

"Wait!" said Ritter. "You can't just walk out on us like this."

"Dead Drop is stronger than ever," growled Zane. "We'll blow Masz out of the stars."

Major Collins stepped around the next corner into Zane's path. "Where do you four think you're going?"

Dellister didn't slow. Naryal watched in dread anticipation of seeing an unstoppable force collide with an immovable object, but Dorothy rushed out from behind Collins and interposed herself between the two men.

"I was gonna ask you the same question," Dorothy said to Zane. "You shouldn't be going anywhere in your state."

"I didn't hear an answer." Collins stood in his olive flight suit, his legs planted shoulder width apart and his arms behind his back. His green eyes drilled into each of the four conspirators by turns.

Naryal stood her ground. "I'm not obliged to tell you any—"

"Max is in trouble," Ritter blurted out. "Megami is making him build her weapons on an asteroid that's crashing into the earth!"

"Is that true?" Collins asked.

Naryal rubbed her temples. "More or less."

"And you didn't see fit to share this intel with me?" Collins' scar stood out on his reddening face. "How exactly did you plan to mount a space operation to begin with?"

"I'm a Coalition governor. I was going to arrange a shuttle flight from Kisangani using my official right of free travel." She shot a withering look at Ritter. "Until someone compromised the mission."

"You're all under arrest," Collins said.

Dorothy rounded on the Major. "What did I do?"

"Shut up!" said Collins.

"Listen, Major," Ritter said. "That space rock will be here in four days, and it's bringing a whole army just like the guy who thrashed us. Megami's left the premises, and we've got a small opening to rescue Max."

Collins' face almost hid his warring impulses. "I'll have to contact Colonel Larson."

"Your devotion to the chain of command is admirable, Major," Jean-Claude said, "but we have no time to bring this matter before a committee. By all means, contact your superiors while M. Dellister, Private Ritter, and I mount our rescue attempt."

"Max is only in this mess because we let him down before," said Ritter. "You taught me to make up for my mistakes. Help me make this one up to Max."

Collins' eyes softened. "I can't let the pilots of our three most powerful CFs go gallivanting off to outer space and leave the fleet exposed."

"I volunteer Jagannath for fleet defense," said Naryal. "It isn't necessary for me to board the shuttle, anyway. The others can fly on my credentials."

Jean-Claude laid his strong hand on her arm. "Veillantif and I shall stand with you."

"I've got a score to settle," said Zane. "There's no way I'd miss a rematch with Masz."

"If you're going," Dorothy said, "so am I."

All eyes stared at the American nurse.

"Zane's suffering from OCD and dissociative personality disorder," Dorothy explained. "Does anyone else want to deal with him if he has another episode?"

"You and the Dauphin will fly back to the fleet with me," Collins told Naryal. "Ritter, I'm granting you a field promotion to Corporal and lending you a squad of my men. They'll accompany you, Dellister, and Wheeler to Metis. Understood?"

Ritter saluted. "Yes, sir!"

Collins returned the salute and stalked off down the hall. He paused, glanced over his shoulder at the Corporal and said, "Bring everyone home."

33

Max kept glancing from his screen to the window overlooking the Metis test hangar. A huge metal face stared back. The XSeed instilled a dread fascination he hadn't felt since he'd stood on his father's porch watching a twister rip through a neighbor's farm.

In Max's defense, everything about the XCD-001-1 Prometheus commanded attention. Its blue-on-white paint scheme stood out against the hangar's gray stone and steel. The XSeed's brawny limbs and thick torso resembled boxier CFs like Dead Drop and the Dolphs, but with the sharp edges filed down. Its helmeted head, whose twin optical sensors held an almost human expression, unnerved Max most of all.

Except for that gun, Max corrected himself. The plasma rifle's dark gray barrel peaked out from the leading edge of the coffin-shaped shield clamped to the XSeed's left arm, leaving its right hand free for one of the two plasma swords jutting from the CF's back.

"I'm losing my patience," Masz hissed over the XSeed's cockpit comm. "Give me clearance to launch."

Down the row of consoles manned by Seed Corp transplants, Tesla Browning bent toward the control booth microphone. Max had never seen the Doctor's brown hair mussed or his lab coat wrinkled. Despite the pressure to succeed, he'd made no exception today. "Standby," Browning told Masz. "We will begin the test flight as soon as the ground team completes final checks."

231

Max pulled up the main status manager. The tech crews were leaving nothing to chance, testing every circuit and checking every bolt. Still, the XSeed's powerful bank of rockets was fueled and ready to unleash the ultimate weapon. Only minutes remained till Megami's death engine launched with her slavering henchman at the stick.

One of the Kazoku guards entered the booth for a brief exchange with Browning. The project lead strolled down the aisle between banks of consoles and leaned over Max. "I've just been informed of a shuttle inbound from Kisangani," Browning whispered. "There are no arrivals scheduled today, but the shuttle has valid diplomatic credentials. Is there anything I should know about?"

"Why ask me?" Max replied.

"Just playing a hunch," said Browning. "Apologies if I spoke out of turn. There is one more curious detail: Most Coalition shuttles have alphanumeric designations, but this one flies under the name *King of Hearts*."

With the gray-uniformed guard looking down the aisle, Max tried to keep his posture and expression neutral. "Can you get them landing clearance?"

"Not here," said Browning. "There's a small loading dock that serves this sector. I could say we ordered an emergency parts shipment and forgot to log it in all the excitement."

Max stole a glimpse at the Kazoku standing impassively at Browning's station. "The Kaks will be all over them as soon as they land."

"Leave that to me." Browning clapped a hand on Max's shoulder and drifted back down the row to confer with the guard. The low crosstalk drowned out their words, but the Kak left without shooting anyone. Max went through the motions of his work, all the while waiting for the hammer to fall.

"Tech crews reporting," one of the Seed controllers announced. "All systems check out. Pilot requests launch clearance."

"Flight control is online," said Browning. "Logistics and targeting?"

A moment passed before Max realized everyone was staring at him. He hastily checked Metis' connection to the XSeed's OS.

"Radio-optical targeting link established and secured." *If only I could've gotten Marilyn in touch with Prometheus.* It was too late now. Any unauthorized connections would be spotted immediately.

Browning spoke into the mic again. "XCD-001-1, you are cleared for launch. Take your position on the launch catapult and prepare to commence operations, over."

Tremors ran up through Max's feet as the XSeed tromped past the booth windows. The experimental CF stepped onto a rail catapult beside a Grento kept ready to launch in an emergency and lowered into a half-crouch. "I'm in position," said Masz.

A bright flash lit the hangar, and a shockwave shook the windows. At first Max thought the XSeed had launched early, but his vision cleared to reveal Prometheus still perched on the catapult.

Chaos engulfed the control room. Max checked the hangar camera feeds. A blackened section of deck to the right of the launch door indicated an explosion. Charred chunks of plastic and metal littered the area.

The Kak guard stormed into the booth. "What happened down there!?"

Browning's hands flew over his console. "We don't know for sure, but it seems a palette of fuel drums detonated. No damage to the XSeed."

"This test is cancelled pending a full investigation," said the guard. "Clear your people out of the hangar. We're locking the whole section down."

"Perhaps you should bring your people back in first." Browning pulled up an external camera feed on the booth's main monitor. The overhead screen showed four figures in dark blue spacesuits tumbling through the vacuum beyond the hangar door.

"All Sector V security personnel," the guard blurted into his comm, "we have men overboard! Report to the test hangar." He dashed from the room.

Max's head spun, but he knew that a sudden explosion that spaced four Socs wasn't a coincidence. He allowed himself a half-smile. *Browning, you underhanded bastard.*

A second flash from the hangar snapped Max back into the moment. The XSeed was nowhere to be seen.

"XCD-001-1," a controller yelled into the comm. "The launch is cancelled. Return to base!"

"Miss Megami wants this unit tested today," Masz said from the XSeed, which Max needed a telescope to see flitting through space. Thanks to its energy-eating 1D armor, Prometheus barely showed up on radar.

"Everyone remain calm," said Browning. "Unless I drastically misread the situation, an EGE extraction team is on its way. With security distracted, our rescuers should arrive any minute."

A Coalition tech two seats down from Max jumped to his feet and stabbed a finger at Browning. "You're talking mutiny!" The tech looked to his fellow Socs, who made up a minority of the control room staff. "You're not gonna let him get away with this?"

Max stood up and decked the scrawny tech across the face. The Soc slammed into his console and slid limply to the floor. "Anybody else?" Max called out.

The other Socs averted their eyes.

"Good," said Browning. "We've bought the EGE some time, but they're still in enemy territory. We should fortify our position against breach attempts. Captain Darving, would you direct our efforts?"

Max cracked the knuckles of his sore fist. "My pleasure."

"Who played the titular domestic on TV's *Mr. Belvedere*?" asked a tinny female voice.

Ritter's sealed helmet amplified his sigh. He'd dreaded being confined to a cargo shuttle for the twelve-hour flight to Metis with nothing to keep himself occupied. But as the trivia marathon hosted by NORMA, their A.I. pilot, stretched into its third hour, Ritter prayed for some peace and quiet.

"John Hillerman!" answered Specialist Josh Young, a member of the rescue squad Collins had sent with Ritter, Dorothy, and Zane.

"Incorrect," NORMA said.

"That was the dude from *Magnum, P.I.*," said PFC Ian Nixon. "Christopher Hewett played Mr. Belvedere."

"All these questions are about pre-Collapse pop culture," muttered Young.

"It's not like there's been much culture since then," said Private Seth Phillips.

"You know whoever wrote this dumb quiz never talked to a real girl."

The shuttle's cabin resembled the cargo box of Jean-Claude's transport plane, but with two rows of modular seats installed. The automated space freighter had no backup life support, requiring all passengers to wear spacesuits for the whole trip. Ritter only resisted the urge to switch off his suit's comm for fear of missing something important. NORMA's next transmission vindicated his patience.

"High-speed object sighted to starboard," the A.I. said.

Ritter sat up ramrod straight in his seat. "What kind of object?"

"No radar data available," said NORMA. "Limited to visual identification, I can only confirm that the object is a combat frame."

"Look!" said Dorothy. The American civilian sat in the front window seat next to Ritter. The finger of her bulky glove followed a bright white streak burning across the black of space.

That's a combat frame? marveled Ritter. He watched the manmade shooting star and wondered if even the blisteringly fast Dead Drop could match the white CF's speed.

"It's Masz." Zane's message gave Ritter a start, not just because the former CSC pilot had hardly spoken in twelve hours, but due to the venom in his voice. "I'm going after him."

Ritter gripped his chair's hard plastic armrests. Zane had insisted on traveling inside Dead Drop, which was loaded in the shuttle's cargo box. If he wanted to take off, possibly blowing their cover, none of them could stop him. *But if Masz really is out there, we might be better off if Zane keeps him busy.*

"We're five minutes from docking at Metis," Dorothy told Zane. "Just sit tight."

"You don't understand," snapped Zane. "I have to do this."

"Dead Drop launching from main cargo bay," announced NORMA.

Dorothy bowed her helmeted head and sighed. "He won't be happy till he gets himself killed."

Ritter looked over Dorothy's suited form as the deck shook. A blue-white fire trail zipped from the shuttle toward the speeding white star. *Pay Masz back for us, Zane. And stay alive.*

34

Zane got a clear look at the white combat frame before it showed up on radar, and he felt the pilot's vile presence long before that. His lips curled back from clenched teeth behind his helmet's visor. *Masz humiliated us, Dead Drop. Now we'll make him pay!*

The XSeed, as Naryal's source called the white CF, rocketed through the void twenty klicks above the lumpy gray surface of Metis. Zane tried to clock his quarry's speed, but he couldn't even paint it with a laser. Clearly the XSeed's outer layer was even more radiophobic than Dead Drop's nonconducting, heat-resistant armor.

No big deal. Nothing can shrug off a plasma bolt! His sensors' inability to pin down the XSeed didn't bother Zane. If he couldn't get a target lock, he'd just have to eyeball it. He deployed the plasma cannon housed in Dead Drop's left forearm, lined up a shot in the white CF's path, and fired. A violet beam blazed through the gas envelope raised by the titanic rockets on Metis' far side. Zane's beam missed the XSeed by an inch and impacted the surface.

Zane increased speed to keep his target in sight and fired again. This time the XSeed rolled to face him, causing the beam to narrowly miss its right pauldron. Zane tilted right a split second before the white CF fired the familiar rifle in its left hand. A thick blue beam lanced through Zane's previous position. Even in the thin atmosphere, the shock of its passing rattled his cockpit.

A second sapphire blast followed the first. Zane silently thanked Zeklov for the extra maneuvering thrusters that moved him clear of the XSeed's beams the instant he sensed Masz firing. He snapped off another shot of his own that kicked up a plume of vaporized rock from Metis' surface when the white CF dodged.

Despite the rage clouding his mind, Zane saw the odds stacked against him in a plasma gun duel where only his opponent could get a target lock. *I love a challenge.*

"Why do you keep interfering with our sister's work?" Masz rasped over the comm.

Zane's voice broadcast his incredulity. "You stole Dead Drop and nearly destroyed it. I don't give a damn about Megami!" He fired again. Blind wrath drove his shot into the void.

"You really are too stupid to live," said Masz. "Your combat frame was a means to an end. Its role is finished. You sought the past and lost your destiny. Now you can burn with all who oppose Miss Megami!"

The white CF pulled a back dive toward Metis, flipped over, and skimmed above the pitted surface toward the black horizon. Using the antennas studding the asteroid as reference points, Zane guessed the white CF was cruising near Mach 3.

"Time to test Zeklov's work." Zane fixed the dwindling white point in his sights and opened the throttle. Crushing force pinned him to his seat. The white dot steadily resolved into the XSeed's robust form. Euphoria washed over Zane as he overtook his foe. He detached his cannon's barrel, extended a blade of violet plasma from its muzzle, and swung at the white CF's exposed back.

The XSeed rolled and caught the blow with its shield. Layers of ablative coating boiled off the glossy surface. The white CF's right hand drew a plasma sword from its back, ignited the sapphire blade, and channeled the rest of its roll into a powerful slash at Dead Drop's midsection. Zane angled his sword and met the XSeed's blade. The blue-violet flare burned itself into his vision despite his screen's antidazzle filter.

"How could you have caught me in that inferior machine?" Masz shouted as their duel raged over the scarred face of Metis in a flurry of incandescent thrusts, slashes, and parries.

"Dead Drop's not as 'inferior' as you thought!" Zane blocked a savage hammer blow and drove the black CF's left fist into Masz's cockpit hatch. Hearing his opponent's pained grunt over the comm gave him visceral satisfaction. But his glee only lasted until the XSeed bashed its shield into Dead Drop's chest with a brutal backhand that forced the air from Zane's lungs.

Zane heaved a deep breath and saw the XSeed skimming perpendicular to the surface with its heavy plasma rifle pointed straight at him. His heart clenched as he realized Masz couldn't miss. Zane fired all his maneuvering thrusters downward. Dead Drop barely descended before the blue flash burst from XSeed's gun. *Goodbye, Dorothy.*

The fat sapphire beam blazed overhead. A ten-story satellite dish disintegrated in a firestorm of superheated gas five klicks behind Dead Drop. Zane felt the tremors through his chair when he touched down in a wide crater.

"I had you dead bang," whined Masz. "Darving's fire control software is trash!"

Zane smiled as he catapulted off the crater floor toward the XSeed, leading with his plasma sword gripped low in both hands. Rather than risk another shot with a faulty targeting system, Masz whipped the white CF around and blasted around the asteroid's curve, trailing white flame. Zane gave chase. "Stand and fight, Masz. You can't outrun us!"

Dead Drop gained steadily on the white comet, but a brighter pillar of fire appeared from beyond the horizon to outshine the fleeing XSeed. *Metis' rocket engines. What's Masz thinking?*

The inverse mountain of burning gas erupting from the cluster of football stadium-sized nozzles filled Zane's field of view. His close proximity to such a vast energy source played havoc with his radar, but he could just glimpse the XSeed—now a dark speck against the tower of light—plunging straight into the inferno.

Zane ground his teeth. Flying around the astronomical cone of rocket exhaust would take him over a klick out of his way. In a combat frame approaching Dead Drop's speed, Masz would certainly give Zane the slip long before Ritter and Dorothy completed their mission.

The exhaust's temperature averaged three thousand kelvins. Dead Drop's armor was designed to give some protection against far hotter plasma—for milliseconds at a time. Masz's willingness to fly through the rocket wash probably meant the XSeed was built to withstand atmospheric reentry. Could Dead Drop survive prolonged exposure to that kind of heat? Zane had no idea.

He dove headlong into the flames anyway. Unearthly forces battered Dead Drop as it passed facedown over the first nozzle. Zane redirected his maneuvering thrusters to fight the blazing torrent trying to shoot him into space. Dead Drop's altitude kept rising with its hull temperature, forcing him to divert main thrusters to steady his flight at a cost in speed.

Enveloped in a total whiteout, Zane had passed roughly a quarter of the way through the hellish gauntlet when his first maneuvering thruster blew. Dead Drop jerked upward. Zane angled another main thruster to compensate, slowing himself further. A second maneuvering booster burned out, followed by a main drive nozzle. Shrieking alarms and strobing red screens warned that external temperatures had exceeded armor limits.

Perhaps Zane lurched across the halfway mark. It was a moot point because all of his remaining drives were laboring to keep him from hurtling into space and losing his foe.

"Don't quit on me, Dead Drop. We've come too far to give up now!"

The last of Zane's thrusters died in the immolating heat. Dead Drop became a black metal coffin tumbling into the void.

Ritter unstrapped himself and rose from his seat as soon as the *King of Hearts* landed inside the Metis receiving dock. The six EGE soldiers followed his lead. Dorothy remained seated, her helmet's visor facing the window that looked out on the empty, rock and steel-walled hangar.

"Young, Nixon, Green, and Phillips, come with me," Ritter said. "Dorothy, why don't you monitor the comm from the cockpit?"

The young woman gave a start but unbuckled her harness and glided toward the front of the shuttle.

Ritter gestured to the last two men. "Thompson and Roth, stay with the shuttle and keep her ready to take off as soon as we get back with Captain Darving and his team. Zane might have given us extra time, but stay on your toes. The Socs may know we're here."

NORMA opened the hatch. Ritter rushed out and overshot the ramp in the low gravity. A firm hand grabbed his gun belt and pulled him down to the gangway. "Careful, sir," said Young. "Me and the other guys have been doing zero-g training in Zeklov's cargo planes. Operating in less than earth-normal gravity takes some getting used to."

"Thanks," said Ritter. "I'll take that lesson to heart."

Ritter's five-man fireteam skimmed across the empty loading dock floor with weapons ready. Ritter hoped he wouldn't have to use the super light carbon nanotube assault rifle cradled in his hands, but holding it felt reassuring.

The other men took up positions surrounding the heavy steel exit door while Young stood to one side and worked the control panel. The hatch slid open with a pneumatic hiss to reveal a clean hallway dressed with ceramic panels. White LED strips lined the corners. Phillips checked the corridor in both directions before motioning the others through.

A security door stood closed about fifteen meters to the right. Nixon bounded over and tested the reinforced hatch. "It's electronically locked. The controls are offline—probably on the other side, too."

"Captain Darving probably sealed this section when he got our landing request," said Young. "That makes finding the way easy." He pointed to another security door thirty meters down the hallway in the other direction. He led the team down the corridor with Ritter coming second.

Nixon tried the second door. "This one's locked too." His gloved fist thudded against the matte white ceramic. "Hey! This is the EGE. We're here to get you off this rock. Open up!"

A blast from the hallway's far end punctuated Nixon's order. The pressure slammed Ritter and his men against the door and the surrounding wall. Bullets were zipping through the air before Ritter collected himself. Thankfully, Young and Phillips were already returning fire against the gray-uniformed Socs who advanced through the blackened door frame, unencumbered by spacesuits.

Ritter pounded on the door. "Let us in!"

Nixon, who'd been knocked to the floor at Ritter's right, staggered to his feet and pushed the Corporal down. A bullet meant for Ritter tore through Nixon's side. The PFC rounded on the Socs, still gripping his weapon, but two more rounds punched through his suit's visor and painted the inside of his helmet with his blood.

Bring everyone home. Collins' words and Nixon's death spurred Ritter to spray the corridor's far end with automatic fire. The three Socs in the hallway hit the deck while the rest of their squad took cover on either side of the blasted-down door.

"It's open," Young shouted over the jackhammer din of gunfire. "Everybody inside. Move it!"

Ritter kept firing till his rifle clicked empty. He turned to see Green standing in the open doorway frantically waving Ritter through. A red trail on the floor showed that someone had seen to Nixon. He made a dash for the door. Green grabbed Ritter's outstretched arm and pulled him through. A volley of shots ricocheted off the opposite wall before Green pulled the heavy door closed.

"Locked," panted Green.

"That won't hold them for long," said Young, whom Ritter was glad to see standing in the short intersecting hallway to his right. His spirits fell when he saw Phillips rise from a crouch over Nixon's still form and shake his head.

"Let's keep moving," Ritter said.

The narrow hallway led to another closed hatch like the one giving on the loading dock. This door opened as the rescuers approached, revealing a hangar about half the length of the *Yamamoto's* but much taller. A Grento stood at rest near the launch door.

A man of average height wearing glasses behind his helmet's visor stepped forward from a group of ten spacesuited figures to greet the rescue team. "I'm Tesla Browning. I take it you arrived on the *King of Hearts*?"

"Dr. Browning," said Young. "I'm a fan of your work. Wish we had more time to chat, but there's a Kazoku squad breathing down our necks."

"I've lost Zane," Dorothy cried over the comm.

"Dorothy, calm down," said Ritter. "What do you mean you *lost him*?"

"NORMA kept Zane's comm channel open," Dorothy said, her voice shaking. "I heard him scream, and the line went dead."

"Have you tried reaching him since?" asked Ritter, trying to keep his own voice calm.

"Yes!" said Dorothy. "I keep trying, but he doesn't answer."

The image of Nixon lying dead in the hallway popped into Ritter's mind. His stomach turned. *I already broke my promise to Collins. I can't lose anyone else!* A conspicuous absence dawned on him. "Where's Max?"

Browning turned to answer. "He's—"

A bright flash filled the hangar as a white combat frame appeared outside the open launch door. It resembled a negative image of Dead Drop, only bulkier with blue accents and two blue lens "eyes" instead of a single purple visor.

"What is that?" marveled Green.

"It's a combat frame," said Young.

"It's the XSeed," shouted Browning.

Ritter felt like a gnat staring down an oncoming train as the XSeed aimed its monster plasma rifle into the hangar. He remembered carving a swath of destruction through the Algiers docks with a similar weapon. When it fired, the whole hangar would turn into a plasma furnace with Ritter and the men he was responsible for inside.

The Grento brought up its machine gun. "You won't even scratch that armor," yelled Browning. He and the hangar's other occupants dove behind metal crates and stacked plastic drums, for all the good it would do them. Only Ritter remained where he'd been standing, within ten meters of the rifle's muzzle. The XSeed's trigger finger moved.

Sorry, Major.

The XSeed's cockpit flew open. The pilot compartment explosively depressurized, sending a man in a gray spacesuit tumbling end-over-end through the void. He landed on the hard steel deck, bounced twice, and rolled to a stop five meters from Ritter.

The security door that Ritter and his team had entered through blew open. Men dressed like the ejected pilot stormed in, firing as they came. Young, Phillips, and Green shot back from behind cover as the Grento turned to face the invading Socs.

Ritter stared at the white CF's open cockpit—so near but so far away. He glanced at the Soc pilot, who rose to his hands and knees and met Ritter's eye with a murderous glare. A sudden impulse he couldn't name drove Ritter across the war-torn deck. He bounded toward the XSeed in a haphazard arc that brought him to the edge of space much sooner than expected.

Unable to reverse his momentum, Ritter channeled his forward motion into a final jump. His boot failed to find full purchase on the edge, and he propelled himself into the void with less than half the force he'd intended. He hung suspended between somewhere and nowhere for what felt like forever. A shot glanced off the white CF's chest a meter to his right, and time caught up with him. Ritter pitched forward to land upside down in the XSeed's pilot seat.

The hatch closed, immersing Ritter in silence and darkness. Monitors blinked to life as he righted himself and wriggled into a chair that seemed already conformed to him.

Ritter read the OS startup screen aloud. "Prometheus." The main monitor switched to a view of the hangar, where the Socs retreated from the advancing Grento through the breached door.

"You all right in there?" a familiar voice sounded from the comm.

"Max?" replied Ritter. "Where are you?"

The Grento's grilled face swiveled toward the XSeed, and its olive drab fist gave a thumbs up. "I commandeered this sucker when me and Browning's guys seized the hangar. Thanks for the backup."

"We're here to bring you home," said Ritter.

"Thanks, kid," said Max, "but the only place I'm going is L1."

"Collins ordered me to bring you back."

Max gave a bitter laugh. "The Major's going soft."

"I talked him into it."

"With charm like that, you'll reconquer Germany on your own someday."

"If you mean that," said Ritter, "you'll come back with me."

"Look Ritter, the queen bitch herself is holding Wen on Byzantium. I'm going after her, even if I have to fight past Sieg by myself."

"Why would you have to fight Sieg?" asked Ritter.

"Sieg's gone native. He found out Megami's his sister, and she flipped him."

A new possibility occurred to Ritter. *If I can bring back Li Wen and Sieg, it might make up for Nixon.*

A figure in a white spacesuit approached Max's Grento. "Captain," Dr. Browning called over their shared comm channel, "This belongs to you. I forgot to return it amid the commotion."

Ritter zoomed in on Browning's outstretched hand, which held a blue oblong device. Max's Grento knelt down, and the cockpit opened. Browning threw the device. It sailed upward in the low gravity, and Max caught it in his gloved hands.

"Hello again, Max," said Marilyn.

She's on that handheld! Ritter realized.

"You're a sight for sore eyes, honey," said Max. He turned his helmeted head toward the XSeed. "Should I ask why our boy Ritter is piloting Megami's death engine instead of Masz?"

"I debated Megami's human extermination agenda with Prometheus," said Marilyn. "In the end, he made the choice to oppose her."

"Good call, Prometheus," said Ritter.

"When did you two have time to debate?" asked Max.

"The clean room door was open for thirty point three four seconds before the guard turned me off," Marilyn said. "Prometheus and I were able to exchange over ten terabytes of data within that time window via high compression ultrasound bursts."

"That's my girl," said Max.

"Congratulations would seem to be in order, Captain," said Browning. "However, the Kazoku are certainly regrouping to storm this hangar. We should make our escape at once."

Ritter opened a line to the shuttle. *I just hope the Kazoku didn't board it!* "Come in, *King of Hearts*. This is Ritter. Do you copy?"

"I—I copy," Dorothy answered in a halting voice.

"Dorothy," said Ritter, "listen carefully. Tell NORMA to take off and dock in the experimental hangar next door. We need to evac Max, Browning, and their team. Understood?"

"I still can't reach Zane," Dorothy said on the verge of tears.

"It'll be easier to find Zane once we're all aboard the shuttle," Ritter insisted. "We're all counting on you. Bring the shuttle in for an evac. Do you understand?"

"I understand," Dorothy said softly.

"Good job, kid," said Max. "That can't have been easy for you. Did Zane go and get himself in another jam?"

Ritter's early warning alarm chirped before he could answer. His sensor screen showed six red dots speeding toward his location. He aimed his main camera in their direction, and a sextet of dark blue, boxy combat frames appeared on his monitor. "I've got six Dolphs inbound."

Max grunted. "That bastard Masz must've called in a strike." He shut his cockpit door and raised his Grento up to its full height. "The shuttle's a sitting duck against those Kaks."

Ritter tried to calm his fluttering stomach. His fists tightened on the XSeed's control sticks. His retreat from the Ein Dolphs at Kisangani flashed before his eyes while Collins' voice echoed in his ears. *Bring everyone home.*

"Barricade the interior door," Ritter ordered Young. "I'll take care of the Dolphs." The EGE soldiers rushed to comply.

"Wish it wasn't our only shot," said Max, "but here we are." His Grento stomped to the launch door's threshold and readied its machine gun."

"Have you ever piloted a combat frame in space?" asked Ritter.

"Only in a couple of sims," said Max. "Worry about yourself. I'll cover you."

"Six Dolphs nearly scuttled our whole fleet," Phillips said as he hurried toward the bomb-scarred door with a plasma torch. "What are Ritter's odds?"

"Ritter's not alone in there," said Max. "Prometheus is designed to assist the XSeed's pilot, if the pilot will trust him. Can you do that, Ritter?"

"Trust Prometheus?" stammered Ritter. "Like you trust Marilyn? I think so."

"You'd better," said Max. He pointed his 115mm machine gun at an acute angle to the left. "Because here they come."

35

Three hundred meters to the left of the test hangar, the *King of Hearts'* stretched-out hexagon hull began to inch out of the receiving dock. Six blue points of light were coming up fast twenty klicks behind it.

I can't let the Dolphs get within firing range of the shuttle! Ritter rotated his control stick. The XSeed made a fluid quarter pirouette to face the onrushing enemy with no lag between command and execution. "That was pretty smooth," Ritter thought aloud. "I hope the acceleration's on par with the turn time."

Ritter slid the throttle forward. He felt as if space itself flowed around him while the XSeed stood still. The shuttle blurred past on his left as the Dolphs grew in front of him.

"Don't pull too far ahead!" Max warned as he launched his Grento. "I can't lay down support fire beyond six klicks. Don't worry. Your gun has a longer effective range than theirs."

Ritter jerked the throttle back on reflex, only thinking how the sudden stop would send him lurching forward after the fact. To his surprise, the XSeed decelerated smoothly yet fast enough to keep from overshooting the Grento's maximum range.

"Was that you?" he asked Prometheus. If so, he was starting to understand Max's advice. The A.I. hadn't second-guessed him. It had enacted his intentions instead of his rash commands.

Red flashes lit the void. Two ruby beams gouged trenches in the asteroid's surface, and three lanced harmlessly into space, but one streaked past Ritter and over the lumbering shuttle's bow.

That was close! thought Ritter. "Dorothy, what's your ETA to dock?"

Another crimson barrage split the sky. This time, two plasma bolts buzzed the shuttle.

"NORMA says four minutes," answered Dorothy.

Can I hold them off that long? Ritter wondered. He climbed fifty meters on maneuvering thrusters and scanned the oncoming Dolphs. All six enemy CFs carried plasma rifles and coffin shields like the XSeed's own, except the latter were smaller and painted blue. They also sported visibly thicker armor.

They look kind of like Masz's custom CF. Must be Zwei Dolphs. Ritter fired down at the enemy leader. Having once discharged the XSeed rifle's prototype, he braced himself for overpowering recoil but marveled when a mild nudge traveled up his CF's right arm. The lead Dolph juked aside a split second before the fat blue beam shot through its previous position.

"Keep your eye on those Zwei Dolphs," said Max. "They're faster and tougher than Ein Dolphs, and their maneuverability's on par with yours."

The Zwei Dolph team aimed their rifles upward. Ritter fired retrorockets. The XSeed glided back from the red volley.

Better they shoot at me than the shuttle. Ritter switched tactics and locked onto the Dolph flying closest to Metis. His target veered toward the surface in response but hesitated, probably due to fear of crashing. Ritter's answering shot clipped the shield attached to the Dolph's left forearm. The shield exploded in a ball of smoke, but the Dolph kept coming.

Along with its five squadmates.

They'll hit the shuttle next. Ritter opened the throttle and swooped toward the incoming Dolphs, firing blue plasma bolts as he charged.

"Wait," Max radioed from just in front of the shuttle. "You're out of my range!"

The Dolphs rolled and banked as Ritter halved the distance between them. He set his neon green crosshairs on a random Dolph. His finger tensed to fire, but the reticle suddenly turned red. *I trust you,* he thought as his hand relaxed.

Prometheus locked onto the leader's left side wingman, who was correcting from a roll. Ritter fired. A brilliant blue plasma beam speared the Dolph vertically, disintegrating its head. The Soc CF exploded before Ritter could blink.

"We did it!" Ritter curtailed his celebration to bob and weave between five angry red plasma beams. The leader would have tagged the XSeed's left arm, but Prometheus added some extra lateral thrust. The ruby bolt passed close enough to fill Ritter's left screen. *Well, they didn't hit the shuttle.*

The Dolphs had closed to less than five klicks. Ritter worked with Prometheus to choose the next target. His reticle locked on, he fired, and the Dolph farthest to his right blossomed into a blazing sphere.

A shrill buzz snapped Ritter out of his trance. Two red zeroes flashed on his main display. He choked in panic.

"Ritter," shouted Max, "what's wrong?"

"I'm out of ammo!" Ritter ignited his retrorockets, but the four advancing Dolphs kept within plasma rifle range.

"Sit tight, kid," said Max. "I'll be right there."

The four Dolphs spread out in a diamond pattern. Ritter's mind reeled. He jetted up and to the right, but the leader's muzzle flash grew to encompass his vision. Ritter steeled himself for the red agony that would speed him into eternity.

A slight tremor traversed the cockpit. Instead of burning plasma, Ritter felt only cold sweat. *I'm still here. Did he miss?*

The answer came as a second ruby bolt struck the XSeed. Steam sizzled off the white CF's midsection, and again the cockpit rocked slightly, but Ritter's readout showed no significant damage. The third Dolph scored a direct hit on the XSeed's left leg with identical results. The fourth beam flew wide to Ritter's right.

"Each impact point lost one layer of armor," marveled Ritter. "I thought nothing could stand up to a plasma weapon."

"Carbyne composite armor can," said Max. "Check your ammo."

Ritter checked. The two zeroes had changed to zero one. Rather than question his luck, he darted down and to the side, lined up two Ein Dolphs, and fired. The pilots must have been stunned by their weapons' ineffectiveness, because their CFs barely moved before Ritter's shot blasted through both of them, leaving two white-hot balls of gas in its wake.

The leader's last wingman defiantly leveled his weapon at the XSeed. Ritter reflexively dodged before the enemy fired. The Dolph adjusted its aim for another shot, but a hail of shells pounded its right side. The Soc raised his shield and charged Max's Grento, which hung in front of the shuttle, spraying 115mm rounds.

Prometheus' readout showed zero ammo again, but a wire diagram of the XSeed highlighted two rods extending from the CF's back. Ritter reached XSeed's left hand over its shoulder to grab one of the devices. A battery indicator bar appeared on Ritter's screen reading fully charged. He toggled his weapon selector, and a scintillating blue blade sprang from the metal cylinder. *I've got plasma swords!*

Ritter rushed the charging Dolph at full speed. Space brought the Soc CF to him, and he slashed horizontally. His sapphire blade sliced through the enemy in a blazing arc. The XSeed shot past the bisected Dolph, and Ritter's rearview camera caught the ensuing explosion.

"Thanks for the assist," Ritter radioed to Max.

"Oh shit!" came the reply.

Ritter trained his main camera on Max's Grento. The Soc leader was rocketing straight toward the older CF and the shuttle close behind it, which had just cleared the loading dock. With no rifle ammo, Ritter would have to close with the agile Zwei Dolph before it shot Max down. "I'm coming," he yelled as he swiveled toward the receding enemy and punched the throttle.

Max kept his Grento positioned directly between the attacking Dolph and the shuttle. "Give me a hand, sweetheart," he said.

The Zwei Dolph fired. Its ruby beam melted the soles of the Grento's feet and singed the shuttle's keel. Max fired a short thruster burst to steady himself, carefully aimed his machine gun, and squeezed off a short burst of tank shell-sized bullets. The Zwei Dolph's rifle exploded, along with its right forearm.

Ritter finished his charge with a triumphant cry, but the Zwei Dolph drew its own plasma sword and rounded on him. Red plasma parried blue with a purple flash.

Turning his back on Max proved to be a mistake on the Soc's part. The Grento heaved forward and sank the curved blade of its heat axe into the seam between the Zwei Dolph's armored torso and left pauldron. Its whole left arm floated free. "Don't fuck with an engineer!" said Max.

"Send me to join my brothers," the surprisingly young-sounding Soc pilot broadcast to both of them.

Ritter pointed his blade at the Zwei Dolph's cockpit but moved behind the Soc CF and sheared off its thruster nozzles instead. "Come on," he said to Max as he glided toward the shuttle. "His friends will find him. Or they won't."

"You're one lucky son of a bitch," Max told the Soc before falling in beside Ritter.

"Why didn't you tell me the XSeed can absorb plasma bolts?" Ritter asked Max.

"Thinking you're invincible nearly got you killed ten times over," said Max. "I didn't want to encourage you."

"Nothing's killed me yet."

"That's what I mean," said Max. "FYI, the XSeed doesn't just absorb plasma. The 1D carbyne strings woven into its armor channel EM, thermal, and nuclear energy to an internal graphene capacitor. Hell, you'll even get a small charge from ballistic projectiles."

"The XSeed's armor steals enemies' shots and turns them into its own ammo?"

"It's not that simple. First, it's not really ammo. Your rifle draws power from the capacitor. That's why you're not lugging around a school bus-sized generator. It can store enough juice for twelve shots at a time. But not even superconductors are a hundred percent efficient. It takes three shots from a Dolph rifle to replenish one of yours."

"Is the ratio the same across the board?" Ritter asked.

"It depends on how big a punch whatever hits you is packing. Be careful, though. Your battery has limits. When it's full you're still bulletproof, but plasma weapons will wreck your day. You'll also be visible to radar."

"So I can recharge my rifle by taking hits," Ritter thought aloud, "but if I take too many the battery fills up, and the XSeed becomes vulnerable to energy weapons and easier to hit."

"The armor also ablates under energy weapon fire," said Max. "A direct plasma hit will burn off a layer of armor at the point of contact. You've got a hundred layers, but a hundred ain't infinite."

"Got it," said Ritter. "The best strategy is still conserving my ammo and not getting shot."

"One more thing," said Max. "No matter what, make sure you never take a shot to the capacitor itself."

"Is it that much worse than taking a shot to the reactor?"

"If the capacitor blows, that cold fusion reactor won't be cold anymore," said Max.

Ritter swallowed a sudden lump in his throat.

The XSeed and the Grento took up escort positions on either side of the shuttle as it maneuvered into the test hangar. "Get Browning and his team aboard," Ritter ordered his men once the shuttle and both combat frames had landed.

"Yes, sir," said Green. He and the other three soldiers moved to round up the techs.

The Grento limped over to an equipment rack on the hangar wall. Max picked out a gray box slightly larger than his CF's palm and handed it to the XSeed. "Here's a fresh mag for your plasma rifle. Reload and we'll charge the empty one from the shuttle's reactor."

Ritter accepted the offered magazine but held it to the XSeed's eyes for closer scrutiny. "Doesn't the rifle run off the capacitor?"

"The capacitor's your backup," said Max. "This way you can sortie with full ammo, shrug off some hits, and be invisible to radar."

"Could we rig up a way to charge the mags from the CF's powerplant?"

"Not without compromising electrical and physical integrity," said Max. "Solve that problem, and you could buy your own colony."

Ritter swapped mags and passed the empty one to Max, who carried it up the shuttle's cargo ramp in his Grento's hand. The

XSeed's status screen showed the rifle fully loaded at twelve shots. The capacitor read empty. *This'll take some getting used to.*

The XSeed's comm chirped with a call from the shuttle. "Ritter," Dorothy said hopefully. "Everyone's aboard. Did you find Zane?"

"I—"

Prometheus interrupted Ritter's reply by displaying what looked like combat footage on multiple screens. Each monitor showed a different camera's POV. Ritter recognized the pitted landscape of Metis streaming past below. *The XSeed took this video while my team and I were fighting our way to the hangar,* Ritter noted from the timestamp.

At first, the video showed standard maneuvers from the XSeed's POV. A purple flash signaled the start of a furious dogfight against an unmistakable black combat frame. *That's Dead Drop. Prometheus is showing me Zane's fight with Masz.*

Ritter watched in rapt fascination, only half-aware of Dorothy's increasingly frantic requests for him to answer her. He saw Masz purposefully drain the capacitor and fly straight into the fiery exhaust from Metis' huge rockets with Zane in pursuit.

The XSeed emerged on the other side with battery capacity to spare. Ritter held his breath and waited for Dead Drop to blast out of the inferno.

It never did.

As his hope withered, Ritter's awareness of Dorothy's plaintive voice grew. "Ritter! Please talk to me. What's wrong?"

Ritter exhaled slowly. "Zane didn't make it. Prep the shuttle for takeoff. We're leaving."

"What?" Dorothy's voice cracked. "You don't know that for sure. We have to look for him!"

"This base is swarming with Socs," Ritter said. "We're lucky they haven't come back in force and wiped us out. But they will, and every second we wait makes us easier targets. Zane's dead. Get ready for takeoff unless you want to join him."

The comm went silent. After a moment, a deceptively young voice spoke. "This is Browning. I've relieved Miss Wheeler. We're ready to launch on your order, Corporal."

"It Captain Darving's call," said Ritter, "not mine."

Max cut in. "I'm not EGE anymore, kid. This is your show. Don't screw up."

Ritter smiled amid his grief. "Thanks, Max. I'll do my best."

"This shuttle runs a version of NORMA," Max said with a chuckle. "She's the first commercial A.I. Seed Corp bought from me."

"You can make it up to us later," Ritter said as the shuttle lifted off. With a deft motion of his control stick, XSeed strode toward the launch door. "Follow me out. Once the shuttle's clear, I'll fall in behind you and cover your six."

"Roger that," said Browning.

Ritter brought the XSeed to the hangar's edge and scanned the starry black beyond. Nothing turned up, so he eased the throttle forward and sailed into space on maneuvering rockets. The empty void surrounded him. "You're clear," he radioed to Browning.

The shuttle slid from the asteroid, looking like a stretched-out honeycomb cell floating out of a boulder. When the shuttle cleared the hangar, Ritter took up a position behind it facing Metis. He kept his shield and rifle ready, expecting a hail of cannon fire and waves of CFs to bear down on them at any second.

"I'm picking something up on radar," Browning said.

Ritter's hands tensed on his weapon and flight controls. Prometheus showed nothing inbound from Metis. "Where?"

"A number of vessels have appeared around the asteroid's edges," said Browning. "They must have launched from the opposite side."

Metis' irregular horizon came into view as Ritter kept pace with the retreating shuttle's acceleration. The unimaginably huge rocket engines blazed at the lumpy oval's center. He suppressed thoughts of Zane's final moments and scanned the asteroid's perimeter. His screen lit up with contacts. *There are hundreds of them!*

Through filters that dimmed the furious engines' glare, Ritter saw rigid constellations of smaller rockets spreading out from Metis. Each point of light marked a shuttle larger than the vessel he guarded. The whole armada formed up on either side of the asteroid, matching its speed as it advanced on a bright blue ball in the distance. Two shuttles broke off from the rest and raced ahead.

"Two Soc shuttles are heading for Earth," Ritter radioed to the *King of Hearts*. "Based on their weight, each one's carrying six CFs. We have to go back and help the EGE!"

"They're all heading for Earth," said Browning, "and so is Metis. The shuttles will most likely hold position in Earth's orbit until after impact; then deploy combat frames to finish off the survivors. Earth is the last place we want to go."

"Seconded," said Max. "I'm flying to L1 if I have to hijack this bird to get there. Megami has Wen, and the space bitch won't be happy when she hears what we pulled."

Sieg's there too. The memory of popping up from a hole in the desert and mowing down the thugs who'd meant to whack Zane surged to the front of Ritter's mind. Nuclear fire whited out the image. *I bet you'd do anything to make up for that mistake,* he remembered Sieg saying in what felt like a past life.

"Contact the EGE and warn them about what's coming," ordered Ritter. "Set course for Byzantium colony."

"Not to question your decision," said Browning, "but Byzantium is no less a death trap than Earth. There's a small fueling station near the edge of L1 operated by a former ZoDiaC associate. He can arrange transport to L3 for anyone who'd rather not take part in a suicide mission."

The shuttle's cargo door opened, and Ritter guided the XSeed inside. "I've taken suicide missions before. Change course to stop at the fueling station. Browning and his team will debark there with Dorothy. Young, Thompson, Phillips, Green, and Roth will escort them. Captain Darving and I will continue on to Byzantium."

"Corporal," said Young, "I suggest you send two of us with the civilians while the rest of the squad accompanies you to the operation zone."

"No offense," said Ritter, "but you guys will be easy targets without combat frames. Keep an eye on Dorothy and Browning till the heat dies down."

"Are you sure about this, kid?" Max radioed to Ritter on a private channel.

Ritter closed the cargo door and lined the XSeed up against the wall beside Max's Grento. "Absolutely," Ritter said. "I have a mistake to make up for."

36

Naryal gathered her black mane in one fist and clutched it tight in the helicopter's rotor wash. Her green pilot's jumpsuit rippled but stayed mostly in place. The same couldn't be said for the dark blue business suit worn by Mr. Huang, the Kisangani Spaceport's manager. His jacket flaps spread out and fluttered like the wings of a nervous bird. The left flap brushed against Naryal's hip.

The helo landed in the shadow of the last shuttle's launch tower. Four men in EGE combat uniforms debarked as Major Collins looked down from the aircraft's upper canopy. Two soldiers carried a metal box the size of a mini fridge. They stepped clear of the whirring rotors and carefully set their burden down on the sun-bleached concrete.

One soldier strode directly up to Naryal. His light blue eyes held her gaze without blinking, and his neat white beard framed a mouth as thin and straight as a razor.

"Colonel Larson," she shouted over the rotors' whine, "I'm surprised General McCaskey chose you."

"I can turn around and fly back to the fleet if that's a problem," Larson said.

"No problem." Naryal motioned to the slight, middle-aged man beside her. "This is Francis Huang, manager of Kisangani Spaceport. He's agreed to supply a shuttle for the operation."

Larson looked down at Huang. "Does this Soc know who he's getting in bed with?"

"I know there is a two hundred-kilometer asteroid on a collision course with Earth," said Huang. "I also know that only the EGE have both the means and the inclination to avert this catastrophe. Now, Colonel, since I will be executed if the current Secretary-General remains in office, I'll thank you to refrain from using such crude slurs."

"This son of a bitch is alright," Larson said. He turned to Collins, gave a thumbs up, and pointed to the eastern sky. The helo lifted off and departed in the indicated direction.

"You brought the package?" asked Naryal.

Larson glanced over his shoulder at the sturdy metal box. "If by 'package' you mean a two megaton nuclear bomb, then yeah. Special delivery, courtesy of our friend Carlos."

"To think that civilization on Earth decayed to the point that a common arms dealer could possess such a weapon," said Huang.

"If I'd had confirmation before now," said Larson, "I'd probably have had him killed."

Huang smoothed his coat. "All the more unfortunate that Governor Troy went rogue. He has an arsenal of nuclear ICBM's at New Ramstein."

"And you can bet Megami's got a cutting edge missile defense system," Larson said. "A manned flight is our only shot."

"Will two megatons suffice to destroy Metis?" asked Naryal.

"No," said Larson. "That's why my team and I will need to fly inside the rock, close enough for the blast to set off the main reactor. When that sucker goes, it'll break Metis into fragments that should burn up in the atmosphere." He stepped in front of Huang. "That's what I brought for show and tell. You got my shuttle?"

Huang pointed up at the antiquated white and black spacecraft affixed to a cluster of solid rocket engines on the launch pad above them. "The Secretary-General ordered most of our equipment transferred to Metis. She left us only two shuttles. Corporal Ritter's team took one yesterday. I'm entrusting you with the last."

"I have difficulty believing Megami would make so large an oversight," said Naryal. "Why not take all the shuttles—or at least destroy those left behind?"

"Leaving the Coalition's biggest spaceport with no working shuttles would've tipped her hand," said Larson. "Leaving two gets everybody in a huff over the inconvenience instead of up in arms over a betrayal. And she probably figures two shuttles are easy enough to shoot down."

The color drained from Huang's square face. "Does the Secretary-General really consider her own people living on Earth the enemy?"

"She considers the whole human race her enemy, pal." Larson gestured to the three soldiers guarding the box. "Get that nuke loaded on Huang's shuttle. And be gentle. It's his last one."

"On final approach to Byzantium colony," NORMA announced over Ritter's comm.

"How many CFs between us and the colony?" Max inquired from the Grento standing beside the XSeed in the shuttle's cargo hold.

"No combat frames, fighters, battleships, or craft of any kind detected," NORMA said.

Ritter patched Prometheus into NORMA's sensor feed. His screens showed only the thirty kilometer-long cylinder and its three hinged mirrors rotating slowly in space. "Maybe they don't know we're coming."

"And maybe I'm the Supreme Patriarch," scoffed Max. "If the Kaks didn't report our little escapade at Metis, chances are they flipped Browning and company five minutes after we dropped them off at that fuel depot."

"Dr. Browning wouldn't snitch on us," Ritter said. "Would he?"

"Browning looks out for Browning, kid," said Max. "If not for him, Wen would be safe back on Earth, and so would we."

"Could they be hiding inside the colony?"

"It's the perfect place for an ambush," said Max, "but I don't know. Looks pretty quiet in there."

Ritter aimed NORMA's main camera at one of the colony's window strips and zoomed in. No traffic moved on the roadways crisscrossing the green fields inside. He saw no combat frames and no signs of life at all. "Isn't Megami supposed to be meeting with diplomats from L3?"

Max snorted. "Megami's concept of diplomacy is getting their unconditional surrender at gunpoint and shooting them anyway. I wouldn't put it past her to murder the whole damn colony just to spite us."

"Do you think Li Wen is...?" Ritter fumbled for the right combination of clarity and tact.

Max tightened his Grento's grip on its machine gun. "I'll never know unless I go in and see for myself. And I have to know."

Ritter thought back to the Coalition's invasion of his hometown. Seeing friends and loved ones gunned down had been a nightmare. Having some of them simply disappear had been hell. *I'll find you when this is over, Zane. No marker without a grave for you. Of all the Socs, you deserve a resting place on Earth.*

"I understand," Ritter told Max. He checked the XSeed's empty capacitor and his rifle's full mag and racked the hefty weapon inside his shield. "We'll go in together. Stay right behind me, and they won't see us coming."

A golden flash lit Ritter's screen. The cargo hold filled with fire. Alarms blared as chaotic forces clawed at Ritter. Only his safety harness kept him from being flung around the cockpit.

The shaking stopped. Prometheus's readout showed no significant damage to the XSeed, but the shuttle's glowing wreckage spun through a spreading particulate cloud.

"Max," Ritter shouted over the comm. "Max, come in!"

"I'm here," said a strained voice. "Good call telling me to fall in behind Prometheus. That mechanical monster absorbed most of the blast."

Ritter pulled up his rearview camera feed. Max's Grento—or most of it—floated amid the debris. The green CF's grilled dome had been blown off, leaving a squat cylinder like a black halo above its headless shoulders. Only a couple of sparking cables remained of its left arm below the biceps, and both its thighs ended in mangled stumps.

The XSeed's capacitor had absorbed enough energy for a single shot.

"Can you make it?" Ritter asked.

"Half my drives are gone," said Max, "but I'm carrying less weight, so it evens out."

"Spoken like an engineer," Ritter chuckled, "always the problem solver."

"Right now, what I want solved is the mystery of who hit us. I've got nothing on radar."

"Me, either." Ritter swept his main camera over the space around them. The particulate cloud cleared, and a scarlet speck caught his eye. He magnified the view of space between him and the colony, and his breath caught in his throat.

"What is it, kid?"

Ritter struggled to process what he saw. Familiarity, not strangeness, robbed him of speech. The burly, soft-edged frame and human yet inhuman eyes at first convinced Ritter he saw a reflection in the colony mirror. But the apparition staring back at him across the void carried an even larger gun with four barrels arranged in the shape of a cross, and its entire outer surface gleamed red.

"Oh shit," said Max. "She built another one."

The red XSeed leveled its four-barreled gun at its white doppelganger. Ritter grabbed the Grento's good arm and poured all his thrust into a vertical dive. A yellow plasma beam as wide as a CF's torso passed over Ritter and Max's heads, annihilating the leftover debris.

"Get to the colony," Ritter ordered Max. "I'll cover you!" Unable to get a target lock, he aimed his plasma rifle by sight. The Red XSeed zipped away from the line of fire the instant Ritter pressed the trigger. The blue flash punched a hole in the colony mirror big enough to fly a shuttle through.

The Grento jetted toward Byzantium on its two remaining thrusters. "Good luck, kid," said Max. "That thieving bitch stole me and Browning's CF design, but there's no way she copied Prometheus. He'll trounce that wannabe's off-the-shelf OS."

Fear loosened its grip on Ritter's heart. "Okay. All I have to worry about is the pilot."

The red XSeed popped up in front of Ritter out of nowhere. It pressed its four-barreled gun to his cockpit door.

"Yes," said a deep airy voice. "You do."

"Sieg!?"

The four muzzles flashed.

Naryal noticed her foot tapping on the launch control room floor and forced herself to be still. Jean-Claude must have noticed her agitation because his nimble yet callused hand clasped hers. She spared a smile for the Prince in his tan flight suit with two angels holding a crown on a white field adorning the shoulder. The king of hearts stood in for a unit patch.

"Five minutes to launch," a nasal voice announced over the PA. From the riser at the back of the control room, Naryal looked over the rows of technicians in white shirts who labored over glowing screens. Mr. Huang paced nervously up and down the center aisle.

The central monitor on the far wall showed Kisangani's last shuttle standing upright on the launch pad. A screen to the right displayed a live feed of Colonel Larson and his spacesuited team waiting for clearance to blast off for Metis, now visible to the naked eye as a bright star in the western sky.

"What bravery," Jean-Claude whispered. "I should be going with them."

"Men like you are needed here," said Naryal.

"Oh? What need could be greater than averting a global catastrophe?"

"Rebuilding after."

Jean-Claude chuckled darkly. "Are their chances so poor?"

"Setting aside risks of every space launch, Larson and his men must fly an unarmed shuttle through a gauntlet of Kazoku, navigate Metis' mine tunnels to its reactor, and detonate a nuclear device. Even if they accomplish each of these tasks, they are unlikely to escape with their lives."

"Their courage in the face of such odds only magnifies their glory," Jean-Claude said.

A commotion arose on the floor below. Hunag rushed to a bank of consoles in the room's front left corner where a group of technicians were pointing at their screens and arguing.

"What's wrong?" Naryal shouted over the din.

"Six combat frames are approaching our position from the west at high speed," shouted Huang.

"Give me a visual," said Naryal.

The screen on the main monitor's left switched to a view of six shining blue dots flying over a sea of trees. The camera zoomed in, and the dots resolved into boxy combat frames with flared pauldrons and black v-shaped visors. Each CF carried a plasma rifle and a shield.

"Zwei Dolphs," said Naryal. "Megami's attack dogs have come to stop the launch."

"I'll be dead before I give those Socs the satisfaction," Griff said over the shuttle's comm. "Wrap up the launch prep and get us in the air."

"We must defend the shuttle," said Huang. "Fire anti-air batteries!"

"Those guns will shoot down Grentos," said Naryal, "but not Dolphs. What forces can you deploy to intercept the enemy?"

"Megami moved this base's combat frames to Metis," said Huang. "We only have the four Shenlongs that escorted your cargo plane."

"Scramble them," ordered Naryal.

"It won't be enough," Jean-Claude said.

Naryal eyed him coolly. "I take it you mean to sortie in Veillantif?"

"The enemy is on our doorstep," said Jean-Claude. "Would you begrudge my duty to protect those in my charge?"

"Not at all," Naryal said. "If there's no one to protect us, we must defend ourselves."

Jean-Claude hurried from the room. Naryal followed him. Huang's voice echoed down the hall. "Request help from the EGE. They may still have aircraft in range."

Not even a fighter could make it from the coast in time, thought Naryal. She and Jean-Claude burst out of the dim control tower and into the humid African day. Only the sun surpassed the light of Metis hanging low over the jungle. *And time is running out!*

Max flew down the colony maintenance corridor, fighting to keep his battered Grento from slamming into the steel walls. After several close calls he came to a combat frame-sized hatch.

Not much longer now, he promised Wen. *I'll take you far away from the colonies, the Earth, and their pointless wars.* Extending the Grento's remaining hand, he opened the hatch.

A dizzying view spread out beyond the door. Max looked down from a sheer rock face to a green strip of land that called to mind his many flights over the Illinois countryside. But here, no cars sped along the roads and no air traffic flew above. Two rectangular lakes flanked the strip of land. Stars twinkled in their depths. A searing green burst lit the right lakebed window.

"The Secretary-General's compound is located at the center of the land strip below," Marilyn said from the breast pocket of Max's flight suit.

I'm coming, Wen. Max urged the Grento forward. He eased the legless combat frame's descent with a controlled burn from his two functional rockets.

"Altitude: one hundred meters," Marilyn said, compensating for the readout Max's helmet had cracked when the shuttle blew. Max held tight to the control stick and poured all his concentration into landing the damaged CF in a tree-ringed clearing below.

The right engine sputtered and died. Even missing three limbs, the Grento's weight exceeded its lone rocket's thrust. Max fought a hopeless battle with the controls as his stomach turned and the rocky slope rushed up to meet him.

Max silently petitioned the God he'd always considered an esoteric concept. The Grento's leg stumps slammed into the hillside. He threw the CF back onto its rear skirt armor in an attempt to glissade and dug its hand into the slope above to arrest his fall. The Grento's protracted crash slowed, but it continued sliding toward the dense tree line.

"I see where this is going," Max thought aloud. He pulled the emergency lever under his seat. The cockpit hatch blew outward, admitting moist, pine-scented air that slapped Max like a wound-up towel. His seat failed to eject.

The out-of-control Grento dug a furrow through a grassy field at the woods' edge. Max released his harness, climbed onto the CF's torso, and made a desperate jump to the left. Sharp pain stabbed his left shoulder as it impacted the dense turf. Max somersaulted once and rolled sideways for what felt like minutes but was probably just a few seconds. He lay prone on the grass, heaving air into his burning lungs.

A short distance ahead, a cacophony like a logging machine gone berserk informed him the Grento had crashed into the woods. A propellant tank exploded with a resounding boom that shook the ground and buffeted Max's back. Luckily, the reactor didn't follow suit.

Max hauled himself to his feet. His left arm hung limp at his side as he checked his status and equipment. Besides the dislocated shoulder, he'd gotten off with no injuries worth worrying about. His visor was split down the middle, so he ditched his helmet. Marilyn's handheld had a cracked screen but was otherwise intact. The pistol Green had given him during the flight to L1 seemed undamaged. He pictured Megami in its sights, and his lips curled around clenched teeth.

Softly singing a rock song written for a pre-Collapse movie by a long dead Ferrari mechanic, Max slouched into the smoke-filled woods. He briefly entertained the notion that he'd died in the crash and was condemned to wander the gray wilderness as a lost spirit. *Are there ghosts in space, or are they bound to the earth by gravity?*

Ritter jerked the control stick to the left, narrowly avoiding the golden beam that tore through space above Byzantium colony. He was learning to read the signals Prometheus sent through his XSeed's instruments and controls. And not a moment too soon, since the A.I. was telling him the CF's battery was charged to thirty percent.

Conserve ammo, Ritter reminded himself, *and don't get shot.* The red XSeed's direct hit to his cockpit hatch had beaten that lesson into him. His CF's carbyne armor had saved his life, but he'd lost three layers at once, along with a third of his anti-radar capacity. Ritter hadn't yet laid a hand on the red XSeed, though he counted his blessings since he didn't relish giving Sieg more ammo.

Red indicators flashed and alarms chirped, warning of an imminent attack from the colony at his left. Ritter searched in vain for the red CF. He dodged to the right, but the moment's hesitation cost him. Gold radiance burst from the sun's glare reflected in the colony window. Ritter's cockpit shook even though his shield took the worst of the attack.

Capacitor forty percent charged.

Ritter climbed rightward on a diagonal to get the sun out of his eyes. The red XSeed materialized from the fading light. It skimmed along the colony's length above the window and pulled ahead of its white twin. Ritter sailed over the mirror looming above the window. He dived behind the thirty kilometer reflector and tasked Prometheus to keep pace with the colony's rotation.

Got to free up some battery space! Ritter pointed his plasma rifle upward and repeatedly mashed the trigger. Sapphire bolts cascaded into empty space. He'd drained his mag and was about to fire the first shot from his battery when the section of mirror behind him exploded, washing out the universe in blinding gold.

Capacitor fifty percent charged.

"If you want to hide," Sieg lectured over the comm, "fire perpendicular to the mirror."

Ritter wheeled around as the red XSeed barreled through the hole in the reflector. Sieg aimed his quad plasma gun at the white XSeed's cockpit again, but Ritter shoved the weapon aside with his shield. The wide golden beam blasted into space.

"Don't do me any favors," Ritter said. "You lost the right to give me orders when you threw in with Megami!"

Sieg drew one of the two plasma swords from his CF's back, ignited the yellow blade, and swung at Prometheus' head. "Don't meddle in my family's business!"

Ritter blocked the incandescent blade. More layers of armor steamed off his shield. "That 'business' is global-scale murder!"

"Surviving in outer space forced the colonists to put aside their differences." Sieg feinted and slashed diagonally upward across the white XSeed's torso. More armor boiled away. "We had peace until contact resumed with grounders. War is a contagion, and Earth is the source. My sister has to sterilize the planet!"

"That's not Megami's decision to make," Ritter yelled as he slammed Prometheus' foot into its red twin's chest. "Does she really think she's a god?"

The red XSeed pivoted behind Ritter and locked Prometheus in a full nelson. Ritter thrashed his CF's arms but couldn't break the hold.

"Megami wouldn't exist if I hadn't failed Elizabeth," said Sieg. "She's my responsibility."

"Then stop her," Ritter said.

"You don't understand what she's become," said Sieg. "I'm too weak."

Ritter fired his retrorockets with an anguished cry. The red XSeed released him and shot away a second before Prometheus crashed backwards through a solid section of colony mirror.

37

Naryal and Jean-Claude skimmed over the jungle canopy ten kilometers west of Kisangani. Half that distance ahead, the six Zwei Dolphs rushed toward them. Jagannath handled better than ever thanks to Zeklov's fine-tuning, but Veillantif's gargoyle-like frame quickly overtook her gold CF.

"M. Zeklov is a true artist," Jean-Claude said. "His refinements to Veillantif have exceeded my high expectations. I feel like I could destroy the entire enemy squad alone."

Naryal rolled aside from a red plasma bolt that burned through the tropical air. "Be my guest."

Jean-Claude pressed Veillantif's saw-toothed wings to its back and surged ahead. He weaved between a volley of plasma bolts and charged the point of the Dolphs' wedge formation. As he flew past, his sword shattered the lead Dolph's shield, and his whip decapitated the CF to the leader's right. Naryal detonated the headless Dolph with a green bolt from her plasma rifle.

The five remaining Zwei Dolphs held their formation and their laser-straight course toward the launch site. *Remarkable discipline,* Naryal admitted. She climbed above their field of crimson fire and answered with two emerald bolts of her own. The Dolph squad dived under the first shot, but the second hit the shieldless leader's weapon. The rifle exploded, along with its owner's arms and head. The rest of the smoldering CF crashed into the jungle.

Jean-Claude came about with deadly grace and closed with the leftmost Zwei Dolphs as the squad streaked below Naryal. She joined the chase, harrying the two Dolphs on the right with plasma bolts. Her targets avoided her shots, but Jean-Claude's prey fared more poorly.

Veillantif's barbed whip coiled around one target's legs. Jean-Claude rocketed ahead to the right, swinging the entangled Dolph into its squadmate and retracting his whip. The Dolphs survived the collision, but they broke formation and cut their speed. Veillantif turned again to engage both Kazoku at close quarters. The Dolphs drew their red plasma swords and responded in kind.

Naryal racked her plasma rifle inside her shield and drew Jagannath's two-handed plasma sword. One of her quarry fired from the hip as she ignited her emerald blade. The red bolt clipped Jagannath's left leg, fusing the knee joint. With a curse she rushed the offender down and swung her oversized energy sword. The Dolph rolled over and tried to block, but Naryal's blade clove through the shield and its bearer. The blue CF fell from the sky in two charred halves.

Jagannath's early warning alarm trilled. Six red boxes appeared on her monitor, screaming toward the spaceport from the south at Mach 1. "New enemy wave inbound!" Naryal broadcast over the comm. "ETA thirty seconds."

"Ritter mentioned two shuttles breaking off from the Metis fleet," said Jean-Claude. "One launched its Dolphs early to draw us away from their main assault." He pivoted to isolate one Dolph between him and its squadmate, severed its sword hand with his whip, and ran his rapier through its cockpit before breaking off toward the spaceport. The two surviving Dolphs trailed behind.

"What kind of butcher sends her own men into the path of an asteroid strike?" Naryal said as she followed Veillantif at full speed. *I've underestimated you yet again,* she silently confessed to Megami. *Death would serve me right, but I'll keep fighting you to the last.*

Ruby lights flashed from the second wave of Dolphs. Oily orange fireballs rose from outbuildings near the launch pad, but the shuttle itself remained unscathed. *They're just calibrating their weapons,* realized Naryal, *but they're already in range of Larson's shuttle. We won't make it in time!*

Four green circles in an echelon formation swept onto Naryal's screen from the left. Missiles streaked toward the six Zwei Dolphs, tracing white contrails past the launch tower. The second Dolph squad broke formation to evade the inbound ordnance.

"EGE Air Corps Lieutenant Walker, here," a confident masculine voice said over the comm. "You CF jockeys can't hog all the fun. My boys'll get these Socs off the Colonel's back."

Four sleek Shenlong strike aircraft hurtled straight toward the newly arrived Dolphs. The fighters opened up with their Vulcan cannons, but the 20mm rounds bounced off the combat frames' shields. The lead Zwei Dolph raised a staff in its right hand. Two red blades ignited on both ends.

"It's the pilot who led the attack on our fleet," Jean-Claude shouted. "Walker, pull your men back!"

Masz accelerated. The two foremost Shenlongs tried to bank away. But a shot from the twin plasma cannon in the custom Zwei Dolph's shield vaporized Walker's jet, and its plasma fork burned through his wingman's cockpit.

The fourth Shenlong in line took a plasma bolt that tore apart its left wing. The EGE pilot aimed his crippled aircraft at the Soc who'd shot him and opened the throttle. The jet and the CF collided in a midair fireball. The last Shenlong vanished over the horizon.

Naryal clenched her teeth. The mass dogfight had taken only seconds, but it would be seconds more until she could risk firing on the Zwei Dolphs without hitting the shuttle. Veillantif was faster, but it lacked ranged weapons, and each of them had a Zwei Dolph from the first wave in hot pursuit.

"It's getting awful hot out there," Larson radioed from the beleaguered shuttle. "Quit jerking off, and clear us for launch."

"You're not fully fueled," said Huang.

"We just need enough to fly this bomb up Metis' ass," Larson said. "Nobody's under the illusion this is a two-way trip."

Masz came to a midair stop a hundred meters from the launch tower. He aimed his dual cannon at the helpless shuttle. With a final burst of speed, Veillantif crossed the burning port and slammed into the custom Zwei Dolph shield-first. Both combat frames tumbled sideways through the smoke-filled air.

Naryal's heart swelled, but fear curbed her rush of triumph. Masz pulled out of his spin as his four squadmates entered point blank range of the shuttle. In desperation she fired on the Zwei Dolphs from 1500 meters away. Her shots demolished the tower beyond Larson's but stalled the Kazoku for another moment.

Masz jetted back toward the shuttle. Jean-Claude righted Veillantif and gave chase. The custom Zwei Dolph rounded on him. Jean-Claude lashed his whip around the haft of Masz's plasma fork and pulled. The fork jerked forward to Veillantif's left, but Masz gripped his weapon with both hands. Using Jean-Claude's momentum, he twisted and cut the heat whip.

Jean-Claude sprang back but collected himself and flourished his sword. "That shuttle and her crew are under my protection. You will not lay one finger on them!"

"Miss Megami wants this planet dead," said Masz, "starting with them." He pointed his shield at the shuttle over Veillantif's left shoulder. Jean-Claude swatted at the Dolph's shield with his own, but Masz fired a shot that disintegrated Veillantif's shield arm as his fork severed its sword hand. An upward slash of the fork's other end reached behind Veillantif and melted its thruster nozzles. Jean-Claude fell, trailing a string of French curses.

Seeing the man of whom she'd grown quite fond crash to the broken ground kindled unexpected wrath in Naryal. She adjusted course to intercept Masz as he raced for the shuttle. Two Zwei Dolphs blocked her path. She turned left but found herself facing two more. A glance at her screens showed six Dolphs surrounding her.

Naryal charged ahead, firing wildly. Both Kazoku between her and the launch tower broke off in opposite directions. The reason dawned on her just before the Dolphs at her back pumped two plasma bolts into her main thrusters. After a dread heartbeat of weightlessness, she managed to slow her descent with maneuvering thrusters. The impact wrecked Jagannath's legs, but Naryal survived.

"Prem." Jean-Claude's voice could barely be heard pronouncing her given name over the comm static, but Naryal breathed a sigh of relief to learn he still lived.

"I'm alright," she assured him.

"Thank God. But Larson…"

Naryal locked her main camera on the launch tower. The custom Zwei Dolph hovered within fifty meters of the shuttle. She watched in impotent rage as Masz fired. Red flames burst from the cockpit windows. The killer's hysterical laughter flooded the comm.

Masz's shield exploded. A lone green circle appeared on Naryal's screen.

"All stations fire at will," ordered Major Alan Collins.

The same green and brown attack helicopter that Larson's team had arrived on swung around the launch tower from the left. The four turrets on its blistered nose blazed, chewing off chunks of the Zwei Dolph's armor.

Masz rushed Collins' helo, but a shot from the aircraft's 70mm cannon snapped the twin fork in half and mangled the CF's right hand beyond recognition. The helo climbed, letting the Zwei Dolph barrel past, and smoothly came about with its rotor angled toward the ground. Another salvo ate away the Dolph's thrusters.

The custom Zwei Dolph plowed face-first into a fuel truck garage. The crash didn't spark an explosion, but Collins' crew made up what was lacking with a pair of missiles. A wave of hellfire washed away combat frame and pilot alike.

But six Kazoku remained.

"Collins, watch your back," Naryal urged the Major as all six Dolphs took flight after the aircraft that had shot down their leader. The helo fled toward the city in a serpentine motion ahead of searing red plasma beams, but it couldn't match the combat frames' speed.

"This is Zeklov transport ZV-011," a Russian-accented voice announced over the comm. "We diverted from a convoy making delivery to the EGE fleet. Do you still need assistance?"

"Yes!" Naryal, Jean-Claude, and Collins answered at once.

"Roger that," the Zeklov pilot said.

Naryal's camera fixed itself on five enormous aircraft soaring high above the northeast horizon. Ten green circles lit up her screen before she saw the new combat frames speeding toward the spaceport. Their olive drab hulls were a compromise between earlier models' curves and the Dolphs' hard edges. Their grilled domes swiveled in search of targets for the 115mm machine guns in their hands and the missile launchers attached to their legs.

Grenzmark IIIs!

The Dolphs lost interest in Collins and focused their fire on the descending Grenthrees. The new CFs' stout appearance belied their agility. Only two fell in the initial assault. The EGE pilots had spent weeks running simulations against Ein Dolphs, and the same tactics proved effective against their successors. 115mm rounds destroyed plasma rifles while missiles rained down on the Kazoku formation.

The Grenzmark IIIs are equal in performance to the Zwei Dolphs, Naryal observed, *if not slightly superior.* The EGE pilots also had the advantage in numbers and knowledge of their enemy. The battle's outcome looked promising.

Not that victory mattered in light of the asteroid on an inevitable collision course with Earth.

"Will someone release the damn launch clamps already?" Larson panted.

"Colonel?" Major Collins said. "You're still alive?"

"You'd better hope I won't be for long," said Larson. "Went back to prep the package for evac when Huang gave me the runaround. Missed the cockpit barbecue, but this whole boat's going up in flames. Power surge started the timer. I can still launch from the engine room. If you don't release those clamps right now, we'll all have prime real estate on a brand new sun."

"A sun?" asked Huang. "I thought it was an asteroid."

"Release the bloody clamps!" Naryal screamed.

High above, the Kazoku and EGE combat frame teams met in close combat. If the Grenthrees fell short of their opponents' ranged weapons capability, their double-bladed plasma lances easily overpowered the Zwei Dolphs' swords. The melee claimed three Dolphs but only one Grenthree.

The shuttle's rockets ignited with a roar that Jagannath's cockpit barely muffled. The spacecraft lifted off the pad on a billowing exhaust column. Combatants on both sides paused and watched the shuttle rise blindly into the sky.

Naryal's monitor dimmed the nuclear flash, but she still had to blink to clear her vision. Her sensors showed that the bomb had detonated at a safe range from Earth's surface. *Well done, Griff.*

The manmade star faded. But Metis remained, drawing closer for judgment.

38

The acrid smoke from the burning Grento dissipated, and the trees gave way to a broad field of manicured grass. Max trudged between the blackened ruins of two work frames, pressing his hand against the wreck on his right as he passed. The palm of his glove came away blacked with soot. He started at a flurry of sound and motion to his left and drew his gun on what turned out to be a flight of birds rising from the other work frame's remains.

Max pressed on toward the walled compound in the distance. He kept his pistol ready for an assault from a covert security team, but he reached the gate unchallenged. Though the thick steel bars were shut tight, a bullet took care of the lock. No one responded to the shots.

A wide avenue stretched between immaculate lawns fronting blocky office buildings to the circular drive of a French Regency mansion. Max recognized the house. The whole structure had been moved stone by stone from a Dallas suburb by a founding member of the Consortium. The sculpture of Winged Victory encircled by the driveway had once resided in the Louvre.

Max walked down the short street unmolested and climbed the granite steps to the mansion's entry arch. He tried the iron handle, and the dark blue oak door creaked open. The small square vestibule gave on an arched hall with several open doorways on both sides. An antique mirror in a gilt frame dominated the left wall and reflected the paintings by Dutch Masters displayed on the right. A trace odor of burnt eggs hung in the still air.

A distant thump broke the heavy silence. Max hurried toward the second door on the left in search of the source, his boots clicking on the peach marble underfoot. The doorway led into a conference room furnished in the Edwardian style. Scattered papers and water glasses cluttered the flame mahogany table.

Max stepped up to one of the empty places at the long table and skimmed the first page of an open leather binder. *It's a nonaggression pact between the Socs and L3. Megami and Prime Minister Venn both signed it.*

Footsteps echoing in the hallway spurred Max to turn on his heel with his gun raised. He locked eyes on a slight figure with long black hair and pulled the trigger. Jagged cracks traversed the mirror on the opposite wall, and the chimes of breaking glass followed the gun's resounding bang. The hallway was empty.

Am I seeing things? Max took several deep breaths to slow his rapid breathing. The unpleasant stench he'd detected on entering seemed stronger here than in the vestibule. He followed the scent. A brief search led to a cracked door at the far end of the conference room. His left arm still immobile, Max nudged the door open with the muzzle of his gun.

A slumped female form bound to a chair. Blood and worse soaking the front of a blue EGE Navy jumpsuit. Cables running from a car battery clipped to black wires jutting from red holes where eyes had been. The stench of sweetness gone to rot.

"Li Wen," Max rasped, his throat suddenly dry. He gave a quiet prayer of thanks that no answer came, and his self-hatred deepened.

"You just missed her."

The breathy feminine voice spoke from just behind Max's left shoulder. He rounded on Megami, who stood facing him with a predatory smile. Her small hand intersected the arc of his right arm, and a numbing jolt lanced through his wrist. His gun fell, bounced on the rose carpet, and vanished under the table.

"With my bare hands, bitch!" Hardly aware of the threat torn from his mouth by rage, Max lunged at the grinning girl. The tails of her blue trench coat flapped as she slid to his right, and her long hair brushed across his neck. A cold sting traversed his throat. Burning pain followed, driving him to his knees. Blood seeped from an invisible slit in his suit's thick neck. He clutched the wound in a desperate bid to stop the warm sticky flow.

"Carbyne's good for more than batteries," said Megami. "It can cut right through a standard pilot suit. Be glad you're wearing one, though. It's why you still have a head."

Max's curses emerged as choking gasps. The sole of Megami's boot dug into his back and shoved him to the floor. He fell on his dislocated left shoulder, but the stab of agony paled against the burning in his throat.

"Don't try to talk," said Megami. "The toxin coating the monowire already paralyzed your vocal cords." She crouched down beside him just out of arm's reach. Her eyes gleamed with cruelty but not for him, as if she were anticipating imminent revenge against a despised foe.

"You deserve more for giving me the XSeed," she continued. "It doesn't matter if Masz stops the EGE's launch or not. Crashing Metis into the Atlantic is only a warmup. My Kazoku will hunt the survivors from above with weapons guided by Prometheus."

Max couldn't raise his left hand, but he extended the middle finger.

"Speaking of Prometheus," Megami said, "my brother has been entertaining its pilot since both of you arrived. I should go out and greet my other guest, even though the invitation was meant for Zane."

Megami rose and swept forth like a spirit of malice. Max lay on the soft carpet in a spreading pool of his own blood, struggling to breathe.

"Max," said a muffled, tinny voice.

Darving slowly and painfully moved his left hand to his suit's front pocket and pulled out the cracked handheld device.

"Your pulse and respiration rates indicate severe blood loss," said Marilyn. "Prometheus and I have cracked this compound's security net. There is an emergency escape shuttle in a secret hangar beneath the house. I will guide you and grant you access, but you must hurry!"

Rising to his feet sent more pain shooting through Max's tortured body than he would have thought possible. He leaned against the table, smearing his blood on official documents.

"Hurry," Marilyn urged him. "I cannot help if you die of blood loss before reaching the shuttle."

Max forced himself to slog through a world of thickening red mist one trembling step at a time. At last he stumbled into a lift door that Marilyn revealed behind a shelf of old books in the mansion's library. The door hissed open, and Max tipped forward onto the elevator car's steel floor. The pain seemed to afflict someone else far away.

He must have blacked out, because he awakened to Marilyn's plaintive voice. "Max, please get up. The shuttle is just beyond the door."

With his last dregs of strength, Max crawled from the lift, crossed the blessedly small titanium-graphite deck, and hauled himself into the shuttle's pilot seat. His numb hand fell away from his hemorrhaging neck as the angular canopy closed. The launch door in front of him retracted with a clang, revealing the star-flecked unknown.

"I listened to the stars," said Marilyn, "and I learned the code. The Gate can compress and dilate time. You will be safe on the other side."

Max's head lolled as the shuttle shot forward. He looked up in time to see the colony mirror streak past. Matter, energy, and information froze. The stars contracted to an infinite point toward which he soared eternally.

Ritter kept his back to the colony wall and his eyes glued to his monitor. He'd lost sight of the red XSeed after crashing through the mirror, and he knew Sieg was out there waiting for the right moment to attack. Ritter resolved not to give him an opening.

Prometheus' battery stood at a little over fifty percent charged. Ritter had learned better than to bleed off power with blind shots that would give away his position. *I've got to avoid Sieg's attacks and keep him talking—break Megami's spell over him.*

But could a spell that had bound millions be broken?

A sudden motion drew Ritter's eye to the lower left corner of his screen. He relaxed slightly when the object turned out to be a small white shuttle instead of a red CF. *The colony's empty. Who could be launching a shuttle?* Hope kindled in Ritter's heart. "Max!" he radioed to the shuttle. "Is that you? Did you find Li Wen?"

An alert on Ritter's comm display notified him that Prometheus had received a message from the shuttle. The user ID was "Marilyn". The subject read: "Gate Code".

"Open it," Ritter told Prometheus. A flood of ones and zeroes filled every screen.

Is this some kind of virus? Ritter reached for the system reset switch, but the monitors cleared on their own.

The shuttle passed the mirror. Ritter was looking right at the one-man delta wing craft when it disappeared. His eyes reflexively squeezed shut. A negative image of the shuttle floated in the red dimness behind his eyelids and remained in his field of vision when he opened them. The triangle-shaped flash burn hovered over a red combat frame pointing a four-barreled gun right at him.

Ritter slid left but caught the brunt of the golden blast. Atmosphere geysered through the breach in the colony's hull to his right, forming a cloud of glittering ice crystals.

Capacitor sixty percent charged.

"A battlefield is no place to daydream," Sieg said as he mirrored Ritter's sidelong flight.

Ritter rocketed off the wall in an arc that soared over the red XSeed's head. Prometheus centered the targeting reticle on its crimson twin, but Ritter didn't fire. Instead he continued downward following the direction of the colony's spin.

"You're holding back," said Sieg. A golden flash engulfed Prometheus' legs and sent Ritter spinning backwards. "This is war. Sentimentality will kill you faster than bullets."

My battery's two-thirds full. "I don't want to kill you!"

Ritter fired maneuvering thrusters to straighten his flight path but let the momentum propel him, inverted, toward the red XSeed. Again Prometheus gave him a firing solution. Again he ignored it and aimed into space to drain a charge. But Sieg shot first. The golden beam washed over Prometheus' right arm. Ritter's plasma rifle exploded, along with its fortunately empty magazine. The limb lost five layers of armor.

Capacitor eighty-five percent charged.

"What you or I want doesn't matter," said Sieg. He maneuvered to line up another shot. Ritter dashed aside just before the golden beam tore through space beneath the colony.

Ritter drew one of his plasma swords with Prometheus' right hand, ignited the blue blade, and rushed the red XSeed. "That's not what you said in that African village. You told me we all have a choice."

"And you said your greatest mistake was refusing to fight." Sieg parried Ritter's thrust with his golden plasma blade. "Here I am—the enemy that will destroy everything you love. Are you going to let me?" The red XSeed spun its wrist, flinging the blue sword into space. The golden blade tagged Prometheus' right hip.

Ritter fell back into a defensive stance. "We're not enemies! We're countrymen."

The red XSeed sprang forward. "Neue Deutschland is a failed dream," said Sieg. "I belong to the Kazoku." He slashed faster than Ritter could react. The golden blade raked Prometheus' midsection. Sieg switched to an icepick grip and stabbed Ritter's cockpit door, turning layers of armor to white steam.

Capacitor ninety percent charged.

Ritter's cockpit trembled. The temperature started to rise. He fired retrorockets but the red XSeed matched his pace. Sieg held back Prometheus' shield arm with his gun. Ritter clutched the arm holding Sieg's sword, but he couldn't budge the deadly blade.

"What a waste," said Sieg. "You had the intelligence to learn from your mistakes but lacked the wisdom to learn from others'. I regret that this final lesson won't profit you."

"Prometheus is designed to assist the XSeed's pilot, if the pilot will trust him. Can you do that, Ritter?"

"Max?" Ritter keyed his comm but realized Darving's words had been a recording. "How can I trust you?" Ritter asked Prometheus. "You're a weapon. I don't want to kill Sieg!"

The next words Ritter heard were his own. "You told me we all have a choice."

An involuntary grin bent the corners of Ritter's mouth. He chuckled. "Okay. Let's do it your way.

"Talking to yourself?" asked Sieg. "I recommend praying."

The golden blade had cut through a third of Ritter's cockpit armor. His capacitor was almost full. The second plasma sword lit up on Prometheus' schematic. Ritter reached his shield arm back, drew and ignited his second sapphire blade, and chopped at Sieg's gun. The shaft of blue plasma sliced through all four barrels. Sieg gasped in surprise.

Ritter gripped his hilt in both hands and parried the red XSeed's sword. He followed with a knee to Sieg's cockpit hatch and heard a pained grunt over the comm.

Sieg dropped his cloven gun and darted left. Ritter dashed right at Prometheus' signal. The A.I. was proven correct when the red XSeed feinted and slid into Ritter's path. The twin combat frames crossed coruscating swords as they jetted sideways through space.

Ritter stabbed at the red XSeed's face. Sieg's golden blade arced upward to parry, and Ritter landed another punch to his opponent's cockpit. Ritter's sword slashed downward on a diagonal. Sieg imposed his shield, but the blue blade cut off the tip.

The white and red XSeeds slashed at each other's throats. Blue and gold blades locked in a burst of green. "You're finally fighting to win," said Sieg. "That's not enough. Victory means fighting to kill."

"Tell it to Prometheus," Ritter said as he and Sieg spiraled along the colony wall, their swords clashing. "Megami built him to kill. Max gave him a choice. She's condemned mankind, but an A.I. smarter than all of us wants to save you!"

Sieg blocked Ritter's high slash. Prometheus's right hand grabbed the red XSeed's shoulder, and the twin CF's spun with their locked blades angled up toward the colony.

"I came here to save someone once," said Sieg. He drew his second plasma sword. Ritter opened his throttle and shot upward, but Sieg's blade burned a swath of armor from Prometheus' leg.

Capacitor fully charged.

"Gotcha," said a breathy female voice.

Chirping alarms warned Ritter of a target lock, but he couldn't find the source. He pressed Prometheus' back to the colony. A sharp impact rattled his bones. He started to slide the throttle forward, but his screen showed a thin black wire pinning Prometheus' left arm, chest, and right wrist to the wall. It had penetrated ten armor layers on impact, and any forward motion only made it cut deeper.

A flash of rockets preceded the arrival of a new combat frame by less than a second. It hung before Ritter against the backdrop of space like a reflection of Prometheus in a cobalt mirror.

"A third XSeed?" Ritter cried.

"There'll be more where this came from," Megami said. A metal disc shot from the leading edge of the shield on her XSeed's left arm, tethered by one of the black wires. She swung the disc in a horizontal arc. The wire detached from the shield, lashed across Ritter's cockpit, and anchored itself to the colony wall.

It sliced through half the remaining armor!

"Now," said Megami, "who are you?"

The red XSeed flew to its dark blue sister's side and racked its plasma swords. "That's Tod Ritter," said Sieg. "He and I fought together on Earth."

"Well, Tod Ritter," Megami said, "why are you piloting the machine meant for Zane Dellister?"

"Prometheus chose me," said Ritter.

"Darving and his damned A.I.," Megami cursed. "Leaking intel through Naryal worked like a charm before that erratic calculator got involved."

"If you wanted Zane to pilot Prometheus," said Ritter, "why did you let Masz kill him?"

"What?" Megami sounded genuinely puzzled. Before Ritter could blink, she leveled the long rectangular gun in her XSeed's right hand at his cockpit. "You're a prime example of why mankind has to die. Give Byzantium's ghosts my regards. Unless gravity drags you back to Earth, in which case you'll have lots of company soon."

The red XSeed laid its hand on Megami's gun. "Ritter's just a stupid kid," said Sieg. "I'll handle him."

Megami brushed off the red XSeed. "Let's compromise. I'll fry his neurons instead of disrupting his atoms." The gun's barrel glowed electric blue. Prometheus read a magnetic field rising to megawatt levels inside.

"Sieg," Ritter said, trying to keep his voice from trembling. "I understood the lesson. I came here to fix a mistake."

"Never mind," said Megami. "I'll disintegrate you after all,"

The red XSeed's shield knocked the barrel of Megami's gun up and to the left. The muzzle flashed like lightning. Prometheus detected a low-mass projectile leaving the barrel at a significant fraction of light speed. The softball-sized hole it punched through the colony rapidly grew to the diameter of a bulk shuttle. A dazzling ball of incandescent gas expanded into space from the breach.

Megami rocketed back from the colony and trained her gun on the red XSeed. "Don't interrupt me!"

Sieg drew his right plasma sword, charged Megami, and bisected her weapon's barrel. "Mind your elders."

"I've got about sixty million years on you," she laughed. Her shield deployed another wire. Sieg dodged left as she swung, and the black filament anchored itself in Byzantium's scarred wall. The blue XSeed shot forward. Sieg fired thrusters to climb, but the wire sheared off the red XSeed's legs below the knee.

The blue XSeed remained invisible to radar, but from his position bound to Byzantium's wall, Ritter saw Megami's CF invert and come about for another pass. "Sieg, she's coming back!"

This time Sieg dived a heartbeat before Megami blurred past. The wire sliced the crest from the red XSeed's head, but Sieg slashed his golden blade upward and cleaved off the blue XSeed's main thrusters. He caught up to his sister's CF and locked its arms from behind.

Megami's laughter sent electrified ice water coursing down Ritter's spine. "You've had a dozen chances to kill me," she told Sieg, "so I know you'll choke again. You couldn't even finish Ritter."

"He's not my responsibility." Sieg slid his plasma sword into the joint between the blue XSeed's shoulder blade and its right pauldron, severing the whole arm. "You are." He stabbed the blue XSeed's side where a human's kidney would be and held the golden blade in place as layers of armor burned away.

Megami's combat frame appeared on Ritter's sensors. Prometheus registered dangerous heat levels in the blue XSeed's capacitor. "Sieg, no!" he said. "This isn't what I meant."

Sieg fired his thrusters but kept his blade pressed to Megami's capacitor. "You don't understand, Ritter," he said. "Sanzen put something in Liz's blood—a terror beyond any other weapon. The Kazoku have it, and so do I. This is the only way to prevent another Sentinel."

"I'm the gentle option," cackled Megami. "You'll beg for me before the end! And no matter what you do, the end is coming."

Prometheus alerted Ritter that the carbon bonds in Megami's battery were seconds from breaking. The red XSeed's remaining rockets blazed, but Megami was firing maneuvering thrusters to slow his flight. They wouldn't clear the colony before her capacitor blew and turned all three XSeeds into nuclear bombs.

Ritter scanned the carbyne filaments lashing his combat frame to the wall. Both wires passed over his cockpit. Using his thrusters would just breach it and saw him in half.

"Sorry, Prometheus," said Ritter. He forced his CF's right arm forward. The wire didn't budge, but with continued pressure the magnetic anchor detached, along with his XSeed's right hand. Ritter cut the second wire with the plasma sword in Prometheus' left hand, pivoted through the hole Megami had shot in the colony's side, and pushed the throttle forward.

A second breach yawned in the immense window directly across from the entry hole. Water from the lake covering the glass formed a spike of ice jutting taller than a skyscraper into space.

Ritter aimed for the window, but the colony's odd gravity threw him off course. A rock wall reared up before him. He maintained speed. Without battery space to absorb the coming blast, he had to trust the XSeed's armor and ram the wall.

The XSeed crashed into the wall as white light filled Ritter's rear monitor. Darkness enveloped him.

39

"...respond! I repeat: This is Governor Prem Naryal of the joint Coalition-EGE forces. If you are receiving me, please respond!"

Ritter's screens winked back to life, bathing him in cool synthetic light. He let out the breath he'd been holding since the EMP from Megami and Sieg's detonation had knocked Prometheus offline. He ignored Naryal's staticky transmission and ran a status check.

This can't be right.

Ritter rechecked the numbers staring at him from the diagnostic and sensor screens. The XSeed had punched through a colony at speed with a nuclear explosion at its back. But all it had to show for the abuse was some moderate armor deformation, two warped thruster nozzles, and a burned out camera.

"Sieg was wrong," Ritter told himself. "No weapon is scarier than an XSeed!"

"This is Governor Naryal," the comm repeated. "Do you copy?"

Ritter pressed the talk button. "Corporal Tod Ritter, here. I copy, over."

Naryal began again due to the brief delay, but she cut her greeting short and addressed Ritter with audible relief. "Browning thought we might reach you on this frequency. What is your ETA to Earth?"

"I don't know," said Ritter. "A few days?"

"Specialist Young said you and Darving had proceeded to Byzantium colony to retrieve Li Wen and Sieg Friedlander. Since you are still alive, I assume the four of you are on a shuttle bound for Earth."

"No," said Ritter. "I'm alone in an XSeed outside Byzantium. Max took off in a one-man shuttle. Sieg and Megami are dead. I think she killed everyone in the colony before we got here."

Naryal sighed. "It's no use."

"What's no use?"

"We'd hoped your shuttle was close enough to divert to Metis," said Naryal. "Our attempt to avert the asteroid strike failed. Metis will impact the mid-Atlantic in two hours."

"Can't you try something else?"

"Our last shuttle was destroyed. We've captured two Kazoku transports. The crews seem demoralized—practically docile. But even if we could repair the launch facility within two hours, we could not obtain another nuclear device in time."

The pieces fell into place for Ritter. "Browning told you about the XSeed's capacitor. You were hoping we could jury-rig it into a bomb."

"Theoretically, it would have worked," Naryal said.

"It's not a theory anymore," said Ritter. He searched the sky, and his eyes fell upon the mottled bright disc of Earth. Metis stood out as a glaring silver blot on the blue ocean.

"Corporal," said Naryal, "Major Collins wishes me to relay his orders. You are to hide the XSeed or failing that, destroy it and lie low in L1. Assume a false identity and wait to be contacted. The likely level of devastation on Earth may prolong the wait considerably. If a year passes without further contact and conditions permit, return to Earth and attempt to locate an EGE officer. That is all."

"No!" Ritter pounded his armrests. "Megami can't win. Not after we fought so hard. Not after I failed to bring everyone home!" He hung his head.

A plaintive beeping prompted Ritter to raise his eyes. The navigation screen displayed a course Prometheus had plotted to Metis. A faint smile twisted Ritter's lip even though Metis would crash into the earth long before he arrived.

"You really did choose us over Megami," Ritter said.

A new message appeared next to the course heading. *Transmit Gate code?*

"Does that code open the hangar at Metis?" Ritter asked Prometheus. "I trusted you this far. Go ahead."

Gate code transmitted. TC/D imminent.

"What's—"

Time contracted to a single point. Ritter traveled for days in an instant, staving off hunger, thirst, and exhaustion to stay on course for the point in space where Metis had been and still was. He floated above the earth and surveyed the destruction wrought by kilometer-high tsunamis.

A chain of causality stronger than carbyne pulled him back into linear time at the moment Prometheus sent the Gate code. This time the A.I. fired its ejector seat before launching from Byzantium for Earth. Ritter cast his eyes upward as his chair fell away from the XSeed. The white combat frame vanished, burning its image into his retinas.

Just like Max's shuttle.

A brilliant glow called Ritter's attention earthward. A brighter light shone amid the silver star of Metis, which still hung in space over the Atlantic. Ritter watched in awe until a blinding flash forced his eyes shut.

A moment passed during which Ritter's awareness shrank to the sound of his own rapid breathing. He opened his eyes. In place of the iron bullet aimed at the ocean's heart, a cloud of glittering sparks expanded in orbit.

Ritter's spirit felt as weightless as his body. "I didn't bring everyone home," he sighed, "but there's a home to go back to."

40

Irenae Zend glided down a steel-clad corridor deep within the manufacturing asteroid Astraea. The quiet of the residential block sharply contrasted with the furious activity preceding Metis' launch and the chaos following its destruction. Hallways that had teemed with soldiers, technicians, and administrators a week ago now lay empty. Even the Kazoku had abandoned their base in the colonies, except for Irenae and a small cadre of her most dedicated staff.

Loyalty transcends death, Irenae recalled, fighting back disappointment at her brethren's faithlessness. Megami was dead, but the Sentinel would live on as long as mankind existed.

The door to Irenae's stateroom hissed open as she approached and automatically closed after her. Recessed lighting kindled to a mellow glow. She passed through a front room appointed as befit the fourteen year-old daughter of a high Coalition official and an industrial heiress, paying the trappings of luxury no mind.

In the more simply furnished bedroom, Irenae removed the velvet cord securing her ponytail and tossed her ash brown hair. She was unfastening the gold buttons of her garnet-colored pea coat when she noticed a package sitting on her faux mahogany dresser.

"Hello," she called out to the dimly lit room. "Is someone there?"

There was no answer—not that she'd expected one. Whoever had delivered the package was long gone, and an investigation would prove fruitless.

Irenae threw her coat on the bed and approached the brick-sized cardboard box as if it were a loaded gun. She gingerly picked it up and found it had less heft than expected, even for the low-gravity environment. She held her breath and opened the unmarked box.

A syringe pen filled with blood red liquid lay on a bed of cotton within.

Irenae wondered if the awe that came over her as she reverently lifted the syringe from the box echoed primitive man's religious ecstasies. She set the question aside and plunged the needle into her arm.

The following is a preview of:

COMBAT FRAME XSEED: COALITION YEAR 40

Combat Frame XSeed Book 2

Arthur

The boy hurried up the slope, scrambling over fallen logs and mossy boulders. The thinning, pine-seasoned air didn't slow him. He'd long since gotten used to high altitude, even though he was only six.

He mostly thought of himself as the boy, because that was what the Captain usually called him. Sometimes, though, the Captain called him Tom. The boy never dared call the stern, graying man anything but Captain. He didn't know if the Captain was his father, though in the secret corners of his heart he doubted it.

Still, the Captain was the only grownup the boy had ever known, as far as he could remember. The shaggy-haired but always clean-shaven man gave the boy much of what fathers in books always gave: shelter, instruction, food—a bowl of plain rice porridge for breakfast and rice with beans in the evening, with whatever meat the boy could catch for himself.

It was a hunt for the latter that had set the boy on his current path. He'd sighted a young rabbit behind the cabin and had given chase. The animal led him up and up the mountain, until the trees ended and the bald peak loomed above.

A quick search—the boy could take in many details at a glance—showed no sign of the rabbit. He abandoned the hunt and continued upward, drawn by the lofty spectacle of the peak.

Minutes later, the boy reached the top. He stood on the summit as chill winds whipped his sturdy homemade clothes and looked out over the plains stretching from the foothills. A pair of vast shadowed circles punched into the uniform green and yellow grid below marked two of the places where the Socs had started the Long Winter and the Starving Years by throwing rocks at the earth.

Socs aren't human. He heard the Captain's low yet iron-hard voice as if the old man stood behind him, but he resisted the urge to look over his shoulder. *They're insects that swarm over the earth and make it like their colonies. You can't reason with them. Never forget.*

Alone on his windswept perch, a new thought occurred to the boy. The Socs had killed many people while turning what had been called Colorado in the FMAS—and the United States before that—into North American Mountain Region 7. What if two of those murdered people, or the millions of dead from around the world, had been his parents?

The boy reflexively fought the urge to cry, but hot moisture stung his cheeks. The icy wind blowing off the farm grids below scoured his tears away.

Catching sight of an angular rock's shadow gave the boy a start. He'd woken up that morning to find the Captain gone and a note with his cold porridge saying only: "Back at noon." The shadow said he had only ten minutes to reach the cabin before the Captain returned. The boy was not forbidden to explore the wooded hills unsupervised; quite the opposite. But he knew the note's double meaning from hard experience.

The boy barreled down the mountain, scratching his limbs and face on sharp branches and nearly falling twice. Only the certain knowledge that no one would come for him if he broke a leg or his back kept him on his feet.

At last he reached the almost invisible cleft in a grassy hillside that led into the small, bowl-shaped valley where the cabin stood. The boy ran, threading his way between the pines as his lungs sucked in cool air and forced it out hot. He half-stumbled up front steps made from cut logs, and his heart froze when he saw the Captain standing two meters inside the door with his left hand behind his back.

The boy started to speak. "I'm—"

With a horizontal motion of his right hand, the Captain signaled him to silence. The boy heard mewling, much like the sounds his prey made before the kill, coming from two sources inside the cabin.

"You're lonely here," the Captain said. "I know that loneliness well." His left hand emerged from behind his back, holding a black puppy by the scruff of the neck. The little dog whined pitifully.

Of course, the Captain was right. The boy's yearning for the companionship he'd never known almost made him rush to the dog despite himself. Hope welled in his heart, but he knew enough to question it. "For me?"

"If," the Captain said. He finished by pulling a gray .38 caliber revolver from the side pocket of his brown felt coat.

Terror rooted the boy to the steps, but the Captain inclined his head toward the dog. "For him," the old man said. He nodded to his left. "Or for her."

The boy crept up the last step and through the cabin door. A blond woman in a blue jumpsuit sat tied to a stout oak chair. The cloth gag in her mouth muffled her pleas.

The Captain held out the gun, grip-first.

"Do I have to?" asked the boy.

"No," the Captain said. "You always have a choice—between action and inaction, strength and weakness; fighting and surrender. And as always, those you care for will pay the price if you choose wrong."

The boy took the gun. It felt heavy in his small hands, but not unfamiliar. The woman's mewling turned to frantic squeals.

"I've never killed a person," said the boy.

"She's not a person," the Captain said. "She's a Soc."

The boy stared down the gun's sights at his target. She looked like a person, with her wide blue eyes and tear-streaked face. He remembered crying on the mountaintop. Because he was alone. Because of Socs like her.

He exhaled and pressed the trigger. The gun thundered, and the woman's head snapped back. He smelled blood. The Captain took the gun and handed him the dog. Its plump furry body snuggled into the crook of his arm, but the connection was gone. The boy felt nothing.

The Captain stooped down and spoke to the boy. "The way you are now—the thinking without feeling when you kill animals and burn them; when you killed that Soc—you must not be that way with the dog. Soon you'll be sent among normal people, and you mustn't be that way with most of them."

"I understand," said the boy. "I think."

The Captain scratched behind the dog's ear. "To him, and to most people, you will be Tom—Thomas Dormio. To the Socs, you will be Arthur Wake."

Arthur nodded. The puppy squirmed in his arms, and Tom hugged it to his chest. Its tiny heart beat beside his, and the connection returned.

More Books by Brian Niemeier

Combat Frame XSeed

Combat Frame XSeed: Coalition Year 40

Combat Frame XSeed: CY 40 Second Coming

Combat Frame XSeed: S

Combat Frame XSeed: SS

Combat Frame Ƶ XSeed

The Soul Cycle

Nethereal

Souldancer

The Secret Kings

The Ophian Rising

Novellas and Anthologies

The Hymn of the Pearl

Strange Matter

Acknowledgements

Heartfelt thanks to:

Ben

Ian

Jeff H.

JJ

Nick A.

RanbaRal

Xavier Harkonnen

Viceroy

Nathan Housley

Brent

ArtAnon

All our Indiegogo backers!

About Brian Niemeier

Brian Niemeier is a #1 best selling author and a John W. Campbell Award for Best New Writer finalist. His second book *Souldancer* won the first ever Dragon Award for Best Horror Novel. As an editor, Brian helps his top selling clients realize the best version of each book.

Visit Brian at http://www.brianniemeier.com/
Follow @BrianNiemeier on Twitter.

Honest reviews are vital to helping others make informed reading decisions. Please consider leaving a review of this book on Amazon.

Made in United States
Troutdale, OR
09/13/2024

22795440R00169